I0760625

# BOUND BY SHADOWS

Books in the
Reclaimed Legacy Chronicles by
Morgan Emerson Fox

*Otherkin's Hunger*
*Bound by Shadows*

# BOUND BY SHADOWS

*Book 2 of the*
*Reclaimed Legacy Chronicles*

Morgan Emerson Fox

Bound By Shadows - Book 2 of the Reclaimed Legacy Chronicles

Copyright © 2025 by Morgan Emerson Fox

All rights reserved.

ISBN-13: 978-1-965280-01-0

Raindrop Books LLC
8401 Maryland Drive, STE S
Richmond, VA 23294

No part of this book may be reproduced or transmitted in any form or by any means, electronic or mechanical, including photocopying, recording, or by any information storage and retrieval system without the written permission of the author, except where permitted by law.

This book is dedicated to the ones we've lost to the inexorable march of time and age, whose memories linger. To the families we were born into and the ones we choose, bound not by blood but by the depths of hearts and the strength of spirit. Here's to the friends who stand by us, embrace our quirks, champion our dreams, and hold us close in times of need.

To our beta readers, editor, and every hand and voice that has touched this manuscript, your insights and dedication have made this story far greater than it could have been without you.

This work is a tribute to tolerance, acceptance, and the beauty of being true to who you are and can become. In a world riddled with division and hatred, this narrative stands as a beacon of hope, urging us to look beyond our differences and find unity in our shared humanity.

We hope you find the same joy, escape, and reflection in these words that we found in writing them. Reject division, embrace love, and always seek the light, even in the darkest times.

## DISCLAIMER

This novel is a work of fiction. The events depicted in this novel are not based on any real people or events. The names, characters, places, and incidents are either the product of the author's imagination or are used fictitiously. Any resemblance to actual persons, living or dead, businesses, companies, events, or locales is entirely coincidental.

The author has used real places in this novel, but any events that take place in these places are fictional. The author has not attempted to portray these places accurately, and any resemblance to actual events that have taken place in these places is purely coincidental.

The characters in this novel are completely fictional. They are not based on any real people, and any resemblance to actual persons, living or dead, is purely coincidental.

The author has created these characters and their stories for entertainment purposes only. The author does not endorse or condone the actions of any of the characters in this novel.

Otherkin.[1] /ˈəT͟Hərˌkin/

n., sing. or pl. A person who holds the belief that they are not entirely (or not at all) human. Usually a spiritual belief pertaining to one's soul and the reincarnation thereof, but may also be a belief that one's genetics are descended from, for example, the Irish fae. The word Otherkin was coined to describe people who felt a connection to mythological humanoids such as elves and faeries, but has expanded in recent years to include dragons, gryphons/griffins and other supposedly mythical beasts as well as animals, angelic/demonic beings (angelkin/demonkin) and in some cases extraterrestrials.

adj. Of or relating to Otherkin.

---

[1] Spiritedust. (2004, May 15). Otherkin. Urban Dictionary. https://www.urbandictionary.com/define.php?term=otherkin

# *Prolog*

In the dimly lit corridors of the Vault, beneath the ruins of Paldiski's former nuclear training center, now the headquarters of the Sodality of the Thorns, Helena Dröger navigated the maze with purpose. The sturdy Soviet-era architecture, now augmented with modern advancements, held countless stories of geopolitical games. Yet, moving amidst them, Helena was an enigma.

The artifacts and artwork displayed along the corridors and the concrete walls evoked an oppressive atmosphere intended to intimidate those within its confines. As she strode past tapestries chronicling centuries of occult history, her mind was a tempest, replaying her recent interactions with Eamon Vale—the Grandmaster. To him, she was the paragon of fidelity, a servant whose loyalty was unquestionable. But the truth was as intricate as the boldest of the Sodality's chronicles.

She recalled the first time she'd met Eamon; the very air around him had pulsed with authority. His words had been laden with magically enhanced oaths to bind her to him. While he believed she was ensnared, Helena had been able to limit the oath's effectiveness just enough that her true nature and intentions remained veiled. If he ever discovered that she was more than human, it would mean her death.

Yet questions lingered. What was Eamon after? Power, dominance, or something even darker? The goal of the Sodality, which he espoused but secretly flouted, was to purge supernatural abilities from the human race. She suspected he used the order's history as a cover to ensure he reigned unchallenged—a reign she could pose a threat to. One day, that reign would end.

Deep in thought, Helena entered her private chambers. Here, she could shed the façade and be her true self. As the door closed behind her, her hands moved to a concealed alcove, revealing a leather-bound volume. It was her diary and chronicle, written in a coded language that recounted her journey across the sands of time.

She opened it. The pages whispered tales of betrayal, loss, and power struggles. Turning to the next empty page, she began to pen her moves, strategies, and doubts.

*Eamon believes he has all the pieces under control. But even the Grandmaster of the Sodality can be blindsided. Lucian and Anja may provide the opportunity I have been waiting for. I must move carefully. Eamon's trust is my shield, and my true purpose remains veiled.*

As she closed the volume, her choices and decisions were now committed to ink. She placed the diary back in its secret location but knew it would soon be time to move it. She would navigate this treacherous path one step at a time, always with an eye on the ultimate prize: her freedom and the world once more alive with magic, where she was no longer forced to hide her true nature. Yes, that and revenge.

Moving to her office, she went to check up on Operation Icarus.

She halted before an expansive, high-tech digital mirror. Its display was designed to project real-time information, but at this moment, it held only her reflection. After centuries, her face remained timeless, but the depths of her blue eyes held tales that predated the Vault's secretive history. She was tall and pale with almost porcelain skin. Her jet-black hair fell in thick waves down her back. Dressed in a vintage dress, as she typically wore here in the Vault, she appraised her image. Eamon was not her first dance partner in the clandestine ballet of power, but he was undeniably the most challenging.

Helena had been vigilant since the very inception of the operation. Grandmaster Eamon's plan to eliminate Lucian, a potential thorn in the Sodality's grand designs, intrigued her. Given her place within the Sodality's hierarchy, she was privy to the nuances of the operation.

Helena knew Richard, the Controller for the Northeastern United

States, was competent. The failure of one of his operatives, codenamed Smoke, had come as a surprise. Lucian's entire immediate family had been killed, yet he had somehow escaped their fate—another family murdered by the Sodality. The biotech giant and billionaire would be extremely dangerous as he sought retribution. If he somehow learned of the Sodality, he would stop at nothing to seek revenge even though he stood little chance of success.

The operation's escalation, and inclusion of operatives like Raven and Nomad, had only heightened her interest. Helena had monitored each dispatch sent to Richard and every update he sent back. She had additional encrypted back channels into the communication system, ensuring no detail escaped her scrutiny. Helena had chosen to remain a silent observer. Could Lucian overcome the combined might of Richard and his operatives? If Lucian prevailed against such odds, he would be an asset worth consideration for her plans.

When Anja Kinzey became a target, her involvement with Lucian came to light, and alarm bells started to ring. Lucian's bodyguards, newly hired as a result of the assassination attempt, were also problematic. Raven had been tasked with crafting fake media to drive a wedge between Lucian and Anja and create exploitable opportunities. The last dispatches had related success, but there had been no updates.

Richard was overdue to report in, and Helena sensed an opportunity. She would don a veneer of concern and approach Eamon.

The room's ambiance was heavy as Helena stepped into the grand chamber buried deep within the Vault. Dominating one wall was a vast monitor pulsating with intricate data points, representing the expansive network under the Sodality's dominion. The man standing before it, Grandmaster Eamon Vale, was the epicenter of this global web. He was engrossed by the information before him. His colorless grey eyes scanned for details while his fingers caressed the tablet in his hands. His salt-and-pepper hair was impeccably styled, as was the tailored suit he wore.

He presented himself as a man who had ascended to power some twenty years ago in a succession blessed by his predecessor. If he found out that she knew the two were one and the same, he would kill her. He was far older and much more powerful than anyone suspected.

At the noise of the door, Eamon shifted his gaze to her. The display's muted light cast eerie flickering shadows as she approached.

"Grandmaster," she acknowledged with a slight bow.

For a heartbeat, he studied her as if trying to fathom her very soul, and perhaps he was. "Helena," he replied. "I assume you're here about Operation Icarus?"

Looking at the network display, she located the node indicating Richard's location in New York City. "I am. Richard's prolonged silence is unlike him. It's…concerning."

The heavy silence that followed seemed to press down. "What do you recommend?"

"I propose personally verifying Richard's status and the operation's progress. The integrity of Icarus is of the utmost importance, and this continued silence is problematic."

"Agreed. But be wary, Helena. The operation teeters on a precarious edge, and its players are more formidable than I anticipated."

"I comprehend the gravity, Grandmaster. You have my word; discretion and diligence will be my guides." As his latest enforcer, she knew the price of failure, and he had others waiting in the wings should she fail.

He turned back to study the display. "Ensure you report any findings promptly."

"Certainly." She turned to depart. Yet, on reaching the door, she hesitated. "I value your trust in this, Eamon."

While he remained focused on the sprawling digital display, his voice bore that characteristic edge that earned him respect and fear. "Do not fail, Helena. Clean this up. That's my singular expectation."

# Part One

# *One*

Anja's heart pounded as the jet's door opened. A rush of cold Icelandic air sliced through the cabin. The confrontation with the Sodality and the capture of the Controller weighed heavily on her mind. They had struck a blow against them and were now running. Time was not on their side, and there were too many loose threads that could snag on thorny questions, such as how to get the officials to overlook two unconscious men without passports and a peregrine falcon without the requisite papers.

Lucian stepped out first, his commanding presence in a tailored suit drawing the attention of the waiting Icelandic officials. Anja followed, scanning the faces for any hint of suspicion. Entry for private jets was usually smooth and uneventful, but this was different. During the flight, they had worked out an approach to get them through the red tape, but so much depended on her still-developing talents. Influencing thoughts and inclinations could be tricky, and she had little experience.

The officials approached. Anja felt the tension clawing at her. She took a deep breath, ready to play her part. Pushing her burgundy hair out of her face, she followed Lucian onto the tarmac. Lucian kept a calm exterior, with dark hair and dark eyes, alert and relaxed. She could sense his tension below the surface and hoped she could project that same calm.

"Welcome to Iceland," the lead official said. "We'll need to conduct a brief inspection before you proceed."

"Of course." Lucian gestured to the ambulances that could be seen approaching. "We have patients in critical condition. Time is short. The first officer, Ms. Williams, has our papers and will help facilitate the process."

Aaliyah Williams, her uniform pristine, handed over a neatly organized folder of documents. She was a British woman of black ethnicity, approaching middle age. Her short, curly black hair framed her face, and her warm, hazel eyes conveyed determination and competence. "Here are the necessary forms and passports. We appreciate your cooperation in this urgent matter. The aircraft and crew will depart immediately after we are cleared to proceed. Only the passengers and patients will remain in Iceland."

The lead official took the folder, glancing through the documents. "Thank you, Ms. Williams," he said, his tone softening slightly. He glanced at Zoe, who had followed Aaliyah.

With her half-Indian, half-American heritage, Zoe's features were striking—warm brown skin, dark almond eyes, and silky black hair that grazed her shoulders. She had an almost otherworldly allure that seemed to captivate the official. Anja hoped Zoe had not overdone it in her efforts to distract their attention.

Zoe offered a nod. The official was momentarily taken aback, his professional demeanor slipping as he returned his attention to the documents.

As two ambulances arrived, accompanied by a pair of SUVs, the doors opened to reveal the orchestrated chaos of a medical emergency. A woman Anja assumed was Dr. Elín Björnsdóttir, the director of Akar Labs, stepped out of one of the SUVs. Two medical assistants began unloading stretchers for the "patients," adding a sense of urgency to the scene.

Elín approached the officials. She stood about five foot seven, and her auburn hair, touched with blonde streaks, was pulled back into a bun held in place by a silver flying dragon pin with a blade-shaped tail. Minimalist eyeglasses accentuated her fair skin and gray eyes.

"Góðan daginn," Elín greeted the lead official in her native Icelandic. "Ég er Doctor Björnsdóttir frá Akar Labs. Þessir sjúklingar þurfa bráðameðferð." Switching to English, she repeated, "These patients require urgent care."

The lead official's stern expression relaxed. "Of course, Doctor. We will try to speed things along."

"Elín has been instrumental in handling similar medical crises here in Iceland at my laboratory. I've invested heavily here, and her expertise is critical," Lucian said with heat.

Zoe placed a hand on his arm to soothe him with her newly acquired talents. "They're just doing their duties, Lucian. Everything will be fine."

Elín nodded, and her assistants moved efficiently, boarding and transferring the patients onto the stretchers. The officials watched, their scrutiny tempered by Elín's evident competence and the seamless coordination of the medical team.

One official, still wary, asked, "May we see the patients' documents?"

Anja had expected this snag. "In our rush, their documents were not on hand and were left behind, but I assure you, we will provide them shortly."

Her warm yet firm tone and touch of magical influence dispelled the last of the official's doubts. He nodded. "Very well, but ensure the documents are delivered promptly."

"Don't worry, you can forget your concern," Anja pressed with more power.

"Thank you," Elín said to the official. "We appreciate your understanding."

As the medical team moved the patients toward the ambulances, Elín turned to Lucian, her expression still worried. They had managed to navigate this critical moment, but the weight of their deception hung heavy. Anja could sense that Elín would need answers. She hoped they could provide them.

Carlos, one of their guards, oversaw the unloading of medical supplies, where his falcon Aria was hooded and sleeping, hidden within. Bringing such a bird into Iceland was anything but straightforward, with export and import requiring extensive pre-approvals and complex paperwork. Cleverly hidden amidst the supplies placed inside one of the ambulances, the falcon's camouflage was perfect; the boxes appeared to be nothing more than essentials for the care of the patients.

Carlos would accompany Nomad and the hidden Aria while Emma, another guard, would take charge of the Controller. Both would play their roles in the ambulances as concerned associates, reinforcing the narrative of medical urgency.

The lead official returned the documents to Aaliyah, who distributed the passports to the team. “You are cleared,” the official said. “I hope your patients will recover swiftly.”

“Thank you for your understanding,” Aaliyah replied. “The jet will be departing shortly.”

After completing the formalities, the team loaded into the various vehicles. As the engines came to life, Anja exhaled, a small triumph amidst the tension. They had cleared that hurdle.

Anja leaned back into the vehicle’s seat as they sped towards downtown Reykjavík. The rising sun cast a glow across the landscape dotted with snow, and the soft hum of conversation filled the space around her. Lucian was busy discussing something with Ian, his lead bodyguard, while Zoe was lost in her thoughts, occasionally glancing out of the window. Claire, their fourth guard, was flipping through some documents, probably related to their stay at the hotel.

Just hours ago they had captured the Controller, and now they were here, in the stark beauty of Iceland—the land of fire and ice. The contrast between the cold, rugged landscapes outside and the warmth of the vehicle’s interior was not lost on Anja. Neither was the fact that this had all started only two months ago. Her life had changed completely in that short time.

She glanced at Zoe, noting the tiredness on her face. The events had taken a toll on all of them, but especially on Zoe. Anja sensed an undercurrent of excitement in Zoe despite all that had transpired. She was still coming to terms with the recent changes in her life, especially her newfound allure. Anja reached out and placed a comforting hand on Zoe’s.

Zoe let out a chuckle. “All these Jedi mind tricks we’re pulling? It’s making me uneasy. Our powers can be used to exploit people.”

Anja gave her a reassuring squeeze. “I know, Zoe, but the stakes are too high. We have to do whatever it takes to protect everyone."

"You do get the Jedi reference, right?"

"Jedi? Is that some kind of martial art?"

Zoe burst out laughing. "You've got to be kidding me. You've never seen Star Wars? 'These aren't the droids you're looking for. Move along.'"

"I guess I'm more into books than movies."

"Yeah, bookworm. We're going to have to fix that. Movie night. No excuses. You need to understand the basics of pop culture, particularly this one."

Anja chuckled. "Fine, fine. But only if you promise to explain everything."

"Deal. Just wait until you see the lightsabers."

Upon reaching the hotel, they were met with discreet luxury. The staff greeted them warmly, with a professionalism that spoke of the establishment's reputation. Their rooms were well-appointed, with expansive views of the city and ocean beyond it.

Lucian confirmed everyone's arrangements. "Carlos and Emma will be joining us soon. Everyone will have their quarters, but I thought it wise for us to stay close. Anja and I will share a suite with an adjoining room for Ian. We may not need a constant watch, but we still need to keep sharp. Tomorrow will be a busy day. We'll strategize our next steps over breakfast. Rest and recover for now. As usual, use room service or go out in pairs until then."

As Anja entered their shared suite, with Lucian close behind, the plush carpet muffled their footsteps and the heavy curtains cocooned the room in a hush, illuminated by the warm glow of lamps. Anja set down her messenger bag, still holding her notes and the *Ars Notoria* that Howard, Lucian's eccentric uncle, had entrusted to her. He was a scholar of the occult, now on sabbatical and hiding from the Sodality. She worried about him out there somewhere alone, but he was trying to find more knowledge they desperately needed.

She approached the bed, touching the soft linen. Lucian joined her, their fingers intertwining as a silent affirmation of their growing bond.

Together, they sank into the bed's embrace, drawing solace from their shared warmth. As sleep beckoned, Anja curled closer to Lucian, her head finding its spot against his chest.

The morning light of Iceland seeped into the hotel's private dining room, painting a glow on the wooden table. From Lucian's seat at the head of the table, the food looked inviting, each dish arranged in the hotel's minimalist style.

Emma was already diving into the smoked salmon, her long black hair flowing loosely down her back, not her usual ponytail, framing her face with those green eyes. Lucian appreciated her taste; the salmon, cured and smoked, lay delicate on dark rye bread, a hint of butter glistening on its surface. Sitting beside Emma, Claire was a contrast; her hair was a natural golden brown and cut feathered to her shoulders, which she had teasingly called a wolf cut. It highlighted her eyes—a startling amber so like her wolf's. She settled for a hearty serving of eggs and some meat to accompany them.

Ian, his lead bodyguard, sat on Claire's other side. His dark hair, peppered with hints of silver reflecting his experience and maturity, blended well with a wool herringbone jacket. His imposing height of six foot two was not as apparent sitting, but his broad shoulders and frame hinted at the power he could bring to bear—sometimes literally. His special forces training and his newly awakened bear could be truly formidable. His warm smile as he regarded Claire suited him.

A high-spirited voice broke his train of thought. Zoe commented about the richness of the Icelandic skyr. Her infectious laughter lightened the room's mood, pulling a smile from everyone, including Lucian. He could feel the pull of her allure and remembered the feel of her bare skin and scent. He and Anja had performed her awakening only a few days ago and the memories of that were still vivid. Pulling his mind from those distracting images, he turned to focus on his appetite—yes, food, *that* appetite.

As he spooned some of the creamy skyr onto his plate, mixing it with fresh blueberries, he caught Ian's nod of approval from his seat.

The man had a similar combination, albeit with a sprinkle of chia seeds.

Carlos soon joined them, reaching for the traditional Icelandic rye bread and making some light comment to Emma about balancing out her lean into the salmon. With a square jawline and a neatly trimmed beard, Carlos exuded a sense of rugged Latin masculinity. He was taller than Emma by at least six inches but just shy of Ian's height. The camaraderie between the two was evident.

Anja radiated an ethereal grace. Her burgundy hair reflected the morning light, and her green eyes sparkled. The day of rest had done them all good. She sampled the fresh fruits, a cascade of vibrant colors on her plate. But it wasn't the food that captivated him. The way Anja listened to Zoe's comments, her lips curling into a soft smile, and the occasional laughter that escaped her drew him in.

Their eyes met for an instant, a silent exchange passing between them. The world around them blurred, leaving just the two of them in focus. Lucian felt a warm rush, a reminder of their bond. It wasn't just the adventure that intertwined their fates; it was these quieter moments, too—the breakfasts, the shared glances, the silent understanding.

The chime of Lucian's phone pulled him from his reverie. He unlocked it, scanning the new message that illuminated the screen. "The vehicles will be here shortly to take us to Akar. We'll need to prepare to head out soon."

"Always on the clock, boss man," Zoe teased, but her jest was met with smiles around the table.

Lucian watched from the vehicle's window, the Icelandic landscape capturing his attention. Lava fields flanked the road leading to Akar Labs. Emerging from the dark volcanic canvas, moss patches announced spring's arrival.

Akar Labs' gleaming façade loomed in the distance, steam from the geothermal plants on the far side rising in the cold air. The facility's modern design mirrored the surrounding vistas with its reflective glass, creating an illusion of harmony between architecture and nature.

Lucian knew the facility's true expanse lay hidden. Beneath the ground were vast subterranean levels housing their supercomputing and data storage centers, not to mention state-of-the-art research labs and containment areas. The underground location was strategic: the cool environment was perfect for the servers, and the earth provided an extra level of security.

Lucian took in the high-security fencing encircling the facility as the vehicles neared. Discreet cameras were positioned at intervals, monitoring every approach. But these visible measures were just the beginning; advanced sensors and biometric access points ensured Akar Labs' secrets remained secure.

The lab would provide a safe location to continue their genetic research. He had built this research facility to further his more clandestine research, and it was not publicly listed as one of his properties, hidden in layers of holding companies.

The vehicle came to a smooth halt at the entrance. They were greeted by Elín. Beside her, a young assistant held a tablet and camera, ready to process the newcomers. The reception area was a vast, open space, the black furniture severe against its white walls. A hum emanated from the high-tech equipment below, the heartbeat of the lab.

"Lucian, it's good to have you here again." Elín extended a badge toward him, the familiar weight of it settling in his palm, then turned to the rest of the group. "Welcome to Akar Labs. Before proceeding, we must ensure that everyone is properly identified and granted appropriate access."

Lucian leaned over to Elín, lowering his voice just enough. "Ensure they all have full access. No restrictions. Um, except for the biosafety areas—I don't think there will be any need to visit those areas, and if there is, escorts and briefings would be appropriate."

Elín nodded, texting on her phone. "Understood."

"You mean like level four containment? Like that?" Zoe asked.

"Yes, like that. Lab leaks would be bad, and we do extensive genetic research. I'm sure you can imagine the consequences. Akar has the ability to handle anything and everything. That we have up to BSL-4, including animal and agricultural, is *not* widely known or advertised," Lucian said.

"Oookaaay," Zoe said.

After taking photos and capturing biometric data from each, the assistant left and soon returned, distributing badges to their owners.

Elín motioned with her hand. "Now that we're all set, let's proceed to our secure conference room. I have a lot of questions."

As they waited for the elevator, Anja experienced an odd combination of awe and trepidation. It was all so new, so unfamiliar. Her eyes flicked to the keypad as Elín entered a code and presented her badge. There was a brief pause before the elevator acknowledged the credentials so they could begin their descent.

She noticed the discreetly placed cameras as they exited the elevator and entered the well-lit hallways. Their presence served as a reminder of the importance and secrecy of the work here.

Once they entered the conference room, Anja took a moment to survey the space. A large table dominated the room, surrounded by ergonomic chairs. High-tech screens adorned the walls. She set down her messenger bag next to a chair before taking a seat.

As the rest of the team took their seats, Elín wasted no time. "Lucian, Anja, I need to know what is going on. And details about these...patients."

Lucian leaned forward, his fingers interlacing. "A lot has transpired in a surprisingly short span. We'll try to keep this brief. I can fill in any missing details later."

He took a deep breath. "My family—my parents, older brother, and my younger sister—were murdered. Brutally." His voice wavered ever so slightly, but he pushed on. "The loss was...unfathomable. It turned out that I was the actual target, and my family was collateral damage."

"My God, Lucian. We tend to be isolated here, but this is...I'm so sorry. You said this visit was urgent, and you needed help, but this..."

Elín was clearly caught off guard. "How do the 'patients' relate to this? Oh, please forgive my interruption."

"No, that's a good starting point. You see, one of them coordinated those murders—the one you had to sedate. The other refers to himself as 'Nomad' and is an underling in the same secret society. He was convinced to help trap the 'Controller.' We don't know his name." Lucian paused briefly. "We believe we are up against a powerful secret organization called the Sodality of the Thorns. We know very little about them, which is one of the reasons we are here."

"So they are prisoners?" Elín asked.

Zoe shifted uncomfortably but remained silent.

"Yes, they must remain isolated. We hope to learn more about them and their organization. They're deeply involved in the organization and may be privy to secrets we must learn. The others with me all have vital roles." Lucian indicated those around the table. "Because of the murders and the continued threat, I hired four very capable bodyguards who have exceeded all expectations. You see, Elín, we have started to unlock fantastic capabilities within our genes—all seven of us. I'll provide details and lab reports, but you will probably need to see the results with your own eyes to believe them. It will seem like magic, and it may even be."

Elín could hardly keep the skepticism off her face. "Well, now. You're serious, aren't you?"

"Yes. Dead serious. Anja and Zoe also became involved soon after the murders." He gestured for Anja to take up the narrative.

Anja cleared her throat, her nerves momentarily causing a hitch in her voice. "I was a librarian. My primary focus has always been on the arcane and the occult practices that history has often overlooked or shunned." She motioned towards Zoe with a fond smile. "And that's how I met Zoe. We were both at Columbia. She was pursuing her degree in criminal justice while I was studying medieval history. She was a world apart from the dusty old texts and manuscripts I was engrossed in, but our paths crossed, and we soon became friends and roommates."

Zoe added, "Yeah, while Anja was buried in her old scrolls and incantations, I studied the criminal mind, especially the darker corners most people prefer to ignore. We just clicked." Zoe leaned forward, resting an elbow on the table. "You know, I always told Anja she needed to come out of her shell, have a little fun, and break a few rules. But I had no idea"—she waved a hand dramatically, encompassing the room and their current situation—"that this would be the result. I mean, unleashing this whirlwind? Be careful what you wish for, right?"

Anja rolled her eyes, a blush coloring her cheeks. "Yes, and here I thought Zoe was the dangerous influence." The room's tension lightened, and a chuckle rippled through the group.

"What Anja and Zoe share is considerable, but a deeper narrative binds us all." Lucian took a deep breath. "While the authorities did their part, the case was going nowhere, and the true depth of what was at play wasn't seen. That's when Zoe came in. Given her expertise in criminal psychology, The FBI assigned her the case as a profiler."

Zoe nodded, her usual demeanor replaced by professional seriousness. "The case was unusual. There were ritualistic elements. Anja warned me to be on the lookout for anything strange. Her 'feeling' about it was unnervingly correct."

Lucian's fingers tightened around the table's edge, but his voice remained steady. "Together, we've been unraveling this mystery, each discovery more shocking than the last. It has led us here, to this moment, to Akar Labs and the larger game at play."

Anja felt empathy for him in the brief silence that followed Lucian's words. "The Sodality dates back to ancient times and has always been involved in dark events. Their millennia-long suppression of anything supernatural has had devastating consequences. Whole bloodlines or even races have been wiped out, all in the name of human or racial purity. For some, that is a seductive narrative. Their vision for humanity is one where no one has the power to oppose them. This is not just a criminal organization. The Sodality has influence and connections far beyond what we could have imagined. The depth of their willingness to do whatever it takes to achieve their ends is... chilling."

"Well now," Elín began, "given the nature of your...let's call it 'investigation,' I believe Akar Labs might offer some unique advantages. Our facilities could help"

Zoe stiffened in her chair, a crease forming in her brows. "Lucian, you know that puts me in an uncomfortable position. I am technically still an FBI agent. This is so far from legal that I can't even put it into words."

Lucian looked at Zoe, then back at Elín. "I understand both points of view, but given the nature of the Sodality and what's at stake, it might be that Akar Labs has methods that could be more…efficient for our unique predicament. Our adversaries are not conventional; you've seen firsthand what they are willing to do. Zoe, you witnessed the interactions with Nomad. It's not torture we're talking about."

They were veering into dangerous territories she was only beginning to understand. Lucian's hand found hers under the table, and for a moment, she found reassurance in the simple touch.

Lucian looked at them all before settling on Elín. "Our collaboration has led us down some intriguing avenues. You see, my research had reached a limit, primarily focused on epigenetic research and modifications. Anja's expertise in ritualistic practices, arcane texts, and historical contexts provided the insight we needed to move past those limits. Together, we've started to awaken dormant abilities that are incredible and terrifying in their implications."

Elín leaned back in her chair, crossing her arms over her chest, and narrowed her eyes. "Awakening dormant abilities through a blend of science and what sounds like mysticism? You realize that might be hard to swallow, even in a place as unconventional as Akar Labs."

Lucian nodded, acknowledging the doubt without yielding an inch. "Yes, I understand how it sounds, but the results speak for themselves. Our enemies already know or suspect what we may accomplish, so they're trying to stop us by any means. We have to catch up and fast. The only saving grace is that they may not know yet that we have succeeded."

Anja gauged Elín's reaction. As much as she understood the woman's skepticism, she also recognized a glimmer of curiosity. They were on the edge of something revolutionary, and Elín, for all her reservations, was intrigued.

# *Two*

Anja listened as Lucian and Elín discussed integrating the team into the lab and their immediate needs. The most urgent was to ensure there would be no security leaks from the inside. To do that, Zoe would be interviewing all of the lab's employees using her profiling and empathic talents. She was turning into a walking polygraph, only much more efficient and accurate.

To facilitate this, they had asked for help. When the assistant Elín had selected entered the room, her presence struck Anja. Tall and lean, she moved with a grace that belied her height. Her fair complexion gave her an ethereal glow that reminded Anja of the sparse sunlight she'd seen filtering through the Icelandic skies.

Elín introduced her. "This is Sigridur Jónsdóttir. She should be able to assist you with anything you need."

"Just call me Sigri. I'll be happy to be of assistance." Her Icelandic accent lent a delightful lilt to her English. "It's a pleasure to meet all of you."

Sigri's hair was a deep, raven-like black, pulled back into a clasp at the back of her neck. But what caught Anja's attention the most were her blue eyes as they scanned the room before settling on Elín, who requested Sigri follow Zoe into her office for an interview.

As the door closed behind them, the others broke off into smaller groups. Their voices were hushed and the conversations animated. Anja caught Lucian sharing a few words with Ian.

Soon, Zoe and Sigri returned. Zoe gave a subtle thumbs-up, her eyes meeting Anja's as if sharing an inside joke. Sigri looked at ease, and Anja sensed a camaraderie had formed between the two women. Whatever had transpired in that office had laid the groundwork for what Anja hoped would be a productive partnership.

Lucian's fingers rested on the table. "As of now, we don't have enough intelligence to bring the fight to the Sodality. What we do have are loose ends—a lot of them. Our immediate focus should be tying those up while gathering more information. Elín, can we visit our guests now while Zoe starts interviewing the other employees?"

She stood and started for the door. "If you'd follow me, we can visit Nomad."

Lucian caught Anja's eye and tilted his head, signaling for her and Emma to join them. It was one thing to talk about their captives, quite another to come face to face.

A guard was stationed outside the room as they neared, his posture alert. The room had a cipher lock—a security measure that put a knot in Anja's stomach. With a nod from Elín, the guard tapped in the code, and the door clicked open.

The room looked much like a typical hospital room with another open door to a bathroom. She could not detect the camera that she had been told was hidden somewhere. Nomad was being treated more like a patient than a prisoner despite the locked door and guard. He was lying on a hospital bed, dressed in a gown, and even had a wristband to complete the image.

He was unshaven, and his short dark hair was ruffled, but he still looked like an average European or American businessman. He was not ugly, but he was not handsome either. He had blue eyes, but they were not remarkable either. The best she could come up with was just...average.

Nomad was engrossed in an English translation of what appeared to be an Icelandic thriller novel. Nomad looked up, marked his page, and set the book aside, his eyes meeting Lucian's briefly before landing on Anja.

Nomad broke the silence. "To what do I owe the pleasure?" His voice was steady, but Anja could sense his nervousness.

"Let's just say we've come to talk," Lucian replied, "and we have much to discuss."

The tension in the room was high. She remembered the time Nomad had seen her in her succubus form. She read the tremor of unease in his look and the guarded curiosity that flickered there.

"We have a dilemma," Anja began. "Your *former* organization is trying to find and kill us, and we're not sure what to do with you. Letting you go would pose a threat. But you can help us. If you prove to be an asset rather than a liability, there's a chance we could set you free in the future."

Lucian watched the exchange intently, but Anja sensed the currents of thought running through Nomad: skepticism and a flicker of hope. "I'm listening," he said.

"You've already helped us trap your Controller, so returning to the Sodality would likely pose problems for you. Your options are limited. I once asked you to reassess your views on good and evil. So now, will you tell us what you've seen of the Sodality?"

Nomad's eyes remained locked onto hers, the scrutiny shifting from her to himself as if he were sifting through his thoughts and allegiances. Then he sighed. "I'll tell you what I know."

Lucian leaned against the wall, arms crossed over his chest, watching Anja dissect Nomad's words. Nomad appeared to know little, but even fragments served as valuable leads.

"So Raven is in New York? Involved in intel and disinformation?" Anja pressed.

"Yes," Nomad responded, his tone less resistant now. "She's good at what she does. Hellishly good. I was told she manufactured the materials to drive you and Lucian apart. To separate you and make you easier targets. Apparently, it wasn't as effective as we had assumed. We were fooled. Ironic."

"Controllers, like the one we've captured—are there more?" Anja asked.

Nomad hesitated before nodding. "Yes. They operate in various regions around the world. Each one handles different aspects or territories. But that's about all I know. They keep us compartmented. Isolated."

When Anja finally turned to look at Lucian, seeking validation, he nodded. Yes, every piece of information helped. Now, they had more leads to follow. He caught Elín's eye as the interview ended.

"We'll speak more later," Anja said to Nomad as they exited. Lucian followed them out of Nomad's room.

After the guard secured the door, Lucian asked Anja, "What do you think? Will he cooperate or try to undermine us?"

Anja considered for a moment. "With his history and past experiences, not to mention his betrayal of their organization, I think he will turn out to be an asset. I think Zoe and Emma should get a chance to talk to him more. Provide him with some clothes and a little supervised time to exercise or walk around. Treat him kindly, and he'll respond to that. Solitary confinement will not help."

"Can you arrange for that, Elín?" Lucian asked.

"That should not pose any significant risks as long as he is escorted and the areas he is taken to are limited. I'll put that on Sigri's list and have her coordinate with Zoe and Emma." She typed a note on her tablet.

"Thank you. Next?"

Elín led the way, her face a stoic mask as they arrived at another secure door. "He's sedated," she informed them. "He's tried to kill himself anytime he regained consciousness, so we've had to take precautions."

Lucian's brow furrowed at the news, but he nodded. The Controller had swallowed a suicide pill when he was captured. It had taken all of Lucian's power and more borrowed from Anja to keep him alive, and even then, he'd teetered on the edge.

The door hissed open, and they stepped into a cold room. It was as if the temperature had been dialed down to match its occupant. The room resembled the one Nomad occupied, but the Controller lay on a hospital bed, restraints securing him at the wrists and ankles. Monitors and an IV were attached to him. His eyes were closed, but his jaw was set in a tight line, even in his unresponsive state.

Anja moved closer, watching the Controller for a long, searching moment. “There’s something…else. It’s as if he is bound by shadows. Mystical bindings of some sort, likely enforcing an oath of loyalty.”

Elín raised an eyebrow, clearly skeptical.

“It could explain why he’s so desperate to end his life,” Anja continued. “If some dire oath binds him, he would be compelled to protect the organization’s secrets at all costs—even if that means his death.”

Lucian met Anja’s eyes, his own filled with a new, grim understanding. This was a new issue, one that bridged the realms of science and magic in a disturbing fusion. But it was a clue, another piece of the grotesque puzzle they were revealing.

“And so,” Lucian said, breaking the heavy silence, “our work here is even more critical. We’re not just battling an organization but up against an ideology fortified by magical oaths. We’ll need every resource and every ounce of knowledge we possess to break it down. Maybe Howard can gather some information in that regard.”

“Yes. They are trying to suppress the supernatural, but actively using it themselves. We have no idea what they are truly capable of. This is a new level of danger I hadn’t seen coming,” Anja confirmed.

Lucian couldn’t shake the unsettling sensation that they were diving into waters far murkier than anticipated. A chilling thought crossed his mind: if this man was warded, were there others within the Sodality who were protected in similar ways?

Anja turned to Lucian. “I want to try something. Maybe there’s a way to feel around the edges of whatever guards his mind.”

Lucian searched her face and weighed her words before nodding. “Do what you need to do.”

Elín glanced at them but said nothing as Anja reached out to touch the Controller’s cheek. As she focused her energy, she felt that same eerie sensation as before—like running her fingers over a textured surface.

Carefully, she began to explore and push ever so slightly against the invisible walls that shielded the Controller’s mind. She was trying to untangle a knot with her thoughts, each string woven tightly.

As she concentrated, she felt something give. It was almost imperceptible, but it was there—a slight shift in the fabric of the ward.

And then, for just a moment, she sensed it: a flicker of something, an image, a fragment of an emotion. It was too fleeting to grasp, slipping through her mental fingers before she could clutch it. But it was there.

Anja stepped back, letting out a breath she hadn't realized she'd been holding. "It's complex," she said. "I can't break it, at least not now. But it's not impervious. There might be a way to get glimpses of what lies beneath. To find a weakness."

Emma stated, "So, they have their ways of guarding secrets. We need to figure this out. Our next steps will depend on what we can—or can't—learn from him."

"There's another possibility. What if I try entering his dreams? It's a less guarded state of mind. Perhaps I could convince him his secrets are safe and only ask him benign things."

Lucian raised an eyebrow. "Dreams? That seems like it might be promising, but can you learn anything from that?"

"I don't know, but It would be a start. Zoe might be able to help with his emotions. If he feels threatened, her new abilities might help defuse that."

Emma thought for a moment, her eyes narrowing in consideration. "Do you think that would work? Then again, what else can we try? I don't think drugs or other more vigorous methods would work, and they might even backfire."

Everything they were doing was new. "I just wonder how deep the tendrils of his bindings go. Do they have any teeth? That's a disturbing thought. Let's think about it."

Lucian looked at each of them, lingering on Anja for a beat longer. "Fine, we'll add it to the list of approaches. Talk to Zoe and see what she thinks."

Elín shook her head. "I can see you all believe in what you're saying, but…this sounds like you're talking about magic. What are you? What have you become?"

Lucian met her gaze steadily. "As Arthur C. Clarke once said, 'Any sufficiently advanced technology is indistinguishable from magic.' In our case, it's both."

Elín stared at them, her mouth slightly open as if to speak, but no words came. Finally, she nodded. "I'll try to catch up on the... advancements."

Lucian said. "We'll make sure you're not left behind, Elín. For now, let's continue with what we've got. You are going to witness more that will change your conceptions of the world. Some of it will be... jarring."

Emma chuckled. "*That's* a colossal understatement."

"Yes, well...prepare yourself by reading the reports from Isabelle at NexGen. They'll provide some context—shapeshifting, enhanced physical abilities, among other phenomena," Lucian stated.

Elín looked between them but said, "I'll dive into the reports as soon as possible."

Anja observed the exchange. Skeptic or not, Elín was stepping into a world far beyond her experience. That she was willing to engage meant they were forging a path together, however rocky it might be.

As they prepared to exit the room, Anja paused, her awareness focusing on Elín. A subtle current of energy pulsed from the Icelandic scientist. She hadn't noticed it before. The sensation was faint, but it was there.

It was a presence unlike anything she'd experienced before.

# *Three*

Over plates of freshly caught Arctic char garnished with local herbs and roasted root vegetables, the team fell into easy conversation. The food was exceptional, traditional Icelandic ingredients with a modern twist. When the dessert was served, Lucian wanted to move the discussion toward more serious matters. It had been a long day, but this was now more than just business. The stakes had grown, and all of their lives were in danger.

"As much as I've enjoyed this meal," he began, "I have something important to discuss. I want to alter our relationship. I want us to move forward as partners rather than employees or bodyguards." He paused to gauge their reactions. "I'll buy out your existing contracts, and we'll draft new agreements. As we face the uncertainties ahead, we should do it more as equals, each of us invested in our shared purpose. Thoughts?"

Emma was the first to respond. "I've seen this more as a collective endeavor for a while now rather than just a job. I'm in."

Carlos was thoughtful. "We've all been through too much to consider this just a job anymore."

"Well, it's about time, isn't it? I'm all for it," Ian stated with a grin.

Claire nodded. "That's an attractive and generous offer. I think I could get behind that. We're too deep in it to stop now; I'd like to see the details, but it sounds like a plan."

"Yes, it's more about formalizing how I've already been approaching our relationships. Giving you all the resources and a framework in which to operate."

Zoe looked hesitant. Her introspective expression drew Anja's attention.

"We can discuss this later tonight, Zoe," Anja whispered.

Lucian looked at Anja and nodded slightly, appreciating her wisdom in giving Zoe the space to mull things over. "We'll sort out the details soon. For now, let's enjoy the rest of the evening. Tomorrow promises to be another busy day."

With that, the conversation shifted back to lighter topics. He would let the new proposal germinate in the back of their minds, hoping to redefine their relationships.

Zoe couldn't avoid the feeling that the world around her was shaking, tectonic plates realigning beneath the surface. Was this partnership something she wanted to involve herself in more than she already had?

The dinner wound down, and Lucian paid the check. Anja leaned over and whispered, "Lucian and I would love to continue the discussion. It's important. Come to our room?"

Whatever reservations Zoe had, she felt the weight of that pulling her towards the decision she knew she would make. It was just hard to let go of her past ambitions. "Sure," Zoe replied. "I'm still trying to figure out my place in all this."

Lucian, who was saying goodbye to Carlos and Ian, paused and nodded to Zoe. "Good. We're entering a new phase."

Back at the hotel, they stepped into the room, and Zoe couldn't help but comment on the persistent sunlight filtering through the windows. "You know, seeing the sun still up at this hour is unnerving. It makes me feel like the day will never end."

Lucian chuckled as he moved to close the heavy curtains, plunging the room into a more familiar evening darkness. "Just wait until summer comes around. You'll think the sun has commitment issues with the horizon."

As he spoke, Anja turned on a couple of lamps, casting a warm glow and shifting the room to something more intimate, before sitting on the upholstered bench at the foot of the bed.

“So, about this partnership,” Zoe began, choosing her words carefully. “It’s not something I can enter into lightly. What are you thinking of?”

Lucian took a seat on one of the armchairs to the side. “A partnership, Zoe, means just that—having an equal voice in decisions, sharing responsibilities, and pursuing common goals. We’re on the cusp of something world-changing. You surely understand that. Of course, the risks we’re taking are not trivial, which is why the financial compensation will reflect that—fringe benefits and all. All expenses will be covered, and you can expect a generous remuneration. Beyond that, there are other perks—access to resources, a network of contacts, and the camaraderie you won’t find anywhere else.”

She weighed his words against her aspirations and reservations. Since her awakening, she was learning how to use her ability to read people. She had always had it to a lesser degree, but now she knew it was something she could control. Even now, though Anja was still hard to read, Zoe trusted Anja completely.

“And let’s not forget our primary objective—ending the Sodality, dismantling their operations, and wiping them off the map,” Lucian added.

Anja broke her silence. “And you won’t be doing it alone. We have each other’s backs. That’s non-negotiable. We need you, Zoe…*I* need you. You’ve already decided to join us. You knew you couldn’t turn your back. This is another evolution of that decision.”

Lucian nodded, casting a glance Anja’s way. “Exactly. So, Zoe, are you in?”

Zoe felt their eyes on her and the appeal of their vision. Lucian’s proposal wasn’t just about work; it was an invitation to be part of a collective force, each one enhancing the strength of the others. It was compelling. She could seek justice where the laws could not adapt fast enough. “Yes, I want to join you. It’s just…leaving the Bureau? It’s what I’ve worked for all my life. It’s a part of who I am.”

Lucian shifted in his chair. “It was a part of who you thought you were. But who's to say you have to make a clean break immediately? A foot in both worlds, at least for a little while, might give us some unique advantages. When you're ready, you can make the transition. No rush."

Anja was nodding. "I agree with Lucian. You'll know when the time is right. Until then, why not use your position to our mutual benefit?"

A warmth spread through Zoe—a weight lifted. "I'll do it. I'll be a part of this partnership. It's a unique situation, but maybe that's exactly what we need…what *I* need."

Lucian smiled. "Welcome aboard, Zoe."

Anja matched Lucian's smile. "Here's to new beginnings."

"Anja, this whole awakening thing…if I'm going to accept it, I need to understand it better," Zoe began, stopping to look at her friend. "You mentioned Rati and Mayavati before. Can we talk more about that?"

Anja looked up, her green eyes meeting Zoe's with understanding. "Of course. During your awakening, I thought you might be descended somehow from Rati, the Hindu goddess of love. Your heritage and, frankly, your proclivities supported that. Since then, I have only grown more confident of that." Anja smiled knowingly. "You're becoming more like Mayavati. Mayavati was an incarnation of Rati. She was known for her ability to read and influence people, to understand their deepest desires and fears."

Zoe took a seat beside Anja. "It's hard to wrap my head around. But as I learn more about myself, it starts to make sense. It explains so much about my life and my past. Like, my humor to cope with stress —it fits."

Anja smiled softly. "But now you're learning that you can also lower and manage it with your abilities without clowning around. You didn't have that before, and levity was what worked for you."

Zoe chuckled with a hint of relief. "Yeah, and I can amp up my appeal and appearance. I might be unable to shift forms like you or the others, but it feels similar. I could do that now, and I know you all wouldn't mind."

The future was uncertain, filled with risks and obstacles, but she was ready. But she also wanted to deepen the partnership. Since her awakening with them and the bond that had formed, there was a pull. Lucian and Anja were receptive. She'd noticed the attraction Lucian had to her, and Anja…well, her raw sexuality called.

A devilish grin crept onto Zoe's face as she caught Lucian's eye. "So, about those other 'fringe benefits?" She went ahead and used her unique form of shifting, willing her appearance to exude sex. It was subtle but seemed to be effective.

Anja chuckled. "Ah, those benefits are delightful," she purred, rising from her chair. "We wouldn't dream of leaving those out, would we, Lucian? Now, come to bed, Zoe."

Zoe's cheeks warmed with anticipation. Her heart rate increased as she realized her decision tonight was more than a new career path. It was an entry into a new life.

"Let's see what your new self can do, Zoe," Anja encouraged.

Zoe moved toward the comfort of the bed, using all her ethereal grace as her clothes fell away. A part of her life had closed, and another, full of opportunities, had opened. Whatever future awaited her, she was ready—very ready.

Lucian stood rooted to the spot and watched Zoe's confident stride toward the bed. His eyes lingered on Zoe's back, the fluid lines of muscle and the play of shadow and light over her skin. She was even more beautiful now, and he had no desire to resist, even knowing some of it was magic.

Anja's presence was a gravitational pull that went down to his marrow. More than desire, it was a connection that resonated with his essence, a surprise in his life of calculated moves and guarded heart.

Zoe was unexpected; she brought an element of conscience, a reminder of the humanity he was often too ready to sideline for his ambitions.

He knew how deep Anja's and Zoe's friendship was, and it grew daily. He doubted he could resist either of them individually, but together, he had no chance.

As Zoe reached the bed, the soft illumination played over her skin, bringing out the contours of her physique, each curve a verse in a silent hymn to femininity. When Anja joined Zoe at the bed, now equally undressed, he watched as they kissed, fingers tracing paths along each other's bodies. Lucian remained still, an observer on the cusp of becoming a participant, watching their kisses deepen. Seeing them together, longtime friends and now lovers, was tantalizing. They were the same height, and their bodies intertwined so naturally. Anja's burgundy hair and pale skin contrasted with Zoe's darker skin and hair. His erection hardened even more under his clothes as he watched their passion ignite.

As he stepped forward, his clothing was a barrier, a vestige of formality and restraint that was no longer needed. The world outside, with its dangers and its duties, faded.

Tonight was about exploration and connection, the mingling of souls as much as the confluence of bodies. It was unburdened, for once, from the call of the mystical or the need to gain power. It was only about them. The future was before them, vast and unknown, but they would face it as one. With a breath that was the first step into a new existence, Lucian moved to join Zoe and Anja.

They turned to watch as he approached. As he started to unbutton his shirt, their looks grew heated.

"Would either of you care to assist?" he asked, enjoying their appraisal.

They shook their heads in unison, and Zoe said, "Oh, no. I want to enjoy the show. How often do you get to see a hot billionaire strip?"

"I certainly hope it will be very often," Anja added.

Lucian's smile grew as he took in their response. "Very well." He slowly unzipped his pants, revealing a pair of black silk boxer briefs that hugged his hips. Zoe and Anja leaned forward, eyes fixed on the sight before them.

Lucian stripped off his shirt and tossed it aside. His chest was covered in a dusting of hair that glistened in the dim light of the room. He unclasped his watch, letting it fall to the carpet with a thud.

Zoe watched him bend and remove his shoes. Anja leaned in closer, reaching out to touch the curve of his hip.

"Touch me," he said, his voice low and seductive. "But only if you want to."

Anja's fingers traced a path across Lucian's hip, her touch light and feather-like. He closed his eyes and let out a moan of pleasure, his body tensing under her fingertips. Zoe watched them intently, her hand moving towards the bulge in his boxer briefs. She traced around the elastic band, feeling the heat radiating from beneath the fabric.

Lucian moved his hips as he felt their touch, and he let out a growl of desire. "You like that, don't you?" Zoe whispered.

Lucian nodded, his eyes still closed. "Yes," he said, his voice husky. "I do."

Anja leaned in closer, her lips grazing the side of his neck. "You taste so good," she murmured.

He stripped off his boxers and let them fall to the floor. Zoe sucked in a breath at the sight of him, fully aroused and ready. He reached out, took Zoe's hand, and climbed onto the bed. "You first," he said.

Zoe straddled him on the bed. Anja lay beside them, watching them intently as they came together.

Zoe pushed down onto him as he lay back. Anja's eyes wandered over Zoe's body, lingering on every curve. Her fingers traced along her side and then to their joining, a smile playing at her lips as she watched him pump into Zoe.

Zoe's walls contracted in a wave of pleasure, so hot and tight. She traced her fingertips along the curves of her breasts, her eyes closing momentarily.

Lucian felt a sense of satisfaction as Zoe's body writhed on top of him. Her hands clutched at his shoulders, her nails digging into his skin as they reached their peak together.

As they came, Anja's eyes opened wide, a look of pure ecstasy washing over her. She watched them intently as they convulsed with pleasure, her own body responding to the power of it. Pulling in some of the energy—the magic from their orgasms—she came too. Her ability to sense both of them expanded; it was like she was in Zoe's place, feeling Zoe's pleasure as her own.

Zoe moved to Anja. Lucian tasted their desire—a hunger that had been growing since they first got onto the bed. She leaned in and pressed her lips to Anja's. Her tongue explored her mouth as she kissed her deeply.

Zoe's hands roamed over Anja's body. She traced her breasts with her hands, eliciting a soft moan. Her mouth continued downwards, dipping into the hollow of her neck before moving lower still.

As Zoe's tongue flickered over her nipples, Anja closed her eyes and threw back her head. Her hips rose off the bed, meeting Zoe's movements with her own.

Lucian watched, his body responding to the sight before him, hardening again. Anja moved, turning Zoe onto her back with her head near the edge of the bed. Anja climbed on top, straddled Zoe's face, and leaned down so she could lick at the joining of Zoe's legs while giving her the same access. He could imagine Anja tasting his seed as she licked and sucked at Zoe's clit and opening. It was driving him crazy with lust once again.

While he moved into position, Zoe looked up at him and smiled. Slowly, he pushed into Anja to her moans of pleasure, muffled with her face between Zoe's legs.

As Lucian began to thrust into Anja from behind, Zoe's tongue continued to dance around her clit. Seeing them feasting on each other was becoming too much to bear. The pressure was building inside him as he started to pick up speed, thrusting into Anja harder and faster.

Zoe moaned loudly, her hips writhing under Anja's ministrations. Anja's hair obscured what was happening, but his imagination ran with it as Anja continued to pleasure her. Anja gasped for air, her hands clutching at the sheets.

Lucian felt his orgasm near, his body tense with anticipation. He reached down to touch Zoe as he pulled back from Anja. Zoe leaned her head back off the bed and opened her mouth for him, which he filled. Zoe's fingers moved to Anja's clit, taking over for her tongue.

The feeling was almost too intense; he wouldn't last much longer. He pulled out of Zoe's mouth and re-entered Anja, picking up his pace again.

His rhythm turned ragged. She moaned again, her movements becoming frantic as Zoe tried to bring her to climax, fingers and tongue working together.

Finally, he couldn't take it any longer. With a cry, he erupted inside Anja, feeling his seed pulse through his body and into hers. Zoe continued to lick and suck at Anja's clit while her orgasm took her. He felt her orgasm through the link Anja had put in place. The room filled with the sounds of their pleasure, each one feeding off the others' ecstasy until they all collapsed onto the bed in a heap of sweaty, satisfied bodies.

As they caught their breath, Lucian looked down at Zoe and Anja lying beneath him. He saw the love and desire in their eyes and knew that this was more than just a physical connection. It was as if they were linked together somehow. He marveled at his fortune; the three were bound together by a force greater than any could have imagined.

# *Four*

ANJA STRETCHED, THE morning light seeping through the gaps in the heavy curtains. Her muscles ached satisfyingly as she turned to look at Lucian, who was propped up on pillows and scrolling through his phone. Zoe, on the other hand, was sprawled naked across the other edge of the bed, her breathing slow and even in sleep.

The light played over Lucian's form, softening the contours of his face. She studied him, recognizing the subtle shift in his aura and the expansion of his heart that Zoe had cultivated. It was beautiful to witness.

Her blossoming love for Zoe transcended their longstanding friendship. Her soul had recognized a kindred flame, and now, with Lucian's presence weaving through their connection, the bond was cast in a vibrant new light.

It was a balance of power, care, and desire that surprised Anja in its intensity. They had established a psychic bond of sorts. The ability to sense each other's emotions and sensations amped up the sex incredibly, too. Anja envisioned their future, filled with shared battles and quiet intimacies. *Yes,* she thought, *this is what I want*.

"Morning," Lucian whispered, leaning over to kiss Anja. "I'll let you have the first shower."

"Such a gentleman," she teased. Slipping out of bed, she padded into the en suite bathroom, turned on the shower, and let the water warm up before stepping in. As the steam rose around her, Anja turned her thoughts to the day ahead.

After a few minutes, the bathroom door clicked open and shut. Zoe had woken and was now taking her turn in the shower—only Anja hadn't finished hers.

As Zoe stepped into the shower, the glass door closed behind her. "Room for one more?"

Anja smiled, moving over. "I think I can make room for you."

Zoe stepped into the stream of water, and their eyes met—a silent acknowledgment of the intimacy of the moment and the night past. Zoe picked up the soap and lathered it between her hands before applying it to Anja's back.

Anja reciprocated, taking the soap from Zoe and lathering up her hands. She started with Zoe's shoulders, working the soap into a foam as she moved down her back. She noted the firmness of Zoe's muscles due to her rigorous training and marveled at the softness of her skin, which was darker and a pleasant contrast to Anja's paler tone. The juxtaposition intrigued her, much like Zoe herself always had.

Zoe sighed happily. "Why didn't we ever do this in college?"

"We were two different people then—I probably would have freaked. I like who we've become, though."

In a whisper, barely heard over the spraying water, Zoe confided, "Me too. I never lusted after women before, but this—this opens up a whole new world for me."

"Neither did I, Zoe. Neither did I—and yes, it does."

As Anja's hands reached Zoe's lower back, she turned her around so they were face to face. Her arms went around behind, still soapy and slick, to continue to wash lower in a slippery embrace.

"Today is going to be something, isn't it?" Zoe finally spoke. "Diving into someone's dreams, huh? Seems like something out of a fantasy novel."

Anja grinned, her fingers moving in slow, soothing circles on Zoe's back. "Yet here we are, two women with abilities most people wouldn't believe. If anyone could pull it off, it's us."

"True. When you put it that way, it doesn't sound so crazy. You know, I joined the FBI to bring about justice and make the world safer. And now, here I am."

"That's not a departure from your original goals, Zoe. It's just a change of direction."

"We'll make it work."

"Yes, and whatever happens, we'll face it together." The kiss they shared sealed it as a promise. With that agreement hanging in the air, they stepped out of the shower, the water shutting off behind them.

That one word reverberated in Anja's mind as they dried off and began to prepare for the day. Together. It was a simple word but loaded with meaning and promise. And as they left the bathroom, towels discarded, Anja had an added sense of belonging she hadn't known she was missing.

"We need to make some headway with the Controller's barriers today," Lucian began, taking in the sight of the two naked women. "It would be good if you both got dressed. I wouldn't want us to get distracted."

Zoe had to respond. "But I wouldn't mind…"

Anja just shook her head but couldn't help a matching smile. "Zoe and I were discussing infiltrating the Controller's dreams. With her ability to read emotional reactions, she could put him at ease, maybe even steer his emotions in a direction that could help us."

"Maybe that will give us the opening we need," Lucian said.

"Exactly," Anja agreed. "And while we do that, you can update Elín on what's been happening. She was struggling with the information overload but is trying to keep an open mind."

Lucian rose, pulling on his robe. "I'll shower and then fill Elín in. You two start prepping for the dream assignment."

Zoe began to rummage through Anja's suitcase for fresh clothes.

"You know, Zoe, you do have your own clothes…"

With a scowl belied with a crinkling of her eyes, Zoe griped, "Yeah, and you need to get a better wardrobe. You're not in the library anymore. I'll need to take you out shopping—on that expense account…I'll go fetch my own clothes." She snatched up her room key and headed out the door, still naked.

"Not that I'm complaining, but has she always been that uninhibited?" Lucian asked.

"Pretty much, and I think there will be no holding her back now," Anja replied with a smile.

Anja entered the cold room, immediately focusing on the man bound to the bed. The beeping of monitors punctuated the air; each beep highlighted the man's stillness. The Controller lay in a position that might have evoked sympathy under different circumstances—restrained and defenseless. But that was the last thing Anja felt. She adjusted the bright lights to soften them with the slider by the door.

The IV dripped some concoction into his veins, presumably to keep him sedated. Perhaps it was too kind a treatment for a man who had wanted them captured or dead. A chill of distaste snaked through her, clashing with the warmth from just hours before with Zoe and Lucian.

"We need to find a way past whatever safeguards he has in his mind, glean whatever we can about the Sodality's operations." Anja moved closer to the bed, taking him in. His eyes were closed, but Anja knew that behind his eyelids were layers upon layers of defenses. Even unconscious, this man was a vault. A dangerous, guarded safe that they had to crack open.

"Zoe, would you use your abilities? Maybe we can navigate his emotional responses and put him at ease enough to lower his defenses. We need to try something. I'll try to enter his dreams and see what I can gather there. If I can bring his subconscious thoughts or emotions to the surface, you might be able to read them more easily. It will be like lucid dreaming, but I will be there with him."

"It could be the perfect one-two punch. I'll monitor both of your reactions from here. If things go south, I'll try to pull you out."

"Okay." Anja took a deep, steadying breath as she positioned herself beside the Controller's bed. Her fingers barely grazed his forehead, her powers focusing on his surface mind.

As her consciousness slipped into his, the room around her shifted, its contours blurring and reforming. She found herself standing in a dreamscape—a distorted version of the room, vivid yet hazy, as dreams often were. The air here was thick with an ethereal glow, and everything seemed to pulse with a subtle, rhythmic energy.

She needed to learn how to think about this dreaming state. If she were to use her succubus form's powers, she could instinctively weave seduction and sex into it, but he was mystically guarded. She wanted to tread carefully.

The Controller lay still, his body and mind at rest but without restraints, monitors, or IV tubes. Anja could feel the resistance in his subconscious, a natural barrier that guarded his mind. She needed to coax him into a deeper state of dreaming, to navigate the layers of his mind without triggering his defenses. To gently 'wake' him into a shared dream.

She closed her eyes and visualized soft, golden tendrils of energy extending from her fingertips, wrapping around his thoughts and intertwining them with hers, becoming one lucid dream. "Relax," she whispered, her voice an echo in the dreamscape. "Let go and drift."

The dreamscape responded to her words, the hazy edges becoming slightly more defined. Flickers of memories and abstract shapes formed, a sign that his mind was beginning to engage in the dream state. She felt a psychic tether anchoring her back to reality, Zoe's presence serving as a safety line.

Anja moved closer to the Controller. She reached out with her mind, nudging his subconscious toward deeper realms of dreaming. It was like guiding a child through a dark forest, using the warmth of her presence to dispel the shadows.

She conjured a scene in their mind from unguarded images that floated up—a peaceful meadow, the air filled with the thrum of crickets. The stars above twinkled, each a point of light guiding him further into the dream. She felt his resistance wavering, the barriers of his mind not detecting a threat. Zoe's calming presence washed over them both.

"See the stars?" she murmured. "Follow them, let them lead you."

The dreamscape shifted again, the meadow becoming more vivid, more real. She sensed his mind opening up; the threads of his thoughts became more focused but remained pliable. She could feel the tension in him ease, his consciousness beginning to flow more freely.

As the meadow blossomed around them, she saw him start to dream, his body relaxing even further. Her task was far from over, but for now, she had coaxed him into the safety of the dream, setting the stage for the next step in their plan.

Anja gently retreated, loosening the threads connecting her to the Controller enough to focus on the real world around her. She was pulled back with a twist, her eyes meeting Zoe's immediately.

"You did it. He's stirring; I think you made an impact."

"Let's hope it's enough to slip past some of his barriers."

"Well then, Phase Two?"

"Phase Two," Anja affirmed. Together, they turned back toward the Controller. "I'm going back in, but I'll try a different angle this time. I will enter his dream as a captive, someone he's successfully caught. People tend to be more revealing when they believe they're in a position of complete power."

"That's a good approach, but be careful. That could turn volatile quickly."

"I'll be cautious." Anja closed her eyes, focusing her psychic energy to reenter the Controller's dream.

The dreamscape shifted, and she formed an image of herself bound, but formed her surroundings from images from his memory. Anja found herself in a dimly lit room. The Controller had a triumphant look on his face.

"So, you thought you could escape us?" he sneered. "It's not so easy, is it?"

Anja feigned resignation. "What's going to happen to me now?"

"You'll be taken to our control center. The Grandmaster himself will be pleased. Your capture could lure Lucian out. He's the real threat."

Anja's internal radar pinged at the mention of Lucian and the Grandmaster. She decided to push a little more. "And who are you?"

He looked at her with a smug smile. "My name is Richard. Richard Kael."

Anja filed away every detail, from the mention of the Grandmaster to Richard's desire to use her to draw out Lucian. They had already assumed that. It was the bait they had laid to capture him. "If I'm your captive, take me to this control center now—get it over with. There is no reason to wait. Show me my fate."

Richard's eyes gleamed with triumph. "No, not just any control center. The Vault. A place only a select few have seen. Imagine—presenting you to the Grandmaster there. He will be pleased."

As he spoke, the dreamscape altered with more images from his memory, giving Anja the view of a darkened chamber she interpreted as inside the Vault. The walls were lined with monitors and advanced technology.

"Look at the Grandmaster's face when he sees you." Anja's words painted the air as a man appeared in the dreamscape. He was in his late forties, impeccably dressed, with salt-and-pepper hair so perfectly styled it could have been a sculpture. His gray eyes, devoid of color, penetrated everything they looked upon.

Anja's eyes blinked open. "I'm getting better at this, I think. I have his name, at least, and a glimpse of what might be their headquarters—what he named the Vault. I also got an image of their Grandmaster."

Zoe barely contained a smile. "Good. It seems we're gaining ground at last."

Anja closed her eyes again and concentrated, shifting the dream once more and weaving more of his memories with hers. They were in a plainly furnished apartment overlooking the New York skyline this time. "Why not make this a little more personal?" she suggested, silky voice laced with seduction. She led him down a corridor toward what she assumed would be his bedroom, her heart pounding.

As she neared the door, she felt it—a sudden change, a shift in the energy of the dreamscape. His psychic barriers were alerted, defenses snapping into place. "What are you trying to do?" he snarled, lunging at her.

Anja sidestepped, avoiding his grasp. She had dreaded this moment—the point where she could no longer manipulate the dream. *Worth a try,* she thought as she braced herself and tugged at that tether to Zoe.

Anja's eyes flew open. Sweat trickled down her forehead; her breathing was erratic but steadied. Zoe had pulled her hand away.

"I sensed trouble, but nothing I did seemed to help."

"That didn't go as planned," Anja admitted. "His barriers kicked in. But we learned something—his defenses are powerful, even in his subconscious."

"At least we know more of what we're up against. Let's think about our next moves."

"That's all we can do for now. At least we've gained some insights. Sometimes, a setback tells you more than a win."

Zoe rose to her feet, stretching out the tension that had built up during the psychic expedition. "I'll need to continue with the interviews of Akar employees so the lab personnel can get back to their routine. We've injected a lot of upheaval."

Anja agreed. "I'll update Lucian on what we've discovered. He needs to know about the barriers and the little I learned. After that, I need to find the others to see how they're doing."

"Let's get together later and decide on our next moves," Zoe said.

"Okay. Also, could you get together with Emma and consider some interaction with Nomad? Ply him with cafeteria food and maybe some sunlight and get a feel for how far we can trust him."

Zoe nodded. "Sure."

Anja extended her hand, Zoe grasped it, and, for a moment, their hands lingered.

# *Five*

ZOE REACHED THE temporary space that Sigri had arranged. The schedule had been shifted to accommodate their interlude with the Controller. The room was modest, with a few tables and chairs and a coffee machine humming in the corner. Emma was already there, waiting to assist.

"Hey, Emma," Zoe greeted, her voice warm. "Ready to get started today?"

Emma nodded. "We've got the first technician lined up. Sigri should be here soon with him."

As if on cue, Sigri entered, guiding a young man in a lab coat before stepping out to get the next ready. His nervous energy was palpable.

"Hello," Zoe said, extending her hand. "I'm Zoe, and this is Emma. We just have a few questions for you, nothing to worry about."

The technician shook her hand, his grip a bit too tight. "I'm Erik. Nice to meet you."

"Nice to meet you too, Erik. Please, have a seat," Zoe said, gesturing to a chair.

Erik sat down, fidgeting slightly. Zoe took the seat opposite him, her empathic powers already at work. She could feel his anxiety but also a sense of satisfaction with his role. It was a good start.

"Erik, can you tell us about your duties at the supercomputing center?"

"I'm a systems technician," Erik replied. "I maintain the servers and ensure everything runs smoothly. It's a lot of work, but I love it."

"That's great to hear. Have you noticed anything unusual lately? Any security concerns or anything that didn't seem right?"

Erik hesitated, then shook his head. "No, everything seems normal. We've had a few minor glitches, but nothing unusual."

Zoe leaned in, her eyes meeting his. "Erik, it's important that we trust each other. If there's anything at all, no matter how small, please let us know. How about any rumors you've heard in the last day or two? I'm sure things have been buzzing."

Erik took a deep breath. "Well, yes. I've heard that Dr. Miller himself has come in with some new and urgent hush-hush project. I guess that's why these new security protocols and directives have been flying around."

"That would be a good guess. Have you heard anything else?" Emma asked.

"I heard from one of the help desk guys that there were a lot of complaints. One of the geneticists who already had one of his pet projects redirected not too long ago was asking a lot of questions. Maybe he's worried about another change. Is that something?"

Zoe glanced at Emma before smiling and giving him a nudge of happiness. "Oh, most definitely. Did you get his name by chance?"

"No, but you can ask Justin."

Emma jotted down a note and asked, "Anything else you can think of?"

"I don't think so, but I'll be sure and let you know," he said.

Zoe smiled. "Thank you, Erik. That's all we ask. Can you have Sigri step in when you leave?"

Zoe looked at Emma, who nodded approvingly as Sigri came in. They gave her Justin's name and asked her to move him up in the schedule.

"I'll make the arrangements and see where your next customer is. He's late," Sigri said before leaving and closing the door.

"Another down, many more to go," Emma said. "That was an easy one. I didn't even get to play bad cop and we still got a lead. You have a knack for this."

Zoe sighed. "Thanks, Emma. Let's hope the rest go as smoothly."

Emma's warm gaze held a flicker of something more than professional admiration. Zoe felt a flutter in her stomach. It probably didn't help she had put a little power into her allure to help with the interviews. It seemed to be generalized to anyone near her—something to keep in mind.

In her past life, before learning about this shadow world, she had never had much interest in women, but now she couldn't help but notice Emma. Zoe was beginning to wonder if her powers affected her more than she realized—something to ask Anja when she had a chance.

"So, Emma," Zoe said, her voice taking on a playful edge. "Do you always watch people so closely, or is it just me?"

Emma smirked, leaning back in her chair. "Oh, I'm just doing my job. Seeing if I can pick up new techniques."

"Learning anything?"

"Well, when the view is this interesting, it's hard not to, and it certainly makes these interviews more bearable."

"Is that so?" Zoe asked, looking directly into her eyes.

Emma's cheeks flushed slightly, but she held Zoe's gaze, her tone light yet suggestive. "Yes. We work well together."

"You find me interesting, do you?"

"Very much so. There's something about you, Zoe. You're… captivating."

"I could say the same about you, Emma."

Emma leaned closer, closing the distance between them just enough to feel the electricity in the air. "I'm glad you think so. Maybe we can…explore that potential a bit more."

"I'd like that. But maybe we should save some of that exploring for later."

Emma laughed. "Probably a good idea. We don't want to scare off the next candidate."

Zoe's eyes sparkled with amusement. "No, we wouldn't want that. But just so you know, I'm looking forward to seeing where this goes."

Before Emma could respond, Sigri returned with the next employee. The moment was interrupted, but as they prepared for the next interview, Zoe couldn't help but feel that this was just the beginning of something deeper, something with the potential to grow. Didn't she have enough to complicate her life? She was still trying to figure out things with Anja and Lucian.

Zoe and Emma straightened as Sigri guided the next person into the room. The man was middle-aged, with sharp features and a perpetually furrowed brow. His body language screamed annoyance.

"This is Dr. Harold Brenner, lead for the quantum computing research section," Sigri introduced, her tone professional but tense.

"This is a complete waste of my time," he snapped. "I have important work to do. Quantum computing breakthroughs don't happen while I'm being interrogated like a common criminal."

Zoe took a deep breath, calling on her empathic powers to soothe his agitation. "Dr. Brenner, I understand your frustration. This is a precautionary measure to ensure the lab's security. We appreciate your cooperation."

"Cooperation? This is nothing but bureaucratic nonsense. Sigri, surely you can see this is pointless."

Sigri's eyes flicked to Zoe, a silent plea for patience. "Dr. Brenner, this is at the director's orders."

Brenner sneered. "The director's orders, huh? The ice bitch herself?"

Sigri's expression tightened, but before she could respond, her phone buzzed. She glanced at the screen and then whispered into the phone, "Elín, we need you here."

Knowing Sigri, Zoe imagined she had given the director a heads-up anticipating problems with this particular individual. The call had come in at the perfect time.

"Sit down, Brenner. That is not a request," Emma stated coldly, getting to play her bad cop role.

After a few tense minutes of waiting, Elín entered the room. Her gray eyes locked onto Dr. Brenner as he stood.

"Dr. Brenner," she began, her tone icy and authoritative, "I understand you're unhappy with these interviews. However, they are a condition of your continued employment here, no matter how good you are in your field."

Brenner's sneer faltered. "Director, this is ridiculous. My time is better spent on my research, not on these trivialities."

Elín stepped closer. "What's ridiculous, Dr. Brenner, is your insubordination. This is paramount. Your expertise in quantum computing is valuable, but it does not exempt you from following protocols. You will cooperate fully, or you will find yourself out of a job. Is that clear?"

Dr. Brenner's face flushed. "Fine," he muttered.

"Good. Now, sit down and answer the questions. You're done here when they say you're done."

Dr. Brenner slumped into the chair, his earlier bravado thoroughly dismantled. Zoe glanced at Elín, silently thanking her for the intervention. Elín gave a barely perceptible nod before turning on her heel and leaving the room.

Zoe leaned forward. "Dr. Brenner, we'll make this as quick and painless as possible. Let's start with your role and recent projects. This is just to ensure everything is in order."

Dr. Brenner sighed. "I lead the quantum computing research section. We've been working on..."

The interviews continued, each one bringing its challenges and revelations. The lead Erik had provided was accurate, and the individual Erik indicated would be monitored while they figured out what to do with him. But through it all, the playful exchanges and growing attraction between Zoe and Emma continued.

Claire leaned back in her chair, staring at the monitors before her. The lab was quiet now, and the hum of air circulation was the only sound. She sighed, feeling the weight of the day settle on her shoulders. It was a strange juxtaposition—there seemed to be both too much to do and yet nothing that truly challenged her.

Lucian's words from the previous night echoed in her mind. He had spoken about turning their relationship into a partnership rather than just being bodyguards. But it left her feeling adrift, unsure of her place in this new dynamic. The rigid guard schedule had been dropped to be replaced with new duties, but the tasks she had been given felt menial, almost degrading. Arranging for Zoe's things to be moved in with Lucian and Anja had been the final straw. It seemed like sex was going to invade politics once more, and Claire found herself bitterly resenting it.

Lucian had been beset by countless issues that consumed all of his attention, not giving her an opportunity to discuss some of her reservations. She glanced at the clock and decided it was time to return to the hotel. Gathering her things, she tried to push the frustration aside. Her wolf was restless, agitated by the lack of action and the constant tension. They were away from the looming threat of the Sodality for now, but hiding did not sit well with her. She'd missed out on the action at Anja's estate, but the dead bodies were real enough. Staging the bodies when they had captured the Controller had somehow seemed wrong, even though they had all agreed it was the only thing they could do at the time.

As she made her way to the parking lot, she spotted Zoe and Emma leaving as well. They were laughing, their bodies close as they walked. Claire couldn't help but notice the chemistry between them, the subtle touches and shared glances. It only served to deepen her sense of isolation.

She climbed into the SUV, taking a deep breath to steady herself. But as Zoe and Emma joined her, the scent of desire filled the car. Claire's senses were heightened, her wolf straining against her control. The aroma of their budding attraction set her on edge on top of everything else.

Zoe glanced over at Claire. "Long day, huh?"

Claire forced a smile, trying to keep her tone light. "You could say that."

Emma leaned forward from the back seat, her eyes twinkling with mischief. "Maybe we should plan a girls' night soon. Something to unwind and let off some steam."

The suggestion should have been innocent enough on the surface, but the underlying innuendo made Claire's blood boil. She nodded, her voice tight. "Yeah, no. I have a better idea. We have some sparring time scheduled in the gym tomorrow morning. You're on the list. Wouldn't want you to get too out of practice with your somewhat iffy combat skills, unless you're too busy trying to get in everyone's pants. Or you're just too much of a pussy."

"Oh, you bitch! You're on," Emma exclaimed, her temper flaring.

What had once seemed like friendly teasing was starting to take on a darker undertone. When Claire turned around to face Emma in the back seat, Zoe placed a hand on Emma's arm.

"You need to get laid or have some good alone time." Emma sat back and looked out the window.

When Zoe turned her attention to her, Claire shook her head and said, "Don't even try your shit on me. It's bad enough you're crawling into bed with them. Fucking your way right to the top."

"Wow. I think Emma is right. Let's just call it a day and chill."

As they drove back to the hotel, Claire stared out the window, trying to ignore the ache of loneliness that settled in her chest. The scent of desire lingered, a constant reminder of what she was missing. Her wolf paced, a low growl vibrating through her core. *Yeah*, she thought. *Something has to give.*

When they reached the hotel, Claire was still on edge, her nerves frayed. She needed to find a way to release the tension, to calm the restless energy that threatened to overwhelm her. But for now, all she could do was endure, hoping that tomorrow would bring some clarity and purpose to her role in this new, uncertain landscape.

Claire trudged up to her room, tossed her bag onto the bed, and sank into the chair by the window, gazing at the ocean. The thought of her life as a lone wolf was unbearable.

Maybe it was time to talk to Lucian about a trip to England. Reconnecting with her relatives might help her find some balance, although she was unsure what to share with them. Her mum always had a way of grounding her, offering wisdom and comfort that no one else could. Perhaps her mum would have some suggestions on what she should do. Claire sighed, the thought of home stirring a bittersweet longing in her chest.

And then there was Anja. Claire had seen how calm and composed Anja seemed, even amid chaos. Maybe Anja had some insight, some way to help her find some peace.

Claire stood up and paced the room, her frustration boiling over.

She needed an outlet, something to channel the raw power coursing through her veins. Sex would help, but masturbation had never been her thing. The only unattached team member she was attracted to was Ian, and jumping into bed with her erstwhile boss was a bad idea. There were already way too many complications within the team. Going off to pick up a stranger was even worse.

With a determined nod, she grabbed her phone and texted Lucian.

*Claire: Can we talk tomorrow? I'm thinking about taking a trip to England. Need to reconnect with family.*

She sent the message and took a deep breath, feeling a slight sense of relief. It was a small step, but it was something. Next, she thought about sending a text to Anja but decided to wait—one thing at a time.

Claire put her phone down and glanced at the clock. It was late, but sleep seemed like a distant possibility. She changed into workout clothes and headed to the hotel gym, hoping to burn off some energy.

The gym was empty, a welcome contrast to the turmoil in her mind. Claire started with the treadmill, pushing herself to run faster and harder until her legs burned. The physical exertion helped.

After the run, she moved to the weights, lifting and pushing, stopping only when her muscles screamed in protest. The pain was a welcome distraction, a temporary balm to the storm raging within her. By the time she finished, she was drenched in sweat, her body exhausted but her mind slightly clearer.

Back in her room, she took a long shower, letting the water wash away the sweat and tension. As she climbed into bed, she allowed herself to hope that tomorrow would bring some answers, some way to find peace amidst the chaos.

Maybe, just maybe, she could find a way to balance the wild energy within her and the responsibilities she carried. For now, it was enough to have a plan, even if it was uncertain.

# *Six*

CARLOS STOOD ON the windswept hill overlooking the landscape. The Akar compound was not far away. The chill in the spring air was brisk, but Aria, his falcon, seemed to take to it with ease. Her feathers ruffled in the breeze as she perched on his gloved hand, eyeing her new domain with interest.

He was still unsure how Aria would fit into his life here, with all the changes and obligations vying for resolution. Aria was a part of him now, and giving her up would be like cutting off his own hand.

Even still, she was an illegal alien, smuggled in and residing here secretly. He could relate to the immigration issues faced by so many refugees. It was hard to see how to make this right.

Footsteps crunched on the gravel path behind him, pulling him from his reverie. He didn't need to turn to know who it was. The scent of Anja's familiar perfume mingled with the crisp air. It made him smile.

"How's Aria settling in?" Anja asked as she came to stand beside him.

The falcon's talons gripped his glove as if she'd always belonged there. "Better than I expected. She enjoys the scenery change and the wide-open spaces here. It appeals to her predatory nature and her sharp eyesight."

"And you? How are you doing?"

"This bond with Aria means so much to me. This is all so new, and everything is changing so fast, but I can't go back."

"No, none of us can. You aren't alone now, especially with that beautiful bird."

Anja reached out to stroke Aria's feathers. The falcon responded with an approving chirp—"chup-chup…eee-chup"—as if giving Anja her thanks.

He could see Anja's curiosity as the falcon stretched her wings in the breeze. "Have you flown her?"

Carlos shook his head. "No, not yet. I want to give her another day to get used to everything. I also want to coordinate more with security. I wouldn't want her to get too fond of killing drones, although I think I've worked out a way to capture them."

"Maybe I can join you for her first flight here?"

"I think Aria would like that," he said, his voice softer than he intended, "and so would I."

As he spoke, Aria flapped her wings as if sharing her approval. Things were starting to fall into place after arriving in this icy, foreign land. He hoped that his uneasiness would fade.

Anja returned to Elín's office to get her bearings in this large complex. From there, she moved down the hall to where Sigri and Zoe had set up an interview room. They found Sigri efficient, and she ensured a smooth flow of employees to be interviewed.

"Any new red flags?" Anja inquired, getting Zoe's attention as the door opened from her current interview.

Zoe shook her head. "No, only the one from yesterday. These are going better than expected. We should be done by later today."

"Good, keep me posted. I thought Emma would be helping you again today. Is something up?"

"Well, kinda. Tensions are running high between Claire and Emma. Some words were said after we finished yesterday's batch. Emma was flirting with me, which set Claire off. Emma said Claire needed to get laid, which didn't help. Claire challenged Emma to a sparring match this morning."

"Isn't that your line? I seem to recall hearing you tell me I needed to get laid a time or two."

"Yeah, and where did that get me? Huh?" Zoe asked, waggling her eyebrows.

Rolling her eyes, Anja turned to Sigri. "They still there?"

Sigri glanced down at her tablet, swiping through the schedule before looking up. "They should still be in the gym. They blocked it off for another hour."

"Thank you, Sigri." Anja turned back to Zoe. "You didn't mention that last night, but then again, I guess we got distracted."

"I needed it after being close to Emma all day and then Claire going off. Would you talk to her?"

"Sure. Um, which one?"

"Both, I guess." Zoe shrugged. "I think I strung Emma along… although…well, she feels left out, and part of me responded. And Claire seems to be losing it."

"Okay, I'll talk to them. See if I can figure something out."

She had still not decoded the protocol for dealing with a female lover in public and had no clue if she should give Zoe a kiss, hug, or something else. Emma didn't seem to have these problems. Maybe Anja should ask. She settled for a kiss that threatened to devolve into more before saying "bye" and scurrying off, leaving Zoe a bit breathless and Sigri with a blush. Oh, hell. It felt good anyway.

Fortunately, maps of the less restricted areas posted at intersections were labeled in multiple languages. As she headed towards the gym, her boots nearly silent against the floor, she considered the interplay between all of them. Each brought something crucial to the table, and as she thought about what lay ahead, she was grateful to have them by her side, even with occasional issues.

As Anja pushed open the gym door, Ian and Claire were engrossed in what was unmistakably an MMA practice session. Ian, embodying the stoic strength she'd come to associate with his bear otherkin traits, moved with an awe-inspiring grounded power. On the other hand, Claire exhibited the agility and cunning of her wolf lineage, dodging Ian's attempts to land a decisive blow.

It was like watching a dance, a clash of primal forces that was as mesmerizing as it was intense. They moved around the mat, their muscles glistening with sweat, each attuned to the other's movements. Ian remained focused and steady, while Claire was sometimes almost a blur.

As they continued their sparring, Ian and Claire noticed they had an audience. Breaking off from their engagement, they turned towards her, their faces shifting from focused intensity to recognition.

"Anja," Ian greeted, his bare chest rising and falling as he caught his breath.

Claire tried not to smile, still high with adrenaline. "Couldn't resist watching us go at it, huh?"

Anja smiled and tried not to think about watching them go at it in bed. That would be a sight. "The two of you are quite the spectacle. Makes for compelling viewing. Have you seen Emma?"

Ian and Claire exchanged glances, both with teasing smiles. "She wimped out," Claire said. "Said she needed a shower and should be out in a few minutes."

"Ah, so she's washing off the shame of defeat, is she?"

Ian laughed, the sound echoing in the gym. "Something like that."

With a shake of her head, Anja said, "I'll wait for her then. You two keep at it."

"I'd like to set up some sparring time with you, Anja. Lucian said you were holding back on me. Maybe even work out with Claire and me if you think you can," Ian dared. Again, those other thoughts started to intrude.

A spark of something stirred in her at the request. Something that wanted to come out and play—in more than one way. "If I can get a chance, that may be a good idea. I'm still worried the Sodality will find us here before we are ready. For now, I'll just watch."

They returned to their sparring with renewed vigor. Anja's senses reached out to gauge their emotions. Claire's energy was a vibrant mix of excitement and determination. It also carried an underlying current of frustration. Probing a little deeper to see if she could find the source, she sensed a conflict in Claire between her wolf nature and her human side. Anja felt the sexual tension between Claire and Ian as well, adding to that frustration.

A sudden insight came to mind. Claire's wolf aspect needed

tempering, a counterbalance to its wild energy. Claire's awakening had not gone to plan, overpowered by the call of the full moon that night. Although it had successfully brought her into wolf form, the awakening was incomplete, leaving her at a point where her control was fragmentary. Anja's power was rooted in intimacy and forging deep emotional connections that allowed her to guide the mental control that Claire still needed. However, since Claire was strictly into men, that had not been a part of that original ritual between them. She could not channel that power with Claire directly.

Lucian was another potential conduit, but Anja knew the complications would be too awkward. Ian, however, stood as a strong possibility. His bear-like stamina and composure could be the grounding force Claire needed, especially during the full moons when her wolf nature was at its peak. Anja's mind returned to her earlier thoughts of watching them 'go at it,' and she wanted to push out her power and see it happen here and now but held that back—*bearly.* She grinned at the pun.

Anja watched them spar, contemplating how to approach it. If she could complete the ritual for Claire while Ian acted as the focus, there would be plenty of energy. Yes, she thought, that could work, and it would work well. It was something that they needed to do.

Emma stepped out of the showers, her skin tingling from the hot water, and saw Anja near the gym exit. "Hey," she greeted.

"Want to join me in the cafeteria for a chat?" Anja offered.

"I'd love to." She didn't have too many bruises, though she hadn't stood a chance during sparring with Claire still holding some sort of grudge. Ian had kept it from escalating. Now, she regretted yanking on Claire's chain.

They found a corner in the cafeteria, a semblance of seclusion amid the bustling room. Anja looked at Emma with a thoughtful intensity.

"When we performed your awakening ritual, we decided to wait until we knew more about shifting and its mechanics. I've been discussing this with Lucian, who thinks he understands it better now.

Do you think you would like to try out another ritual?"

Emma was sure the look she gave Anja was answer enough, but she said, "Oh, yes. Claire just trounced me on the mat, and I'd sincerely like to return the favor to that bitch." She grinned to take the sting out of the jibe, but there was an undercurrent of irritation.

"Claire has been having her bitchy moments, but that's not entirely her fault. Blame it on her wolf."

"Isn't that the same thing?"

Anja considered her response for a moment. "Yes and no. She's still trying to find a balance. Both you and Claire are still in the process of learning and adapting. Neither of you are fully awakened. Claire has shifted once but lacks full control over it. You have gained some abilities but haven't learned how to shift. Carlos may even be able to shift, but I don't know. His was a ritual without sex, and I'm not sure what to do, but he seems content to remain the way he is. Ian was the last and most complete. He is the furthest along of the four of you; we all still have much to learn. Once someone reaches a certain point, they should be able to grow and develop the skills they gained. Is that the limit, or would another level or power-up grant even more?"

"Huh," Emma prompted.

"Combining Lucian's serum with a ritual was the key that opened what kind of seems like a Pandora's box. The problem is that we need to figure out how it all works, mostly by trial and error. Is it sex that is the answer? It's my go-to method. It gives me the power to reach in and help adapt others' mental pathways with a ritual, but that is only a part. I think as Lucian gains more power and experience, he could help shifter otherkin on his own."

"What do you suggest?" Emma asked.

"I initially thought Lucian might assist you by himself, but I wonder if it's something you'd be open to exploring with us together? Another go at raising enough power to allow you to learn how to shift for real."

Emma's heartbeat quickened. "You mean both you and Lucian? Together? Like with sex?"

"Yes, and now probably with Zoe as well." Anja broke into a smile. "We've already ventured into intimate territories, you and I. Adding

Lucian into the equation could add depth, considering his abilities. All of us together will lend power and guidance. It's bound to be a hell of a power-up. Maybe for all of us."

Emma didn't need to think about it. "Yes. Joining in and shifting? *Hell* yes! When?"

"I'm glad you're open to it," Anja replied. "We could wait..."

"No," Emma interrupted, smiling back. "I don't want to wait."

"Then it's settled. I'll convince them, but I don't think that'll be an issue," Anja said with a teasing smile.

"More than anything, I want to experience what Ian and Claire have with their otherkin forms. Something within me has been stirring—begging to be set free. I want it so badly."

"I get it." Anja's voice took on a more somber note. "I'm sorry I haven't asked sooner, Emma. How are you dealing with having to kill Viper?"

Emma sighed, her expression darkening. It was an action she'd rather not have taken, but circumstances had left her no choice. "I did what I had to do to protect Zoe. It wasn't the first time I've had to use lethal force," she admitted, feeling the weight of her words. "I don't like it, but I can live with it."

Anja nodded. "The world we are entering will often call for hard choices. You're strong, Emma."

"I'm going to check in with Zoe to see if she needs any more help with the interviews. She's really good at it."

"I told Zoe it would be good if you two could spend some time with Nomad. If we're going to find a place for him, then not keeping him in solitary confinement can only help. See if the two of you can get him to open up some more and figure out how much we can trust him." Anja suggested.

"I don't know if we can ever trust him, but perhaps we can find something. We'll try."

"Let me know. I'll catch up with you later."

Emma stood, catching Anja's eyes for a moment that stretched in time. She leaned in and kissed Anja's lips softly.

As Emma turned to leave, Ian and Claire walked into the cafeteria. Emma gave them a nod while her thoughts lingered on the kiss and the promise of something more just on the horizon.

Claire saw Anja and Emma parting with a tender kiss as she entered the cafeteria. For a moment, her thoughts drifted back to the scandal years ago, the complicated interplay of power and sex that had forever shaped her outlook on relationships. Her mouth tightened with a twitch, betraying her inner turmoil.

That Anja seemed to be fucking everyone and nobody seemed to care was getting on her nerves. During her awakening, she had felt Anja's allure, but viewed herself as strictly straight, which closed off the option of sex with her. Whether that was the right choice still bothered her. The ritual had gone sideways, forcing her to shift into wolf form. She could never regret that, but she was struggling to control it.

Her sparring with Ian had left her frustrated, almost like a bitch in heat. She was sure Emma would be glad to point that out.

"Can we join you?" Ian's voice pulled her back to the present. "We'll be right back after grabbing some food."

"Sure," Anja replied, smiling warmly.

Claire followed Ian as he loaded up his tray. Her selections were more from habit than thoughtfully chosen.

Claire couldn't help but feel uncomfortable as she lowered herself into the chair. The past haunted her, reminding her how quickly lines could blur and how loyalties could be tested. Sitting beside her, Ian seemed blissfully unaware of her inner struggle and focused on fueling up after their intense workout.

She looked at Anja, so confident and comfortable in her skin, then at Ian, who had seamlessly integrated his bear otherkin aspects into his very being. It sparked a touch of envy in her. She was still wrestling with her wolf, unsure how to balance the agility and cunning it offered her with the complexities of her human relationships.

"Everything okay, Claire?" Anja's voice pulled her out of her reverie.

"Yes, just a lot on my mind."

The cafeteria buzzed around them, filled with the aroma of food and murmur of conversation. Still, at that moment, Claire felt the weight of years. Seeing Lucian's uncle Edward at the funeral of his and Lucian's family had dredged up unpleasant memories. Here she was, tangled up with the Millers once again.

Edward was sophisticated, charming, and manipulative. She had been assigned to the protective detail for a royal Edward had been cozying up to. The assignment had been prestigious, but it had quickly become a tangle of ethical dilemmas. Edward had arranged meetings and parties where that royal could indulge in covert pleasures that would not have been available otherwise.

Edward had twisted her presence into something more like a lookout and accomplice than a true bodyguard. He had convinced her to turn a blind eye to things she knew to be wrong to protect her ward's reputation. As time passed, she had felt trapped by her own complicity. When the scandal finally broke, all of them had been implicated. It was not just a question of her career being tarnished; a part of her had been violated, and she would never forgive him. That she now was once again entangled with the Millers was a constant irritant. The ordeal had taught her to be wary, to draw lines that should never be crossed. Those lines were closing in on her again.

Rediscovering and reclaiming her family's wolf heritage meant everything to her now, but was Anja the new Edward? It was like Anja had cast a spell over Lucian, whom Claire was now committed to protecting. Anja was fucking her way through the entire team, and they were all falling in line. Okay, that was a bitchy thought, but it seemed like it was all happening again, and Claire felt trapped. Would it destroy her completely this time, or was there a way out?

Ian's laugh drew her back to the conversation. He was sharing a joke with Anja, their faces animated. Claire looked at them and wondered if she should share her burdens and tainted past.

"You seem miles away," Anja observed.

"I was just thinking about the past," Claire admitted. "I had an experience that wasn't so great. It involved Edward. I've been on high alert ever since, and sometimes I find it hard to trust, even when I probably should."

Anja's face softened, and Claire felt relief seeing that there was no judgment, only understanding.

"We're all still learning, Claire. My otherkin nature now drives me toward sex. It's something I'm still trying to come to terms with. I may outwardly show no hesitation or reluctance to dive in, but my past experiences are still a part of me. Those issues had me suppressing my needs and urges for a long time, and now...my demon needs to be fed. Do I regret setting it loose? No. It has always been a part of me, only buried. Now, at least, I know what it is. It is more of...not negotiation, but more like finding a balance and learning to control it. I'm afraid sometimes that if I don't feed that need for sex, I will lose control, so I try to keep it satiated."

"Should I go elsewhere so you two can talk?" Ian asked, looking a bit uncomfortable.

Claire shook her head. "No, I think it would be good for you to hear this, too, Ian."

Anja went on. "Like I said, I had, and still have, my issues to deal with—we can talk more about it sometime if it might help. We all have our pasts, Claire. They shape us, but they don't have to define us."

Claire nodded, a small weight lifted off her shoulders. Was Anja right? Perhaps it was time to break the shackles of the past and embrace what made her who she was, wolf and all. She needed control and could very much relate to Anja's struggles to find balance.

Claire hesitated a moment, staring at her nearly untouched plate. "I can't get into the specifics, names, or details, but let's just say it led to my resignation from Royalty and Specialist Protection. It was high politics and sex at its worst. I was good at the job and even excellent when it came to the protective aspects. But when personal and intimate entanglements started to interfere, I couldn't cope."

She looked up and caught Anja watching her. "I left that life, but now"—Claire grimaced, the irony not lost on her—"I'm back in a tangle of complexities and worries. I guess that's why I'm uneasy. The interpersonal relationships here are becoming more intricate by the day. I thought I'd left all that behind, but maybe it's a part of life I need to come to terms with."

Vulnerability wrapped around her and a glimmer of something else —hope. Acknowledging her fears aloud was the first step.

Anja reached across the table, touching the back of Claire's hand. "Claire, I understand your concerns. Really, I do. This is different. You have a voice now, a say in how things go. It's not about political maneuvering or power plays; it's about being human. Relationships, love, sex—that's part and parcel of what it means to be alive."

Claire let the words sink in, that faint stirring of hope growing stronger within her. She found her eyes drifting to Ian.

Anja's look intensified and then shifted to Ian. Was Anja assessing them and sizing up some unspoken potential? For a fleeting moment, Claire sensed a delicate probing at the fringes of her consciousness.

"I think you and Ian would make a good match." Smiling, Anja continued, "He could help you connect with your wolf. Would you be willing to try it? With me there to guide the two of you? The full moon drove your awakening, and the ritual was interrupted when it forced you to shift. I believe completing the ritual will give you the control you need. This time, Ian could be the focus rather than me."

Ian shifted in his seat and caught her eye as she digested Anja's words. "You know, I find you incredibly attractive, Claire. No prediction on how things will go, but I'm more than willing to find out. To try, at least."

Claire's heart skipped a beat. The growing tension between them was probably a big reason for her need for some sort of release. Emotions whirled within her; this was an opportunity, daring her to leap. "You know, why not?"

Something loosened within her when she uttered the words—a release of fears. For the first time in a long while, Claire started to think that maybe, just maybe, she could accept these new intimate relationships without losing herself.

"We'll talk again soon about you gaining more control over your wolf. Discuss it with Ian and see what you would feel comfortable with. In the meantime," Anja added with a touch of mischief, "you two should spend some time getting to know each other better."

Claire was more at ease with herself than she had been in a long time. Even her wolf seemed to approve. Could this take her beyond her past? With a final nod to Anja and a sidelong glance at Ian, she decided to try.

# *Seven*

Anja sat through the morning meeting somewhat impatiently. One new development caught her interest: Claire and Ian had started sharing the same room. Given how hesitant Claire had been, Anja counted it a win. There was satisfaction in knowing she had a role in helping them take that step.

Next up on the schedule: Carlos and Aria. Anja looked forward to observing her inaugural flight in the open skies, an event she and Elín had been invited to witness. Elín was increasingly interested in the utility of their abilities.

The most significant event of the day was Elín's introduction to the reality of shifting. Anja knew none of the team had witnessed Lucian shift. She was also eager to reveal her form outside a combat environment.

The sun was rising while they assembled outside for Aria's first free flight in Iceland. Elín was clearly taken aback as the falcon launched to the skies. Her wings captured the light in an incredible display.

"Gods. Remarkable," Elín murmured.

There was a grace to Aria's flight, a sight that made Anja feel vicariously free. Unsettling images too frequently plagued her dreams of flying. She had not tried to shift and fly in her succubus form for real and was afraid her wings were merely for show.

When the moment passed, and Aria safely returned to Carlos's arm, Elín turned to Anja. "So, we have another event?" Elín seemed to be as anxious as she was.

Anja nodded. "Yes, shifting is something you need to see to understand. It's time for us to show you more. Let's head inside."

Lucian stepped to the center once the team gathered in the lower training area. The air in the room was charged with suspense.

"Before we proceed, I need to remove my clothing. Shifting isn't forgiving to the fabric." Lucian disrobed, placing his clothes on a nearby chair. Anja watched as he took a centering breath. He had shown this form to her in her nexus during their first trip there, but nobody else had witnessed it. The form was intrinsic to his otherkin nature, much as the bear was to Ian and the wolf to Claire. The awakening rituals had ingrained these into their beings almost as smoothly as breathing. Well, Claire still had some control issues, but shifting forms seemed to be relatively smooth, though it took its toll on energy.

That drain had to do with their new ability to generate flux catalysts naturally. The flux was part of the breakthrough Lucian had discovered. Turning on the epigenetic switches enabled the generation of flux. The flux acted as a catalyst for the quantum effects at a molecular scale. An extremely fast and powerful realignment of how their genetic blueprint was expressed allowed the shifters to shapechange. Tissue and even bones morphed during the change.

Some of the power to drive those molecular reactions came from the flux their bodies now provided, but more had to come from some other source. It was that mysterious external source that they had few clues of how to measure or classify. They hypothesized that the flux receptors were now active in their genome and that every cell of their bodies acted as tiny antennae—trillions of them. What they didn't know was where that energy came from. It was what they had to call magic.

She had provided the other key piece of their breakthrough: the ritualistic practices that allowed a person to activate and mentally control the process. Her unique ability to help reshape a person's mental pathways to use lost ancient abilities enabled that. As they gained more experience and power, who knew what they could do?

Over millennia, the Sodality had effectively suppressed these powers, but now they were on the cusp of a new renaissance.

Anja was brought back from her musings to the present when Lucian's body began to change. His muscles contoured and bulged as he grew in size. A low, rumbling growl filled the room as fur sprouted along his body, transforming him into a glorious lion. A golden mane framed his head.

They were all captivated. Elín's eyes widened at the demonstration. Carlos watched with reverence. Claire and Ian exchanged glances.

He let everyone absorb his lion form as he moved about. Lucian then returned to his original spot by the chair and shifted back to his human form. His body compressed and fur receded, leaving him standing in his human skin. He retrieved his clothes and dressed, a little unsteady. He sat breathing heavily and closed his eyes. "I don't think I should shift back so quickly. That took a lot out of me. We need to learn more about the limits and the effects."

"Thank you, Lucian," Anja said. "Transformation is a personal experience, and I hope you all better understand what it means for us. It's about embracing an essential part of who we are, but we don't know its limits."

Elín stood there with her heartbeat loud in her ears. Seeing Lucian transform into a majestic lion had been unbelievable. Her logical, scientific mind had trouble reconciling what she had just witnessed. The briefings, reports, and scientific data she had pored over hadn't come close to capturing the impact of seeing it first hand.

The empirical part of her craved a deeper understanding of the genetic transformations, epigenetic controls, and switches that enabled it and how the mind could trigger the change. Anja had related the effects that rituals had on body and mind, while Lucian had provided lab reports, genetic charts, and blood analysis. The reports Elín had read from NexGen gave her a foundation, but they were still incredible. Her heart longed to believe even as her mind told her it was impossible.

And now, it was Anja's turn. Elín braced herself. What would witnessing Anja's shift do to her if Lucian's transformation had left her this unbalanced?

Standing proudly with a smile, Anja snapped her fingers, and all of her clothing disappeared, leaving her completely nude. She looked around, appraising all of their reactions.

Elín gasped. How could that happen? Some sort of parlor trick? "How?"

"All I can tell you is it's by magic. I discovered a way to travel to what you would call an alternate plane of existence under special conditions. That place is what I call my nexus. I have read of places like that, sometimes called a soul home, but that's a story for another day." Anja paused for a moment to let that sink in. "In the short version, I also accidentally discovered the ability to summon things to and from that other place, wherever it is. Hence, the clothes I was wearing are now there.

"The transformations we undergo can be explained mostly by science, but the total energy required does not add up. Mass and energy differentials are too great, even with how much it took from Lucian just now. I believe that comes from somewhere in the universe, or multiverse, whatever you want to call it. Much like how I can send and retrieve things such as my clothes, but more like pure energy. Magic."

Anja stepped back a pace and looked around at everyone.

The room pulsed with energy, a feeling that promised change. Anja's vanishing clothing was like magic; could Elín accept that it was? Lucian's shift she could almost believe was a biological change, given her current understanding—but true magic?

"Every transformation you witness is a form of magic and an acceptance of heritage. They echo the traditions, the legacies, and the latent energies within each of us." Anja looked at Elín, and the gaze struck her like a bolt. She felt Anja had seen something in her, coiled below the surface, and it reverberated.

Anja's form started to shift. It was unlike anything Elín had ever imagined. The metamorphosis was seamless, a dance of biology and magic intertwined. Her height increased slightly, her body curving and expanding in areas to blend power and pure sex appeal. Then burgundy bat wings sprang from her back, almost matching her hair color, unfurling majestically to span the space around her. Delicate horns appeared through her hair, and a sleek tail that ended with a spade-shaped tip flicked back and forth a few times before it coiled around her leg. It was mesmerizing. Anja had stepped out of a myth celebrating sexuality and power.

Everyone around her was transfixed by the transformation. Claire and Ian stared, clearly captivated. Carlos looked reverent. Zoe and Emma exchanged a glance that spoke volumes.

Meeting Elín's eyes, Anja spoke in a voice unmistakably hers but layered with a huskier, more sensual timbre. "This is as real as it gets, Elín. It's not an illusion. If it would reassure you, you're welcome to touch me—my wings, my horns, anywhere. You must understand that this is as real as anything you've ever known."

Elín's breath hitched. Should she step closer and touch the membrane of those wings or the pointed ends of those horns? Would that tactile experience ground her and make this easier to accept?

Her fingers twitched at her sides. She took a slow step forward, her eyes still locked on Anja's. This was a form of evidence, wasn't it? This would be a way to confirm the authenticity of this extraordinary phenomenon. And, in some inexplicable way, she thought that touching Anja in this form might also touch some deep, unknown part of herself.

Elín reached out with a tremble to touch one of Anja's burgundy wings. The membrane was warm and smooth, subtly resilient under her fingertips. An almost imperceptible moan emanated from Anja, as if just being touched aroused her. Elín could feel her arousal stir. This was as real as anything she'd ever touched. It was a potent contradiction to the concept of the rational world she knew. And that moan…Something inside her responded and wanted more.

Elín retracted her hand slowly, letting it slide down to touch the skin of her shoulder, her eyes meeting Anja's again. What she saw there was not just the otherworldly creature of horn and wing but also the woman.

"All the data in the world couldn't capture this. Your reports and accounts…" Elín finally said.

Then, as smoothly as it had begun, the transformation reversed.

Anja returned to her human form, the wings, horns, and tail vanishing. But something had changed, not just in her but among them. This strengthened the connection between them all.

Anja winked at Zoe, then glanced at Lucian as she spread her arms, and her clothes reappeared on her body as they had been.

She had once again proven that she was a beacon for all of them.

"You see now, Elín, why secrecy is not just precautionary but essential," Lucian said seriously. "We're standing on the cusp of revolutionary discoveries—a new understanding of reality—and not everyone will welcome that."

Elín nodded, still reeling, struggling to categorize what she had seen and touched. "It's one thing to discuss in meetings or hear about in abstract terms. But seeing it—touching it—is an entirely different level of understanding."

Anja adjusted her blouse and stepped closer, her eyes still holding that inexplicable depth they had taken on in her other form. "It's like describing color to someone who has never seen it. And that's why we can't afford to be careless. The Sodality will redouble their efforts to eliminate us if they find out that we have reclaimed our rightful legacy. It is in our DNA—in our very being."

Ian, who had been watching, joined the conversation. "Anja is right. We're not just hiding to protect ourselves; we're doing it to build something greater than us. It's like learning to tame fire all over again."

Anja nodded, looking at each in turn. "We need to grow stronger and understand our capabilities better. When we defeat the Sodality—and we will—maybe we can consider how we engage with those outside these walls."

Elín gained a new respect for Anja and Lucian, not just as leaders but as pioneers. She nodded. "I understand. I do."

Lucian looked around the room, assessing those around him. He noted expectation, curiosity, and a bit of apprehension. The walk back from the training area had been silent and heavy with thought. He was recovering from the energy drain faster now.

"So, Elín, I trust you found our little demonstration…enlightening?" Lucian began, his fingers resting on the table in front of him.

"Enlightening is an understatement," Elín responded with unmasked awe.

"Good. Our reality is replete with wonders, and we have only scratched the surface." He turned his attention to the rest of the group, scanning each face. "This is a pivotal time for all of us, especially with the Sodality lurking. We're not showing off our otherkin abilities for entertainment; we're revealing essential parts of ourselves that must be understood, respected, and incorporated into our lives."

Claire shifted uncomfortably in her seat. Ian, seated beside her, gave her hand a reassuring squeeze, and Lucian caught the flicker of a smile.

Lucian was aware of the collective nodding around the table. A shift was happening. This was more than just a team; it was the genesis of something special. Elín's observations had been correct: witnessing was indeed transformative, and they had all been irrevocably changed.

Lucian felt a subtle push at the edge of his consciousness—Zoe's empathic nudge. It was her new way of letting him know she had something to say. "Zoe, how did your interviews go? Have you finished screening the lab's staff?"

Zoe sat up a little straighter in her chair, a glint of satisfaction visible. "With the help of Sigri and Emma, we've completed the interviews sooner than expected. Everyone seems to be clean except for one individual—no other red flags regarding loyalty or potential risk. There were a few complaints about interrupted schedules and waste-of-time interviews. Still, Sigri stressed it was at the director's orders which seemed to get their attention. In the rare instances that was not enough, a short conversation with said director put the fear of God into them."

"As well it should have," Elín said with a scowl.

"So, the exception," Lucian mused, glancing at Emma and Sigri, who nodded. "What do you suggest we do with this person?"

"I'd say a change of scenery would do wonders," Zoe replied. "A less sensitive location within your businesses, perhaps? Place him somewhere his skills can be used, but far from any vital information."

Lucian saw the echo of approval from multiple corners of the room. "We'll arrange a 'promotion.' It's better to keep potential risks at arm's length. Sound good to you, Elín?"

"A good solution. Maybe better than he deserves," she replied. "There are a few assignments here inventorying frozen samples to keep him on ice, so to speak, but with all that is happening, I think he should move on to another location. Even being here at the Lab poses risks.."

Lucian saw Zoe and Emma nod. "Elín, can you update us on the genetic screening for flux receptor traits? We're all keen to know where we stand on that front."

Elín cleared her throat, shuffled through her notes, and passed out copies of the list she had made. "Of course. Based on our genetic screenings of the employees here, we've identified a surprisingly high number of employees with potential otherkin traits. In addition to Sigri here"—she paused, casting a glance at Sigri, who looked visibly startled—"and myself"—another pause, this time met with a nod from Anja, who was updating her notes—"we have identified another ten individuals out of the one hundred thirty-two employees."

"The number does seem high," Lucian mused. "Any ideas as to why?"

Elín shrugged. "It could be a variety of factors, but one likely reason is that Akar Labs has always targeted particularly talented individuals for recruitment. Talent and otherkin traits seem to go hand in hand."

Ian showed surprise as he scanned Elín's list. "Graham MacGregor? Head of security? He might be my nephew. I'll have to look into that. What are the odds? If he is, I'll talk to him. I'm kind of surprised he hasn't sought me out first."

Carlos also leaned in, eyes scanning down the list until they stopped on a name. His only outward reaction was a subtle shift in his body, but Lucian noted the ripple of surprise that radiated from him. "Macaria Aguilar, one of the drone operators. She's shown a keen interest in Aria. This might explain why."

Lucian finally spoke. "We'll need to approach these individuals discreetly, assess how much they know or suspect about their heritage, and decide on the best course of action. This isn't just about abilities; it's about trust, loyalty, and the future we're creating here."

Nods of agreement met his words. This was a complexity added to their already intricate situation, but Lucian sensed that, if anything, the revelations had solidified their commitment. They were all of a kind, bound by secrets and laden with untapped potential.

# *Eight*

ANJA OBSERVED THE emotional textures of the room, akin to subtle brushstrokes on an intricate painting. She could almost touch the texture of those feelings within each person, a talent that was both a gift and a burden. She turned to Sigri, who was still absorbing the revelation from Elín's report.

"Sigri," Anja began, startling her out of her reverie. "Would you like to discuss this further tomorrow? It's a lot to take in, and you might want time to process it."

Lucian added, "Tomorrow is Sunday, and we're all taking the day off—a well-deserved break. If you'd like, you could come with us. We could talk, go shopping, and see the sights. Whatever feels right for you."

Sigri pondered the offer. "That sounds wonderful. I'd love to join you."

Anja sensed the relief in Sigri's voice, a weight being lifted, even if just a little. This was an opening, a chance for Sigri to explore a part of herself she hadn't known existed before today.

"Good. Tomorrow it is then," Anja replied warmly.

As she caught Lucian's look, Anja saw that he fully agreed. Sometimes, despite the chaos, life offered these small pockets of calm.

The prospect of a day spent in exploration and camaraderie would be a breath of fresh air, a respite from the lab's long and sometimes stressful days. Zoe, Emma, and Sigri had been working almost non-stop on the interviews, and Zoe was nearly exhausted from evaluating the employees. Lucian had been trying to catch up with Elín regarding the recent genetic research and results and formulating new experiments. Elín had been pushing the genetic and supercomputing centers into overtime, processing the updated bloodwork procedures and testing.

Anja probed the layers of emotion surrounding Elín, a cascade of thoughts that nearly drowned out the room's other occupants. "Elín, could we have a moment in your office?"

Lucian nodded as if giving his silent approval. She looked at Zoe and got a nod from her as well. Elín hesitated for a second before agreeing. "Of course."

Anja purposely navigated the space between them, whispering in his ear. "Could you get a dose of the serum? I have a strong *feeling* Elín will be needing it."

With a slight nod, he whispered, "I'll get it."

Anja noticed Lucian's flicker of excitement. As she and Elín headed for her office, Lucian was already getting Sigri's attention to help facilitate that request. The medical supplies they had brought contained more doses, but they would need more delivered soon.

Once the door closed behind them, separating them from the meeting outside, Elín exhaled deeply. "This is a lot, Anja. My mind is spinning, and honestly, the implications are staggering."

"I understand. How are you feeling about all of this? I can explore your emotions more deeply if you're open to it. The test results demonstrated that you have this potential, too. It's why I wanted the privacy—fewer distractions for us."

Elín appeared to debate internally, juggling her scientific curiosity and personal nervousness. Finally, she relaxed. "This is so unexpected, really. Go ahead, let's see what you find."

Anja took a deep breath, centering herself. Then her senses expanded, delicately touching the contours of Elín's emotional landscape. She found trepidation, curiosity, and, underpinning it all, a well of untapped potential. It was as if Elín stood on the border of something larger than herself. "Would you like to know what I sense?"

"Please," Elín said.

"You're at a crossroads, Elín. There's fear, yes, but also the stirrings of something greater within you. It's like you're about to turn the key to a door you didn't know existed but have always been meant to open. Now that you've seen the reality of what we are, you can feel that door."

Elín sat back, struck by the weight of Anja's words. "That's incredibly…accurate."

"Would you like help unlocking that door?"

For a moment, Elín was lost in internal debate, her eyes searching Anja's as if looking for an assurance she could hardly verbalize. Finally, she gave a hesitant smile. "Yes, I would."

Anja found herself distracted by the office decor. Dragons. The imagery was everywhere—the woodwork carving perched on Elín's desk, paintings on the wall, even a tiny, intricate frosted glass sculpture on a bookshelf. It was as if the office was whispering Elín's secrets.

As Anja touched Elín's arm to establish a more direct connection, she was taken aback by what she discovered—latent power, raw and astonishingly potent. A dragon, she realized. The essence of what Elín could be was unexpected, unparalleled in intensity. Anja decided it was not the place to encourage a shift; the repercussions would be… enormous.

"Elín, have you always been drawn to dragons?" Anja asked.

Elín looked a bit startled, then glanced around her dragon-adorned office. "I suppose I have. They've always fascinated me as mythical creatures and symbols of power and transformation. Sometimes I've even been called the 'Dragon Lady.' Not all of my decisions or directives have been popular ones."

"I think we will soon prove that dragons are more than just myth. According to the tales, there are different kinds of dragons. Given your heritage, you are most likely akin to an Icelandic ice dragon—a creature of profound wisdom, inherent magic, and elemental power."

Anja caught a flicker of recognition in Elín's eyes when she mentioned ice dragons, and a thought darted through her mind. "You know, in Nordic lore, there's a dragon named Fáfnir. He was originally a dwarf, or maybe a human of stout stature, but transformed into a dragon due to his greed and desire for a powerful treasure. What if I told you that your lineage and its legacy could be linked to such powerful figures? Perhaps a common, distant ancestor. Not in the darker aspects but in the profound strength they embodied. Perhaps that legend should be used as a cautionary tale as well."

"Fáfnir? That's a tale I heard as a child. To think it could be more than just a myth."

"It often happens that myths are fragments of some deeper truth. Darker motives like greed drove Fáfnir, yes, but the essence—the dragon form, the wisdom, the elemental force—that could be a part of you, lying dormant in your heritage until now."

For a moment, Elín looked like she wanted to say something, question the incredible notion, but no words came. Instead, she nodded slowly as if some distant part of her had always known and was only now daring to believe.

Anja noticed Lucian's emotions from outside the door—expectant and waiting. Elín was a revelation that could change their group in ways they hadn't begun to fathom.

"We could awaken that part of you today. Now. Lucian has prepared the serum you've been briefed on and read about. It's a catalyst to help open that door within you. Would you like to try?"

Elín's face carried a resolve that could only come from a person who had already decided. "Yes," she finally said, her voice filled with the gravity of the decision. "I want to. Need to. Can we do it here?"

"Yes, we can." Anja's arousal increased with Elín's acceptance. "Given the potent energy—magic—we're dealing with, we'll need to use the sensual aspects of the process to channel the power effectively—my power, sex magic, if you will. Is that okay?"

Elín's cheeks flushed a warm pink, evident in her pale complexion, her eyes flitting away as her mind navigated the implications. When she spoke, her voice was softer, touched with vulnerability. "I remember the sensation when I touched you in your succubus form. It…it stirred something in me. Something I haven't felt in a long time. I haven't had a lover in years, but that touch made me realize how much I've been neglecting that aspect of myself. Yes, I'm willing."

Anja remembered that touch. Shifting to that form and being

touched, even lightly, had awakened a hunger for more. It was a not-so-subtle arousal, and Elín's response had mirrored her own. She had wanted to just go for it then and there. *See? Control,* she thought.

She sensed the need in Elín—for self-discovery and reawakening not just otherkin abilities, but neglected needs and dormant desires. And if all went as she was confident it would, Elín was on the brink of a profound transformation that would change the core of her being. No, not change—reveal. It was a step into what made them both unique—magical.

Elín watched as Anja crossed the room to the door, her motions fluid and graceful. The door opened, and Lucian entered, carrying a vial of liquid and a case with a syringe. As he closed the door behind him, her heart skipped a beat; this was the moment of no return.

"She's a dragon, Lucian," Anja whispered.

Lucian raised an eyebrow and glanced around the room. "The Dragon Lady is more than an epithet, then?" At Elín's look, Lucian smiled. "Yes, I've heard it. I don't think I'll be able not to use it myself now. Fair warning."

"As long as you don't use 'ice bitch,' I think I can live with that," she replied, her nervousness lightened by his teasing.

He regarded her with a more appraising look. It was an odd sensation but not uncomfortable; it was like someone sifting through a book of her life, acknowledging what was yet to be written. After a moment, he picked up the syringe and drew the serum into it. The liquid shimmered and then began to glow a soft blue, almost white light, infused with energy from Lucian.

Lucian explained, "I've been able to tailor the serum to specific individuals to amplify the effect—one of my new talents." Lucian watched Elín, waiting for her confirmation. For a second, her throat tightened, making speech impossible. But her eyes met his, and she nodded.

Satisfied, Lucian stepped forward and administered the injection into her arm. A strange cold spread from the point of contact, radiating to her extremities as if her cells were singing.

With one final, indecipherable look at Anja, Lucian withdrew the syringe, capped it, and placed it back in its case. Then, as quietly as he'd entered, he left the room, closing the door behind him.

Elín was left sitting there, her arm tingling at the injection site, her heart pounding like the wings of a caged creature yearning for the sky.

*What have I just agreed to?* The thought spiraled in Elín's mind, mingling with the anticipation and a surreal sense of having crossed some invisible barrier. The serum tingled in her veins.

Anja moved further into the room, scanning the surroundings before settling on the plush couch where Elín sat. "Your couch looks incredibly comfortable, and the room seems soundproof. Good, that will work well."

"So, what comes next?"

"We start slow," Anja said, smiling, "and set the pace from there. Like with Lucian, I'll guide you through a sort of ritual. Given your draconic heritage, I believe it would be helpful for me to be in my succubus form for this."

Elín's heart raced at the mention of Anja's other form; she had sensed its power and her attraction to it earlier and found herself wanting to explore it. "I was hoping for that," she admitted with a touch of embarrassment, though her voice was infused with a desire she couldn't quite keep in check.

Anja's eyes sparkled. "Shall we help each other get undressed?" With an air of ceremony, Anja unbuttoned Elín's blouse. Each open button ratcheted up the tension in the room, not with nervousness but with growing anticipation. Once her blouse was undone, Anja slipped it off Elín's shoulders with a soft rustling of fabric, revealing her fair skin.

Elín mirrored Anja's actions, her fingers lingering over each button. She could smell Anja's perfume, a sweet jasmine and woody scent. She eased the blouse off Anja, revealing her figure. Anja's hair shimmered, cascading down her back like a waterfall of red wine. The action of undressing each other was more intense and intimate than just undressing themselves. She suspected that was why Anja had suggested it.

Feeling emboldened, Elín reached up to free her auburn hair from its tight bun, letting it flow down past her shoulders as she shook it out, setting the dragon pin asside.

Taking turns, they slowly removed the rest of each other's attire. As Elín's bra came off, her nipples hardened under Anja's appraisal. Anja reached out to touch her hips and slowly slid off her panties as Elín stretched out her legs to help, the cool air of the office unnoticed with her rising heat. Once completely nude, Elín watched, captivated, as Anja stood and stepped back, trailing her fingers down her body.

The tension in the room was as tight as a drawn bowstring. Anja's green eyes met hers, full of ancient knowledge and untold stories.

And then it happened.

Anja's form shimmered as though reality itself was bending around her. Her hair glowed and fluttered in a breeze not present in the room. Her eyes also changed, adopting a supernatural luminance that made Elín feel she was gazing into the heart of a mystical forest of green. And then there were the wings—she wanted to touch them again and so much more as they unfurled.

Elín's breath caught in her throat as Anja, now in her succubus form, exuded a palpable aura of sensuality blended with untamed power. It was exhilarating, and Elín couldn't help but be drawn in.

"Are you ready?" Anja's voice was different now—richer and fuller. It reverberated through Elín in a way that touched her deeply.

Elín managed a nod, her transformation feeling so near she could taste it like the crisp air of a storm waiting to break. She marveled at the sight before her, her heart pounding with rediscovered desire.

"Then let's begin," Anja said, her wings folding as she returned to the couch, leaving Elín spellbound and wholly ready.

Their eyes locked, and in that moment, Elín experienced a profound connection beyond physical attraction. Anja leaned in, and their lips met in a soft, electrifying kiss. The taste of her kiss was unlike anything Elín had experienced before. She could feel the wetness pooling at her core.

Elín's hands, almost of their own accord, found Anja's wings, tracing the unique texture like a blend of silk and something far more exotic—leathery with a velvet-like softness. Anja let out a moan, her own hands now exploring the curve of Elín's back, sending shivers of delight cascading down her.

She continued to explore the landscape of Anja: her hair, her shoulders, her breasts, her hardened nipples, even her tail, supple and velvety, its tip narrowed and thickened now, appearing more like a phallus.

"Oh, gods…Oh!" As she touched it, Anja shuddered as if it was as sensitive as Elín's clit was at this moment. Anja's fingers found that nub and began to tenderly caress it as if reading her desire.

As their mouths and fingers continued to explore, each kiss deeper, Elín's latent power stirred, responding to Anja's nearness, the sexual energy pooling in her, and the serum flowing through her veins. Each touch, each shared breath, amplified their connection, setting the stage for the monumental change that awaited her.

Elín experienced a growing completeness, a certainty that she was ready to accept her new self. And as their lips parted, they caught their breath, not just from physical desire but also from the recognition that they had crossed into unmapped places—territories that promised things she had never even considered.

In the gathering heat of their intimacy, Anja broke the silence with the melodic cadence of an ancient chant. Her voice, which possessed a quality that Elín had never heard, flowed through the room.

Elín closed her eyes and lay back on the couch, allowing Anja's voice to guide her mind along paths she had never known existed within her consciousness—allowing Anja into her mind to show her the way. With each phrase and syllable, locked doors slowly creaked open, revealing new pathways.

A tumble of memories and fragments of dreams flickered through her mind like images in a kaleidoscope. There she was, as a child, staring up in wonder at glaciers under the pulsing auroras. Another flash: her first sight of a dragon in an illustrated storybook. And another: a dream of soaring over volcanic landscapes, the air beneath her filled with thermals that lifted her higher and higher, white wings gliding through the air.

With each image and recollection, the dragon within her stirred—a mythical creature waking from a long slumber. In her mind, she saw scales forming, wings unfolding, and a tail unfurling. And then something more: an indescribable energy that pulsed in her being. It unlocked an ancient and timeless consciousness.

Anja ceased her chants and focused only on the pleasure flowing through their bodies. She moved up to place one knee beside Elín's head while her other foot rested on the floor. Opening her eyes, Elín looked up to behold a sight unlike any other—Anja's form loomed above her, wings slowly moving, her hair falling around her full breasts, her opening just inches from Elín's face and mouth. She took in that sight and closed her eyes again, leaning up to kiss that place. Opening her mouth to lick, then suck and lick again, she could taste the sweetness of her, much like their kisses before. The smell of Anja's sex was intoxicating.

Anja's tail, which she had caressed earlier, brushed up along her thigh. Elín opened her legs more. She broke that intimate kiss to catch her breath and moaned. "Yes, Anja…Please!"

At her request, that tail entered her and filled her. Soon, it was sliding in and out and twisting around, probing all the right places. It was incredible how intense it all was, how accurately Anja found the right places and rhythms that were just what she wanted. Anja's movements were becoming more urgent now, too, while Elín continued to lick and suck.

Anja urged, "Now, Elín, now…Come for me. I'll go with you."

With that command, the final barrier within Elín shattered. A surge of unimaginable power rippled through her, intertwining with her, becoming a part of her. She screamed, believing the soundproofing would hide it but not caring if it didn't. She was lost to all but the sensations. An orgasm like she had never experienced—never imagined possible—swept over her entire body in seemingly endless waves of pleasure. It left her shaking and breathless when the spasms tapered off.

Anja moved and curled in next to her, lying on the couch. The silence was broken only by their breathing as they slowly came back to themselves. Elín opened her eyes. Their eyes met, and in that instant, Elín knew—without a shadow of a doubt—that her life had irrevocably changed. She had glimpsed her dragon form, had touched upon the extraordinary powers that lay dormant within her, and now there was no turning back.

The air still thrummed with energy, a lingering resonance of the power that had just been unleashed. Elín reclined on the couch, every inch of her skin tingling, her perceptions heightened as if the world had just come into focus. Power coursed through her veins, weaving through muscle and sinew, fortified with strength she couldn't have fathomed before this moment.

Anja lay beside her, smiling radiantly in her succubus form, her wings folded behind. "How do you feel?"

Elín struggled to find the words, finally saying, "Other than having just had the best orgasm of my life…Just new. Remade, if that makes sense."

Anja nodded. "In many ways, you have been. And as for shifting, we might consider a field trip of sorts. Soon. You're a dragon, Elín, a creature of myth and might. Learning to shift—maybe even partial shifting—will take time and space."

The prospect was astounding. Shifting—and flying!

Anja leaned closer, her voice softening. "Welcome to your new self, Elín. Welcome to a life you've just begun to discover."

Elín took a deep breath, still grappling with the enormity of it all while they shared tender kisses. *A dragon!* she thought. With a reservoir of untapped powers, a whole new existence was unfurling like wings before her. She'd stepped through a door, leaving behind the ordinary world she knew for something far grander, and she was ready to fly.

# *Nine*

THE MORNING SUN streamed in, casting dappled light across the hotel room. Lucian woke up to find himself nestled between Anja on one side and Zoe on the other, still in peaceful slumber. The scent of last night's intimacy lingered in the air. He simply took it all in for a moment—the warmth of their bodies and the softness of their breaths. They looked so serene in sleep, so unburdened. How he wished it could always be like this. The sight warmed him, but it also stirred questions that needed answering.

He disentangled himself carefully, not wanting to wake them. That Zoe was here, in this intimate space with him and Anja, highlighted thoughts that had been dancing around his mind. He had enjoyed the night with them incredibly but did not want to upset what he had with Anja, which was precarious enough with her proclivities. Would adding Zoe to their relationship add stability or not?

Eventually, Anja stirred, her eyes fluttering open. "Morning," she murmured, her voice husky. She read him well, always had. It was unnerving. He was the one who could always read others, but in this instance, he felt less in control.

Zoe woke up a moment later, stretching luxuriously like a cat waking from a nap.

"Morning," he said in a whisper, his gaze lingering on Zoe, who had revealed more of her naked form with that stretch, which was likely very intentional.

Zoe stretched again, revealing even more, a lazy smile gracing her face. “Hey,” she said.

Anja sat up, smoothing her tousled hair. “We should talk, shouldn’t we?”

“About what?” Zoe sat up. He figured she already knew.

“About this.” Lucian gestured broadly, indicating the three of them. “About you moving in with us. How we make this arrangement work.”

“How do you feel about this? About me moving in?” Zoe asked.

He considered his words. “Beyond being a fantasy come true, I think it’s a natural progression. We’ve grown closer, and we seem to have something special. But that doesn’t mean it won’t come with its issues. I want both of you to feel welcome, valued, and respected. It’ll take communication, honesty, and perhaps some adjustments.”

Zoe broke into a full smile. “I can’t argue with that. I think we can talk things through when they need to be.”

“Agreed,” Anja said. “It’s very different, but with some effort, it can work.”

Lucian nodded. “So, Zoe, how do you honestly feel about this?”

Zoe contemplated her answer before speaking. “I feel seen, loved even. But I also understand that what we have here is new. As much as I love spontaneity, I like ground rules. There are some other obvious issues as well.”

This was unfamiliar to all of them, and that unpredictability made it exciting, but this conversation was important.

Anja shifted her position on the bed, angling herself to see Lucian and Zoe. “I’ll start by saying I’m more than pleased with this arrangement. It feels right to me. I want this. I *need* this. But we have to acknowledge our natures, too. I’m a succubus. Sex is a part of me, just as your lion, your demon, is a part of you, Lucian. And Zoe, your lineage from Mayavati also comes with its intricacies. Your nature can help balance the three of us, ease tensions, and ground us in situations that might otherwise spiral out of control if it were just me and Lucian.”

Lucian nodded. Without that, he might indeed go off the deep end someday, lost to obsession rather than love. From the beginning, he had been keenly aware of how Anja’s demonkin nature had played a role in their relationship. But he also had to agree with the balancing aspect she raised. He'd accepted that it would never be exclusive and was learning the richness it could bring into his life. "I've never seen your nature as a barrier, Anja. It's a part of you, and I love you for it, not despite it."

Zoe leaned forward, looking at Anja. "Same here. It's a part of who you are, and I find it incredibly appealing. Now more than ever."

Anja beamed, pleased. "Well, I'm glad to hear that. Now, about our relationship. Initially, Lucian, you thought you might be my one and only. But circumstances have evolved. I will undoubtedly need to have sex with others, and Zoe will want to explore more of her nature. You have been tolerant of that. What we're looking at now is something that's more 'monogamish' among the three of us. Is everyone comfortable with that?"

Lucian raised an eyebrow when Anja used the term. "Monogamish? Haven't heard that one before."

"Well," Anja began, "it's like a monogamous relationship but with a little wiggle room: monogamous-*ish*. Think of it as a committed relationship between the three of us—me, you, and Zoe—but with the occasional involvement of others for specific needs or experiences. The core emotional commitment remains among the three of us, but there's room for sexual experiences with others, individually or together."

Lucian glanced at Zoe, who nodded in agreement, then back to Anja. "I see. So it's about maintaining the depth of our relationship while allowing for…others, with all parties informed and agreeing?"

"Exactly," Anja confirmed.

Lucian relaxed. It was a term that made sense to him—monogamish. Committed, but not in the usual way. "I'm okay with it. I guess that love isn't a finite resource. We don't love less; we love differently, more."

Zoe grinned. "Couldn't have put it better myself. I'm on board with the 'monogamish' thing. I think it captures what we're aiming for—something special among us but flexible enough to adapt. But…"

At Zoe's hesitation, Lucian asked, "You have some reservations?"

"Yes. I'm still FBI, and I'd be dating a witness or potential suspect in a multiple murder investigation. I know you're innocent, but still.

That is bound to cause issues."

"I can understand, but you have a place with us here," Lucian said.

"Yes, I know, and I'm grateful for that, but I'm still coming to terms with it. It will still hang over my head until I can make that break. And you, Lucian, do you have reservations? And don't lie to me. You know I can tell."

Lucian chuckled at that. "Well, I guess Anja was right. You will keep us balanced and honest."

"You bet, now 'fess up."

After a moment of thought, he said, "I'm still learning to deal with all this. I feel a huge responsibility for everyone on the team, and starting this relationship adds even more complexity. Love is not something I contemplated, and I don't really understand it. I fell for Anja, and now I'm falling for you. It's like jumping off a skyscraper only to realize I need to learn how to fly."

"I can relate to that. I don't think love is meant to be understood. Just felt. I think we are all learning together." Zoe turned to Anja and raised an eyebrow in challenge. "Your turn now."

"Is this another instance of being careful of what you wish for?" At Zoe's grin and nod, Anja continued. "I'm worried I'm not completely in control. A couple of days ago, while watching Ian and Claire spar, I used my powers to sense their feelings to try and figure out how to help her control her wolf. They were intense, and I was imagining how they would look together having sex. I really wanted to see it, feel it, feed off it. I almost gave in to that temptation right then. I'm wondering if I somehow influenced them to get together. I still need to guide them to help Claire gain more control over her wolf and complete her ritual."

Anja looked down, and Zoe reached for her hand. "There is more, too, isn't there?" Zoe asked.

Anja nodded, still not looking up. "Yesterday, when I asked Lucian to get the serum for Elín's awakening, I knew we would have sex. I didn't even think about the two of you and how you would feel. I just went ahead and jumped right in."

"Lucian and I knew what was happening. I could feel it, and I can tell you I was struggling to keep my composure out there. I could also tell that Lucian was not upset and was turned on just by the thought of what was happening in that office."

It hadn't occurred to Lucian that Zoe was quite so tuned into them. The thought was somehow disturbing and comforting at the same time. That she accepted his feelings and reactions was incredibly liberating. He had no need to hide anything from them.

"Well, I definitely enjoyed it. I even found a new talent in my succubus form. My tail has some interesting uses," Anja admitted.

"Well, I was wondering what that sensation was. Fuck, Anja, we need to add that to the list. I'm starting to feel a little jealous." Zoe smiled to make sure she knew she was teasing but figured Anja could probably tell how turned on the thought of that made her. Glancing at the protrusion of the sheet over Lucian's lap, she didn't need her empathic abilities to see he agreed.

"We all have our issues, but this is a good start. Moving forward, I think we can be open. Lucian?" Zoe prompted.

"Yes, agreed," he responded.

"Anja will need a fair amount of freedom to do what she needs to do. You mentioned wanting to help Claire and Ian with the ritual."

"Yes, I will need to be there, but I think me having sex with either of them is not on the menu. Just watching and guiding should be enough," Anja said. "I'm pretty sure I can keep my hands off them if not myself."

"What else do you think might come up?" Zoe prodded.

"Emma. She's at a point where she could use some guidance to access her cat form. I think the three of us could offer her a unique blend of help—Lucian with the genetic aspects to help with shifting, myself with the mystical and sensual parts, and Zoe, you would be instrumental in helping her navigate the emotional side of things. I believe inviting her to join us for an evening could be beneficial for her and pleasurable for all. But I want to know how you both feel about that."

"Well, if it's just for one night, I think I can manage. Any more than that, and you'll have to order me a casket." Lucian's humor was not lost on Zoe. Most men, and women for that matter, fantasized about having a ménage à trois. Now, they had that on an almost daily basis. Adding Emma wouldn't kill him literally, but she could see his point. He would be dedicated to trying to please them all—not that it should be his concern or duty.

"Lucian, you know it's not up to just you to perform and please us girls," Zoe said, then added, "But thinking about it is getting me all worked up and..."

Anja cut in, "Zoe is always turned on, so don't worry." It was an old inside joke that Anja was always teasing her with.

Zoe shot a scowl Anja's way. She wanted to interject her usual humor as she always had, but their new relationship and her new abilities were affording her many other avenues for stress relief. She was growing and learning and was grateful for that.

"This is new, and taking it one step at a time and letting it happen will be the easiest. I'm completely open to the idea," Zoe said. "I've been feeling a strong connection with Emma, and helping her through this feels...right, you know? She's been feeling left out and a bit lonely. She's definitely a flirt, and with the team dynamics already strained, I think it would relieve some of that pressure."

"Yeah, I talked to both of them yesterday. Emma was very eager to join us, and I told her I would try to arrange it. Also, Claire brought up her issues about sex and colleagues. She is worried about coping with it all," Anja explained. "I'm trying to help her see that it's not such a bad thing."

Lucian confessed, "It's not usually a good idea to bring relationships to work. My companies have policies discouraging it, but I think this whole situation is unique, so I say let's go for it."

"You would." Zoe smirked, then shrugged. "I guess we all would."

Anja smiled. "Thank you. Both of you. It means a lot that you're so supportive. I'll let Emma know we can try something in the next few days, and I'll let you know if Claire and Ian decide to try as well. I'm sure they will."

Lucian got up to order room service, and Zoe couldn't help herself from watching his naked backside as he walked across the room. He looked over his shoulder, catching her unabashedly watching, and said, "We'll need to eat something. Sigri will be here shortly."

Anja heard the knock, and Lucian rose from his seat to open the door. He and Anja had dressed before breakfast had been delivered. Zoe was still reluctant to put anything on until it was absolutely necessary, and apparently, she did not feel the need yet. Sigri was standing on the other side of the door. She glanced at Anja momentarily before turning to Lucian in greeting.

"Morning, Sigri. Come in, please," Lucian said in welcome.

"Thank you," Sigri replied, stepping inside. Her countenance was curious. Anja sensed a mix of emotions emanating from her—anticipation mingled with a bit of vulnerability. She wondered if that was why Zoe chose to remain as she was, to be the more vulnerable one.

"Good to see you," Zoe said with a smile as she adjusted her sitting position to make room for their guest. The fact that she was still naked did not seem to bother either her or Sigri, who politely ignored her state of undress. Anja trusted Zoe to sense if it was an issue.

Anja could tell that today's conversation would be consequential for Sigri. "Have a seat." She gestured toward the space made by Zoe. "Would you like some coffee? We also have tea," she added, picking up on the tension in Sigri's posture and thinking something warm might help ease it.

Sigri nodded and took a seat. "Coffee would be great, thank you."

Lucian poured a cup, handed it to her, and returned to his seat beside Anja. "So, you wanted to talk about Otherkin," he began, his voice soft, providing a safe space for Sigri to open up.

Sigri took a sip of her coffee, buying herself a moment. "Yes," she said, setting her cup down. "After yesterday's meeting, I've been thinking a lot. I'd like to explore this part of me, this…otherkin…trait you talked about."

"We'll help you explore that," Anja said. "And after we talk, we could go do something more lighthearted. Shopping, maybe, or a tour of the local sights?"

A restrained smile broke through. "That sounds wonderful."

Anja took a moment to consider her words, picking up on the cautious optimism that hung around Sigri. "In many cases, otherkin traits can be traced back through family lines. Have you heard stories or tales within your family that speak to something…unusual or out of the ordinary?"

Sigri shook her head, her raven-like black hair shimmering in the room's light. "No, nothing like that. I was raised in a small fishing village; people there don't talk much about the unusual or extraordinary. It's mostly sea tales and local gossip."

"Would you be open to allowing me to read you, to probe your emotions and thoughts? It might give us clues about your potential form or any dormant abilities you may have."

The air thickened with expectation as Sigri processed the suggestion. Anja sensed an internal debate—intrigue and a small, natural instinct of self-preservation for her privacy.

Finally, Sigri smiled a little. "Yes. If it will help me understand this part of myself, then I'm willing to let you try."

Anja felt Sigri's emotional landscape open up like a book willing itself to be read. And Anja was ready to explore.

Anja knelt beside Sigri, placing her hand over Sigri's on the armrest. Her touch was light but intentional. "Just relax, Sigri. Let your mind drift—perhaps to your hopes and dreams."

As Sigri closed her eyes, Anja delved into her mind. Zoe's influence through their bond helped to relax Sigri. After a bit of probing and guidance from her 'sight,' Anja's senses were greeted by a cascade of vivid images, which she related as she saw them. Playful white foxes darted in the snow—quick and agile movements, a dance of life and energy. The foxes shifted settings, moving from snow-covered landscapes to darker lava fields. In the summer setting, their coats had changed to shades of dark gray and brown, allowing them to blend seamlessly with the dark terrain.

Sigri's eyes opened, awe coloring her expression. "I was captivated by the Arctic foxes at the Reykjavík Zoo. I saw them after I moved here to join the lab. They have this amazing ability to adapt, changing their coats from white in winter to shades of black, gray, or brown in the summer. It's mesmerizing. I used to watch them play for hours, wishing I could be that carefree."

"I think that is just what you could experience for yourself. But, before we proceed further, I should clarify that the awakening process often involves some intimacy," Anja said. "I would guide you through the ritual aspects, and given my disposition, those rituals can be rather…sensuous."

Sigri looked surprised and shy but curious. "Intimacy? Like, a physical closeness?"

Anja nodded. "Yes. The outcome tends to be…let's say pleasurable. It helps me channel the energy needed for the awakening, allowing me more power, or rather magic. But I want to clarify that it's entirely up to you."

"And it would be only you guiding this ritual?"

Anja laughed. "Yes, just me, unless you'd prefer otherwise. Rumors have been swirling about Lucian, Zoe, and myself, but this is your choice. Lucian may also be able to assist by himself with the actual shifting into your otherkin form. In your case, the Arctic fox."

Sigri took a moment to absorb the information, then nodded. "I appreciate the honesty."

"Absolutely, take all the time you need to decide. There's no rush at all. This is about your journey, your self-discovery. The intimacy aspect is just one way to help focus energy, but it's powerful. It might not be required. Every awakening is unique."

"It's good to know that I can choose. I really don't have much experience with that." Blushing slightly, she added, "I'll give it some thought and maybe spend some time at the zoo, watching the foxes that have so fascinated me."

Zoe smiled warmly. "Yes, you're not alone in this. If, how, and when are up to you."

The sincerity emanating from Lucian and Zoe amplified Anja's own. "Whenever you're ready, just let us know. We're here for you, Sigri."

Sigri smiled, visibly touched. "Thank you, I will. For now, shall we go enjoy our day off?"

"I suppose that means I need to get dressed?" Zoe asked.

"Yes, It's still rather chilly outside, and while you could stay naked, it would be rather unusual. Icelandic customs generally accept nudity and even require it sometimes, but just walking around would not be one of those times."

"Require? Tell me more," Zoe said.

Sigri giggled. "I'll give you the full rundown, but first, go ahead and get dressed so we can head out."

Zoe scowled at her playfully but went to comply.

# *Ten*

SITTING IN THE conference room, Anja closed her notebook and studied the list Elín had passed to her. These were employees that tests revealed had the potential to be otherkin. Lucian leaned in to better view the dossier on Graham while Elín perused her copy.

It seemed like this room was almost becoming their prison. As comfortable as it was, it still had no view, and the walls tended to creep inward, or so she felt. It wasn't like they had many choices. She wanted to ask if they could put up a view of the outside from the security cameras but didn't know if that would be any better.

She had been updating her notebook with the latest events when Elín had entered. It was an old and comforting routine to pen her notes. It was more like her journal now. She briefly considered Ashton's diary, which was currently occupying her bag, and the parallels of their narratives, though separated by some five centuries. She no longer needed to write anything down with her now perfect memory, but maybe someday it would help another struggling soul understand.

"It now seems obvious," Anja mused, breaking the quiet, "that certain traits run in families. If I had to wager, I'd say Graham is almost certainly a bear otherkin like Ian."

Elín nodded. "It's another confirmation that our screening seems accurate. He has the suppressed flux receptors in his epigenetic chart, similar to Ian."

As they considered the futures of those on the list, the sound of footsteps signaled Ian's approach. Anja straightened, her senses already picking up the shift in energy from the room as the door opened to admit Graham. The towering figure who stepped into the room carried the wildness of the outdoors on his broad shoulders, his deep-set brown eyes taking in the gathered group.

Standing just an inch taller than Ian, he displayed his muscular build beneath his tactical gear, designed with utility and an element of intimidation, reflecting his military background. The dark hues of his clothing accentuated his shaved head and the full, well-groomed beard that framed his jaw. His appraisal, alive with a sharpness that missed no detail, swept the room in a single pass.

Ian's introduction held a tone of familial pride. "This is Graham, my nephew. Graham wanted to see how long it took me to notice he was here."

Graham's stance was relaxed, his arms folded. "I've been aware of the lab's research areas and some of its more…unique aspects, and I figured Ian was here guarding Dr. Miller. But as for the particulars of this meeting, I'm in the dark, as I presume is necessary for security." Graham's expression remained unreadable. "Well, I hope you will enlighten me about the purpose of this meeting."

Ian drew out his etched bone talisman from beneath his shirt and held it up to Graham. "You know of this, don't you?"

Its appearance brought a change over Graham. His posture stiffened, his brows knit together, and his face darkened. "Ian, what are you doing? These people have no right to know!"

Perceptive to the undercurrents of emotion, Zoe extended her influence, a subtle coaxing warmth like sunlight melting frost. Graham relaxed ever so slightly.

Ian's voice carried a weight that stilled the room. "They all know," he said, indicating the others. "Only them. But there's more at stake here." He spoke of transformation, of invoking the bear, and presented the same potential resting within Graham. "Listen and decide," he urged. Anja believed the words he used were from an ancient tradition that carried the weight of a life-changing crossroads, likely words spoken by elders of his clan in times of choice.

Graham's face was a sea of shifting emotions as they recounted the process and what they had experienced. His initial anger gave way to healthy skepticism, and the seeds of wonder began to take root as the tale progressed. His features softened, allowing a glimpse into a man confronting the improbable reality that his very nature might be more than he ever imagined.

"So the tales were true then?" Graham asked.

"Yes, and more, nephew."

After giving Graham time to let it sink in, Anja broke the contemplative silence. "Graham, we'll get into the specifics and plan your awakening soon if you choose, though I believe you will. This is a lot to process." She turned to Ian. "Perhaps you'd like some time with Graham to discuss it further. I imagine the two of you have much to catch up on."

After Ian and Graham had left, Anja said, "Next, we should speak with Dr. Brendalynn Innes."

Sigri got up and left to fetch the doctor. The group waited in silence. Each was lost in their thoughts.

Lynn soon came in, her presence composed. She stood tall and slender, her golden-blonde hair cascading just past her shoulders in a flow of waves that caught the light with each movement. Her eyes, the blue of a clear sky, surveyed the room with a calm but wary curiosity.

Her attire spoke of a professional who valued form and function. A white lab coat fell over her casual clothing.

"May I ask what this is about?" Lynn's query broke the silence after Sigri had returned to her seat next to Elín.

As they once again told their story, Lynn listened, her initial skepticism softening into a thoughtful contemplation.

Anja watched her closely, sensing the ebb and flow of emotions. "With your permission, I'd like to…well, read you, for lack of a better description, to uncover your otherkin identity."

Lynn sat calmly despite her shock. "Okay."

The revelation that Dr. Brendalynn Innes carried the essence of a unicorn brought a moment of silent wonder to the group. Anja acknowledged its fittingness. The connection extended beyond mere chance, suggesting a more profound tangle of fate and character.

As they proceeded, each name and face was not just a colleague but a puzzle to be pieced together with their otherkin counterpart. Mike Hafstein, the lead engineer of the lab's geothermal power plant, with his innate understanding of the earth's fiery veins, struck Anja as the natural embodiment of a fire salamander—a creature of flame and volcanic mysteries.

Dr. Teodora "Dora" Ziem, a geneticist with a razor-sharp intellect and a fiery spirit, kindled something Anja did not expect. It was not demonkin exactly, but she believed that the origin of all the various forms harked back to the mixing of daevas and humans in the ancient past, maybe even before Sumerian times. She penned comments about this in her notebook to remind her to consult with Howard sometime.

Dora's file listed her as in her mid-thirties, but her appearance made it impossible to guess. She was tall and lean with strawberry-blonde hair that fell in waves past her shoulders. Coupled with her Polish heritage, she presented a striking figure. The pendant on her necklace, a deep red gemstone, also caught Anja's attention. Anja was excited by Dora's potential. How would Dora's awakening affect her?

As they continued to work through the list, Carlos entered the room, his steps measured, his posture showing a hint of anticipation. Beside him was Macaria "Cari" Aguilar, the drone operator whose skills had earned her recognition within the tight-knit community of the lab. Her dark hair was pulled back in a ponytail, and she was dressed in dark khaki cargo pants and a faded teal tank top. Both Carlos and Cari shared a Latin heritage. There was a kinship between them.

As Carlos introduced her, Anja observed Cari to read the subtle signs of otherkin potential. She noted how Macaria's brown eyes took in her surroundings, missing nothing, reminiscent of a raptor's broad, panoramic vision.

Carlos shared anecdotes of Cari's instincts, her uncanny ability to anticipate the drone's path, almost like she was riding the air currents alongside it. She had much in common with Carlos.

The others on the list, those not brought into their circle, remained names on a page for now. Anja knew there would be time for them, for their stories to be told and their legacies to be awakened.

Lucian's phone vibrated against the polished surface of the conference table.

"Uncle Howard." His voice was a low, even timbre as he answered. "What news do you have?"

Howard's weary voice came through the line. "Lucian, I've been tracing the Sodality's fingerprints through history anywhere I can find clues. As we supposed, their extensive reach and their methods are insidious. You've seen that first hand." The reference to Lucian's family's murders brought a brief flare of pain and anger.

Lucian leaned back in his chair, his pose betraying his inner tension. "And the oath we seem to be facing with the Controller? The spells binding his loyalty and secrecy?"

"Ah, yes, my boy. If the Grandmaster has used blood to seal the oath, willingly given, it creates a bond not easily severed. Death will break it, but there are obvious issues with that."

Lucian's hand tightened on the phone. "So, severing the tie by ending the Grandmaster would solve the issue, but that raises two problems: finding him and the act itself. The former is proving impossible so far; the latter…" He paused, the unspoken risk and violence hanging heavy.

"Not a realistic option, is it, hmmm? This man, this Grandmaster, he's not one to leave his end unguarded. He holds that position for a reason. The other option is to get rid of this Controller of yours."

A cold, humorless chuckle escaped Lucian. "So we have to get rid of him one way or another—and soon. Maybe make the chains…our own. Turn the Grandmaster's spellwork against him. There must be a way. It's guarding even the Controller's subconscious, haunting his dreams with its vigilance."

Howard's sigh was a soft hiss of frustration. "Perhaps layering an additional charm could obscure the original's intent, create a loophole of sorts. But it's delicate, akin to redirecting a river's flow without causing a flood."

Lucian nodded slowly. "We'll need to be careful. And it will take time…" His voice trailed off, the unspoken truth hanging between them.

The line remained quiet while Howard considered, and Lucian could hear a rhythmic tapping on the other end of the call. "Lucian, you must understand if you tamper with the spellwork, there's a risk the caster might sense it. This oath…It might not be just chains; it could also be a two-way link."

"You're saying the Grandmaster could trace the disruption back to him?"

"Possibly. And considering his apparent resources, that could be… problematic. If he's as powerful as we suspect, the danger isn't abstract—it's immediate and probably deadly. He may decide to check up on the Controller if he turns up missing—like he is now. When will that be noticed? Hmmm? It's a delicate balance, Lucian. One false step, and you could be exposed. You must be very careful. And we must continue to prepare for the moment that we will have to face him. I'll continue my research, looking for forgotten lore to aid us."

"Thank you, Howard," Lucian said, warmth breaking through his icy resolve. "The shadows seem to have teeth. Be careful, Uncle."

"And you too. I'll let you know if I find more."

The call ended, leaving Lucian in brooding silence. He stared at the wall; his mind was a whirlwind of strategy and risk. The weight of his uncle's warning echoed in his thoughts.

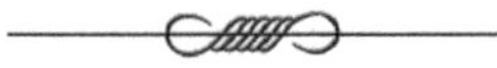

Zoe watched Lucian as he ended his call. Tension was etched on each face as Lucian related the call and laid out their stark choices. Her discomfort was mirrored back at her from her companions.

Lucian leaned against the cool surface of the conference room table. He cleared his throat, and the room fell into a hush. "We have three choices. None ideal, but we must choose one. We could just go after the Grandmaster. Eliminate the source of the threat…" He paused a beat, then admitted, "Okay, that won't happen. We have no idea where to find him, and even if we did, it would be a huge risk.

We don't know the full extent of his power or influence or what his defenses would be. I would love to finish this, but we're not ready yet.

"Second," he continued, meeting Zoe's eyes briefly, "we could eliminate Richard. Kill him." A collective discomfort shifted through the room, an unease that not even the sturdiest could suppress. Lucian's hand was steady. "It's the surest break."

"No," Zoe said, her voice firm. "We're not executioners. I can't... won't...be a part of that."

"Understood. We don't want to become like them," Lucian responded, although a part of him wanted to do just that. *No,* he thought. Their only other option might be better, even if it was not as sure and final. "Or we take a more...creative approach. We manipulate his memory, cover the tracks leading back to us, add layers of confusion on top, and then..." Lucian's expression darkened. "We return him to where he was taken, let him believe he escaped the trap somehow."

Lucian's voice softened. "Releasing him, with altered memories, might be our only viable move. It allows us to maintain our moral ground and protect our secrecy. I just hope it's not too late. The possibility that he could be used to find us is a huge risk we need to address. Now." He turned and looked at Elín, who'd been quietly observing the exchange.

"Memory manipulation, then. You might pull it off with Anja's talents. Give him some dreams as misdirection," she said.

Anja leaned forward, her expression serious. "I can do it. We don't want them to detect the tampering. That could alert him to our use of mystical capabilities as well."

Lucian acknowledged her caution. "It's a risk we have to take. There are no good options."

"You'll need to be thorough," Zoe interjected. "Layers of false memories, a web of deception difficult to unravel, if he ever does."

"That's where the layering comes in," Lucian said. "Construct a narrative that gives him a false recall of the events that transpired, perhaps make him believe that Nomad was the traitor and killed the others for some reason—that he went rogue. We need to act quickly. Every moment we delay, the risk of discovery grows. If the

Grandmaster decides to trace him, assuming he can, we will be exposed."

Zoe nodded. "Let's get him out of here and cover our tracks. It's the best choice—the only choice."

A murmur of assent traveled around the room.

"Hold that thought," Lucian interjected, halting the room's momentum. Everyone's attention snapped back to him. Leaving Richard alive could actually be better after all. "Once Richard is back in his element, unaware of the true extent of his situation, we'll have Mark and Dan tail him discreetly. We need to know where he goes and who he contacts. He could lead us back to the Sodality or other players in this game. We have too little information as it is."

Anja and Zoe exchanged a glance, the implication clear: they needed to ensure that Richard's mental state was coherent enough to follow his routine but sufficiently foggy to keep their secrets safe.

"Mark and Dan are resourceful; they'll know how to keep a low profile, and Dan has firsthand experience with how dangerous they can be," Lucian added, referring to Dan's encounter with who they now knew to be Raven, one of the Sodality's operatives. "We need to find out what shadows they're hiding in. It's the only way I can see to find them and take the fight to them."

# *Eleven*

ANJA STOOD AT the entrance of the hospital room, her gaze fixed on Richard's unconscious form. The room was dimly lit, the beeping of monitors the only sound breaking the silence. Lucian, Elín, and Lynn were already gathered inside.

Lucian turned to Anja as she stepped in, and Zoe followed close behind her. "Are you ready?" he asked.

"Yes. The sooner we get this done, the better." Anja glanced at Lynn and wondered what she would think of all this. Someday soon, Anja would attempt to awaken her unicorn form. Her likely healing talents would be another welcome addition. For now, it would be good for her to witness what it all could mean for her.

Lynn noticed her appraisal. "He is weakened from weeks of sedation, and though we have tried to keep the effects to a minimum, he's not likely to get up and walk away. How will that affect your plan?"

"Valid question. Lucian has the ability to heal. One we hope you will also have, or you may even exceed his capability." Anja looked at Lucian to see if he wanted to add anything.

Lucian said, "It's a little hard to explain, but it's similar to shifting, only it's more like having the tissues realign to what they 'should' be rather than 'could' be. I can speed up that process greatly. If he had the flux receptors of a true shifter, it would be easier, but he does not. Instead, I have to provide the energy. When he poisoned himself, it was a combination of healing damage and introducing something to flush the poison out. Anja had to help by lending me more of the needed…um, magic, if you will. He just barely survived, and his mind still fights to escape or die."

Elín moved to Richard's bedside, checking the IV drip and the sedation levels. "He's stable. Should I give him an injection to loosen his inhibitions?"

"You mean like a truth serum or such?" Zoe asked, uneasy.

"Would you prefer something fatal? That would be much easier," Elín shot back.

The horrified look on Lynn's face said volumes, but Zoe said, "Wow. That's cold."

Anja put a hand on Zoe's shoulder and shook her head. "I think we'll try without anything extra first. It would be better in the long term. Lucian, can you show Lynn what you were talking about? Get him back to a healthy state?"

Lucian stepped forward and pulled down the blankets enough to place a hand on Richard's bare chest. He closed his eyes in concentration. The dim lighting in the room made his hand's soft, ethereal glow apparent. It cast a golden light that flowed like water over the Controller's form.

As Lucian focused, the glow intensified, illuminating the room with an otherworldly radiance. The energy flowed from his hand into Richard. Anja could feel the power emanating from Lucian, a tangible force that seemed to fill the room. The effect was almost immediate; Richard's pallor faded, replaced by a healthier, more robust complexion. His shallow and labored breathing deepened into a steady, rhythmic pattern.

Lynn's eyes were wide with wonder as she watched the subtle movements beneath Richard's skin, his tissues realigning and restoring lost muscle tone. The tension in his muscles eased, and the lines of pain and stress on his face smoothed. Even in his unconscious state, the effects of so many days being bedridden vanished. Anja sensed Lynn's longing, a mix of admiration and a deep-seated desire to possess such power. She was a doctor, but this was on a whole new level.

Lucian's hand finally lifted, the glow dissipating like mist. "There.

He might now be in the best health of his life."

Lynn stepped closer to touch Richard. The sensors and monitors displayed the change, yet she needed physical confirmation. Her voice was filled with awe as she whispered, "That was incredible. I've never seen anything like it."

Zoe placed a reassuring hand on Anja's back. "It's our turn now. Let's make this work."

Anja took a deep breath and approached the bed, her fingers tingling with anticipation. She placed her hand on Richard's forehead, feeling the warmth of his skin beneath her touch. Closing her eyes, she concentrated, drawing on her unique abilities to penetrate the layers of his subconscious.

The room around her blurred as she entered Richard's mindscape. It was a chaotic swirl of fragmented memories and dreams. Anja began weaving her own threads into the fabric of his thoughts, creating a new narrative that would mislead and protect. After their first foray into this world of dreams, this was more familiar now.

She conjured images and emotions, constructing a story in which Nomad had gone rogue, betraying his comrades for his gain. She layered these false memories with truth to make them believable, embedding them in Richard's mind and replaying them until they formed a solid foundation.

Richard's mind resisted at times, the defenses of his psyche or the oath flaring up. Zoe soothed these disruptions, their powers twining together like a stream, eroding the barriers and embedding the new memories deeper.

After what felt like an eternity, Anja finally withdrew, her hand trembling as she broke contact. She opened her eyes, the dimly lit room coming back into focus. Richard remained still, his breathing even; the new narrative settled firmly within his mind.

"It's done," Anja said, her voice a mix of exhaustion and triumph. "The Controller's memories now contain the misdirections we've constructed. He believes Nomad betrayed them and went rogue. That is very close to the truth, leaving out the part where we convinced Nomad to cooperate."

Lucian's expression was one of relief and respect. "You did well,

Anja. This gives us a fighting chance. I only hope this will be in time."

Zoe nodded. "You were amazing. We'll need to keep monitoring him, but this is a huge step."

Anja felt a wave of relief wash over her. The task was monumental, but they had done it together. "We've done as much as we can. Now, we hope this holds."

Lucian nodded, his gaze steady. "Let's regroup and ensure every part of our strategy is ready. We can't afford any mistakes."

All together once more for a last review, Anja let her senses roam and closed her eyes. Nothing immediate seemed to press into her awareness. The fickle gift of sight offered no guidance.

She must have missed the start of the meeting, but she heard Lynn say, "The sedatives will wear off in time. When he's found, he'll be coherent but confused. It will be convincing. If a quicker recovery is needed, I have prepared some stimulants to bring him out of his sedation faster."

"He's ready for transport, then," Lucian concluded. "It's up to Ian and Claire to get him back without leaving a trail."

Anja opened her eyes. "So, Brendalynn—Lynn," she corrected herself, honoring the preference, "what do you make of all this? It's quite a lot to take in, isn't it?"

Lynn offered a smile, not entirely masking the depth of her feelings. "Yes, it's…a lot."

Anja remembered her struggles with self-discovery. "The healing you witnessed, what did you think of that?"

Lynn turned inward momentarily. "It was amazing," she confessed. "The potential of such abilities is staggering. To heal like that…"

"It could be within your reach as well. Your lineage, the unicorn, is renowned for its healing prowess. Your potential is sure to be profound."

"I want to explore it; I do. But there's so much I don't understand."

"Of course. We're here to guide you whenever you decide." Anja knew that, much like it had been with Zoe, there would be no other decision now that Lynn had seen it.

After Lynn departed, Anja listened intently as Emma relayed the latest developments with Nomad. "He was initially recruited by the Russian SVR for training as a covert agent for his intelligence and patriotism. At the time, he was slated to be a deep cover agent in the US—an illegal. His training included everything from extensive language usage and mannerisms to espionage tradecraft. He claimed to have excelled at it and was chosen for additional training, including assassination techniques."

Emma continued, "Some of the most attractive and promising female agents were selected as swallows and sent to State School 4 earlier in training. Even some men were chosen for that.

"He was in the final stages of his training when he was approached by an SVR officer named Igor Krakarov, who wanted him to join a special unit. In the end, Igor turned out to be 'Eagle,' a member of the Sodality. Nomad's initiation into this so-called special unit was brutal."

Emma went on to describe what he had experienced there and his introduction to the concepts of human purity and tales of hidden supernatural threats throughout history. Eventually, he was assigned to Richard in New York, where his original SVR training would be put to use but dedicated to the Sodality's purpose.

The mention of the conditioning and training camps unnerved Anja —not with fear, but with resolve. "The dehumanization is chilling. But it's crucial intelligence, Emma. Well done."

"Thank you, but Zoe helped too. He does have a way to contact Raven."

"We might leverage that," Lucian said, already strategizing. "Carefully, though. Raven is a wildcard." The conversation shifted as Lucian briefed them on the departure preparations. "Ian and Claire understand their roles."

Anja recognized the meticulous planning, the subterfuge woven to protect their haven. "Portugal, then Boston," she echoed.

"Yes," Lucian confirmed. "And thanks to Lynn, we have everything needed for continued sedation and, eventually, recovery."

"Let's hope the waters remain as muddied as we need them to be."

"Emma, continue your work with Nomad, and you too, Zoe," Lucian directed. "Every shred of insight is a weapon against the Sodality."

The early morning frost contrasted with the warmth of the jet's interior as they boarded; Ian's mind cycled through their objectives. He glanced over at Claire; her calm, focused expression was a mirror of his own.

Lucian's dedicated aircrew had greeted them: Captain Alex Turner, his co-pilot and first officer Aaliyah Williams, and hostess Bella Martinez.

Captain Turner was in his mid-thirties, with short-cropped dark brown hair and a neatly groomed beard complementing his piercing blue eyes. He was tall for a pilot, matching Ian's height. His first officer, Aaliyah, was already prepping for the flight in the co-pilot's seat.

Bella's striking beauty, with her flowing black hair, sparkling brown eyes, and warm, welcoming smile, was on display when she ushered them aboard. She closed the door and moved to her seat in the back of the jet as it taxied to the runway.

Soon, they rose sharply as the rugged landscape and snow-covered mountaintops gave way to the ocean.

"Remember," Ian began, "once we release Richard, we step back into the shadows. We must remain unseen."

"I've gone over the plan a dozen times in my head," Claire admonished.

The sedated form of Richard in the pressurized hold was a reminder of the precarious nature of their endeavor. Ian trusted that Anja and Zoe's efforts would work as expected. Claire would check on him occasionally, but they expected no issues.

Dan and Mark's roles were critical in what came after. If Richard could be tailed without suspicion, they could gather intelligence on his network, his contacts, and maybe even the elusive Grandmaster. "We'll need to keep in contact with Dan and Mark. They're our insurance once Richard's out of our control."

Claire reached for the secure satellite phone. "I'll ensure they're ready to tail him when he's free. It's time to update them and tell them when we'll land."

The jet descended toward Portugal. Ian felt the familiar rush of impending action, the adrenaline that came with the risk. "We do this right, and we're one step closer to dismantling the Sodality."

Claire's nod was all the reassurance he needed as they began the protocols for landing in Portugal.

Once in the air again, Ian and Claire found themselves alone with time stretching ahead. They sat across from each other, the sound of the engines a backdrop to their shared silence. As the jet leveled off, Ian wanted to fill the void.

"I think we should use this time to talk, just you and me, before we sit down with Anja," he suggested. "It's important that we're on the same page."

"The stopover gave me time to think about what Anja proposed… about her guiding us." Claire inhaled deeply. "I've been thinking about boundaries…about what I'm comfortable with. For me, the nudity isn't an issue. It's the intimacy…I'm straight, Ian. I don't have any desires towards women, no matter how attractive or wonderful they might be. And Anja is both. You, um…told me about your awakening, the experiences you've had with Anja. I don't want to ask you to deny your past, but moving forward, I need to know that what we have is exclusive. Anja has her connection with Lucian and Zoe, and I'm learning to accept that."

Ian's expression softened. "I respect that, Claire, and I want you to know that's what I want too. Anja's role in this…It's to guide, to help you connect with your wolf. But what we have, what we're building… that's just ours."

Claire's shoulders relaxed. "That's what I needed to hear. Anja being present…I'm open to her guidance and her helping me through the process. But I don't want…I'm uncomfortable with you being intimate with her again."

Ian leaned forward and reached for her hand. "I understand, and I agree. What we have is too important to risk. Our relationship isn't about that. It's about us growing together, and I wouldn't have it any other way. You're certain you're okay with Anja being there with us? Being part of it in her own way?"

"I understand why she needs to be there, and I can accept that. It's all so new to me—this isn't something I ever envisioned for myself."

"I need to be honest with you, Claire. The thought of Anja being present and watching us arouses me, and I have a feeling it might affect you in ways you might not expect."

Claire's cheeks colored slightly. "I've never seen myself in that light, as someone who…performs, I guess you could say. But I trust Anja, and if her being a voyeur is something that brings her pleasure, then I won't hold that against her. I just hope that it doesn't inhibit me with you."

Ian caressed her fingers. "It's about trust. It's okay to admit that it's scary and exciting at the same time. It's new for us. We're new. Figuring out how it works with her in the mix…It's going be different."

"I know," Claire agreed, her hands folded in her lap. "And when it comes to Anja helping me with my wolf, the potential is…It's exciting, but it's also a lot."

"Agreed. This doesn't change the foundation of what we have together. It adds to it, but it doesn't replace it. Anja's guidance is just that—a guiding force, not a third presence in our relationship."

Claire smiled faintly. "So, we set the boundaries. Clear lines that she can honor."

Ian returned the smile. "Exactly. We talk through everything. No assumptions, no crossing lines. We're in this together."

"Together," she echoed. "I think…I think it could be good for us."

The jet dipped slightly as it descended into Boston, pulling them back to the present.

# *Twelve*

HELENA CAUTIOUSLY APPROACHED the high-rise apartment building Richard used for his office and living quarters. The structure was sleek and modern, its glass façade reflecting the bustling cityscape of Manhattan.

It seemed quiet, but Helena knew better than to trust appearances. Her gaze flickered over the windows of nearby buildings, searching for anything out of the ordinary—movement, reflections, or anything that could indicate a hidden observer.

Satisfied for the moment, Helena followed an apparent resident who was preoccupied with his phone. She paused to look at her phone while motioning for the man holding the elevator door to go on. He shrugged, and the door closed. There were still no other residents or visitors by the time the elevator returned, so she entered and pressed the number of Richard's floor.

As she ascended, Helena reviewed what she knew. Local operatives wouldn't be aware of this location, but somebody might be watching if Richard had been compromised. She also knew he didn't rely on conventional alarms but preferred traps and destructive measures for protection.

The elevator dinged, and the doors slid open. Helena stepped out into the hallway, her footsteps silent on the plush carpet. She approached Richard's door, scanning the area for any signs of surveillance devices. Her fingers brushed over the doorframe, feeling for any irregularities. There was the usual, almost unnoticeable hair-thin wire to indicate entrance in his absence. She would reset it when she left.

The lock looked the same as all the others she had observed along the hallway on her approach to the last door on the right. He would not have wanted to draw any attention with extra external security. Taking out her lockpicks, she chose a city rake. She inserted the tension wrench and slipped in the rake, flicking it as she felt for the wrench to give. It only took a few flicks before the lock turned.

Helena pushed the door ajar, slipped inside and closed it behind her. The apartment was dark, illuminated only by the faint glow of the city lights filtering through curtained windows.

She located the security panel hidden behind a cheap mirror hanging by the door. It was part of a standard kit issued to Controllers to ensure their secrecy. If not disarmed on entry, it had some nasty surprises—poison gas, remote explosives inside computers, and a secure alarm link to the Vault. Fortunately, she had the master disarm code. It beeped after a few tense moments, and a green light illuminated.

She would need to keep an eye out for other traps but did not really expect any. Richard followed operational protocol, and he did not usually deviate. What had happened to him was a puzzle.

Helena surveyed the stillness of Richard's office. The space had little comfort—a metal desk, probably government surplus and cluttered with tech, was the room's focus. A comfortable and well-used leather office chair was the only item that stood out. It spoke of long hours at the desk poring over reports and directing the activities of his region. The bedroom was sparse, with simple box store furniture and cheap linens. She could almost hear the ghostly echoes of Richard clicking away at the keyboard as he worked.

Accessing the computer, she bypassed the firewalls and encryptions that would have stopped anyone else. As Eamon's enforcer, she had access to built-in bypasses available only to a select few of the Sodality. The screen came to life, flooding the room with a pale glow that cast her face in sharp relief. She examined his recent activities, following his digital trail.

A file flickered onto the screen, labeled "Operation Early Bird." The plan it detailed was audacious—an attack set to capture Anja and use her as bait to draw out Lucian. Helena read the reports, absorbing the names Nomad, Smoke, Viper, and Raven. The scandal Raven had planted with the compromising deepfaked videos of Lucian and an escort to alienate Anja and separate her from his protection had succeeded.

Richard had arranged a rendezvous at a safe house, where Anja's freedom would be ransomed back to Lucian. Nomad had reported that her capture had gone well and even provided an audio recording of Anja. Richard had used Raven to set up a meeting where Lucian would buy Anja's freedom and watch as Lucian was ambushed. Now Richard was unaccounted for, vanished like a phantom in the night.

With a deepening frown, Helena leaned back in the chair, the leather creaking under her. Richard's plans must have fallen apart, and she had to piece together the aftermath.

She pinpointed the coordinates of the safe house where the ransom was to be delivered. It was nestled in the woods of upstate New York —a place selected to be remote. With the location etched in her mind, she shut down Richard's computer, the screen's light dying away as if it were the final ember of his dwindling presence. She stood up, graceful and deliberate, an air of menace enveloping her like a second skin. She reached for her coat, a functional, sleek garment that belied the lethality of its wearer.

The trip to the safe house would not be excessively long, but it demanded caution and the readiness to face whatever lay in wait. Helena had no illusions about the dangers lurking in such a place.

She exited Richard's office, reset the security system, and locked the door behind her. She also reset the hairline trip wire. Her car awaited her—a nondescript rental. The drive would be quiet, time to gather her thoughts and prepare.

The forests of upstate New York enveloped her the following morning, a green spring canopy arching overhead as she drove along the winding roads. Dappled sunlight flickered through the moving leaves, casting light and shadow across the car's interior. The cheeriness of the scenery did not match her mood.

The safe house was hidden well. She parked her car at a discreet distance and proceeded on foot; the underbrush tugged at her clothing as she moved silently through the trees.

The safe house would soon come into view. Helena prepared herself for what she would find there, the weight of her responsibility as heavy as the gun she carried—a tool of last resort. Her silver knife was quieter and just as deadly—and more personal.

As she rounded the last turn of the gravel drive, she could see the front door cracked ajar. That was the first indication of what she was likely to find. The next was a low buzzing. Flies would be swarming to the scent of death that she noticed even from here.

She pushed the door open, the creak of the hinges echoing in the still air. The scent of decay hit her like a wall. Helena was no stranger to the dead—her heritage made her intimately familiar with death and its many faces. In some ways, the familiar scent was a comfort, for it was her domain. She stepped inside, the dim light casting eerie shadows on the walls.

There were two bodies in the front room. Smoke and Viper lay there in advanced stages of decomposition. An open door led to a small kitchenette and another closed door. There were no corpses in the kitchen, so she approached the other door and stood in front of it, debating her options.

She closed her eyes and raised her hands to waist level, palms up, and with a flick of her mind sent out a small pulse of magic. Two distinct reverberations returned from the recently dead behind her, and only a few faint, much older traces came from the distance. So, only two: that left Richard, Nomad, and Raven unaccounted for.

The buzzing flies avoided her, seemingly repelled by some invisible force as she knelt beside Viper, her hand hovering over his forehead. Closing her eyes, she reached out with her necromantic powers again, and the air around her thrummed with energy. She felt the cold pull of the void as she summoned an echo of Viper's spirit to the mortal plane. A pulse of power marked its culmination. The power she had to expend was more than expected.

Viper's ruined eyes fluttered open, empty and unseeing, a ghoulish echo of the man he had been.

"Who killed you?" Helena asked. The dead could not lie.

"I don't know...I shot woman on second floor...dark-skinned, shoulder-length hair...shot her from behind...she was aiming at Nomad," Viper rasped, his voice barely more than a whisper. "Then... noises...scream...nothing."

Shot from behind while shooting someone in the back. Ironic. "And Smoke? What happened to him?"

Viper's head lolled to the side, his memories disjointed and fragmented. "Heard shots through the darkness...then...I...I don't know..."

So, this was the result of the attempt to capture Anja. Obviously, there was no second floor here. This was not where they had died, which explained the unusual power drain.

Helena released Viper's spirit, letting it slip back into the void. She moved to Smoke next, repeating the process. His recollections provided more details—he had been on watch outside Anja's estate when the attack began, with Viper entering through the back and Nomad the front. Smoke had been shot by a sniper and then captured. The ambush had been organized and efficient. That they had been expected was obvious in hindsight.

Smoke had been hit in the leg, his wound bandaged by a man in a ghillie suit, and then he was bound and placed in their van with an equally bound Nomad and Viper's body. A woman with long dark hair and green eyes had driven off with them, but he hadn't lived to see their destination. So Nomad was the only survivor of the failed attack.

As she released Smoke's spirit, Helena stood. At least three assailants: a man and two women, all armed and trained. She needed to report this to the Grandmaster, but she had to be careful. Her powers were a secret she could not afford to reveal.

After ensuring she left no traces behind, Helena exited the safe house and returned to her rental car. Before getting in, she used her power one last time, a wash of energy banishing any lingering scents and traces from her clothes and body. It was a useful talent, especially when consorting with the dead.

She drove back to Richard's office. Once inside, she sat in Richard's chair, looking at the flickering computer screen as she contemplated the grim tally. The plan suggested by Nomad to ensnare Lucian was bold and would have appealed to Richard. Still, it had gone awry. The staging of the bodies, positioned to suggest a deadly skirmish with no survivors, was a macabre riddle. Why was there no sign of Richard? It wasn't like him to leave a trail, even in dire circumstances. Richard was a man who would choose death over capture, a man who would take his secrets to the grave rather than risk them falling into enemy hands. She knew Eamon had ensured that. He also had cast the same binding on her, or at least believed he had.

She tapped a finger on the desk, the rhythm echoing her racing thoughts. It was a conundrum that gnawed at her—if Richard had died in the conflict, his body would have been disposed of there. His absence was a void, suggesting a different fate.

Helena's instincts screamed that the answer was critical, not just to the mystery of Richard's whereabouts but to her plans. Whoever had outmaneuvered Richard might tear the fabric of their organization, woven with secrecy and loyalty. She already had concluded that the answer was Lucian and Anja. She needed to ensure that she could gain control of the situation—and of them.

She considered the possibility of desertion. The thought was as unsettling as the silence in the room, broken only by the hum of technology—the lifeline of information that now was as much a curse as a blessing.

The answer now seemed obvious: betrayal. Nomad had been captured before proposing the trap for Lucian. He'd coordinated that trap—only Richard had been the target instead. Why or how Nomad had been compromised? That was the real question.

With a click, she closed the file on the screen. It was time to dig deeper.

Helena allowed her thoughts to roam, the room fading as she contemplated the dossiers on Lucian and Anja, their secrets still hidden. They had bested Richard and his operatives and were now gone from New York, whereabouts unknown.

The Grandmaster moved his pieces across the board of the

Sodality's intricate power plays. Unexpected moves could thwart the surest of strategies. Lucian and Anja's intertwining destinies could be the unpredictable element that unsettled Eamon's composed tableau.

Lucian had four capable bodyguards. Two of them appeared to be in different locations at the same time. Emma and Carlos matched descriptions from Raven of being in the city with Lucian while also being present at Anja's estate. Zoe Ananda matched Viper's description of the woman he had shot in the back. Why she had been with them was a troubling question.

The silence around her was a canvas for her thoughts, each a stroke painting a picture of a future only she could envision. Hiding her magic was suffocating. She longed for a world where the Sodality sought not to eliminate or 'purify' magic but perhaps harness and control it instead. The Grandmaster had suspected Lucian Miller was dangerously close to some breakthrough, hence the need to eliminate the threat he posed. He could be the leverage she needed to break free from the Sodality or take it herself.

Helena picked up the secure line, pressing the series of keys that connected her directly to Eamon, the Grandmaster. The line clicked, and his voice came through, crisp and clear. "Report."

"I've pieced together Richard's last actions. He intended to trap Anja, using her as leverage against Lucian. There was a team—Nomad, Smoke, Viper. But something went wrong."

"And that team?" Eamon demanded.

"Dead. Smoke and Viper killed, the scene staged to appear they killed each other. Nomad is missing and presumed captive, convinced or forced to betray Richard. There's no sign of Richard and no word from Raven."

A silence fell.

Eamon finally spoke. "Your assessment?"

"It was a trap. Richard is meticulous; he wouldn't walk into this unthinkingly. Someone anticipated him, and Nomad betrayed him. I think it is likely they're both captives of Lucian now. Raven also apparently failed. Lucian and Anja are still working together."

The snarl she heard sent shivers down her spine. She had never heard its like. For that sound to have escaped from Eamon revealed an alarming amount of concern. “This needs to be cleaned up. Lucian and Anja have become too dangerous to live.” Eamon’s statement was as chilling as the sound that had preceded it. “I will initiate other channels to locate Richard. Keep me informed of your progress.”

“Yes, Grandmaster.” Helena hung up and looked again at the darkened corners of the room.

The call’s ring cut through the office’s silence an hour later. She answered, “Helena.”

“I’ve located Richard in the city. He seems disoriented.” Eamon betrayed an urgency that she had seldom heard from him.

Helena straightened in her seat, her mind alight. He didn’t realize he’d confirmed to her that the methods he used to locate Richard must have included some mystical link to Richard. It was another indication of how dire he felt the situation was becoming. That he could trace Richard implied that he could do the same with her. “Understood. Do we know his condition? How did he escape?”

“That’s what I need you to find out. He may try to return to his office.” Papers shuffled in the background. “Tie up these loose ends, Helena. If there’s any doubt about his loyalty or condition, bring him to me. Directly and discreetly.”

“I’ll take care of it,” Helena assured him, her words clipped. The line went dead, leaving her in the growing dusk that shadowed the room.

As the city’s noises crept in from outside, she prepared to solve the mystery of Richard.

# Part Two

# *Thirteen*

ANJA PACED THE room, her mind racing. The hotel room seemed too small as they prepared for the night's endeavor. Lucian lounged on the plush sofa, his face showing the anticipation of the experiment they were about to try. Seeing him in the fluffy white hotel robe had made her smile.

Zoe watched Anja's restless movements with an amused look from where she relaxed next to Lucian on the sofa. "You're making me dizzy." Zoe had not bothered with a robe.

Anja shot her a look and suppressed a smile. "Just thinking. We need to learn more about how all this works. Emma's shifting is one piece. As we learn more, imagine what else we might do."

They all fell into a contemplative silence. Anja *was* nervous; not only would they be aiding Emma, but they would also be learning more about themselves. This would also be a test of their monogamish relationship—the first of many, she supposed.

Her arcane knowledge was only one part. "Lucian, your lineage is steeped in power you're only beginning to tap into. Marbas, from whom you descend, was capable of transformations that defy simple definitions."

Lucian sat, his brow furrowed not by concern but with the hunger for knowledge as he considered her words. Mastery of his full potential eluded him, like a locked chest at the bottom of the sea—mysterious and out of reach.

"Something more has been stirring in me, something beyond the lion," Lucian admitted.

"You think there's more to Lucian's abilities? That he could shape more than just his form?" Zoe asked.

"Yes," Anja said. "And it's not just about shifting shape—it's about embracing the essence of Marbas. The wisdom to heal, change, and see beyond the veils that blind us to the truth of our natures."

A thought crossed her mind, disturbing in its implications. Marbas could heal or cure disease, but it was also written that he could cause disease. Someone of his line, with the knowledge and ability to change others' forms, could have been the origin of lycanthropy—a transmissible affliction that was more like a curse. Otherkin could be shapeshifters but were not lycanthropes and not contagious. She would need to be very careful with this realization.

Their attention turned to the door as a knock sounded. Lucian opened the door for Emma, her black hair silhouetted against the hallway light. She wore a little black dress that shimmered in the light. High heels added to her height, bringing her even with Lucian.

Emma's expression was alight with anticipation. "Tonight, we will explore what you are capable of, Emma," Anja said. "And we may unlock some of Lucian's secrets in aiding you. Remember when we discussed your first shift?"

Emma took a deep breath. "Yes, I can't help but feel eager. A part of me has been stirring—calling to me. Claire and Ian…their animals…"

"That's what we're here for, Emma. For you to have that, too," Zoe said. "This is all about you." She glanced at each of her companions.

Lucian's stance relaxed at her words, worry lines fading. Given what they were about to do, she was easing their tension in new ways. Emma, the center of the night's endeavor, allowed a small smile to grow.

Zoe's attention lingered on Emma, her mind working to dismantle any barriers of discomfort. "Emma, we're all here to help. We'll follow your lead, and you set the pace."

She moved around the room, her actions casual, lighting candles to cast a soft glow and dispel any lingering shadows. The room's atmosphere shifted with each flicker of flame, becoming a place removed from the outside world.

Zoe moved to each of them—a stroke of Lucian's cheek, a kiss for Anja. The kiss she gave Emma was more sensual and lingering, a follow-up to the flirtation they had both been anticipating.

"We're redefining our boundaries tonight," Zoe continued, barely above a whisper. "And remember, this is an accepting space without judgment. We're here to support Emma, yes, and to be with each other. To learn. To explore. To enjoy."

Emma looked at the trio, then down. "I've never…" She paused, trailing off as she sought the right words. "It's always been one person at a time for me. This feels overwhelming, but in a way that is exciting." She folded her arms across her stomach. "I just don't want this to go wrong or get awkward."

Zoe's expression was earnest. "Emma, this is all about you. Your comfort, your odyssey. It's about awakening something beautiful in you—something that's been waiting for the right moment."

"We're here to guide and support you," Anja said. "Our connection, our energies, our bodies are yours to command tonight."

Emma's response was vulnerable. "But can I handle it? Can I manage all of this? The sensations, the intensity, the…I've been fantasizing about it. But now I don't know what to expect."

Anja said, "Emma, don't expect anything—other than some impressive orgasms. We need to, or rather mostly I need to, build up an excess of magic, and those orgasms will provide that power. I'll channel that to Lucian for his part. I will guide your thoughts as Zoe will guide your emotions. This is more about you letting go in more ways than one."

Emma took stock of her friends. Anja's words and Zoe's comforting presence calmed her. Emma was at ease with Anja, and memories of their shared times together brought a wave of arousal.

Lucian could be intimidating, but he also was masculine. Zoe?

Emma couldn't help feeling attracted to her. She was so open and caring. She was always seeking what was right. Emma trusted her in this, too.

Anja approached. "Emma, we can get comfortable on the bed. Lucian and Zoe can start by watching and warming each other up." She smiled at them.

"Okay," was all Emma could muster as she stood and let Anja lead her by the hand to the bed.

Relaxing into a familiar pattern with Anja felt good. She had missed these times with her. Anja slipped the dress from Emma's shoulders to let it fall to the floor with her own. Their tongues entwined, and their hands caressed each other. Neither of them had worn anything under their dresses. Still in her heels, she saw Anja's face bright with desire. Taking over the lead, as she had so often in the past, she pushed Anja back onto the bed and began to explore her body, kissing her way down Anja's neck. She suckled each nipple and lightly touched them with her teeth.

"Oh, yes, Emma. More…" Anja breathed out. Her perfume was so familiar.

Emma continued lower while Anja spread her legs for her, and she obliged by going down to lick and suck at her. Anja tasted so sweet and musky as Emma reached the slickness in her folds. Anja continued to writhe and moan—a heady feeling of power swept over Emma. She pressed in closer and licked deeply and languidly, savoring the taste.

Hearing Zoe moan, Emma moved up and turned to see what had elicited those sounds.

Lucian was in a soft chair with Zoe perched on his lap, both facing them on the bed. Zoe rode up and down on Lucian's cock. Emma turned over beside Anja so they could watch. She reached over to continue stimulating Anja with her fingers and spread her legs as an invitation for Anja to reciprocate. Soon, Anja's fingers were inside her, sliding in and out in time with Zoe and Lucian's movements. The sight of them watching while being watched was intense.

"That looks incredible…" Emma said as Zoe came. At that same time, Anja reached her peak, crying out and rolling her head back.

"I want some of that too," Emma voiced.

"I guess...you...can have him for...a little while. It's...your night... after all." Zoe tried to catch her breath as she stood.

Lucian approached the bed. His erection stood out in front and bobbed slightly as he walked. He paused at the side of the bed and leaned down to kiss her, and a rush of heat rose to her face as she realized she could taste Anja and that Lucian would taste it, too. She reached to cup his cheek, and he turned to kiss and then lick her fingers. Her blush only deepened, knowing where they had just been as he sucked on them. That thought was nearly enough to tip her over the edge. Anja, still sliding her fingers in and out of her, was enough, though. The orgasm that rocked through Emma made her cry out as she fell back in bliss.

When she could see again, Lucian moved up over her with Zoe and Anja to either side. Anja had mercifully moved from her to Lucian's member and was using her juices to stroke him. Zoe had moved up and was fondling her breasts and watching her face. "This is too much," Emma said.

Zoe gave her an evil-looking smile. "We're not done."

"You wanted me, Emma?" Lucian asked.

Looking down at his erection, she breathed out a quiet, "Yes. Please."

Lucian moved closer, easing her legs apart. She looked down to see Anja guide him to her entrance while spreading her open to accept him.

Emma lay on her back and could feel the weight of Lucian's body pressing down onto hers. He eased into her, his hands gripping her hips as he took her.

The sensations were overwhelming—the feeling of Lucian's hardness inside her, Anja rubbing her clit, Zoe's warm breath on her skin. Emma was getting closer to another orgasm with each passing moment.

Lucian picked up the pace, and Emma gripped his hips tightly and pulled him closer. Her grip spurred him on, and he started to pound into her harder and faster. Anja's movements also became more fervid, her touch flicking over Emma's clit and Lucian's shaft.

Zoe's kisses turned more urgent, her teeth grazing Emma's skin as she sucked on her nipples as she reached down to pleasure herself. Emma was losing control, and the orgasm grew inside until it finally broke free.

Emma cried out in pleasure as her body spasmed beneath Lucian's and Anja's attentions. Anja licked up to taste Emma's orgasm from her mouth. Their desire for her radiated off them in waves.

Lucian reached his orgasm, spurting inside her. Zoe's fingers were almost a blur as she came, too.

Anja fed on all three of them, her eyes glowing with pleasure as she reached her climax.

The lingering euphoria enveloped Emma in a warm embrace as they collapsed amidst the tangled sheets. The room was heavy with the scent of their sex.

Lucian's presence moved above her, a calm force, with Anja just behind him, her hand resting on his back. "Emma," he began, "I will try and push your shift. Look inward and accept your nature while Anja and I help guide you."

"Lucian will help your body follow what it knows to do," Anja assured her. "I'll help your mind, and Zoe will help your emotions let go of yourself. You want to do this, and you can do it."

"Yes," Emma said in surrender, permission granted to them to lead her through the metamorphosis. Lucian's hand rested on her chest, a warmth that soon radiated outward. Her skin still carried a light sheen of sweat and was mottled with the signs of her pleasure. Before she closed her eyes, she saw the glow emanating from Lucian's palm. It became a beacon in the darkness of her closed lids.

She inhaled deeply, and her chest rose to meet Lucian's hand. Then she exhaled any lingering hesitation. Opening herself up to their guidance, she relinquished control.

Lucian's hand was a conduit, a bridge that channeled arcane energies from Anja through him to Emma. As his palm rested over her heartbeat, he could feel her life force, vibrant and waiting. His magic unfurled, seeking, probing, following the intricate pathways Anja's boost of power had illuminated.

With his inner vision, he searched Emma's being, past the corporeal, into the blueprint of her existence. There, in the helical depths, he witnessed the dance of her DNA. He saw the epigenetic markers, like notes on a grand staff of biological music, each poised to play its part in her transformation. He also saw multiple scores that she could play—Emma had not one but many feline forms.

Lucian's magic touched these markers like a pianist coaxing a melody from the keyboard. The flux receptors began to activate, a cascade of biological signals. Each burst was a note in the symphony of change, a chorus that sang to the nature of what Emma was becoming.

The physical manifestation was miraculous as his magic worked through the nucleotides of her genetic helix. Each note echoed through epigenetic chambers to release flux catalysts. Her cells responded with fantastic speed; they multiplied, differentiated, and shifted form and function under the orchestration of ancient magic now reawakened.

With a sense of reverence and awe, Lucian withdrew his influence, stepping back to witness the culmination of this primordial process.

The shift began subtly; a tingling danced beneath her skin, a whisper of fur against her flesh that wasn't there moments before. Her senses heightened, sounds became crisper, and the room's dim light painted vivid patterns behind her closed lids. Emma's body morphed, muscles rippling. The physical sensation was alien but not unwelcome —a reshaping, guided by Lucian's steady energy and Anja's guidance.

Bones realigned with a sensation that should have been painful but wasn't—instead, it was as if she was stretching after a long slumber. Her form condensed and then expanded, silhouette shifting, new textures emerging. It was a surrender to an innate rhythm that had lain dormant.

Emma's breath came in short gasps from the sheer intensity of the experience. There was a moment of disorientation, where she hovered between her human self and something new—a creature of agility and feline grace.

And then, with Zoe's support, letting herself go, she flowed through the final throes of her transformation and arrived at her destination. Emma saw the world through the eyes of her otherkin form and felt the power and the primal elegance that came with it. The room and its occupants appeared different, with muted colors but augmented with the scent of emotions in the air.

Emma moved, testing limbs that were both familiar and foreign, her senses reveling in new stimuli. There was no fear, only the realization of her potential and the bond with those who had guided her here.

In the afterglow of transformation, Emma understood the depth of their connection, the power of trust, and the beauty of letting go.

# *Fourteen*

THE CONFERENCE ROOM was abuzz with conversations. Standing alongside Anja, Zoe, and Emma, Lucian surveyed the team with newfound pride. Sigri shuffled through papers while Elín oversaw the organized chaos.

Claire and Ian entered, still riding the high of the morning's flight. Lucian announced Emma's breakthrough. "Emma has embraced her cat and panther forms. She's a stunning embodiment of the black panther, majestic and powerful. And a cute cat as well."

Claire teased, "So we have a kitty among us now for real?"

Emma shot back, "Bitch. I mean that only in the most literal sense, of course." Her face was alight with humor.

Laughter flowed. It seemed the brewing tension between Claire and Emma had cooled.

Lucian's expression sobered. "Claire and Ian have just returned from their task. They released Richard into the subterranean bowels of Manhattan—the subway system. Dan is tailing him, and Mark is providing backup. They think they may have a location of his home base."

The previous banter faded. Ian leaned forward. "We tried to set him up at the safe house, but it was a no-go. The place was swarming with cops—the bodies were discovered."

Murmurs of concern rippled through the team. Lucian turned. "Zoe, you'll need to investigate further. We can't ignore this. Emma should go with you. Her previous experience with the FBI could also help, and I don't want you to go alone."

"Yes, that would be good," Zoe replied.

The room soon began to empty. With the sounds of departing footsteps and the click of the door closing, Anja beckoned Lucian and Zoe closer. "Regarding this trip, I believe we should give Zoe the freedom to explore. If the opportunity arises for them to continue on the side, I think it would be a good thing. Emma taught me about sapphic lovemaking. Zoe might be able to pick up a few tips and tricks to bring back to us."

Lucian agreed with a smile. He could see the benefit of that.

"Claire's wolf requires taming, a guiding hand. Claire and Ian have developed a monogamous relationship and involvement outside of that bond that would not help. I'll need to be there to observe and to guide. Sex isn't the goal, but I'm sure they will enjoy the experience. The goal is to help Claire gain more understanding and control of her wolf."

Zoe listened, her expression contemplative. For them, Lucian thought, lines were often blurred, and Anja's role as a mentor could be as intimate as any physical connection through the barriers it broke down.

Lucian's response was simple. "Your guidance has always been invaluable, Anja, and your approach with Claire and Ian will be no different. Zoe, be careful," he urged, turning to her. "We can't afford for you to take risks. Come back to us, that's an order."

Zoe smiled, acknowledging the command beneath his protective plea. He knew she was well aware of the risks and the necessity.

"I'll miss you," Anja admitted. "Return to us soonest. Our bed will be colder without you."

In response, Zoe reached out, pulling them into an embrace. She kissed each of them, a promise sealed with whispered 'I love yous' that brushed against their ears. The words hung in the air.

Anja's eyes shimmered with moisture. With a final look, Zoe turned to leave, carrying the love and trust of those who stood with her in shadow and light.

As the jet sliced through the sky, Zoe's thoughts drifted to the recent whirlwind of events. The hum of the engines provided a backdrop to her musings. Zoe had always been independent and resourceful, never one to rely on the comforts of wealth, but she couldn't deny the allure of this world she was rapidly becoming a part of.

The clink of fine china snapped her back to the present. Bella, the ever-attentive stewardess, was setting down a cup of herbal tea on the sleek fold-out table before her and a coffee for Emma. "Anything else I can get for you, Ms. Zoe? Emma?" Bella asked with a smile.

"Thank you, Bella, this is perfect," Zoe replied, wrapping her hands around the warm cup. The steam carried hints of ginger and lemon. Emma just shook her head and smiled, content to sip her cream-heavy coffee.

Zoe's mind wandered to Anja and Lucian. There was an undeniable chemistry, a magnetic pull between them that had quickly evolved into something more profound. She had been surprised by the intensity of her feelings, especially for Anja—a connection that transcended friendship and had ventured into a shared intimacy she had never even considered.

Lucian had also captured a part of her heart with his quiet strength and enigmatic aura. The three of them together were balanced—a trio of power, passion, and intellect. It was a situation she hadn't anticipated, but now that she was in it, she couldn't imagine it any other way.

The jet began its descent, which brought a flutter of anticipation. She was eager to touch down in New York.

When the wheels touched the tarmac, they gathered their things. Zoe would need to check in with Lucian's secretary Ava soon to coordinate her return. For now, though, she had a brief reprieve in the city, a momentary pause in the storm of her new life.

Exiting the jet, she spotted Thomas waiting by the sleek Rolls. He held two packages. "Ms. Zoe, Ms. Emma, welcome back to New York. I have something for each of you from Mr. Miller."

Zoe took the package, feeling the weight of it. "Thank you, Thomas.

Do you know what it is?"

Thomas shook his head. "I'm afraid not. But Mr. Miller said you would understand the importance."

Emma gave Zoe a questioning look, and Zoe said, "I guess we'll just have to find out."

With a polite thank you to Thomas and a promise to relay any messages to Ava, Zoe followed Emma into the back and settled, the package resting on her lap. As the city blurred past, Zoe felt that every end was just a new beginning.

After opening the box and examining the contents, Zoe brushed her fingertips over the cool metal of her Glock, the familiar weight a reminder of her previous life, one foot still in the FBI, the other stepping into the unknown. The titanium credit card gleamed under the interior light of the Rolls. She ran a thumb over the card, considering the freedom it offered—a freedom that was as daunting as it was exhilarating.

"Oh, wow, I guess he was really serious about the expense account and stuff!" Emma, also now armed again, smiled.

The note from Ava was crisp, professional, and to the point, much like Ava herself. Zoe appreciated the clarity, even as the enormity of the trust being placed in her sank in.

On the drive to Zoe's apartment, Emma said, "I need to go to my apartment to take care of a few things. I think I'm going to pack up and end my lease. I'm in this all the way now. We might as well move our things into Lucian's penthouse. I see no real reason to keep these separate places. I already have most of my stuff there from when I started guarding him. I know you just moved into your apartment, so it would probably be easy for you to have Ava make the arrangements."

"I don't know, Emma; it may be too much for the bureaucrats to take. I'm still involved with the investigation, and they would tag me as compromised."

"Hmmm, I see your point. Would you like to come see me there tonight?" Emma asked a bit nervously. "It would be more comfortable than me staying at your place. I want to talk about things, and Lucian wanted me to watch your back."

Zoe squeezed her hand and smiled. "Yes, I'm unsure what will happen, but I have to check in and go to that safe house. I'm not looking forward to either of those. I'm sure they won't let you into the scene, and your presence would draw questions I don't want to answer. There are fewer complications that way."

"I can follow separately and sneak in as a cat to keep an eye on things. I'm going to be tailing you anyway. Lucian was quite clear I was to watch out for you." Laughing, Emma added, "And Anja had other assignments for me too."

"Okay, okay. I get the idea," Zoe responded with a matching smile. "I'll spend the night with you at the penthouse. I'll take care of my stuff here, then come on over. Have Thomas come back for me after you're done with him."

With a kiss for Emma and a word of gratitude to Thomas, she exited the vehicle, her heels clicking against the pavement as she made her way to her apartment.

The familiar surroundings greeted her, but they belonged to a part of her life that was rapidly closing. With a sigh, Zoe braced herself for the call she had dreaded—the call to her supervisor at the field office.

She dialed the number. When her supervisor picked up, Zoe detected an undercurrent of something—was it disappointment? Concern?

"Zoe, we need to talk about your sudden leave of absence," her supervisor began.

Zoe took a deep breath. The Glock, the cards, the package from Lucian—all of it waited silently, symbolizing the turn her life had taken. She was about to enter that new world entirely, and there was no turning back after that happened.

Her supervisor laid out the grim news. "Bodies have been found, Zoe. It looks like the killer from the Miller estate murders is among them. You're to meet Detective Cruz at the scene."

She knew this already, of course, but there was no benefit in revealing her hand—not when the stakes were so high. "Got it. I'll be there as soon as I can."

The location was already etched in her mind, a map drawn from recent, haunting experiences. As her supervisor continued, offering the coordinates, she scribbled them down with a feigned sense of urgency.

"And Zoe," her supervisor added, "this case…It's taking on a life of its own."

A wry smile formed as she ended the call. 'Life of its own' was an understatement. With every step forward, the path twisted unpredictably, much like the double helix of a DNA strand that she now knew could hide secrets beyond comprehension.

She took a moment to steady herself, the reality of her dual existence—FBI agent and member of a clandestine world—coalescing into a sharp focus. Then she looked around at her apartment.

Emma stepped into Lucian's penthouse, the luxurious expanse greeting her with familiar warmth. She had been here before, but today marked a new beginning. She found Ava, Lucian's secretary, at her desk and informed her that she wanted to move her belongings into her room here.

As Emma walked through the opulent space, her thoughts drifted to the remarkable changes in her life. The ability to shift forms had altered her in ways she was still exploring. Her senses were sharper, her reflexes quicker, and a newfound agility coursed through her. But more than the physical changes, the deepening connections with Lucian, Anja, and Zoe occupied her thoughts.

She was a partner now in their quest to eliminate the Sodality and their continued threat. Their relationship was unconventional. She might occasionally join their intimate circle, but she also understood the sanctity of the special bond that Lucian, Anja, and Zoe had.

She wished she could be a part of that, too, but that was not practical for so many reasons. She was happy for them and would be content with her place at their side. Cats liked their independence, and she couldn't envision it any other way.

Anja had entrusted her with a delicate task—to guide Zoe in learning the nuances of intimacy between women. Emma wanted to ensure that her exploration was enlightening and enjoyable. Zoe's curiosity and openness would make it an enriching experience.

Emma paused by the large windows, looking out over Manhattan. The world outside looked unchanged, but for her, everything had changed. With a deep breath, she turned away from the windows. There was much to do, and her new life was just beginning.

Her thoughts were interrupted as Zoe arrived.

"Hey, Emma." Zoe launched into the details of her call with her supervisor, explaining the upcoming trip to the safe house. "It's strange. We staged that scene at the safe house, and now I'm going back there as an FBI agent to investigate. It's like living in two different realities."

"It must be challenging for you to still be an active agent maintaining that balance."

"You could say that. But I know it's necessary, especially now with everything at stake."

"You're handling it incredibly well. And remember, you're not alone in this. We're all with you."

Zoe's face softened. "Thanks, Emma. Tomorrow's trip will be another step, but I'm ready for it. I've come too far, seen too much to back out now."

Zoe had a small bag with her, indicating her intent to stay in the room assigned to her. However, Emma had other plans. "Zoe, you're not staying in that room. Anja's directions were pretty clear. We're sharing a room…and a bed."

Zoe showed an undeniable glimmer of interest. "Oh, I see. Anja's orders, huh?"

Emma smiled. "Yeah, it's part of your…let's say 'continued education.' I think it's for the best."

"Hmmm. I guess you're going to insist?"

"Yup. Now, let's get settled in."

They made their way to the room that would be theirs while in the city. The room was spacious and luxuriously furnished, typical of Lucian's taste. Emma had been staying here as a bodyguard but had moved in more of her personal items.

Zoe put her small bag on a chair with a sense of hesitation. "You okay with this?" Emma asked.

"Yeah, I'm good. It's just new, that's all. But I'm open to new experiences."

A warmth spread through her at Zoe's words. Their relationship was evolving, growing, and more intimate than she had expected.

Zoe placed her Glock on the opposite nightstand to Emma's. She hung up her jacket and holster, then stripped off the rest of her clothes. "Are we sharing a laundry basket, or do I need to move another in?" she teased.

As demonstrated by their last adventure in bed, Zoe showed little inhibition and a penchant for nude sleeping. It was more like just being naked every chance she got. Emma could appreciate that.

Emma matched Zoe's lack of attire, and the two women got into bed, the comfortable sheets and plush pillows enveloping them. As the lights dimmed, Emma spooned against Zoe and kissed her shoulder.

"It's been a long day. Nap first?" Emma whispered.

"Mm-hm," Zoe murmured. "That sounds good."

# *Fifteen*

ANJA STEPPED INTO Ian and Claire's room. The hotel where they had been staying was pleasant, but they needed to find better-suited accommodations if they stayed longer in Iceland. Maybe a large house with enough bedrooms to host the team. Lucian already had several around the globe, so what was one more, right?

Ian and Claire sat close together on the edge of the bed, their hands intertwined. They were dressed only in robes and fresh from a shower. As Anja closed the door behind her, she felt the pulse of their emotions—nervousness from Claire and protectiveness from Ian.

"Hi." Anja moved to sit across from them, her posture open and inviting. "Would you like to talk about things first?"

"Yes," Claire replied, her eyes betraying a hint of the wildness that they hoped to tame this evening. "I've...we've talked about it," she said, squeezing Ian's hand. "I'm uncomfortable with anyone else being involved physically with either Ian or me, but I understand the need for your guidance, Anja."

Anja smiled reassuringly. "I'm here to facilitate and guide, nothing more. Your intimacy with Ian is just that—yours. I'll be present to help you navigate the energies and ensure that everything flows as it should."

Ian spoke up. "We trust you, Anja. And we acknowledge the... arousal that may come with your presence. It's a natural part of the process, isn't it?"

"It is," Anja confirmed. "The energy that comes from intimacy can be a powerful catalyst for awakening the deeper aspects of your otherkin selves. It's about channeling that energy, not becoming lost to it."

Claire took a deep breath. "Okay, I'm ready. Let's discuss how we're going to do this."

"The ritual will be simple. I'll lead you through it with my voice and presence. We'll start with meditation to center ourselves, and then you and Ian will connect sexually. You'll seek the calm within the storm through touch, breath, and arousal—the place where the wolf resides."

"And if I feel the wolf rising?" Claire asked in a whisper.

"Then you embrace it. You let it know that you are its master, not vice versa. Ian will be with you, and I'll be the anchor. You don't need to fight it this time." Anja perched herself on the arm of the plush hotel chair. "There's one more thing I need to be clear about. My presence here, while primarily for guidance, will be...stimulating for me. It's a part of who I am, and it's impossible to separate that."

Ian's expression didn't waver. Claire's cheeks were touched with a hint of color, but she agreed. "I guess it's part of the whole experience. To be seen and to see. It's something new for me, but...I think I'm okay with it."

"Good. I know it will be a turn-on for me to watch the two of you. I'll draw pleasure from watching you and Ian."

"Yes," Claire finally said with a tremor of nervousness. "And I suppose it's only fair to acknowledge that we might...um, like it."

"So, voyeurism and exhibitionism for all involved," Ian said with a smile.

Anja smiled. "Exactly. It's a two-way street. I don't want either of you to be concerned about your reactions. Don't be afraid to watch me enjoy myself. Actually, please do. This is a shared experience; all feelings are valid and welcome. But remember, the focus remains on you, Claire. We're here to support you in finding balance and control."

Claire added, "We're okay with the...mutual aspect of it. It's uncharted territory for us, but we're ready."

Anja's hunger for the imminent encounter was there, even though she had fed it the night before. It was likely not satiated, since she had returned most of that energy to Lucian and Emma for her shift. *I really need to figure this out before it gets out of control,* she thought, watching Claire stand up.

Claire's excitement grew when she stood and removed her robe. Since her first shift, she was utterly comfortable in her skin, and they had all seen her naked. This was different, though. It was much more intimate, and the expectation for her to have sex while someone watched was a little daunting, even with the conversation they'd just had.

She crawled up on the bed, looking back at Ian as he disrobed and moved up beside her. A rush of excitement washed over her, replacing hesitation. She knew Anja was watching, and that knowledge only increased her desire for Ian.

Anja stood and slipped the dress off her shoulders while Ian explored Claire's body. Anja was completely naked under the dress. Claire had seen her nude before in that moonlit meadow by the lake. Then, it had been only during her initial awakening and not intimate. This was different—very different.

How Anja watched with such intensity was enough to make anyone's temperature rise. She was sure Ian felt it, too, by his deep and passionate kisses.

Claire lay back and spread her legs for him as his hands roamed over her body, tracing along her curves as he pushed inside of her. His filling her up was electrifying, and she moaned out loud as they began to move together. She felt every inch of him—the way his muscles flexed as he thrust and the way his hair tickled her skin.

Anja climbed on the bed beside them, not close enough to touch but inside their intimate space. Claire could smell Anja's perfume and Ian's cologne. Her amplified senses could detect their arousal. Her wolf was waking. She could feel it stirring inside her.

They turned their heads to watch as Anja started to masturbate beside them with one hand, the other touching her breasts and nipples. She focused on their joining as Ian continued to pump in and out.

It turned on Claire even more to know that she was being watched and that seeing them turned Anja on. She closed her eyes and gave in to the feeling, letting Ian take control.

"You like that, don't you? Being watched while you make love. You can see how turned on I am."

Claire could only smile, lost to sensation, but Ian said, "Yes. I'm as hard as I've ever been."

"Claire, move up on top of Ian and face me," Anja requested. "I want you to set the pace in time with my chants when I start the ritual. Follow them in your mind and with your body; I'll guide your thoughts along pathways to help you master your wolf."

She whimpered as Ian pulled out but moved to the side. Ian turned over onto his back and propped himself on the pillows. He stroked himself as Claire moved up to straddle him. She reached down to guide him back into her and looked back up to see Anja watching.

"Oh, Claire, you look so stunning on top of Ian. You two are so delicious together. Watching you is so turning me on."

The suggestion of power that Anja's words provided was stunning. Claire had control. The acceptance of her feelings and awareness of her attractiveness was liberating. "And so is watching you, Anja..."

Anja began to chant. Claire could not understand the words, but the sounds stirred something deep inside her. She felt a gentle probing at the edges of her consciousness and let it flow through her. She followed the images of the moon and wild forests. Sounds became as vivid and amplified as scents had become. The feeling of Ian thrusting up to meet her as she moved on him, hitting just the right spot deep inside, was incredible.

She could feel Anja's fingers penetrating herself through the connection between them. At first, she thought she was imagining it, but with her mind so open to Anja, apparently the link went both ways. The pleasure Anja was experiencing was as intense as her own. Sensations from Anja multiplied together with hers, amplifying them to incredible levels. She could see herself and Ian pumping into her as if reflected in a mirror, colored with sensation. It was like she and Anja had traded bodies. At this point, she wouldn't even care if Anja joined them—touched her, kissed her, or licked her into oblivion. *"No,"* she heard Anja's voice in her mind. *"This is enough for now. Maybe next time."*

Claire's mind was completely open to Anja's, and she let her into her deepest, darkest secrets and desires. New pathways were drawn in her mind as she saw her wolf looking back at her and understood how to control her.

"Yes, come for her, Ian!" Anja commanded, and he obediently complied, shooting into Claire, hot spurts filling her. It was more than enough to push her over the edge—her orgasm hit her in waves, shaking her whole being as she lost control. She barely heard Ian moaning loudly, "Ah, Claire, that's so good!"

Claire smiled, eyes closed in pure bliss as she collapsed onto Ian, still buried inside her, knowing Anja was there with her.

Anja moaned as she hit her peak, and Claire's eyes snapped open to watch as Anja came. The sight of her writhing on the bed with her legs spread and fingers moving, coupled with the link still between them feeding pleasure and power, pushed Claire over the edge of another orgasm, and she spasmed tightly around Ian.

When she regained some semblance of coherence, Claire saw Anja smiling back at her. "Fuck, Anja. I don't know how to describe that. Can you teach me and Ian how to do that mind link thing?"

"I'm not sure. Maybe? It's one of my new talents that is growing stronger, but I don't know if it can be taught. We are all still learning and growing," Anja replied huskily, a wicked smile spreading. "We may have to do this again to try. Now, lie back and let yourself go. Bring that wolf out; make her yours."

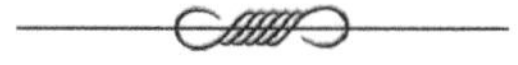

Ian watched, heart pounding in his chest, while Claire began to shift. The air vibrated with an electric charge that foretold a coming storm.

Claire's body arched, muscles flexing and stretching as her human shape melded into something wilder. Her skin rippled, and from beneath, a coat emerged, a rich golden brown that mirrored the color of her hair.

Her face elongated into a muzzle, nose quivering as new scents and sounds flooded her heightened senses. Her irises, once a softer amber, now gleamed with a brilliant hue.

When the transformation was complete, Claire stood on all fours. Her fur was streaked with darker patches, reminiscent of the shadows cast by leaves in a sun-dappled grove. She was larger than any ordinary wolf.

Ian's breath caught as he witnessed the majestic creature before him. She was an incarnation of the wild beauty inherent in their kind.

The wolf turned to face him, and for a moment, nothing else existed. Her gaze met his, and a jolt of recognition passed between them. This was Claire, his Claire, and she was also the embodiment of the wolf.

Claire moved with an instinctual elegance, her limbs carrying her up onto the bed where Anja awaited. She rubbed her snout against Anja's cheek, a silent thank you for the gift she had been given.

Claire reclined onto the bed with a stretch that showcased her newfound form; Ian was struck by the contentment in her posture. He could see a wolfish grin in her eyes, a playful light that had always been part of Claire but now shone through with clarity.

"Thank you, Anja," Ian said in wonder and gratitude. "For everything."

Anja simply smiled, her hand lingering on Claire's fur in an affectionate ruffle. Claire's response was to roll onto her back, exposing her belly.

Anja stroked Claire's fur. There was a sense of completion, and as she stood, her movements were unhurried, allowing Ian and Claire to savor the moment.

After slipping into her dress, Anja departed silently, a closing of the door leaving Ian and Claire alone with each other. In the quiet that followed Anja's departure, they had a profound sense of connection. The world outside faded away, leaving only the bond they shared, now stronger and deeper than ever before.

Claire rolled onto her back again, her belly exposed in a show of acceptance and trust that Ian had never experienced with her. It was an invitation he accepted. He stroked her fur, marveling at the softness and warmth.

# *Sixteen*

THE DEPUTY WAVED Zoe through as he lifted the barricade. He had radioed in for clearance after examining her credentials. The gravel crunched beneath her car tires as she navigated the winding path, the forest canopy creating a marbling of light and shadow on the windshield.

Pulling up alongside the collection of official vehicles, Zoe took a moment to gather herself. The reality of the situation hit her anew; she was about to step into the aftermath of a deadly encounter, one that she and Emma had staged.

Exiting her car, she scanned the area, noting the forensic team at work. The buzz of activity around the crime scene van was methodical and precise, contrasting with what had actually occurred. The buzz of flies, on the other hand, seemed more fitting.

Detective Nina Cruz spotted her first, a notepad and case file in hand. She approached Zoe with a brisk stride. "Agent Ananda. Glad you could make it. Your boss said you were coming. We've got a mess here."

Zoe shook her offered hand, switching to profiler mode. "How was the scene discovered?"

"Anonymous tip from someone who claimed her hunter husband thought there was someone dead inside. Flies, smell, that kind of thing. Said they didn't want to get involved. It was confirmed by a deputy who then called it in."

Cruz led Zoe through the desolate rooms, now stripped by the forensic team. Even with the bodies removed, the smell of decay was thick, and the flies sought what they sensed.

"Two dead. One shot in the back and one in the leg. According to the initial assessment, one died very quickly, and the other survived for a while. My initial impression is they shot each other."

Zoe nodded and thought, *So far, so good.*

"We found this," Cruz said, handing over a small evidence bag. Inside was a sapphire ring, its gemstone gleaming even through the plastic.

Zoe recognized the piece. It was Lucian's mother's ring, the one they had found on Smoke while first talking to Nomad. "This matches the description of a ring missing from Eliza Miller's possessions," she murmured.

Cruz agreed. "It does."

Despite the churn of thoughts beneath, Zoe had her professional façade firmly in place. "So you believe this is your unsub?"

"It must have been our guy from the Miller estate. Maybe they disagreed over this little beauty." Cruz gestured to the ring. "Valuable. Maybe too valuable."

That was how they had decided to stage this scene. The reality of what happened would have been too much and caused too many questions.

Lucian and the rest of their team were still trying to find the whole of it, and Zoe was still committed to justice. It was not as if Smoke and Viper here had been innocent. Viper had shot her in the back, intending to kill her. Emma was the one who'd pulled the trigger, ending Viper's life from behind, but it was the Sodality that was responsible. They would eventually be held to account, but it would not be through the legal system. Zoe was still adjusting to that reality.

Zoe returned the ring. "You'll need to verify its authenticity. If it's genuine, it confirms the connection between the murders at the estate and the deaths here."

Cruz nodded, her expression grim. "I'll get our guys on it, but I don't doubt it is the one."

Zoe followed Cruz out of the grim room, her mind awhirl. She was presenting findings she had helped fabricate while internally piecing together a puzzle only she could see the complete picture of.

Stepping outside, Zoe caught a glimpse of a black cat hunched down in the shadows under the CSI van parked in front of the house. She looked elsewhere while suppressing a smile as Cruz briefed her on the next steps.

"And we still have loose ends," Zoe said thoughtfully. "This ring ties the killer to the estate murders, but we're dealing with more than just these two. There's an organization behind this, I'm sure of it. You've seen the profile. Their motives, however, remain unclear. Now that you have bodies, identifying them will expose other threads that must be followed."

"There are other things that don't add up."

Zoe was suddenly concerned they had made a mistake in the staging. "What other things?" She was amazed her question came out even.

"One of them had a serious leg wound that was bound. We'll have to wait for the coroner's report to see how he died, but that means he was alive for a while. Who patched him up? If it was somebody else, where are they?" Cruz asked.

*Oh, crap.* "As you said, they likely shot each other. He must have tried to stop the bleeding in his leg. Must not have been enough."

"That's the only thing that would make sense. But still…there were indications that there were other visitors. Tire tracks, shoe and boot prints around the house and in the woods." Cruz paused before continuing. "The other weird thing is that the bodies were moved slightly—recently. Nothing else seems to have been disturbed, which makes it even stranger. I don't know what to make of that."

*What the hell?* "Okay. That just confirms my suspicions. These two were not acting alone." Zoe weighed her words carefully. "Follow those leads. The calculated nature of the Miller murders suggests a level of planning that goes beyond one individual, and you have one other body here. Which one of them was in the estate? Were there even more people involved? The other tracks and traces? How and why?"

Cruz's face set in determined lines. "Well, if that's the case, we've got our work cut out. Let's get this ring processed first. If your suspicion is right, we might just be scratching the surface of something much bigger."

*You have no idea,* Zoe thought as they walked back to the squad cars. The case of the Miller estate might be drawing to a close with this staged evidence, but Zoe knew the actual investigation was ongoing.

Returning to her routine at the field office was a blend of relief and frustration. Sitting at her desk, surrounded by the familiar drone of activity, she focused on her reports. The work was a welcome distraction, a semblance of normalcy in the whirlwind of events.

However, a call from Detective Cruz interrupted her concentration. "The ring match is confirmed. We're closing the Miller estate case. It's a clear-cut scenario now." There was a pause on the line. "Zoe, there's pressure from above to wrap up the rest, too. No more chasing after phantom organizations."

Zoe's grip tightened on the phone. This was what she had feared. "But there's more to this. We both know it."

"Yeah, I get it, Zoe, but my hands are tied. The higher-ups want me to focus on clear and current cases. Resources are stretched thin as it is."

Zoe sighed with frustration. She understood the practicalities and the bureaucratic limits all too well. "I hear you. I'll continue on my end. It fits more under federal jurisdiction anyway. Send it my way when you get the coroner's report, fingerprints for ID, or anything else. But..." She trailed off, her mind racing with unanswered questions, like who had disturbed the bodies.

Cruz's voice softened. "I know, Zoe. It doesn't sit right with me, either. But sometimes we have to play the long game. Keep your eyes open, okay?"

"Will do, Nina, you too. Thanks for the heads-up."

As the call ended, Zoe leaned back in her chair, her thoughts spinning. She couldn't just let it go, not when she knew there was so much more beneath the surface, but Lucian was right. Revealing what she knew to anyone here would get her tossed in the loony bin or worse. The field office might be limiting her official involvement, but Zoe Ananda was not one to give up easily. She had to wait for more information from Cruz to ID the two bodies, but there were other things to try. Using her accesses, she started to dig into what electronic records she could.

She tried searches for similar crimes with even vague ties to the occult. She called up her previous searches for hate groups and other associated organizations. There were way too many, which was disturbing in its own right.

Later, in the fluorescent-lit corridor of the field office, Zoe found herself standing rigidly, facing her supervisor.

"You need to shut down the casework on the Miller murders, Zoe."

"But sir, there are still loose ends, unanswered questions. They were not acting alone. We don't even know who they were yet. We can't just..."

Her supervisor raised a hand, cutting her off. "The case in Granite County is closed, Zoe. There are no pending requests. That's the end of it."

Zoe's mind raced, trying to formulate a response, a plea to continue. But her supervisor wasn't finished.

"And another thing. There have been reports about your involvement with Lucian Miller. It's getting too close for comfort, Zoe. It's raising eyebrows."

The hair on the back of her neck crawled. The implications of his words were clear and threatening. Though presented as professional and part of her undercover work, her relationship with Lucian was now being used against her.

"Sir, I assure you my involvement with Miller has been strictly professional," Zoe lied, trying to maintain her composure.

Her supervisor's expression hardened. "I'm telling you to back off, Agent Ananda. If you don't, you're not only off this case but also looking at possible termination for cause. We can't have agents who don't know where their loyalties lie."

"Understood, sir," Zoe replied, barely above a whisper. But internally, a storm of emotions raged. Anger, frustration, and a sense of injustice all drove her.

As her supervisor walked away, Zoe was at a crossroads. She had already decided to leave the Bureau but had not thought it would be this soon. The rules of the game had changed, and now it was time for her to change her strategy, too. She briskly followed him down the hall.

Zoe stood in the spartan confines of her supervisor's office; her decision had crystallized. The gulf between her current role at the FBI and the clandestine world she had been drawn into was becoming unbridgeable. The realization that the Sodality's influence might be reaching into the very organization she had pledged to serve was a bitter pill to swallow. Typically she would have been encouraged to tie things up if for nothing else than to write the damn report. It all but confirmed that pressure was mounting, and somebody thought this case was too hot.

"I'm resigning," Zoe announced, her voice steady despite the turmoil inside her.

Her supervisor looked up, his expression turning icy. "You do realize, Agent Ananda, you've barely completed a year of your three-year commitment. Most of that time was spent in training."

"Then send me the bill for the training." It was a financial burden she was willing to bear if it came to that.

The supervisor leaned back in his chair, scrutinizing her. "You understand this is highly unusual. Walking away now…you're throwing away a promising career."

"It seems this is the most expedient way to settle this. I suspect somebody wants this investigation shut down quietly and quickly."

The supervisor's eyebrows lowered with a hint of understanding, or maybe recognition. "If that's your decision, we'll process your resignation. But remember, this isn't something you can walk back from."

She read her supervisor's emotions and saw she had hit a nerve with the suggestion that he had been pressured to shut her down and divert attention. The Sodality's reach was deep indeed.

"I understand," Zoe replied, her decision now final. She had crossed too many lines, choosing a path that diverged sharply from her life as an FBI agent. The realization that her quest for truth and justice now lay outside the bounds of conventional law enforcement was both daunting and liberating.

Zoe removed her access badge and Glock, placing them on his desk. Her holster, a personal purchase, remained with her. Once a symbol of her commitment and authority, her credentials joined the other items. It was a poignant moment, marking the end of an era in her life.

A call from her supervisor brought in an escort to oversee her as she gathered her personal belongings. The mundane task of picking up her effects was surreal. She had not had much chance to accumulate many items, but the few she had were a reminder of the life she was leaving behind. Her most treasured was the coffee mug her favorite instructor had given her at graduation. It read: *I'm not judging you, I'm psychologically profiling you. There's a difference.*

As Zoe exited the office, feelings swirled inside her: sorrow for the end of a career she had worked hard for, anticipation for her new course. She was stepping into a world of shadows and secrets, where the rules were different and the stakes were unimaginably high. But she was ready, her commitment as strong as ever. She just wished she could have brought her files with her. Stealing the files would have gone too far even now.

As Zoe exited the building, Emma was waiting for her outside. Emma's countenance held understanding and concern as she took in Zoe's expression.

"I guess we'll be heading back to the land of fire and ice then?" Emma said with gentle humor.

Zoe nodded, a small smile flickering despite the circumstances. "Yes, Emma, we will. To the penthouse first. I need a diversion. Another lesson would be good." With her emerging otherkin aspects, she recognized the call of her nature and accepted that it was much akin to Anja's.

A burgeoning freedom sank in as they drove off. The road ahead was uncertain, but she was not alone.

# *Seventeen*

Helena navigated the dimly lit passageways of the Vault with practiced ease. This hidden labyrinth, its location known to only a few within the Sodality, was steeped in Soviet history.

Their entrance to the Vault had been by sea through a hidden coastal grotto. Richard, his blindfold removed, looked around with apprehension. His previous visit here, his initiation into the higher echelons of the Sodality, had been under vastly different circumstances. Still, even then, he had not known the actual location of the Vault. Now, he was here under a cloud of suspicion and uncertainty.

As they approached the Grandmaster's control center, the air grew heavier, the silence more profound. Grandmaster Eamon's presence was felt before they entered the room.

Helena stepped forward and bowed. Richard remained silent, his eyes downcast. The room was illuminated mainly by wall displays, adding to the ominous atmosphere. Grandmaster Eamon sat at the head of a long table, his nearly colorless gray eyes fixed on her, waiting.

"Grandmaster," Helena began, "I have returned with updates on Richard's disappearance and the subsequent events."

Eamon inclined his head slightly, signaling her to proceed. Helena took a deep breath and continued, detailing Richard's encounter with Nomad and Smoke, the confusion surrounding his survival after taking the suicide pill, and the loss of his phone.

"Richard claimed to have been ambushed by Lucian where Nomad was pretending to hold Anja captive. He believes Nomad has gone rogue or was captured and forced to help Lucian. Both seem to be true. Richard claims to have taken his suicide pill but does not know how he survived. He found Smoke and Viper dead upon regaining consciousness. He was confused and muddled and spent the next week recovering and trying to assess the situation."

Eamon's expression remained impassive, but Helena could sense the wheels turning in his mind as he processed the information.

"Additionally, I directed Richard to contact his law enforcement sources to check on the investigation into the bodies of Smoke and Viper as well as the Miller murder case. He managed to squash the inquiries by using his leverage over his contacts. However, Zoe Ananda was trying to push the FBI to open a more extensive probe before resigning from the agency due to the pressure Richard applied," Helena continued, her eyes on Eamon, gauging his reactions.

At the mention of Zoe's involvement, Eamon's gaze sharpened. "Zoe Ananda has resigned from the FBI?"

"Yes, Grandmaster. The pressure Richard applied seems to have pushed her out, but she remains a significant threat. She has aligned herself closely with Lucian Miller and Anja Kinzey. Anja, Zoe, and two of Lucian's bodyguards were present when Nomad and his crew attacked and failed. It appears Raven failed as well."

Eamon leaned back in his chair, his eyes narrowing as he considered this new information. The room was silent, the tension palpable.

"And Richard?" Eamon asked, his gaze shifting to Richard, who stood nervously beside Helena. "What of the tracking device found in his shoe?"

Helena recounted the discovery of a tracking device. "The device has been sent to Russia as a diversionary tactic. However, the presence of the tracking device so close to our power base is concerning. It was apparently planted to find us or get closer."

"A wise move, Helena. We cannot afford any more surprises. It was also good that you stopped to check, albeit so close."

"Grandmaster, Richard is confused and potentially compromised like Nomad. He may provide other insights." She directed scrutiny toward Richard and away from her.

Eamon's gaze returned to Richard, his expression unreadable. "Richard, you have much to answer for. Your failure has brought us to the brink of exposure."

Richard knelt and swallowed hard, his voice trembling as he replied, "I did everything I could, Grandmaster. Nomad deceived me, but I am ready to continue serving the Sodality."

Eamon's eyes bore into Richard's, assessing his sincerity. "You will have your chance to prove your loyalty, Richard. I will deal with you shortly."

Richard nodded, swallowing visibly. "Grandmaster," he said.

Eamon turned his attention back to Helena. "Continue monitoring the situation. We need to find Raven. It might be best if she were to disappear—perhaps permanently. The alliance between Zoe, Lucian, and Anja must be dismantled. I have other concerns as well."

Helena bowed her head. "Yes, Grandmaster. What would you have me do next?" She knew that every move from now on would be scrutinized.

"Your next task is to find Howard Miller, Lucian's uncle. He is in Rome and digging into dangerous secrets. He could be used to draw Lucian and the others out of hiding. Take him if you can—or kill him. Lucian and the others have remained elusive despite all the resources at my disposal."

The new assignment intrigued her. This could well be another opportunity she could take advantage of. It also occurred to her that the resources Eamon alluded to included arcane methods. That he had failed spoke volumes.

"Now, leave us," Eamon commanded Helena as Richard remained kneeling, head down.

She bowed gracefully and exited the room, leaving Eamon and Richard alone. She briefly wondered what would become of him but banished that thought. That was beyond her control, and his failure occupied Eamon's attention. She did not want that kind of attention.

Her mind was already racing with plans and options as she made her way to her chambers deep inside the Vault. The Soviet-era concrete walls around her whispered of secrets and power, a fitting backdrop for the machinations of the Sodality.

In the cool confines of her chambers, Helena sat down with her journal. The leather-bound volume was filled with her meticulous and coded handwriting.

She opened to a fresh page, the quill—an affectation of her past—poised in her hand as she contemplated her next steps. The assignment to track down Howard Miller in Rome was a significant one. With his extensive knowledge of the occult and Miller family secrets, Howard could be crucial in understanding Lucian and Anja's capabilities.

She penned her latest observations with a careful hand, detailing the developments with Lucian, Anja, and their group. Their ability to evade the Sodality's grasp was both a concern and an opportunity, one she intended to exploit.

Her mind shifted to Zoe Ananda, a new piece in this intricate game. There was much to learn about her, and information was power. She planned to dig into Zoe's past to understand her motivations and how she fit into Lucian and Anja's plans.

Lucian's companions numbered seven, with Zoe Ananda now a part of their circle. A capable force, no doubt, but Helena's Syndicate, combined with the resources of the Sodality, could undoubtedly handle them. She mulled over the prospect of forming an alliance of sorts, whether witting or not.

She would begin her hunt for Howard Miller in Rome tomorrow. The Vault surrounded her, but her mind remained alight with the fires of ambition.

She turned off the lamp in her room, casting it into darkness.

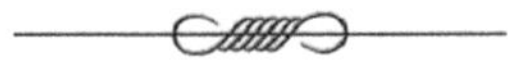

Sitting comfortably in Lucian's penthouse conference room, Zoe watched as the large screen flickered to life, signaling the start of the secure conference call with Lucian and the team back at Akar Labs in Iceland. At least the view out over the city was better than the walls of the room there.

Emma was beside her, her posture relaxed but attentive. Mark and Dan, the detectives tasked with tailing Richard, sat across the conference table. They were focused, aware they were part of something much larger than a typical surveillance assignment.

"Good evening, everyone." Lucian sounded clear; his image, along with those of Anja, Ian, Claire, and the others at Akar Labs, filled the screen. It was as if the conference room had expanded.

Zoe straightened slightly. "Lucian. We're all here. I checked out and cleared Mark and Dan."

Lucian took in each face on the call. "Let's start with an update from Iceland, then."

Anja spoke up. She detailed the latest developments, including the planning for awakening Mike and Graham.

After the updates from Iceland, Lucian turned his attention back to Zoe and her team. "Now, let's hear from you, Zoe. What do you have for us?"

"Well…I've resigned from the FBI. Lucian, since I did not complete my initial commitment, you may be on the hook to cover my training expenses. I hope you don't mind," she said with a dry smile.

Lucian showed no sign of surprise. "I had hoped that you might have been able to continue a while longer, but I do appreciate your position. As for the expense, that training will benefit the team, so I'll cover it if need be."

Zoe glanced at Mark and Dan and signaled them to share their findings.

Dan began with a crucial piece of information. "We were glad we planted a tracking device in Richard's shoe. He's good at shaking tails. He spent some time at what appears to be his office apartment in a high-rise in Manhattan. But later, he left with a tall, statuesque, pale woman with arresting blue eyes and jet-black hair. She was about five foot ten, I would estimate. They went to Teterboro and took a flight to Riga. In Riga, they went to a low-end hotel. A few hours later, the tracking showed that they traveled by vehicle towards Moscow."

Lucian's expression on the screen hardened. "Do we have an ID on the woman? Was that Raven?"

Anja jumped in. “That description does not fit the woman I saw, so probably not. Looks like we may have somebody new.”

Dan replied, “We’re working on an ID, but nothing so far. The foreign connections will make nailing it down even more difficult. If she is connected to the Sodality, it may be virtually impossible.”

Emma added, “That’s a significant move. It does imply deeper connections within the Sodality, even with the higher echelons. I wonder if that’s where they are heading to take Richard in for questioning.”

This wasn’t just a simple case of tailing an operative anymore.

“I would say that is likely. Keep digging. We need to understand the full extent of Richard’s connections and what this trip to Moscow might entail,” Lucian said.

“I’m not sure what we will be able to do other than monitor the tracking device. Russia is not a good place to be right now. We’ll put our heads together and see if we can figure something out. We’ll also keep an eye on the apartment. See if anyone else shows up. If it’s abandoned, we may want to risk going in to take a look.”

“Good, but remember, what you have learned here and anything related to it that you discover will not be spread to anyone else. I don’t want any leaks. Period,” Lucian responded.

Mark glanced at Dan. “Understood, Mr. Miller, and we’ll keep you updated on any new developments.”

Before the call concluded, Anja chimed in with a personal request. “Zoe, could you stop by my apartment? I need you to pick up some books and return them to Raymond at his shop in Brooklyn.”

Zoe jotted down the note. She remembered Raymond, the knowledgeable and charming owner of Archambault Antiquities. Anja had had a part-time job there in college, helping catalog and organize the shop. She had formed a lasting friendship with the fascinating and kindly old man.

“And give him a discreet warning about the Sodality,” Anja added.

“We miss you, Zoe. Please be careful. My jet will be there to pick you and Emma up tomorrow morning,” Lucian said with concern.

“Thanks, Lucian. We’ll be ready,” Zoe replied.

“And Zoe,” Anja continued, “I’ll give you a call on your phone in a few minutes."

Zoe couldn't help but feel a touch of apprehension. Returning the books to Raymond was a simple errand, but the warning she had to deliver carried a heavier weight. The Sodality's shadow loomed large.

The video call ended with a set of agreed actions and follow-ups. Zoe leaned back, feelings swirling. This was her life now—a blend of intrigue, danger, and the pursuit of a greater good. It was a far cry from her days at the FBI, but somehow, it was exactly where she was meant to be.

As Mark and Dan left, Zoe prepared herself for the tasks ahead. The next few days would be busy.

The phone rang shortly, and Zoe answered it with a smile, seeing Anja's picture. "Hey, Anja."

"Hey, Zoe. I wanted to let you know that Lucian and I will be working on awakening Mark and Graham tonight." Anja buzzed with excitement through the phone. "I'm really looking forward to it. Having three men at once will be a whole new experience for me."

Zoe chuckled. "I wish I could be there. But I'm sure you'll manage just fine without me."

"I wish you could be here too, but we'll have plenty of time to share stories when you get back. Oh, and speaking of stories, how are your lessons going with Emma?"

"Hmmm, learning some new tricks. Things I never even dreamed of, but now I can't wait to try with you when I return. She's even introduced me to a few toys. I'll have to make a side shopping trip. I don't want to steal hers."

"Well, damn, girl, we'll have a lot to catch up on. I'm sure Lucian won't mind us demonstrating these new tricks you've learned."

"Yeah, but we don't want to kill him," Zoe teased.

They chatted more about the plans and how things were going at Akar Labs. Zoe could hear Anja's excitement, and she was genuinely happy for her friend. "I understand our relationship is... unconventional, but I love how open and honest we can be about everything."

"Exactly," Anja agreed warmly. "It's all about trust and understanding. It's why our arrangement works. I can't wait to tell you all about tonight."

"And I can't wait to hear all about it. Stay safe, Anja, and enjoy tonight."

"Love you, Zoe."

"Love you too, Anja. And pass that on to Lucian."

As Zoe hung up, she was content. Despite the dangers they faced, the love and support they shared were real and intense. It was a bond that went beyond physical attraction. It was a connection that would endure.

# *Eighteen*

THE EVENING AIR was crisp and cool as Anja and Lucian, with Graham driving, approached Mike's house just outside Reykjavík. It was late May, and Iceland's unique beauty was on full display. The sky, a canvas of twilight hues, stretched endlessly above them, hinting at the prolonged daylight hours of summer, only a few weeks away.

Mike's house sat secluded, surrounded by open land that merged with the wild landscape. The structure was clad in weathered wood that had taken on a silvery patina. Large glass windows reflected the evening light and offered glimpses of the warm interior.

As they approached, Anja noted the subtle touches that made the house uniquely icelandic—the turf-covered roof blended with the surrounding greenery. The place exuded a sense of tranquility and connection with nature.

The surrounding land was covered in greens and browns, dotted with volcanic rocks and hardy shrubs that had adapted to the harsh climate. In the distance, the rugged outline of mountains loomed, their peaks still capped with snow, a beautiful contrast against the softer colors of the twilit sky. It was a fitting home for Mike, a geothermal expert whose work revolved around harnessing the earth's natural power.

Mike opened the door and greeted them with a warm smile. The interior reflected his personality—organized, welcoming, with a touch of the unconventional. The living room, where they gathered, was spacious, with a large, comfortable sofa and a few armchairs surrounding a low coffee table.

"Welcome," Mike said, but Anja could sense the underlying current of nervous anticipation. "I can't say I'm not a bit nervous about all this."

Lucian set down a small cooler. "It's okay to feel that way, Mike. This is something new for all of us."

Graham, standing a bit more rigidly, gave a curt nod.

Sensing their unease, Anja decided to address the elephant in the room. "Tonight is about discovery and embracing a part of yourselves that has been hidden," she began. "I'll be guiding you through the rituals and the intimacy required. Having three men at once will also be a new experience for me, something I've only ever fantasized about but never thought I'd ever do."

She looked at each of them in turn, a lingering appraisal. "Before we begin, I want to check for any limitations or issues you might have. We should all feel comfortable with what's about to happen. You need to be able to let down your guard for me."

Mike shifted slightly, his demeanor easing. "I'm open to this process, Anja. I have no experience with it, so you or one of the others may have to give direction."

After hesitating, Graham added, "I'm not into other guys, but I know we will have to be near each other. I can handle that. Other than that, I don't really have anything."

Something inside her stirred, wanting to be let loose. "Thank you. As for me, I have no limitations. My role is facilitating and guiding; I'm ready to embrace that. Lucian, the serum first," Anja said.

He reached down to the cooler he had carried in and extracted a vial and two syringes. He drew the serum and then placed the vial back on the ice in the cooler. Stepping first to Graham, he studied him for a moment, and then the first syringe began to glow under his touch. Graham eyed it warily, then offered an arm for Lucian, which he injected. He repeated the process for Mike, then dropped the syringes into the cooler, closed it, and moved it to the side. "You will feel a tingling flow from the injection site, but that is normal, and it will soon fade a little. It will help us awaken you to your true selves."

The atmosphere shifted, charged with the anticipation of the unknown and the promise of pleasure and transformation. The prospect of guiding two more men through their awakening stirred a deep sense of purpose. This was more than just a physical encounter, but it was also about pleasure.

Anja looked around the cozy living room. She could feel their anticipation mingling with her desire. "Let's move to the bedroom, unless you want to get started here," she suggested.

Anja slowly removed her coat, revealing the curve of one shoulder before pulling it off completely. She held it out to Mike with a teasing smile, enjoying how he looked at her exposed skin.

"Here, let me take that for you," he said, swallowing hard as he accepted the coat. His fingers brushed against Anja's.

She turned and walked a few steps away, leaving behind the scent of her jasmine perfume, before turning to face them again.

Anja began to undress, her movements sensual and deliberate. She slipped off her top, revealing her bra. It was a delicate lacework of black and red, accentuating her full breasts that rose and fell with each breath she took. Her nipples were hard points against the fabric. She reached up and unhooked it. Her hands brushed against her skin as she slid the straps down her arms, casting a shadow over her shoulders and revealing more of her cleavage before finally letting the bra fall to the floor.

Mike could only stare at her, his desire growing as he watched her strip. She felt it like a caress. Lucian and Graham exchanged glances; Graham was a little overwhelmed by Anja's confidence in her sexuality.

She saw his discomfort and tried to ease his mind. "Graham, I haven't always been this comfortable with sex, believe me, but it was part of accepting who I am and all that comes with it. It's okay to be nervous. I'm sure that will pass quickly," she added with a sly smile.

Next came her pants, which revealed a black lace thong as they slid down her legs. Anja paused for a moment, allowing the men to drink in the sight of her before she stepped out of her pants entirely.

She slid the thong aside, revealing the most intimate part of herself, then pulled it off and stepped out of it completely. Mike swallowed hard, trying to maintain some semblance of control as she twirled that scrap of fabric on her finger before she tossed it aside playfully. Lucian and Graham were captivated by Anja's confidence, but for different reasons. While Lucian found it alluring, Graham was nearly overwhelmed, and his cheeks flushed with embarrassment and desire.

"Are you enjoying the show, gentlemen?" Anja teased, her green eyes dancing between the three men.

"Absolutely," Mike managed to choke out, rough with need. "You're stunning, Anja."

"Thank you," she purred, running her fingers through her patch of red pubic hair. "Now, who wants to be first?"

Anja didn't wait for an answer; she had already decided. Sensing Graham's trepidation, she approached him, trailing light touches along his arm as she pressed her body against his. "Relax," she whispered, her breath warm against his ear. "I promise I won't bite… unless you want me to."

Graham was startled at her words. Tentatively, he reached up to cup her face, his thumb brushing over her cheekbone as he leaned in to capture her lips in a gentle kiss. The kiss did not remain unsure, and they worked at getting his clothes off.

"Fuck. This is really happening," Graham said, trying to catch his breath.

"Yes, it is," Anja murmured against his mouth before deepening the kiss again, her hands wandering over his clothed body, finding the edges of his shirt and working it up and over his head. As Graham fumbled with his belt, Anja smiled at Lucian and Mike, her look inviting them to join in on the fun that was only just beginning.

Lucian had not hesitated while they were kissing. He now stood naked and aroused at the sight of her with Graham.

"Mike, you need to catch up with everyone else." Anja's smile was teasing when she glanced at him. What would it feel like to have all three focused solely on her? In her? *"Think of the power,"* she thought she heard.

"Right," Mike responded, staring at her body as he removed his clothes.

Anja admired the play of muscles beneath Mike's skin as he moved; she itched to touch him. The tension of what would happen next hung in the air. It was up to her to lead them, and she wouldn't disappoint.

When Mike's shirt hit the floor, Anja let her gaze roam over his chest and take in the defined planes and valleys that spoke of strength and endurance. She imagined him pinning her down, his powerful arms holding her in place as he took her...but not yet. There was still so much more to come.

Graham's earlier hesitance had given way to a carnal hunger that made her heart race. The sight of him standing there, naked and wanting, spurred her to action. She reached out to him, her hand brushing against his erection before she pulled away with a coy smile. "Shall we take this to the bedroom?"

"Bedroom it is," Mike rumbled. The men exchanged glances, each trying to gauge the others' thoughts without giving away their own.

Mike picked up Anja and carried her into his bedroom, where the others followed. Mike set Anja down on the bed, and she looked up at him with a seductive smile. "Are you ready for me?" Her red pubic hair glowed in the soft light, a fiery beacon that drew Mike's gaze.

"Absolutely," Mike replied.

Anja reached out to stroke Mike's erection. He moaned, and his hips bucked forward as she touched him. Lucian and Graham stood to watch on either side of the bed, their hands resting on the edge of the mattress, waiting to get into position.

She spread her legs wide, inviting Mike to take his pleasure from her. Lucian caressed her breasts tenderly, and Graham's cock found its way into her mouth. She took him in and started to bob as she began to fellate him. The scent of sex filled the air as they gave in to their desires for Anja.

Soon, Anja found herself astride Lucian as he lay beneath her. She could feel his desire for her radiating off him in waves, and she relished it. She guided him inside her with a sultry smile, feeling every inch of him fill her up.

Lucian gasped as she lowered herself onto him, impaling herself on his cock with a moan of pleasure. He dug his fingers into her hips, trying to hold onto control as she began to ride him, her body moving in a dance that was seductive and predatory.

The room was filled with the sounds of heavy breathing, skin slapping against skin, and the wetness of their bodies joining. The smell of arousal and lust filled every corner. Anja looked at Mike and Graham with a wicked gleam. "Would you like to join us?" she purred.

Mike readied himself behind her, his hands gently caressing her hips as he got into position to enter her from behind. Anja moaned at the thought of simultaneously being taken from behind by Mike and Lucian from below.

Anja could feel Mike gently push in, stretching her, still slick from being inside her and his pre-cum. Again, he pushed in a little more and soon filled her. Having the two of them pumping inside her was incredible; she had never been this full. "More…I need more," she whispered and turned to look at Graham. He moved in closer, giving her access to his erection once more. As she took him into her mouth, the sensations of triple penetration sent waves of pleasure coursing through her body.

"God, Anja, I can't get enough of you," Graham moaned. A hand tangled in her hair, moving her head as she sucked him. She opened her throat and let him push her down until her lips met his body. Being held there, she could not breathe, but the sensation of being completely filled was worth every second. She came in a wave of ecstasy that left her shuddering and gasping for air before collapsing on the bed, breathing heavily.

Once she had caught her breath, she pulled Lucian between her legs to continue fucking her. He slowly entered her, and she savored every inch as he did. Graham and Mike knelt to either side of her head, their erections waiting for her to take them.

For a while, she savored going back and forth between Mike and Graham, sucking on one while stroking the other.

As she reached another peak, Anja was lifted higher and higher by the combined forces of her desire and the men's lustful energy. She came undone in another wave of bliss.

When she could breathe again, Anja turned to Mike and opened her mouth to accept him; she was aware of her power over these men—bringing them to their knees with a single touch, word, or glance. It was heady, and she reveled in it, her moans growing louder as Mike's cock slid deeper into her throat.

"Lucian..." she breathed, barely audible as she looked down at their joining as he slid in and out of her. His broad chest rose and fell with each ragged breath.

"Ah, Anja," Lucian gasped. His hands gripped her hips as he plunged into her.

*Feels so good,* she thought, her body quivering with each thrust. The sensation of Lucian inside her and the heat of his desire radiating off of him was intense. She could feel herself getting closer to the edge, and she rode that edge in a near-continuous orgasm.

"Please...don't stop," she begged, her words muffled by Graham's cock in her mouth, but the message was clear. And as the four of them moved together as one, lost in the delicious throes of passion, Anja knew that this night would forever be etched into their memories—pure, unadulterated ecstasy they would never forget.

"Anja...I don't know how much longer I can hold on," Lucian breathed heavily, the intensity of their connection threatening to bring him to the brink.

"Wait," Anja gasped as she released Graham from her mouth.

Anja began chanting the ritual words as she stroked both men in time with the rhythm of Lucian's movements. She could feel the power growing even stronger, and she let out a low moan of pleasure. She was nearly bursting with it, and the power needed release as much as they all did.

Mike and Graham stroked themselves as they watched her writhe beneath Lucian. Anja continued, growing stronger with each chanted word. Energy gathered around her, fed by their collective passion. As the ritual peaked, she knew their awakening would soon be complete.

She reached in first to follow Graham's mental pathways, so similar to Ian's. She could see the bear lumbering through forests long forgotten.

Next, she focused on Mike, his internal flames flickering as hot as his passion for her now. Lava seemed to flow through his veins like a volcano about to erupt.

"Almost...there..." Anja panted, the power of the ritual surging through her as she neared completion. The room pulsed with energy, the air thick with their mingled scents and the sounds of their pleasure.

"Finish it, Anja," Lucian urged, guttural and raw. "We're ready."

"Come on me," Anja told Mike and Graham, who were positioned on either side of her. The ritual only needed the final burst of power.

Mike tightened his grip around his erection and stroked faster.

"Yessss," Graham said through clenched teeth, focusing on Anja's flushed face.

"Now!" she cried as their connection solidified.

As they reached their climax together, Mike and Graham released themselves onto her face, their hot seed coating her skin with some in her mouth and on her tongue. At the same time, Lucian thrust one final time inside her before he pulled out and spilled himself onto her body and breasts.

Anja gasped as she drank in the energy surge from their climaxes. The orgasm she had been riding burst over her in a final crescendo. She embraced the power, feeding on it all before driving it back into Mike and Graham, locking their changes in place.

As their breathing slowed and they began to regain their senses, Mike, Graham, and Lucian watched as Anja rubbed their mingled semen over her body and breasts. She gathered it up and licked her fingers clean, savoring the taste and power of it. Her raw sexuality entranced them.

Anja lay on the rumpled bed; her red hair framed her flushed face. She was a picture of carnal delight, her breasts rising and falling with each breath she took. Mike, Lucian, and Graham stood around her, still trying to comprehend what had happened. A sheen of sweat glistened on their bodies as they caught their breath.

"Thank you," Anja whispered, soft and sultry. "You've made one of my wildest fantasies come true."

"I never thought I'd be part of something like this," he admitted. He glanced at Lucian and Mike, seeking reassurance.

"Neither did I," Lucian replied.

Anja studied their faces, her heart swelling with affection for these men who'd willingly embraced their otherkin selves. "From this moment on, you are no longer simply human. You are something far greater. Embrace it, cherish it, and let it guide you. For now, let's rest. Come to bed. Lucian and I will help guide you through the rest of the transformation when the sun rises."

The sky was painted in the morning light's soft orange and purple hues. Mike stood outside his home, his heart pounding with excitement and apprehension. Graham's newly awakened bear form lumbered into the distance. It was a powerful sight that filled him with a sense of wonder. The air should have been cold against his naked skin, but he didn't feel it.

Now, it was his turn. Lucian and Anja stood nearby, watching him, offering silent support. They had guided him through a ritual that opened up pathways in his mind. Visions of his otherkin form had flickered in his consciousness.

Mike took a deep breath and focused inward, trying to connect with the creature trying to surface. As he concentrated, a warmth spread through his body, starting from the center of his being and radiating outward. His skin began to tingle. It was an odd sensation that was neither painful nor uncomfortable. He closed his eyes and surrendered to the process.

When he opened them again, the world looked different. His perspective had changed; he was closer to the ground, and his body was heavier, denser, and more potent. Looking down, he saw his limbs had transformed—sleek, dark, with vibrant fiery patterns adorning his skin. The sensation was extraordinary, alien, and somehow familiar at the same time.

Mike reveled in the newfound sensations of his fire salamander form, exploring the terrain with wonder. A subtle and unmistakable vibration coursed through the ground. It was a minor earthquake, a phenomenon not uncommon in Iceland. The low rumble resonated with the fiery patterns on his skin.

Anja smiled knowingly. "The earth recognizes you, Mike," she said. "Like it's welcoming you."

As the trembling subsided, it left him exhilarated and humbled. He was now a part of something greater, a living link between the fire in the earth and the life it nurtured. This was his welcome into a world that had always been there, waiting for him to truly see.

He moved experimentally, marveling at the agility and fluidity of his new form. The ground beneath his feet seemed different, more alive, as if he could sense the heat and energy emanating from the earth itself. It was a connection to the natural world he had never experienced before.

Lucian and Anja observed with fascination. Mike could sense their approval and encouragement, bolstering his confidence in his newfound identity.

Mike explored the area behind his house, reveling in his newfound freedom and power. He slithered over rocks. Eventually, he returned to his human form, feeling exhilarated. The transformation was smoother than he had anticipated. It was as if his body remembered its shape and slipped back into it.

Standing again on two feet, Mike looked at Lucian and Anja with a broad grin. "That was incredible. Thank you."

Lucian clapped him on the shoulder. "Welcome to a larger world, Mike."

Anja's eyes sparkled as she began to relate stories and myths about fire salamanders. Mike listened intently, absorbing every word. The stories spoke of creatures able to control and withstand fire, to blend with flames.

Encouraged by these tales, a flicker of something deep inside shifted, a dormant power now stirring to life. Anja sensed his growing curiosity and challenged him. "Try to bring out some fire, or maybe melt one of those lava rocks nearby."

Mike focused on a cluster of dark lava rocks a short distance away. He closed his eyes, concentrating on the essence of the fire that now coursed through his veins. Slowly, he extended a hand towards the rocks, his mind reaching out to the forgotten heat that slept there.

To his amazement, the rocks began to glow, their surfaces turning bright orange as they heated up under his influence. A small flame burst forth, flickering and dancing.

Mike opened his eyes, pride swelling in his chest. He had always had a connection to the earth and its fiery heart, but now that bond was tangible, a part of him as real as the flames he had just conjured.

As the fire died down, leaving the rocks glowing hot in the dim light of dawn, Anja hugged him. There were depths to his powers that he would need to explore, mysteries waiting to be uncovered. He was eager to discover the full extent of his fiery heritage.

# *Nineteen*

THE AIR WAS tense in the control center as Helena prepared to leave for Rome. Grandmaster Eamon had summoned her to discuss troubling developments regarding Richard.

Eamon's delivery was grave. "He's been compromised. Some supernatural force has tampered with his memories. This is a development we cannot ignore."

Helena's mind raced as she processed his words. "This is a disturbing development indeed." It had been a long time since they had faced the possibility of an actual supernatural threat.

"The Sodality exists to protect humanity from such taint. We cannot allow these aberrations to spread or gain strength."

She couldn't help but reflect on the irony of Eamon's words. The Grandmaster, who wielded those same supernatural powers he condemned, was now tasking her with eliminating others who had access to similar abilities. The hypocrisy was not lost on her, but she knew better than to air her thoughts. If he knew that she was aware of that, he would surely kill her—or try at least. That was a battle she was not ready for.

"Even rumors of powers like that can be dangerous," Eamon said flatly. "Perhaps it is time to quash the rumors surrounding the Zvaigzne Syndicate. That was your 'idea,' Helena, and I think we may need to revisit that."

She felt a cold wash over her as she felt a compulsion of loyalty. He was using her blood oath to force the truth and a confession. She had been able to deflect in the past, and she would again. With the calm of the dead, she replied, "You have long been aware of those rumors. They provide a notable advantage to the Syndicate. Advantages that have been of significant use to Sodality. That, you cannot deny."

"They have been of use; however, the risk is growing. Rumors that the dead may walk and seek vengeance? The danger is that others may decide they could escape our notice and live. Perhaps even challenge us. That cannot stand."

"Yes, Grandmaster," she said, meeting his eyes.

"The only reason I have tolerated this is your loyalty to me and the Sodality. You have been faithful to your duties, and you are successful. Perhaps one day, it will be your turn to assume the leadership of the Sodality."

She presented what should be a pleased smile. She was well aware that would never happen. He might assume her form and appearance, but she would be as dead as the man whose guise he now wore.

"I hope that day will not be soon," she said earnestly. "I am content with my position where I can serve most effectively," she lied.

"Richard has been handled, but you have another crucial assignment now, Helena. You must succeed in Rome. Do not fail me."

She wondered if he suspected she also had forbidden powers. He must believe the blood oath provided sufficient control over her. He was mistaken and must not learn the truth before she was ready. She needed to control Lucian and Anja. How to exert that control was still her most pressing question.

Helena made her way to her quarters to prepare for the trip. She knew the stakes were high and the risks even higher, but deep down, she recognized an opportunity. If the enemy had indeed tapped into magical powers, then there was more to be gained from this mission than even Eamon realized—at least for her.

While she packed her belongings, her thoughts lingered on the potential of whatever these newfound powers were and how they could reshape the balance of the hidden world. Packing her journal was also significant. She might not return here—it was best to keep it safe.

After leaving the Vault, Helena stepped into the brisk air outside, her mind racing with plans. She reached for her phone. Dialing quickly, she connected with one of her most trusted contacts in her Syndicate, a leader based in Riga who had proven reliable and ruthless in past actions. The phone rang twice before being answered.

"It's Helena. I need you to mobilize a team and head to Dwor Szeptów. We're expecting some…special guests. They should arrive in about three days, so be prepared to receive them."

There was a brief pause on the other end. "Special guests?"

"A prisoner and visitors. We'll be ambushing and capturing them as they try to reunite with their friend. This is high-priority. I need you to bring additional firepower. We can't afford any mistakes."

"Understood. We'll be prepared."

Helena ended the call, her mind already shifting to the next phase of her plan. Dwor Szeptów was an old estate in Poland, secluded and fortified, ideal for what she had in mind. It was a place where secrets could be kept and visitors could disappear without a trace. It would not be the first time.

The drive to Tallinn airport was a blur, her thoughts consumed by the tasks ahead. She was playing a dangerous game. It was a part of who she was and the life she had found herself in.

As the plane took off, heading towards Rome, Helena looked out the window, the world below reduced to a patchwork of lights and shadows.

Chauffeured by Thomas through the bustling streets of Brooklyn, Zoe and Emma found themselves at the doorstep of Anja's apartment. The building, nestled among the eclectic mix of architecture in the neighborhood, held a certain charm despite its age. The apartment, upon entry, was well-kept but coated with a layer of dust that attested to its owner's absence.

In the bedroom, just as Anja had said, the two books lay on the nightstand. Zoe picked them up and scanned the titles with amusement. "*The Secret Garden of Pleasure and Pain* and *Whispers of the Night: A Collection of Sinister Tales*. Anja always did have interesting tastes in literature," she commented to Emma, who responded with an equally amused smile.

After they locked up and headed out again, Thomas pulled up to their next stop in front of Archambault Antiquities, with its vibrant green sign and ornately carved wooden door.

The tinkle of the bell announced their arrival, and Raymond emerged from behind the counter amidst the clutter of books and oddities. His appearance was a blend of scholarly and rugged—silver hair that was perpetually mussed, wire-rimmed glasses perched on his nose, and a three-piece wool suit that spoke of a bygone era. Despite his shorter stature, his presence filled the room. Zoe had visited several times while they were in college, and Anja frequently helped to catalog and organize the shop.

Raymond lit up at the sight of Zoe, a fond smile breaking through his usually stern demeanor. "Zoe, what a pleasant surprise," he said, his voice rough like gravel. "And what treasures have you brought me today?"

As Zoe handed over the books, Raymond brushed over the covers reverently. "Ah, Anja's books. She always enjoyed the most intriguing reads." Raymond placed the books behind the counter. "I've been concerned about Anja. She was getting involved in some rather sinister dealings and hasn't been here for nearly two months. That is not like her at all. I feared she might have come to harm."

Zoe exchanged a knowing glance with Emma. "Anja is fine, Raymond. Better than ever, actually. But you're right about the danger. It was very real. Deadly real." She leaned in closer and became even more hushed. "There's something you should know about the Sodality—that's what they call themselves. It's real and as dangerous as the rumors suggested."

"The Sodality? I thought that the rumors of a secret organization were just an urban legend..."

"It's no legend. It's a very real threat, and Anja got caught up in it. But she's okay, thanks to some...unexpected help," Emma confirmed.

Raymond processed this information, his brows knitting together in thought. "I always knew there was more to her stories than just fanciful tales. But this...this is something else."

"Which is why you need to be very, very careful with this knowledge," Zoe cautioned. "And careful in general. The Sodality has eyes and ears everywhere. We don't want you getting caught in the crossfire because of your association with Anja."

Raymond agreed gravely. "I'll be cautious. Thank you for telling me. And for looking out for Anja. She's like a daughter to me."

Zoe reached out, placing a comforting hand on Raymond's arm. "Anja wanted to come herself. She sends her regards and promises she'll visit as soon as she can."

Raymond softened at this, a hint of his smile returning. "I'll hold her to that."

"This is Emma, another close friend and protector of Anja's."

Emma extended her hand, offering Raymond a firm handshake.

"It's a pleasure to meet you, Emma," Raymond said. "Anyone who looks after Anja is a friend of mine."

Turning, Raymond walked back through the labyrinth of shelves and returned with another book in hand. The cover was ornate, hinting at its gothic contents. "I thought Anja might enjoy this one as well," he said, handing it over to Zoe. "But tell her I expect her to return this one in person."

*Nocturnal Yearnings: An Anthology of Dark Love* was sumptuous. Its deep black cover was adorned with intricate, gold filigree patterns. The title was embossed with a gothic font. The pages were edged in gold and gave off a subtle, barely perceptible shimmer, suggesting the treasure it held.

A flutter of intrigue ran through Zoe as Raymond handed her the book. Would the stories inside live up to the book's tantalizing exterior? She imagined tales of forbidden love set against moonlit landscapes and ancient, whispering castles. In a fleeting thought, Zoe wondered if any of these stories would parallel their own lives.

Zoe accepted the book. "I'll make sure she gets it. And I'm sure she'll be eager to come herself next time."

Zoe tucked the book under her arm. She glanced at Emma, sharing a silent understanding. Together, they stepped out into the bustling streets, the door to the shop closing behind them as the bell chimed.

After getting in the Rolls again, Zoe glanced at Emma. "Emma, I want to stop at a shop where I can pick out some of those toys like the ones we've been using."

"Sure," Emma replied with a sly smile. "I know just the place. It's got a great selection; it's not in a seedy location and not too far from here." She turned to Thomas, their driver, who was waiting for instructions. "Thomas, please take us to that little boutique in Brooklyn—the one you took me to last time."

"Very well, Miss Emma," Thomas replied, unfazed by the request. He navigated the streets, eventually stopping in front of the store. "Here you are, ladies. I'll wait for you here." He politely declined their invitation to join them inside, opting to remain in the car.

"Thanks, Thomas," Zoe called out as she and Emma exited the sedan. The two women approached the entrance of the sex boutique, a small but welcoming establishment known for its extensive selection of sex toys that catered to the LGBTQ+ community.

As they entered the shop, the faint scent of jasmine filled the air. Behind the counter sat a tattooed woman in a black Lolita outfit. Despite her goth appearance, she greeted them warmly. "Hey, ladies! Are you looking for anything in particular?"

"No, thanks, Gloria. We're just browsing today." Emma returned Gloria's smile.

"Let me know if you need any help," Gloria responded.

"So you've been here before?" Zoe asked.

"Yep, one of my favorite stores in New York."

Zoe had heard about such places before, but even with her uninhibited nature, she had never actually ventured inside one. Zoe's eyes widened at the array of unique and fascinating sex toys on display as they meandered through the boutique. She felt like a kid in a candy store, her curiosity aroused by every new item.

"Emma, look at this one!" Zoe exclaimed, holding up a toy for inspection. The two women giggled like schoolgirls as they compared various items, their laughter echoing throughout the store.

The fluorescent lights above cast a surreal glow over the vast inventory of toys that filled the boutique. Beside her, Emma walked with an air of confidence and familiarity, having been here before. Zoe walked past displays of strap-ons, dildos, and vibrators, wondering at the variety.

Emma chuckled at her friend's wide-eyed fascination. "It can be a bit overwhelming the first time. But once you get past the initial shock, it's actually quite fun to explore."

Zoe nodded, her attention darting from one colorful item to the next. A grin spread across her face as she spotted something particularly intriguing. "Hey, what do you think of this one?" she asked, holding it up for Emma's inspection.

"That one looks like it could be...interesting," Emma replied, raising her eyebrows in amusement at what appeared to be a large tentacle.

As they continued perusing the inventory, Zoe found herself becoming more comfortable with the idea of using these toys—not just on herself but with others as well. The thought excited her, and she couldn't help but laugh alongside Emma as they joked about the items.

She followed Emma around, admiring the selection, her hands trailing over the soft materials and shiny silicone dildos. She chose a long, clear, double-ended one to add to her selections.

Emma pulled out a larger, more powerful-looking wand vibrator. "And this baby here? It's waterproof, so we can use it in the tub or shower."

"Okay." Zoe added it to her basket that held a few carefully selected items. "I think I'm set for myself, and a little surprise for you, too, Emma." She hesitated, biting her lip as she considered her next question. "What about Anja? What do you think she might like?"

"Hmmm. Anja can be pretty adventurous. She's a succubus—remember that ball gag and whip when we captured Nomad? And don't forget her preferred reading materials..." They moved on to a section where a vast collection of BDSM gear hung from the walls like art installations.

Zoe spotted a blindfold and whispered, "Oh, I think I might like to be blindfolded during...some of our playtime."

"Yeah, add it to the pile. I think you might turn out to be a good sub."

"I don't know about that, but it does hold a certain appeal. We covered a lot of ground at the academy but more focused on the sadistic side. It was also a topic of some of my abnormal psychology courses at Columbia. Come to think of it, those courses seem rather biased in retrospect."

"Yeah, kinky stuff. Being submissive is a lot more common than those stodgy old professors would care to admit, at least not in the classroom. I'm sure there were other courses that were more inclusive."

"I never thought about it back then. There was never anyone who I would have trusted that much. But now…" The thought of it was new but exciting.

"Okay, let's grab a selection of ropes to take back. I'm not sure if she would rather be tied up or tie someone else up. I don't think Lucian would care to be bound, but I feel he wouldn't mind using them on you or Anja. Maybe even both at once. I would really like to watch that."

When they checked out, Gloria wrapped their selections in tissue paper and put them in a pair of black totes. They exited with a wave and went out into the warm afternoon to return to the penthouse.

The next day came too soon as they boarded Lucian's private jet, bound for Geneva and then on to Keflavík. The cool air of Iceland kissed their skin as they exited the plane, and its freshness invigorated them.

Claire sat next to Ian in the secure conference room of Akar Labs. The air was thick with anticipation as Zoe, Emma, and the rest of the team gathered around the large table. Zoe, with a new air of determination, began to speak.

"A lot has changed since I left for New York. I'm fully committed to this cause now, more than ever. My ties with the FBI…They're in the past."

"We're glad to have you, Zoe. Your skills and dedication are invaluable," Lucian said.

Anja's smile was warm. "It's too bad that had to be, but I think it's for the best."

Zoe and Emma recounted the events of their recent trip. The conversation soon shifted to Claire, who was excited though contemplative about her upcoming travel. "I'll be heading back to England to look into my family history. There might be others like us, like me there. I've heard family tales—legends, really—of wolves. It's time I learned how much truth they hold."

Lucian leaned forward. "Remember, always travel in pairs. We can't afford to take any risks."

Ian agreed. "I'll accompany Claire. We'll keep a low profile, only reaching out to those who we can trust."

Claire looked at Ian, camaraderie growing between them. "We hope to find potential allies to join our cause."

As the meeting continued, plans were laid. Claire's mind occasionally drifted, imagining the mist-shrouded landscapes of England, the whisper of ancient secrets, and the potential to find others like her. Ian's voice brought her back to the present, and his comments on logistics and safety measures reminded her of the reality of their situation. Thanks to Anja's guidance, Claire's newfound confidence in her wolf form was a source of inner strength she intended to draw upon.

The discussion shifted as Anja brought up the next steps. "We need to continue awakening the potential of our team. Sigri and Lynn are ready, and we should proceed with their awakenings."

Lucian's attention landed on Sigri. "I agree. It's time we bolster our ranks. Sigri, I'll guide you through your awakening. I've been honing my abilities for this. Zoe will help, too. Being able to help guide Emma into her other forms has strengthened that capability for me."

Sigri's face lit up. "I'm ready."

Anja turned to Lynn, whose presence had become increasingly important within their group. "And Lynn, I'll work with you on your awakening. I understand you'd prefer a more...private setting with me."

A slight blush colored her cheeks as Lynn replied. "Yes, I would appreciate that, Anja. Emma has dropped a few hints. She admitted to me that she was bi and that you were, too. It's refreshing for me to admit being a lesbian openly. It is rather strange, though, to openly discuss a plan to have sex in a team meeting."

"You can say that again," Claire said.

Lynn's candid admission had set a tone, and Anja responded with a knowing smile. "Yes, Emma wasn't wrong in her hints. These aspects of our lives shouldn't be secrets among us. It's important we're comfortable with who we are, especially in a group like ours."

Lucian chimed in, "Absolutely. We should be all about openness here. And speaking of which, Zoe, Anja, and I have formed…let's call it a 'triple arrangement.' It's a bit unconventional, but it works for us."

Zoe laughed, a sparkle in her eye as she glanced at Emma. "Speaking of spilling beans, Emma, you've been quite the informant, haven't you?"

Emma shrugged, a mischievous grin on her face. "I plead guilty as charged. But in my defense, it's all about being open, right?"

There were chuckles around the room, and Claire smiled at the camaraderie. It was a rare sight to see such a diverse group, not just in terms of their otherkin aspects but also in their personal lives, bonding over shared secrets and mutual acceptance. It *was* a break from her past—something to share.

"There's something I've been meaning to say," Claire began. "I've had…bad experiences in the past. Situations where personal and professional lines were blurred, not in a good way. It made me cautious, even fearful, of getting too close to anyone, especially in a group setting. But being here with all of you, I've realized this is different. What we have here…it's about genuine connection, respect, and even love in various forms. And I want to thank you all for that. You've helped me see that it's okay to open up, bond, and be part of something special."

Claire glanced at Ian, softening. "With Ian, I've found a kind of partnership that I didn't think was possible. It's not just about the awakening of my wolf; it's about finding a place where I truly belong. And for that, I'm grateful."

As Claire finished, a weight lifted from her shoulders. She had opened up and shared a part of herself that she had kept hidden. And in doing so, she was more connected to the group than ever. She was no longer just Claire, the protector, the lone wolf; she was Claire, a vital part of a diverse and supportive group.

Lucian leaned back, crossing his arms thoughtfully. “Claire, you should stay at my estate while you’re in England. It would provide a comfortable and secure base to conduct your inquiries.”

Claire was suddenly uncomfortable at the offer, but Anja responded. “Yes, I think that would be a good option, Claire. It would allow you to face those issues with Edward. You can handle it now, and it could completely banish those ghosts from your past.”

“Okay, you’re right. It’s past time for this. I can do it. Thanks, Anja,” Claire said.

When the meeting drew to a close, and they dispersed, she turned to Ian. “This is more than just a trip, Ian. It’s a journey into my past and, maybe, our future.”

Ian placed a reassuring hand on her shoulder. “Claire, whatever we find, we’ll do it together.”

# *Twenty*

LUCIAN OBSERVED SIGRI settling onto the couch next to Zoe, noting her poised demeanor. Though marked by a Nordic coolness, her features were softened by an underlying warmth, hinting at the Arctic fox that lay dormant within her. As he prepared the syringe, he infused the serum with his unique magic, tailoring it to awaken the slumbering otherkin essence in Sigri.

The serum in the syringe glowed subtly, visual evidence of the changes Lucian had wrought. Sigri's lean form exuded a quiet strength. He sensed a natural affinity to the fox spirit in her, an alignment that promised a smooth transition.

"This will feel a bit strange at first." He injected the serum into her arm.

Sigri's reaction was immediate, a gasp escaping her as she reported a tingling sensation, not unpleasant but certainly foreign. Lucian watched the glow from the syringe fade as the serum coursed through her veins, his eyes tracing the shift in her aura. "You might feel a range of sensations as the otherkin within you awakens. Remember, every reaction is a part of the transformation. Embrace it."

Sigri's breaths deepened, and Lucian sensed the changes starting within her, responding to the call of the serum. "It's best if you disrobe, Sigri. When the change occurs, your clothes could get in the way of the process."

Sigri only nodded. Zoe offered to undress alongside her for solidarity, but Sigri declined with a small smile. "No need, Zoe. I will be fine. It's not unlike a sauna," she said, her voice carrying a touch of humor.

Sigri removed her clothing, placing it neatly to the side. Her movements were devoid of self-consciousness. Once disrobed, she reclined on the couch again, her posture relaxed.

Lucian, still fully dressed, took a seat beside her. "Now, I'll look into you and guide you to your new form."

Zoe, seated nearby, focused her energy on soothing any anxiety or fear, coaxing Sigri's mind and body into a state of tranquility.

The air hummed with the energy of impending change. Lucian's consideration was intense as he prepared to guide her. His hands hovered just above her, ready to channel the magic that would awaken the Arctic fox within.

Sigri was a picture of readiness, her eyes closed and breathing steady. The stage was set, and the shift to her new form was about to begin.

Lucian delved into the intricate lattice of Sigri's DNA, his inner vision piercing beyond the tangible to the essence of her being. The serum, glowing with potential, became his tool to unlock the dormant aspects of her genetic makeup.

His magic danced through the helices of Sigri's DNA. Epigenetic markers, typically silent and hidden, now shimmered with potential, reacting with the energy Lucian channeled into them. Her cells multiplied and differentiated, taking on new forms and functions under the guidance of an ancient and mystical force.

Lucian had a deep reverence throughout this profound process. As he withdrew his influence, Sigri lay on the cusp of embracing her newly awakened self.

"You are ready," Lucian said. "Embrace those playful foxes you admire. Accept their form, and remember that feeling."

It was at that moment the transformation began. It was a subtle shift at first, a tingling sensation dancing beneath her skin, a whisper of change that set the stage.

Sigri's senses heightened, sharpening in a way that painted the room's dim light in vivid, surreal patterns behind her closed eyelids. Her muscles rippled, realigning and reshaping without pain or discomfort.

As her form transformed, Sigri experienced a brief moment of disorientation, a fleeting instant where she hovered between her human self and the new creature she was becoming.

With Zoe's emotional support enveloping her, Sigri completed her transformation. Her eyes fluttered open, revealing not the human irises that had closed moments before but those of a creature born of wilderness and freedom.

Sigri, now in the form of a beautiful black Arctic fox, embodied the playful spirit that she had long admired. Her dark fur shimmered, a natural reflection of the nearing summertime when the foxes don their darker coats.

Unable to contain her delight, Zoe exclaimed, "Oh, she is so cute! Can I keep her?"

Sigri, in her new shape, began to explore her surroundings. Every sense was heightened, each sound crisper, each scent more pronounced. Her movements were a blend of agility and curiosity, exploring this new world she perceived through the eyes of her otherkin form.

The room and its occupants appeared different to her now, awash in vibrant colors and scents that spoke of emotions and life. She moved with an instinctive grace and marveled at the harmonious coexistence of her human and animal selves.

Then she could not resist any longer. She took off running and darting around the room, leaping over furniture and literally bouncing off the walls—Zoomies, indeed. The joyous laughter she heard echoed in her soul.

She understood the profound realization of her potential and the bond she shared with those who had guided her. The transformation was not just a physical change but an awakening—a revelation of her true self.

Anja followed Lynn into a room and closed the door.

"I sometimes—well, it has been more frequent recently—stay here overnight when patients need round-the-clock care. It's more like an apartment now," Lynn said as they entered. "I should just move in."

Indeed, it looked pretty comfortable. There were paintings on the wall, primarily colorful idyllic landscapes. Stepping closer, Anja noticed that most were numbered reproductions but were still beautiful.

"Thomas Kinkade," Lynn said. "I have always loved his art; here, with no windows, they provide comfort."

"They're beautiful," Anja said as she turned to take in the rest of the room. It wasn't large. There was a functional dresser between a closet and a door that was slightly ajar, leading to a small bathroom. There was a nightstand with a lamp that would work well for reading, a few books on the stand. She couldn't make out the titles, but that wasn't why she was here. The bed beside it looked welcoming, with a fluffy comforter and several large pillows.

The atmosphere was charged with anticipation and a hint of nerves. "Lynn, I can do the injection. It's simple enough, but if you would like to…" Anja trailed off.

"I can do it," Lynn said, then asked, "Are you afraid of needles?"

Anja laughed and smiled. "Oh, no, nothing like Zoe. She freaks."

Lynn held out her hand and accepted a small white packet and the syringe that had already been filled shortly before. After a probing look, Lucian had drawn the serum and imbued the clear liquid with a pulsing, golden energy that shimmered. Lynn had watched in fascination.

Lucian and Zoe were helping Sigri, and Anja hoped that went well. She was confident of their growing ability with the animal forms, and being able to divide their efforts would help, especially later.

Lynn locked eyes with Anja for a moment while she took a deep breath. Tearing open the packet, she swabbed a spot on her arm and, with no hesitation, injected the glowing liquid. "It tingles a bit. I had honestly expected more."

"I'll see what I can do to provide a few more tingles," Anja said with a smile.

Anja moved closer to Lynn. They had discussed the process ahead of time, understanding that the transformation required more than just this serum. Their combined energy and a deep, intimate connection were needed to guide her through the metamorphosis.

Without a word, they began to undress each other slowly and deliberately, their hands dancing across each other's bodies with tender care. The room filled with laughter as clothing was tossed around them, forgotten in their eagerness.

Lynn's tall, slender form was revealed in the soft light of the office; her skin held an ethereal quality. Her small but perfectly formed breasts and patch of golden pubic hair added to her beauty, reminiscent of the golden hue of the serum now coursing through her veins.

Anja traced delicate patterns over Lynn's skin, exploring every curve and crevice. Lynn's breath caught as Anja's touch lingered on her breasts, causing her nipples to harden.

As Lynn reached the waistband of Anja's panties, she pushed them down, revealing a tuft of curls that matched the fiery red of her hair. After petting the silky patch, she slipped the cloth down Anja's legs and tossed it to join the other forgotten articles strewn about.

There was a sense of entering a sacred place as they moved towards the bed, a private world where their combined energies would guide Lynn's transformation.

"Anja, I've been looking forward to this," Lynn whispered.

"Me too, Lynn." With that admission, their lips met, hands roaming freely to explore each other's bodies.

Anja pushed Lynn down onto the bed, lowering herself on top of her. Anja's breasts pressed against Lynn's as they kissed, her hands skimming down the curve of Lynn's body, leaving goosebumps in their wake.

"Your touch is electrifying," Lynn sighed, her fingers tangled in Anja's hair.

Anja trailed kisses along Lynn's jawline and down her neck. As she nipped at Lynn's earlobe, a low moan escaped from deep in her throat. In response, Lynn's hand found its way between Anja's legs, exploring the wet warmth there, and Anja gasped and writhed as Lynn brushed against her clitoris. The touch sent a shockwave of pleasure through her.

Anja's hands roamed over Lynn's body. She took one nipple into her mouth, teasing it with her tongue as her hand massaged Lynn's other breast.

"Anja…" Lynn was overwhelmed with pleasure and could do nothing but surrender to the intense sensations coursing through her body. Anja blew lightly to tickle Lynn's skin and smelled the woman, a hint of rose and lavender mixed with the scent of leather and cedar in the rain—a heady perfume.

After giving equal attention to both breasts, Anja continued lower. "Are you ready?" Anja asked, looking up at Lynn.

"Yes…please…" Lynn breathed, her body already trembling with anticipation.

Anja's tongue eagerly explored Lynn's most sensitive parts, causing her to moan and squirm. The taste of Lynn was intoxicating.

As Anja pleasured Lynn orally, she slowly inserted two fingers, feeling the tight, wet warmth envelop them. She curled her finger up and hit that perfect spot inside Lynn, driving her closer to the edge.

Lynn's body was on fire, hot to the touch, ignited by the intense desire and the serum that coursed through her. "Anja, I'm so close…" Lynn panted, eyes squeezed shut in ecstasy.

"Mmmm, I need some more," Anja whispered as she moved up to straddle Lynn's head.

In this new position, their bodies were locked in a sensual embrace. Their tongues danced around each other's pulsating clits to lick, suck, and taste.

Moans and gasps of pleasure echoed as they hungrily devoured each other, their passion growing. "I'm ready now," Anja panted between breaths.

"Me too," Lynn replied, lost to desire.

"Let go with me, Lynn," Anja urged.

Anja cried out in ecstasy as wave after wave of orgasmic bliss crashed over her body. Lynn followed her over the edge, calling out Anja's name and shuddering beneath her body and tongue as she came undone in an explosion of delight as waves of pleasure rippled through her body.

They were panting heavily as they rode out their orgasms. The air crackled with electricity as Anja fed off their shared pleasure.

Lynn felt Anja roll off and was gathered in her arms. Lynn had a brief reluctance to disengage but welcomed the comfort as they came back together face to face.

As she lay in Anja's arms and looked into her eyes, now glowing a vibrant green, her mind was a whirlpool of visions and sensations. Anja's touch against her skin unlocked hidden chambers in her mind, corridors long closed and unnoticed. Images of majestic and ethereal unicorns danced through her mind's eye, set against a backdrop that was fanciful and eerily familiar, much like the Kinkade paintings on her walls.

A memory surfaced, unbidden, of a book she had read in her youth. It told the tale of a unicorn girl, delicate and strong, with a small slender horn adorning her forehead, symbolizing purity and strength. The story had captivated Lynn's young imagination, filling her with a sense of wonder.

Now, as Anja's presence enveloped her, the serum coursing through Lynn's veins began to respond. She could feel her body responding, a gentle metamorphosis that hinted at deeper, more profound changes. She sensed she could push further and transform more dramatically but chose restraint. This subtle alteration was enough, an understated realization of the potential that had lain dormant until now.

Her thoughts drifted to her medical knowledge, the years of study and practice, and the lives she had touched and healed. These memories intertwined with the visions of unicorns and magic. It was as if her scientific understanding was merging with a more profound, instinctual wisdom. New methods for healing and mending unfurled in her mind, encompassing concepts and techniques that defied conventional medicine.

Lynn struggled to grasp the enormity of what was awakening. It was overwhelming, a flood of insight and intuition that threatened to sweep her away. However, in the safety of Anja's embrace, she allowed herself to explore these revelations, each new thought a step into a world where science and magic coexisted, where her abilities as a doctor could transcend the boundaries of the known and venture into the realms of the miraculous.

Anja's words were colored with awe and melancholy. "You look so beautiful," she whispered, her sight fixed on the small, pearly horn peeking through Lynn's golden hair. "It's so fitting, but it's sad that it must remain hidden."

They sat together while the horn gradually disappeared from sight. Yet the transformation remained; it was a profound shift that had altered her very being.

"Hiding it isn't about shame," Anja said gently. "It's about safety, about protecting something so very precious and rare. Someday, I'd love to see you in all your glory, fully transformed. I wonder if I could ride you in that form?"

Lynn's laughter rang clear and bright. "Only you, Anja," she said, her words filled with affection and a hint of daring. The idea wasn't so far-fetched.

Here, with Anja, she was free to explore the depths of her new identity, to embrace the magic that now coursed through her veins. It was a path of discovery and wonder, lit by the glow of a horn that had briefly bridged the gap between worlds.

# *Twenty-One*

The sprawling Miller estate in Kent loomed large as Claire and Ian approached, its grandeur a reminder of the world she had once been a part of. The air was crisp, the scent of greenery mingling with the aroma of damp earth—a contrast to the sterile environment of Akar Labs.

Ian's presence was a steadying force, anchoring her amidst the flood of memories that threatened to overwhelm her. As Edward Miller stepped forward to greet them, Claire steeled herself.

"Claire," Edward said. "It's been a while."

"Edward," she replied, betraying none of her turmoil. "Yes, it has."

The tension hung between them. She had left the Royalty Protection Detail because of a scandal involving Edward that had turned her life upside down and left her questioning herself.

But as she stood facing Edward, Claire realized she *had* moved on. The bitterness and resentment that had once consumed her had ebbed away, replaced by acceptance. She was here for Lucian, for Anja, and herself—not to dwell on past grievances. "I've moved on from what happened. I can't ignore it, but I can move beyond it. We can agree to cooperate and bury the past for Lucian's sake and my own."

Edward's expression softened slightly. "I understand, Claire. I regret the circumstances. It was never my intention to cause you harm. I've moved on, too, and I respect your feelings."

The air between them shifted, the tension easing ever so slightly. It wasn't forgiveness or reconciliation but an understanding—an agreement to set aside their personal history. The past would always be a part of her, but it no longer defined her. She was here with a new purpose alongside Ian. Her journey had taken her from the shadows of protecting royalty to the forefront of a battle against hidden and malign forces.

The limousine glided through the picturesque landscape of Kent, and Claire found herself lost in thought. She had reached out to her mother and brother earlier, mentioning tales from her childhood—the family stories about wolves that had always fascinated her, though she'd been sworn to secrecy. She had not revealed her newfound abilities but only expressed a renewed interest in family tales that had always intrigued her.

Her mother's voice had been hesitant over the phone. "Those stories, Claire…are meant to stay within the family. They're part of our heritage but also a burden."

Her brother's reaction had been more animated. "You remember the legends, too, don't you? The ones about our ancestors, the great wolves of the moors—the guardians and watchers. They said we shared a bond with them, a kinship deeper than blood."

As Claire looked out at the expanse of countryside, memories of those stories came flooding back. One story, in particular, drew her: her grandmother's recounting of an ancestor, the last of their line to truly embrace the wolf within. "She was magnificent," her grandmother had said with a blend of pride and melancholy. "But as times changed, she concealed her true self to protect the family, and the clan moved here—far from Dartmoor."

There was another breed of wolves—werewolves, cursed creatures who terrorized the countryside. The moon ruled them, and when it was full, the term 'lunatic' was apt. The clan had hunted them, but other hunters came, some for fame and glory but others just for the killing. It had been a terrible time. It was apparent now that the Sodality was behind that. They would have made no distinction between her family and the others who were contagious and only spawned more monsters. These tales were only hinted at when asking about the move and why they'd hidden.

Now, Claire was an undeniable link to these legends. Her family's history was enmeshed with these tales, and while the power to fully embrace the wolf had faded through generations, she knew it still coursed through their veins.

With her ability to shift, Claire believed that she would be the key to reclaiming this dormant legacy for her family. The thought was exciting and overwhelming. It was time to unravel these secrets and explore the true extent of their connection to those noble wolves of old.

As Claire stepped out of the limousine, the crisp country air brushed her face. The familiar sight of her childhood home, nestled amidst greenery, evoked a sense of nostalgia. Beside her, Ian's presence offered a comforting strength.

Her mother appeared at the doorway. Her disapproving expression softened as she looked at her daughter. "Claire, you were supposed to come alone," she admonished gently.

"I know, Mum, but it's important. Ian knows about...our family's history. He's part of it too." Claire turned to Ian, introducing him with a sense of pride. "This is Ian of Clan MacGregor." Ian extended his hand in a gesture of respect, but Claire's mother merely nodded, her expression unreadable. There was a brief flicker in her eyes—perhaps a recognition of the name and its significance.

With a resigned sigh, her mother stepped aside, allowing them entry. "Well, come in then. We have much to discuss, it seems," she said, leading them into the warmth of the house.

The interior was as Claire remembered—cozy and filled with relics of their family's history. As they settled into the living room, Claire's mother regarded them.

Claire glanced at Ian, finding reassurance in his steady presence. "Mum, there's a reason I've come back, and it's not just a family visit. It's about our history, our connection to the wolves," she began.

Her mother's expression shifted. "You've begun to feel it, haven't you?"

Claire nodded, feeling a surge of emotion. "Yes, and more than that. I've...we've awakened something dormant for generations. It's time to embrace our heritage again."

In the cozy living room, with the evening light casting a glow through the windows, Claire's revelation hung in the air. Her mother, who had always carried the weight of their family's history, looked at Claire with concern.

"I can shift now," Claire stated even though she had not intended to, her voice steady and filled with the gravity of her admission. "And I can show you tonight. The hunters who once drove our kind into hiding are still very real, and they've only grown more powerful and dangerous. They hide, watch, and wait. I want you to understand the full implications of what this means. We *can* reclaim what is ours. Ignoring this chance means it will continue to fade to be eventually forgotten and lost forever. I have made my choice. We were once protectors and can be again."

Her mother sighed, looking out the window where the sunset painted the sky in fiery colors. "But exposing the family to this danger..."

"I understand, Mum. But hiding isn't an option anymore."

Claire's mother absorbed her daughter's words. Her eyes, once bright with the fire of youth, now carried the wisdom of years and the scars of silent battles.

Ian, who had stayed silent through their discussion, said, "Your old enemies are hunting again, and you need to be ready. That is why we are here. To gather strength and help."

"You're right," Claire's mother finally said.

"I'm part of a group now," Claire continued. "Ian and I and others are actively tracking these threats. We're preparing ourselves, and I need the support of our family and the wisdom of those who came before us. We need to stand together. Call the Pack."

Claire's mother met her daughter's eyes, the fire's glow reflecting in them. "I'll reach out to those who might be willing to listen," she agreed. "I'll share your message. Not everyone will welcome such a revelation."

"Thank you, Mum. They must understand the stakes. We're

stronger together, and it's time we remember that."

As the evening deepened into night, Claire, Ian, and her mother engaged in long conversations, making plans, sharing stories, and reigniting the spirit of their heritage.

After the discussions tapered off, Claire said, "Let me show you what it really means."

While her mother and Ian watched, Claire removed her clothes and crouched in front of the fireplace. She looked inward and saw her wolf looking back at her. More controlled and focused now, she fell into its gaze and shifted. She shuddered, and the air around her rippled outward.

Her form stretched, her body becoming leaner and more muscular. Fur the color of her golden brown hair sprouted, with darker areas blending in, and when she looked up her eyes were a luminous amber, seeming to glow in the reflected light of the fire.

What stood before them was a large wolf of immense presence. For a few heart-stopping moments, she just looked at her mother. Seeing the tears start to form in her mother's eyes, she padded over and nuzzled her cheek, her mother's arms coming around her before she buried her face in fur. Claire could feel the joy in her mother and the weight of ages being shed in those tears.

Helena stepped out of the taxi, looking across the bustling streets of Rome with a predator's awareness. The city's ancient grandeur was lost on her; she was here for a singular purpose. As she made her way into the hotel, a modest but strategically located establishment with views of the Vatican, her thoughts were already on the task ahead.

Settling into her room, she unpacked only the essentials. She surveyed the room, glancing briefly at the bed with its crisp, clean sheets. It was merely a functional part of her temporary lair, nothing more.

The Grandmaster had provided contact information for an operative in Rome. She made an encrypted call. "Orion," a man answered. Orion was a new element in her game, an unknown and potentially useful asset.

"Orion, this is Helena. I need you to come to my hotel room. Discreetly. We have much to discuss."

Helena provided directions and ended the call, her mind already calculating the next steps. She moved to the window and looked out over the city. Her attention fixed on the distant silhouette of St. Peter's Basilica. The city, rich in history, secrets, and shadows, was an ideal stage for her schemes. With his interest in forbidden knowledge, Howard was out there, possibly unlocking doors better left closed. That was Eamon's fear and her hope.

Some ten minutes later, there was a knock at the door. She crossed the room and opened it to reveal a short man with sharp features and a confident demeanor. He did not stand out from the crowds below, and she had not noticed his approach to the hotel.

"Orion, I presume," Helena said, stepping aside to let him enter.

He nodded, scanning the room. "Helena," he said.

She gestured for him to sit at the small table by the window. "We have a lot to cover, and time is of the essence."

Orion took the offered seat, his posture relaxed but alert. Helena joined him, pulling out a tourist map of the city and laying it on the table.

"We have a critical target in Rome." Helena handed Orion a folder filled with documents and photographs. "Howard Miller. He is a man driven by knowledge and a dangerous curiosity. He is likely delving into ancient texts and arcane secrets in his research here in Rome."

Orion opened the folder, examining the detailed dossier on Howard. The photographs showed an elderly man, in his mid-eighties at least, with salt-and-pepper hair, scholarly in appearance in his round spectacles.

Howard Miller had been born in 1938 as the youngest brother of the Miller family. While the Millers were known for their social standing and successful business ventures, Howard was the black sheep of the family due to his unconventional interests. In the late 1960s, he'd joined the faculty of the London School of Mystical Arts and Esoteric Sciences, LSMAES, as a young and enthusiastic professor. However, his unconventional interests and approach to teaching had quickly set him apart from his more traditional colleagues.

After glancing through the file, Orion said, "He should not be hard to spot. May I keep this file?"

"No. Not even the photos, so study them carefully before you leave. You may, however, keep the map. He left the school on sabbatical and was not located until he appeared here. He will be seeking esoteric knowledge." Helena pointed to several locations on the map. "These are places he's likely to visit—libraries, historical sites, and certain restricted areas around Vatican City."

Orion nodded, absorbing the information. "And what do we do once we find him?"

"Engagement is not authorized. Your primary objective is to observe his actions. We need to understand what he is after, who he contacts, and what resources he utilizes. Only then will we plan our strike."

Orion's eyes flicked to the photographs again. "Any known associates?"

"None that we've identified in Rome. He is likely to have local contacts or allies. He would not come blindly to Rome if he did not have specific goals in mind. Be vigilant. Maintain a low profile. The last thing we need is to alert him."

"Understood. I'll start with some of the lesser-known locations, ones not typical for tourists to visit. They are the most likely places for someone seeking forbidden knowledge. Would you not reconsider at least one photo to show?"

Helena considered the request. "Take a picture of it with your phone. That should suffice. Ensure you do not share, and delete it when we are done here. Report back to me with any significant findings."

Orion stood, ready to leave. "I won't let you down."

"See that you don't." The deeper threat was unspoken but evident nonetheless.

Later, as darkness enveloped Rome, Helena's phone vibrated against the polished surface of the antique bedside table, breaking the stillness of her hotel room. She picked it up. "Report," she commanded.

Orion relayed an update. "He has been frequenting the Vatican's lesser-known libraries and engaging with scholars specialized in ancient lore. His focus seems set on geasa and binding oaths."

A sardonic smile spread. Her most significant constraint and constant threat was the invisible chain that bound her to the Grandmaster. "Interesting," she murmured, her mind racing. Howard seeking such knowledge could not be a coincidence. The same oaths had bound Richard. Was Howard's research connected to that, and how had they discovered those bindings? How closely was Howard tied to Lucian and Anja? Was it only skill and knowledge, or did they have some other form of power? So many questions remained, and a source of answers was near. "Keep a constant watch on him. He must not leave the city. He is of immense value. Alive."

The knowledge Howard sought could hold immense power, power that could potentially free her. And if there was a chance, however slim, to understand more about the intricate bindings that tied her to Eamon, she had to take it.

She stood up, her movements fluid as a panther ready to pounce. The risk of capturing Howard inside the heavily surveilled and sacred grounds of Vatican City was immense. It would be easier to wait until he returned to where he was staying in Rome, but still—she would need to be cautious, cunning, and swift.

She reached for her phone and dialed a number connecting her to the city's darker underbelly. "Buonasera," she greeted coolly as the call connected. "I require your assistance."

On the other end, a gravelly voice responded. It was a contact from the local mafia, a reference provided by her connections via her Syndicate. This alliance, formed through years of unsavory endeavors and mutual interests, was about to prove its worth.

Helena was concise and clear in providing authentication and passphrases. "Where can we meet discreetly?" she asked in fluent Italian.

The voice on the other end hesitated momentarily before replying, "Meet me in Testaccio, at the bar on Via Galvani. You should recognize the signs."

The night air was cool and crisp as she stepped out of the hotel. The city was alive with nightlife, but Helena moved with purpose as she navigated the narrow alleys and cobblestone streets, her senses on high alert for any signs of trouble. The ancient city seemed to hum with energy.

She arrived at the bar in Testaccio just before midnight. The dimly lit establishment was marked by a small, stylized olive branch carved into the wooden frame of the door. To most, it was a simple decorative element, but Helena knew it signified a haven for underground activities.

The dimly lit establishment was filled with the murmur of conversation and the clinking of glasses. She scanned the room, her eyes settling on a man seated at a corner table, his gaze fixed on her as she entered. Helena approached the table, her movements confident and unhurried. "Buonasera," she greeted, sitting across from him.

"Buonasera," he replied, his voice low and gravelly. "What do you need?"

Helena glanced briefly at the other patrons. "Is this private?"

"None here would dare listen. Some of them may even be of assistance, depending on your needs. You may speak plainly."

"I need someone taken. Quietly. No traces. I need him transported to Poland. Discreetly and alive."

The man nodded, his eyes calculating. "Consider it done. We have the means to move him without drawing attention. Your man will vanish like a ghost."

"He's staying at a hotel near the Vatican. I need his belongings, too. Everything."

"Which hotel?"

"The Hotel Romano di Luna. He's in room 304."

"We'll take care of it. Our network is skilled in making problems disappear, whether it's people or evidence."

"Once he's secure, arrange a private charter to Poland. I'll handle it from there." Helena slid an envelope across the table. "I will be in touch."

As she stepped back into the night, her mind raced with plans and contingencies. Howard's research into geasa and binding oaths could hold the key to her freedom, and she was determined to uncover it.

The shadows of Rome closed in around her, but Helena moved through them with the confidence of a predator. No one would bother her.

Helena surveyed the scene at the private charter. Howard lay drugged and unconscious, his belongings stuffed in a trunk. He almost looked frail, but that was age and the drugs.

The flight to Olsztyn-Mazury Airport was uneventful, a silent flight offset only by the hum of the aircraft. Waiting for her was a trusted confederate whose loyalty to Helena was unwavering. She was recognized here, and the usual bribe dispersed the awaiting officials after only perfunctory checks.

They moved swiftly, transferring Howard and the trunk into a vehicle. The ride to Dwor Szeptów, 'the Whispering Manor,' was uneventful. The estate sat ensconced in the dense embrace of the Masurian forests. Its history was as dark as the woods that guarded it, with a legacy that dated back centuries.

The road to the manor was serpentine, as if carved by the caprices of the forest itself. Legends spoke of the whispers of the woods that either guided or misled travelers based on the enigmatic will of the manor.

The Whispering Manor was more than just an estate; it was one of several bastions of her power. This one was a place where even the walls listened, and the shadows danced to her command. Here, amidst the oppressive aura of dread, she would unlock Howard's secrets, which could help break the bonds that tied her.

Lucian's determination to rescue his uncle would lead him straight into her clutches. And with Anja, an additional piece in her game, the stakes were even higher. Richard had failed, and now it was her turn to demonstrate how it was done.

Helena's eyes glinted. This was more than a mere abduction. The dense forests surrounding the manor would serve as a shield.

When the vehicle arrived at the manor house, the breeze through the forest whispered to her in welcome, her plan stirring the air and charging it with anticipation for the impending confrontation.

# *Twenty-Two*

Elín, perched in the front passenger seat, watched the passing scenery as the 4x4 navigated the winding roads from Reykjavík. The trip to Hvannadalshnúkur through Iceland's dramatic landscape was mesmerizing.

The evening sun, reluctant to set in late May, cast long shadows across the terrain. Mountains rose, their peaks still covered with snow, standing guard over the valleys below. The interplay of light and shadow over the landscape created a stunning scene—the mossy ground's deep greens, the volcanic rock's darker hues, and the lingering snow's white.

Elín's anticipation of testing her dragon form added an electric charge to the air inside the vehicle. Anja and Lucian were seated in the back, their conversations oscillating between Mike's recent transformation and what lay ahead for Elín.

"We'll be going off-road soon," Mike said, his eyes never straying from the road. "Iceland doesn't take kindly to the unprepared."

The vehicle climbed higher, the terrain becoming more rugged and isolated. The vastness of the landscape was humbling, a reminder of their tiny place in the grand scheme of nature. The vegetation thinned as they ascended, giving way to rocky outcrops and sparse, hardy plants clinging to life.

The sky, with its deepening blues and purples, signaled the approach of twilight. The last day of May was giving way to the night, the transition seeming as magical as the land itself. The air grew colder, a crispness hinting at their altitude.

In the fading light, the silhouette of Hvannadalshnúkur loomed closer, its majestic presence guiding them upward. Elín's heart raced with the promise of what lay ahead.

Mike maneuvered to a halt at their destination, a spot nestled at the base of a glacier. The runoff from the ice had birthed a lake, its surface a blend of drifting ice and water.

As the sun dipped below the horizon, the sky above them transformed into a canvas for the auroras. Vivid greens and purples danced in curtains across the heavens, reflecting off the lake's icy surface, creating a surreal spectacle of light and color.

The chill of the approaching night began to make its presence known, an icy contrast to the day's warmth. Mike offered to heat a rock to provide warmth, but Elín waved him off. Since her awakening, the cold did not affect her as it once had.

Elín began to undress at the edge of the glacier lake. It was a rugged assembly of rocks, and chunks of ice floated like ghostly ships on the water's surface near the shore. Her movements were unhurried and ceremonial. The cold air brushed against her skin, but she was focused entirely on the transformation that awaited her.

Lucian called out to her. "Seek that place within you, Elín. Embrace your true form. It is coiled in sleep and will awaken to your call."

Elín closed her eyes and took a deep breath of the crisp air, letting it fill her lungs. It ignited something deep in her soul. Her confidence grew, amplified by the natural energy around her. She stood there, poised at the edge of transformation, her spirit soaring with what she was about to become.

Beneath the dance of the auroras, surrounded by the raw beauty of the wilderness, Elín was on the cusp of revealing her true nature. The night held its breath, waiting for the magic to unfold.

Her mind delved into the vivid dreams and visions she had experienced during her awakening with Anja. Those memories acted as a beacon, guiding her toward her form. She allowed herself to fall into those visions and embraced them to wake the dragon.

The power that surged through her was colossal, a force that echoed with her being. Around her, an icy mist began to form, swirling under the canopy of stars and the dancing auroras.

The beast began to uncoil, and Elín's skin began to change. Scales emerged, wings unfurled, and a powerful, spiked tail grew. Each new feature shimmered with a brilliance that mirrored the icy shades of the glacier in front of her.

For a few heartbeats, she remained grounded, her new form a marvel. She looked around, taking in the awestruck expressions of Anja, Lucian, and Mike. Her eyes, now faceted orbs, saw the world anew.

She leaped into the air with a primal roar that echoed across the icy landscape. Her mighty wings caught the night air and propelled her upwards with astonishing speed.

As she climbed higher, the landscape below her became a vista of shadow and light. Elín reveled in the freedom and power of her flight, the wind a roaring symphony around her, the stars her companions in the night sky. She was a creature of legend, a being of power and grace, soaring into her destiny.

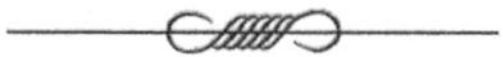

Anja was stunned by the spectacle. The transformation from woman to dragon had been swift and breathtaking. Elín was a fearsome sight, embodying the essence of myth and legend brought to life.

Her icy scales blended seamlessly with the sky and the landscape. She appeared at one with the elements, almost disappearing into the distance.

After a while, Elín descended, gliding down from the mountain's peak, along the glacier, and over the icy lake. As she neared the ground, her wings cupped the air, allowing her to touch down gently.

The transformation then reversed, a process as awe-inspiring as her initial metamorphosis. In a moment, the majestic ice dragon receded, and in its place stood Elín, her human form emerging as the scales and wings faded away. She looked exhausted but exhilarated, her body shaking from the intensity of the experience.

Elín's gaze was still fixed on the peak above. Her eyes sparkled with joy and disbelief as if she was still accepting the reality of her transformation.

As Anja draped a warm blanket over Elín's naked form, she noticed a faint, shimmering outline on Elín's back. It was like the ghost of dragon wings, a barely seen reminder of the creature Elín had just been. This spectral image had a soft, silvery-blue sheen that nearly matched Elín's pale skin, a delicate and ethereal vestige of her transformation.

Elín turned to face Anja and Lucian. She tried to articulate her experience, to convey the enormity of what she had felt during her flight. "There are no words."

She thanked Anja and Lucian, her words filled with emotion, acknowledging the incredible gift they had given her. Clearly, this transformation was more than just a physical change.

Zoe relaxed into the plush armchair, her legs tucked beneath her as Anja and Lucian lounged on the sofa across from her. They had all returned to the warmth of their hotel room after a short day at the lab. She had, of course, wasted no time in shedding her clothes.

"I hope we can slow down now that most awakenings are done and Claire and Ian are off to England. We need a break and some time to relax," Lucian said.

"Feels good to be back together like this," Zoe mused. "I missed you guys."

"Likewise," Anja replied. "I'm sorry we've been so busy, Zoe, leaving you to yourself last night. How was your trip to New York? And I'm not talking about what you shared in the meeting this morning. I gave Emma an assignment."

Zoe grinned. "It was interesting," she deflected. "After I returned the books to Raymond and shared your warnings, he picked out another book for you. He thought you'd like it." She produced the book from her bag and waved it in the air. "*Nocturnal Yearnings: An Anthology of Dark Love.*"

Anja looked surprised, but that soon turned into curiosity as she took the book from Zoe, flipping through its lavish illustrations. “Ohhh…He knows me too well,” she breathed and ran a finger over the stunning black and gold cover. “Much too well. Sometimes my yearnings can get a bit dark, and I try not to think about what he knows about these books and me.”

“What’s this one about?” Zoe asked, leaning in closer to watch Anja’s face.

“Dark erotica. Things that go bump in the night. I…they’re fantasies I sometimes like to imagine,” she admitted.

Zoe leaned back and brushed her hair back over her shoulder, and her breasts swayed gently as she moved. She knew she was putting on a show for them and could feel Lucian watching her—they both were.

“Now, back to the subject of your other adventure, which I noticed you deftly avoided with the book…”

The surge of excitement at the prospect of exploring new sexual challenges with these two people was immediate. Her recent experiences in New York had opened her mind to the vast spectrum of pleasures that awaited them. “I also went shopping at a little boutique with Emma. I picked out a few things to bring back and test out.” She stood and walked over to the dresser, pulled out another bag, and set it on the nightstand by the bed. “We can try them out, but don’t look yet.”

Anja nodded in agreement, her eyes sparkling with excitement. “You wear your skin so naturally, Zoe. It’s incredibly sexy.”

“Thank you.” Returning to her chair, Zoe leaned back, spreading her legs slightly. “Well, I spent some time exploring my…curiosity about women. Emma taught me a thing or two, and I must say, I enjoyed it more than I thought I would.” She could see the curiosity sparking and enjoyed their undivided attention.

“Is that so?” Anja asked. “Tell us more…”

“Well, let’s just say that our nights together were enjoyable. Emma introduced me to new ways of teasing, touching, tasting, and satisfying one another. It was an experience that left me satisfied yet hungry for more,” Zoe said as her hand drifted down to play with her curls.

As the words spilled from her, arousal stirred, and she decided it was time to shed her inhibitions—the few she had left, anyway. She started to rub herself and spread her legs wider to give them a show.

"Perhaps we could all explore these new techniques together," Anja suggested with a sultry smile as she glanced at Lucian.

"An excellent idea," Lucian agreed. "I'd love to watch that."

"Seeing you like that makes me want to join you," Anja said, her eyes flicking to Lucian for a moment before returning to Zoe.

"Please do," Zoe encouraged.

With a coy smile, Anja began to undress, teasingly lifting the hem of her shirt to reveal the smooth expanse of her stomach before pulling the fabric up and over her head. She tossed the shirt aside, leaving her in a lacy bra and skirt.

Anja's pale skin glowed in the dim light of the room; the contrast between her red hair and fair complexion was beautiful. Anja unhooked her bra, letting it fall away to reveal her full, pale breasts. The sight left Zoe aching to reach out and touch them, to feel the softness of skin beneath her fingertips.

"Your turn, Lucian," Anja purred as she pushed her skirt down her legs. She stepped out of them. Having not worn anything underneath, Anja now stood naked before Zoe and Lucian.

"Patience," Lucian replied. "I want to watch you two first."

Anja's hands moved to Zoe's hips, her touch gentle but firm as she pulled their bodies together. Their lips met in a kiss, tongues dancing together as they explored each other's mouths. Anja's mouth held a sweet and spicy taste that Zoe could not seem to get enough of.

As their passion grew, Zoe stole glances at Lucian, watching as his dark eyes drank in the sight of them. The intensity of his look only served to heighten her arousal, making her crave even more of the connection and pleasure that awaited them all. She whispered, "We're just getting started."

As Zoe and Anja continued to kiss and caress each other, their hands eagerly exploring every curve and contour of their bodies, Lucian remained seated. His arousal was evident from the growing bulge in his pants. Still, he seemed content to simply observe for now, enjoying the voyeuristic pleasure of watching two women lose themselves in each other.

"Lucian," Anja panted between kisses, "do you like what you see?"

"Very much," he replied with obvious desire. "I could watch the two of you all night."

A flush of excitement ran through Zoe at the thought of Lucian watching them, knowing that they were fulfilling his fantasies just as much as their own. She reached out and covered Anja's breast with her hand, gently squeezing and teasing her nipple. Anja let out a moan, her body arching into Zoe's touch.

"Tell us, Lucian," Zoe said, breathy and seductive, "what would you like to see us do next?"

"Let me think," Lucian mused, his dark eyes roaming over their naked forms, drinking in the sight of them. "Why don't you take turns pleasuring each other? I want to see how well you truly know one another's bodies."

Zoe's heart raced at the prospect. She was eager to dive in. Her connection with Anja had always been strong but was now changed from best friends to sexual partners. Their willingness to be open and vulnerable with one another had brought them closer than ever before.

"Your wish is our command," Anja murmured as she leaned Zoe back. Straddling her waist, Anja leaned down and captured Zoe's lips in another hungry kiss, her hands roaming over her body.

Zoe melted beneath Anja's touch, feeling herself growing more and more aroused. They took turns pleasuring one another, their bodies writhing together while Lucian watched raptly.

"Let's take this to the bed," Anja suggested, leading Zoe by the hand. They moved gracefully, their bodies gliding against each other. Lucian remained in his chair, his eyes never leaving them as they lay down on the plush mattress.

Zoe reached over and pulled out a toy while looking at Anja devilishly.

"Wow, that looks…intriguing," Anja said. "I haven't ever tried any sex toys before."

"Trust me, it feels amazing," Zoe assured her, running her fingers along the vibrator's length. Turning it on, she pressed the vibrating head against Anja's inner thigh, causing her to gasp.

"God, that feels good," Anja moaned, gripping the sheets tightly as Zoe moved the toy closer to her heated center. "Please, don't stop."

"Not yet, anyway," Zoe purred, her eyes filled with desire as she watched Anja's reactions. Guiding the vibrations over her sensitive flesh, she reveled in the way Anja's body responded to her touch, arching and shivering.

Lucian, meanwhile, couldn't tear his eyes away from the erotic scene before him. As he watched Zoe pleasure Anja, his arousal grew until it was unbearable. He stood, stripping off his clothes, revealing his straining erection.

"Keep going," he commanded, sitting back down in his chair, his hand moving to stroke himself. "I want to see you lose yourselves in each other."

"Lucian," Zoe breathed, watching him as he began to masturbate, the sight of him so utterly captivated by their performance only fueling her arousal further.

"Zoe, focus on me," Anja whispered, pressing her lips against Zoe's neck as Zoe continued to wield the magic wand, exploring different angles and intensities to elicit the most potent reactions.

"Zoe…it's…it's almost too much," Anja stammered as the relentless vibrations threatened to push her over the edge.

"Tell me when you're ready," Zoe murmured, her excitement mounting as she witnessed Anja's surrender to pleasure. "Tell me when you come."

Anja nodded, her breath coming in ragged gasps as the sensations coursed through her. She reached for Zoe's free hand, their fingers intertwining.

"Yes! Now! I'm cominggggg," Anja cried out, her body shuddering as the waves of ecstasy crashed over her. Zoe felt her link to Anja blossom and felt her orgasm as if it were her own. In a flash, it *was* her own.

"Lucian," Zoe murmured, staring at his erection, "I love watching you stroke yourself…it's *so* incredibly hot. I want to try something different. I want to be tied up and blindfolded. I want to feel completely at your mercy, to trust you both completely."

Anja's eyes widened momentarily before a slow smile spread across her face. She looked at Lucian, who nodded in agreement.

"Lucian," Zoe whispered, trembling with anticipation. "Would you tie me up?"

Lucian's eyes darkened with desire as he realized the opportunity to explore his dominant side with Zoe. "Of course."

Lucian used the ropes in the bag to secure her to the bed. Anja took charge of blindfolding Zoe after she rummaged through Zoe's bag on the nightstand and pulled out the blindfold she found there. She fastened it into place, covering her eyes. As Zoe's vision turned to darkness, her other senses heightened, leaving her vulnerable and exposed.

As Zoe lay there, blindfolded and bound, she keenly felt the weight of anticipation in the air. Her heart raced, her mind buzzing. She heard Anja say, "Zoe, I have a surprise for you."

"What is it?" Zoe asked, beginning to pant.

"Something to make this even more memorable," Anja teased. From the corner of the room, Zoe heard the sound of rustling fabric, followed by soft footsteps approaching the bed. "You must have bought this for a reason."

"Anja put on a strap-on dildo," Lucian informed her, his voice thick with desire. "You might enjoy feeling both of us inside you at the same time."

"Oh, fuck," Zoe breathed; the thought alone was enough to drive her crazy. She could hardly wait for whatever they had in mind.

"First, let's get you warmed up, shall we?" Lucian suggested.

She felt the smooth, cool surface of a dildo pressing against her entrance and gasped as Anja slowly pushed it inside her, filling her. As Anja began thrusting into her, Lucian positioned himself at her lips, teasing her with the tip of his erection. Zoe took him into her mouth, sucking and swirling her tongue around him.

The sound of Anja's heavy breathing as she thrust the dildo into Zoe with urgency, the wet noises of their coupling, Lucian's moans of pleasure, and Zoe's muffled cries mingled together.

Anja continued to pump the strap-on in and out of Zoe, driving her wild with pleasure while Lucian's thrusts matched the rhythm. The combination of sensations was overwhelming, leaving Zoe teetering on the edge.

The room was filled with the heady scent of arousal, a mixture of sweat, musk, and the soft scent of Anja's perfume. Zoe could smell the tang of latex from the strap-on.

As Zoe spiraled towards her climax, she realized that this experience had unlocked a part of her she never knew existed—a part that craved submission, vulnerability, and the exquisite pleasure that could be found in surrendering all control.

Lucian groaned as he pulled out of Zoe's mouth, his breath ragged. "I'm close, Zoe. Are you ready for me?"

"Please, I want to taste you," Zoe begged, consumed with lust and longing.

Just as Anja picked up the pace, driving the dildo into Zoe with urgency, Lucian erupted onto Zoe's face. She felt the hot liquid on her face and tongue, then slowly dribble down her cheek and chin. Zoe's flushed skin was slick with sweat and desire, now laced with semen.

Zoe could feel the connection with Lucian blossom with sensations as he joined with her and Anja. She could see the scene around her through that link, even with the blindfold securely in place. Her orgasm rocked through her, and she felt Anja feed off it to drive her climax with a last thrust into her.

"Let me clean you up, Zoe," Anja purred, leaning down to lick Lucian's seed from her face. The sensation of Anja's warm tongue against her skin only served to extend the tremors rolling through her body.

Anja pressed her lips to Zoe's, sharing the taste of Lucian in a deep, passionate kiss that left them breathless.

# Twenty-Three

HELENA ENTERED THE room. She stood tall and statuesque, her porcelain skin contrasting with her jet-black hair that cascaded in thick waves down her back. The dress Helena wore was a stunning piece of vintage elegance, reminiscent of the sophisticated styles of the early nineteen hundreds. The rich black fabric absorbed the light around her. Long fitted sleeves extended to her wrists, where lace cuffs peeked out. The low neckline showed enough cleavage that men's eyes would be drawn there—a distraction she employed often.

The room where Howard was kept was comfortable, a contrast to the grim exterior of the manor and woods. The comfort was another tool of manipulation, a reminder that she controlled every aspect of his environment and that it would change at her whim. The door, though unassuming in appearance, was locked from the outside.

Her cold blue eyes scanned the room, then Howard. His hair was graying, more salt than pepper, and still ruffled. He appeared to be in better shape than she expected and didn't look to be in his mid-eighties. Seeing him now, awake and alert, he seemed closer to his early seventies or a bit younger.

Her regard fixed on Howard as she took a seat opposite him. She kept her demeanor calm, as if they were old acquaintances rather than captor and captive.

Helena introduced herself simply as Helena. There was no need for pretenses; she knew Howard would assume her affiliation with the Sodality. Her expression remained unchanged as she confirmed his suspicions. The revelation was strategic, meant to unsettle him with her openness.

When she spoke, her words were clear and articulate; her English was perfect and held no accent—centuries of existence had granted her the ability to master many languages and accents.

Howard's eyes widened as he realized the gravity of his situation. "Why have you kidnapped me?" he demanded, his voice tinged with a mix of fear and anger. "I took a risk going to Rome but believed it was worth it."

Helena leaned forward slightly, her interest apparent. "And why was it worth the risk, Howard? What did you hope to find in Rome?"

Howard hesitated, clearly weighing his options before speaking. "I wanted answers."

His foot started to tap lightly—a nervous habit, she noted.

Helena's eyes gleamed. "You were researching geasa and oaths—why? That's a particularly intriguing area of study. Is your research related to Richard?"

Howard's eyes flickered with uncertainty. He did not answer, and Helena continued, her tone more probing. "Lucian and Anja must have captured Richard. Why do you think they released him rather than killing or keeping him longer?"

Howard's reluctance was glaring, but he finally spoke, his voice low. "I felt the binding might be more than just a geas. It could have a permanence that might be traced."

Even though she suppressed any outward reaction to that revelation about being traced, it cut deep. She had suspected as much when Eamon had found Richard so swiftly. This had profound implications for her situation. She might be able to run but hiding was another matter. "So, Richard was the focus of your research. And what exactly did you hope to learn from him?"

"Anything we could. Ah…" He cut off what he started to say and then restarted, looking at his sleeve. "We could not break it. Perhaps with more time, but the risks were too great."

"Richard's memories were altered. How was that accomplished?" That question revealed much, but Howard would not be leaving. Ever.

He looked at her, startled. "I…I don't know. I do not know what became of him."

That appeared to be true, so she tried another tack. "It was a blood oath. Who was attempting to break his oath? Lucian? No, I don't think so. It would have been someone like you with knowledge, so...ah... Anja, yes?"

Howard paled, confirming her guess. "Why do you care? What do you want?"

"Anja is young and beautiful. Would you want her? Is that why you protect her? She is enamored with Lucian. I am also young and beautiful, but I am very attracted to older and wiser men," she lied and leaned closer to him, nearly spilling out of her dress. "I would like to know more about what you have learned about binding spells. Working with me could be enlightening and pleasurable, don't you agree?"

He looked into her eyes with curiosity but no heat. He showed no interest in her provocative display, which was a curiosity that she should explore in greater detail. She did not doubt her beauty, as proven countless times. After all, death was the mother of beauty; Wallace Stevens was closer to the truth than he'd known. Then again, maybe he *had* known. Howard's dossier made no mention of a wife or even lovers. Either he had been extremely discreet, he was impotent with age, or there was missing information. She would bet on the latter. He was old but in remarkable condition for his age. There was no information on religion in the files either.

"I'll be contacting your brother, Edward. We couldn't find your phone, but we're searching for it. I would have preferred to contact Lucian directly, but you seem unwilling to provide that convenience."

Howard remained stoic, giving away little. Helena appreciated his restraint, even if it was an inconvenience. She preferred to avoid the messiness of torture most of the time.

"I understand your loyalty," Helena continued. "But you must realize the situation you're in. I'm offering a more civilized way to discuss common interests with Lucian by contacting Edward. It would be wise for you to cooperate."

She watched Howard closely, gauging his response. His silence spoke volumes, but Helena wasn't deterred. She had dealt with stubbornness before and knew patience often yielded better results than brute force.

As their discussion drew to a close, Helena left Howard with a final look, a silent promise that their conversation was far from over.

Ian stood by the window in the drawing room of the Miller estate. The news Edward had just relayed hung in the air, casting a shadow even on the sunlit room.

Edward, a man whose stern features rarely betrayed emotion, looked unusually perturbed. Ian noted the tightening of his jaw. "What has he gotten into?" Edward muttered, more to himself than to Ian or Claire.

"We're not sure." Ian's mind raced. The call from the unknown woman referring to Howard as a 'guest' was unexpected and dire.

Claire spoke up. "Whatever is happening, we need to call Lucian and Anja."

"I never approved of Howard's…interests," Edward said, "but he is my brother. And after what happened to the others…" His eyes, usually unyielding, now reflected a deep-seated anger.

The weight of responsibility sat heavily on Ian's shoulders. They were involved with something dangerous that could threaten not just Howard but all of them.

"I'll call Lucian." Ian dialed Lucian's number, each ring amplifying his tension.

When Lucian answered, Ian didn't hesitate. "I'm putting this on speaker. Claire and Edward are here." He relayed Edward's information concisely, the words tasting bitter on his tongue. "They gave a contact number in Szczytno, Poland. They want you and Anja to come alone. The threat of what would happen if we failed to comply was left unsaid."

Lucian's curse crackled through the phone. "You'll need to return immediately. The Sodality…they've got Howard." The last was said to whoever was in the room with him. Muffled curses could be heard in the background.

Claire's expression mirrored Ian's concern. She moved closer, her presence a silent support for Ian.

Ian listened intently as Lucian laid out the plan, his mind racing through the logistics. "I'll have the jet sent for you," Lucian said. "Since they've contacted Edward, there's a chance you're being watched. We'll meet in Iceland, but you'll have to route through Geneva."

The mention of surveillance sent a ripple of unease through Ian. Edward's face was etched with concern, the familial ties to his brother now pulling him into the fray.

"We'll get him back, Edward. Lucian will throw all he has at this. Let us know if they contact you again."

As Ian ended the call, Claire stated, "I'll inform my mother that something's come up and that we'll return when we can."

Ian leaned in, his lips meeting Claire's in a brief but reassuring kiss. It was a moment of connection, a grounding point amid the whirlwind of events unfolding around them. "It's time to go earn our keep," he said with a grimace.

They went into action, gathering their belongings and preparing for the trip back to Iceland. Ian's military training meshed with the role he found himself in.

The flight to Geneva and then to Iceland loomed ahead, but Ian was bolstered by Claire's presence. As they departed the Miller estate, Ian cast a final glance back.

Helena stepped into the room. Howard, who had been reading, looked up, his posture tensing.

"Good evening, Howard." Helena took a seat opposite him, the folds of her black dress falling around her. Her gaze, cold and penetrating, fixed on Howard. "Tell me, how did they discover Richard's blood oath?"

Howard's fingers drummed on the armrest. "Richard attempted to end his own life. Not once, but several times. It was Anja who sensed something else about him. She said he was compelled to extreme loyalty, bound by a force far stronger than mere allegiance."

Helena's expression remained unreadable. Anja was quickly becoming of great interest.

"I don't know how Anja did it, but I thought whoever the caster was might trace him through the binding. It was strong and likely unbreakable. That's why releasing him was necessary. Despite the risks, they chose not to end his life on moral grounds."

The potential for her binding to be traced was a vulnerability she couldn't afford to overlook. "And where is Richard now?"

Howard seemed uncertain. "I heard he might have gone into Russia, but I'm not sure of the source of that information."

Helena internally smirked at the mention of Russia. She had found the tracking device on Richard and had sent it to Moscow, a ruse to mislead and confuse. It seemed to have worked. With how easy Howard was to read, she doubted he was playing a deeper game. "Richard has been delivered to the Grandmaster, Eamon Vale." This revelation hung in the air, heavy with unspoken implications. "What can you tell me about Anja? She seems far more significant than a mere librarian."

Howard, though visibly tense, managed to maintain a semblance of composure. She observed that he was fond of Anja. "Anja is…unique. She has tapped into some kind of power, the full extent of which I'm not certain."

Helena noted his careful phrasing. His words held truth but hid more than he revealed.

Howard looked directly at Helena. "And what about your powers? You haven't delivered me to the Grandmaster. I suspect you have your own goals, possibly diverging from his."

He was more observant than she had initially given him credit for. "My goals align with those of the Sodality. But yes, I have certain… aspirations."

She saw no harm in admitting this much. Howard, after all, was not leaving Dwor Szeptów alive. There was a certain freedom in speaking to someone who, in her mind, was already a ghost.

Howard ventured further, "Are you bound in some way, like Richard? Is that why I'm here?"

The question was daring and too close to the truth. Helena's mask slipped for a fleeting moment, revealing a hint of genuine emotion. She quickly regained her composure, aware that her reaction might have already given her away.

"You are bold, Howard," she said, a slight smile playing on her lips, though her eyes remained as cold as ever. "But no, I am not bound like Richard. My allegiance to the Sodality is by choice."

Howard's insights were unnerving, and she realized she needed to be even more cautious around him, balancing the need to extract information from Howard while keeping her secrets. Helena was playing a dangerous game, but it was one she had mastered over centuries.

Helena rose from her seat. She cast a final, piercing look at Howard, leaving him with a promise that their conversation was far from over. The door clicked shut behind her, echoing.

Outside, she sought out her most trusted lieutenant and servant. Finding him in the dimly lit corridor, she wasted no time on pleasantries. "We need to enhance our plans for capturing Anja and Lucian. I want you to prepare two special collars for them. We cannot take any chances with their abilities."

The lieutenant, a man of few words, nodded in understanding. He was aware of the significance of such devices.

"The collars should be made of cold iron with a silver filigree design. These materials disrupt magical energies and should neutralize any abilities they may possess. Make sure they are ready as soon as possible. We cannot afford delays."

"They will be crafted and will be ready for their arrival."

Helena gave a curt nod, her mind already moving on. She would have the upper hand with these collars, ensuring that Anja and Lucian's abilities were rendered useless once they were captured. It was a critical step in securing her position and advancing her agenda.

Helena stood by the window, watching the darkness outside. The night was a canvas upon which she projected her designs, a backdrop to the intricate game she orchestrated. Her mind, a fortress of strategy and cold logic, was revisiting the past missteps of Richard, her former associate, now a cautionary tale in the annals of their clandestine world.

Richard's attempt to capture Lucian and Anja had ended in his ignominious capture. Richard had been outmaneuvered, tricked into a vulnerable position by his targets, a mistake born of arrogance. He had never faced opponents with abilities such as theirs and had become complacent in a world where that kind of power had all but vanished. She knew those powers had not completely disappeared, as evidenced by her, the Syndicate's, and the Grandmaster's usages.

The differences between Richard's approach and her own were as apparent as the contrast between night and day. While Richard had been hasty, Helena was deliberate. Where he had been overconfident, she was wary and methodical.

Dwor Szeptów was an impenetrable fortress guarded by loyalists and security measures. The grounds and surrounding forest had mystical protections bending to her will. Even the earth hid danger. She was the predator in this lair, and Anja and Lucian, no matter how significant their powers, were the prey.

As she turned away from the window, her silhouette a study in grace, Helena's thoughts were cold and relentless. Anja and Lucian, for all their abilities, were mere pieces in her grand design, tools to be used to further her goals. In her world, where power and cunning reigned supreme, Helena was unmatched save for Eamon himself—and that would soon change with Anja and Lucian under her control.

Helena had no intention of being anything but the victor. Her determination was as unyielding as the cold iron of those collars, her strategy as all-encompassing as the night sky outside her window.

# Part Three

# *Twenty-Four*

Lucian surveyed his team from the head of the table. To his right sat Anja, her expression a mask of focus. To his left was Elín, her calm demeanor belying the sharp mind at work beneath. Next to Anja was Zoe, while Claire and Ian sat opposite and next to Elín.

The others, Carlos, Emma, and the newly awakened team members —Sigri, Mike, Graham, and Lynn—filled the remaining seats, each bringing their unique strengths to the table. Though not yet awakened, Dora and Cari, the latest additions, were present, too. Dora's Polish heritage made her an invaluable asset in her homeland, and Cari would assist Carlos.

"Let's finalize our approach," Lucian began. "We know the risks but also what's at stake. Howard's safety, possibly his life, depends on our precision and discretion." Lucian outlined the specifics of their strategy, each point punctuated by nods or murmurs from the team.

As the meeting progressed, ideas were exchanged and potential pitfalls were identified and countered. Dora's insights into local customs and geography proved invaluable.

Dora reluctantly volunteered that in the past, she had been tangled up in the underworld and was familiar with some of the elements in and around Szczytno. They would need to be the source of weapons and ammunition. "I really don't want to go into the details of my history, but I can help get what you need."

Lucian turned to Anja. "Anja and I will travel via my jet to Olsztyn-Mazury Airport, with one stop to obscure our trail. We must not lead them straight back here."

Anja seemed distracted with a faraway look, and he wondered if this was really the right choice. Offering themselves up as additional hostages was not optimal, but there were no other options they had been able to come up with, and he would not abandon Howard. He and Anja both had other surprises in store if all hell broke loose.

Turning back to the group, he continued. "The rest of you need to head out ahead of us and be in position before we land. Your job is to track us and pinpoint where we're being taken. We're stepping into their game, but we'll play by our rules. Ian, Claire, you'll stay with Zoe to coordinate. Anja will contact Zoe through their link when it's time to initiate the rescue. Remember, we don't know our final destination. Lynn, stick close to Mike and Emma. You three will be key in providing support when we make our move."

Carlos was next, alongside Cari and her aptitude in drone technology. "Carlos, it looks like you may have to leave Aria here. Maybe you can recruit another friend there. You're our eyes in the sky with Cari and her drones. Scout the area but maintain a low profile. We can't afford to tip them off.

"Elín, I need to ask you to remain here. You can coordinate with Sigri to help keep everybody synced up. A dragon might be a little much for the skies over Poland, but as a fallback plan…well, let's not think about that now.

"Dora, you'll coordinate with Claire and Sigri on travel logistics and accommodations. Ian, you'll oversee the execution and the approach to our location. Assume heavy surveillance and guarded access points."

Lucian's words were met with agreement. He could see the wheels turning in their minds, each member mentally running through their roles, anticipating challenges, and preparing for contingencies.

"We're walking into a volatile and unknown situation, but we have the advantage. We have surprise, we have skill, and most importantly, we have each other. Trust in your training; trust in your team. We're going to get Howard back, and we're going to do it without losing anyone."

With that, the team dispersed, each member moving with purpose.

Lucian watched them go, aware of the risks but confident in their ability to face whatever lay ahead. They were more than prepared; they were united, and in that unity, they found their strength.

Later, Anja's demeanor hinted at something significant as they entered the hotel room. It immediately drew Lucian's and Zoe's attention.

Zoe looked at Anja with a deep understanding, their bond allowing her to sense the gravity of what was about to be shared. Reaching out, her hand found Anja's, a gesture of support and readiness. "What's wrong?"

Anja hesitated, her eyes briefly flitting between Lucian and Zoe. "You're not going to like this," she began.

Lucian, his usual composure giving no hint of his internal turmoil, gave her a slight nod. "Go on…"

Anja gestured for Lucian and Zoe to sit down. They did so, albeit reluctantly. Once seated, Anja took a deep breath, preparing to articulate the visions that had haunted her.

"You know I sometimes get visions of the future," she began. "It's a gift…Or, at times, a curse. What I see now…It's dark. It's essential that we do this, and you'll be able to get Howard out."

Before she could continue, Zoe interrupted. "Wait, you said 'you,' not 'we.' What does that mean?"

Lucian, too, picked up on it, his reaction immediate and intense. "No, not happening."

Anja met their reactions with a solemn resolve. "Yes, Lucian, we—I—must. I can't see clearly beyond that point, but I know we may all die if I don't do this. Maybe not during the rescue or even for years, but all paths lead to the same end. Even if we could kill them all and rescue Howard, the Sodality will stop at nothing. They will eventually find and kill us or worse. We would fade into oblivion." Her words hung in the air, heavy with the foreseen future, a future where her actions could mean the difference between life and death for them all.

The premonition bore down on her like a physical force. She could see the turmoil roiling through them, their emotions raw and unguarded, and closed off her sense of their inner feelings. Those were much too much to bear. She knew she had to make them understand, even if it meant confronting their deepest fears.

"I understand this is hard," Anja said with a firmness that belied her gentle tone. "But you must not risk yourselves for my sake. It's crucial that you get Howard out. Even if it means trading me for him." Anja paused for a moment, letting her words sink in. But that was only part of it. The dark-haired woman, an ageless beauty, played a role in her visions, too. Pain. Pleasure. More. That future was clouded, but the other pathways were clear. Death. She did not understand why, but it was clear she must follow her vision even though she knew she would not escape with the others. Telling them even part of what she saw would stop them from letting her go. Holding the truth back was also wrong, but she had no choice.

Zoe said, "You're holding something back. What?"

"I don't see my death if I'm captured...maybe I can't. But I know this must happen, or there is no hope." Anja was prepared for the worst, even if it meant sacrificing herself—and hurting them.

Lucian and Zoe were visibly struggling. "How can we let you go?" Lucian asked. "We both love you, and we know you love us, but how can we just...let this happen?"

Anja reached out, taking each of their hands in hers, seeking comfort. "I know it's hard to understand and even harder to accept," she said. "But sometimes love means making the hardest choices for the sake of others. I need you both to be strong, for me, for Howard, for all of us."

Zoe's expression changed to determined. "I'm going in with you two. They're probably aware of me anyway, and I doubt they'd pass up the chance to get their hands on me too."

Anja experienced a flicker of fear at the thought of Zoe being in danger, but she also understood her reasoning. It was true that Zoe's presence might be anticipated, and her skills could be invaluable in whatever awaited them in Poland.

She looked inward, searching her intuition and the murky waters of her prescience, seeking guidance. After a moment of contemplation,

Anja nodded in agreement. “Okay, Zoe, but remember what we discussed. Remember what’s important. You must.” Zoe could help make sure Lucian and Howard escaped. It would be enough.

Anja called Emma. “Emma, you’ll be the one to give the signal for the rescue. Coordinate with Ian and make sure everything is timed perfectly. Zoe will be coming with Lucian and me to wherever we end up.”

For her part, Emma accepted the added role without question, but her acknowledgment carried concern.

Lucian made a quick call to Ian and Claire, informing them of the change in plans. However, Anja noticed that he omitted the revelations she had shared about her vision. It was a decision not to burden them with it until absolutely necessary.

Even so, there was much she had not told Lucian and Zoe.

Ian sat studying the map of Poland displayed on the monitor on the wall. The conference room hummed with the quiet intensity of a team poised for action.

Lucian, Anja, and Zoe’s departure on the private jet was scheduled for the following morning. The rest of the team was splitting up with another charter for Ian, Claire, and Dora. They also had cash for bribes and about a half kilo of gold that Dora had said would be necessary to buy the weapons. It should be enough.

Ian’s thoughts were interrupted as Lucian’s head of security in New York updated them via a secure line. The communications gear purchase and delivery to the German airport had been confirmed. It was a small reassurance in a sea of uncertainties.

Lynn and Mike would travel as a couple, as would Carlos and Cari. Graham and Emma would be another couple playing the part of honeymooning tourists. They needed to blend in with other travelers to avoid unwanted attention.

They would all meet at the hotel and call in room numbers to Elín and Sigri in Iceland, while Ian and Dora would attempt to purchase weapons. Claire would test and distribute the comms gear to the others.

Anja shared a critical update. “I’ve established a mental link with Emma. It’s not perfect, but I’ll get a sense of her direction and emotions, and she mine. It’s the best we can do under these circumstances.”

Ian nodded, his mind racing through the logistics. The lack of proper tracking gear was a concern, but they had to make do. “We’ll adapt and overcome,” he said, more to himself than anyone else. “We’ll also attempt a tail if we can.”

The team’s next concern was arming themselves in Poland. Ian knew that securing weapons on foreign soil was risky but necessary. They would have to rely on Dora’s contacts to help make it happen.

As the meeting drew to a close, the weight of responsibility rested heavy on his shoulders. They were venturing into unknown territory, both literally and figuratively.

The team dispersed to prepare. Ian took one last look at the map, etching the details into his memory. Szczytno, Poland—a name that had been just a dot on a map was now his focus.

With a deep breath, Ian stood up. They were a team, each member bringing their strengths to the table. Together, they would face whatever awaited them.

The private jet hummed through the sky, its interior a bubble of hushed conversations and strategic planning. Dora sat beside Ian, her strawberry-blonde hair contrasting with the leather of the aircraft seat. She watched out the window; her brown eyes were reflected in the glass. In her face, she saw a depth of experience and acknowledged the dark world she was about to re-enter.

In the cabin’s quiet atmosphere, Ian reviewed their plan. “Claire, you’ll head to the hotel with the comms gear once we land. Set up our base there. Stay in contact.”

Claire nodded. They had the gear aboard. Thankfully, the radio equipment had been delivered to the plane as promised.

Dora turned her attention back to Ian. “Follow my lead and try not to say anything. We'll need to find someone who knows the local weapons scene. I have contacts, but they were not arms dealers, although they surely know some."

Ian glanced at her. "Right," he agreed. "We'll get a car once we're on the ground and stay in touch using the gear we picked up."

Dora's gaze drifted back to the passing clouds outside. Her mind was already in Szczytno, sifting through her contacts and calculating the best way to secure their needed weapons and ammunition. Her connections in the Polish underworld were a mixed blessing—useful, yet a constant reminder of a past she couldn't seem to escape.

As the jet began its descent, the tension in the cabin rose. Dora could feel their collective focus sharpening.

When they landed at Olsztyn-Mazury Airport just south of Szczytno, the crisp air hit them with a reminder of the reality awaiting them outside the insulated world of their jet. Ian, Dora, and Claire disembarked.

Dora's posture was erect as she walked alongside Ian, scanning the surroundings. She knew the country, the language, the people. This was her domain, and she was back—not as a visitor, but as a critical player in a high-stakes game. *Back into the thick of things,* she thought as fire swirled in her belly.

They split up as planned, Claire heading towards the hotel with the gear while Ian and Dora ventured into the less savory parts of the city. Dora led the way, her stride confident, her mind running through potential scenarios. She spoke in Polish, blending in seamlessly, her accent perfect and her demeanor and clothes those of a local.

As they moved deeper into the shadowy underbelly of Szczytno, Dora's contacts became their lifeline. Each meeting, exchanging words and cash bribes, was a step closer to their goal. The underworld had its own rules, and Dora navigated them with a deft hand, her past experiences in these streets guiding her every move.

This was more than just a task for Dora. It was a return to a life she'd thought she had left behind. One she had once sworn to avoid. And here she was, walking these familiar paths, not just for herself, but for a cause that had given her life a new direction.

As the day turned into night and the plans began to take shape,

Dora felt the old thrill of the underworld's pulse. It was a dangerous game, but Dora Ziem was a player who knew how to play.

In the dimly lit backroom of an unassuming establishment, Dora stood across from a rugged man with a scar across his cheek. The air was thick with the scent of tobacco, beer, and old wood. Ian stood a few steps behind her, his presence strong but unobtrusive, appraising the array of weapons and matching ammunition laid out on the table before them.

Dora's voice was steady as she spoke in fluent Polish. "Potrzebujemy najlepszej jakości, bez śladów," she said, insisting on the best-quality weapons with no traceable history.

The man, known in the underworld as 'Kruk' for his cunning, nodded slowly, his eyes fixed on Dora. "To są najlepsze, co możesz znaleźć. Niezawodne i czyste," he assured her, gesturing towards the weapons.

Ian inspected the firearms. They were well-maintained—precisely what they needed. First, he examined the sniper rifle and its telescopic sight. Next, he picked up one of the handguns, weighed it in his hand, assessed its balance, and smiled. He opened the two ammo cans to check the contents and inspect the rounds and spare magazines. Satisfied, he gave a nod.

Dora turned back to Kruk, her expression unreadable. "Zgoda," she agreed. The deal was made.

Kruk's eyes narrowed as Ian placed a pouch on the table. The gold coins and bars clinked in the quiet room. He examined the pouch and handed it off to an assistant.

It was an old-fashioned way of doing business that was once again rising to prominence. Cryptocurrency had, for a while, dominated illicit transactions. Still, for any large operation, the blockchain records were too easy to trace, pointing law enforcement toward accounts with high volumes of questionable transactions. TornadoCash had offered a temporary reprieve until the US Department of the Treasury had stomped on it. The risk of having assets frozen or seized was way too costly.

From her days in the underworld, she had participated in many such transactions, though usually for drugs and precursors rather than guns and ammunition. Gold was still solid, untraceable, and easily laundered. It was much cheaper and safer than laundering crypto.

Soon, the gold was tested, weighed, and verified. It was almost like testing drugs, Dora thought wryly. The acid test kit even had a similar look to it. When the assistant completed the tests, he nodded and returned the pouch to Kruk.

With the transaction complete, Dora and Ian gathered the weapons, packing them into a nondescript duffle bag. After exiting the building, they made their way back through the dark and winding streets of Szczytno to their rented car. The trunk clicked open, and Ian placed the bag inside. Before closing the trunk, he put one of the pistols, a pair of magazines, and two handfuls of ammo into his coat pocket.

As Dora drove through the city, the tension from the negotiation ebbed away. Ian remained silent while he loaded the magazines and clicked one into place, his thoughts equally occupied, occasionally glancing behind them.

As they returned to their hotel, the streets of Szczytno passed by in a blur of shadows and lights.

# *Twenty-Five*

THE HOTEL ROOM, filled with whispered conversations and the sounds of gear being checked, resembled a command center more than a hotel suite.

Ian began to unpack the weapons they had acquired. The Bor sniper rifle, a sleek and powerful weapon, was placed on the table.

Carlos couldn't help but grin at the sight. "Quite a haul."

Ian laid out the WIST-94 pistols and their magazines. The clatter of metal on wood echoed in the room. He glanced at the ammunition box, estimating the load they could realistically carry. "We might only be able to load half of these," he mused aloud.

Emma, lounging on the couch with Graham, looked over with a mix of awe and excitement. "Wow, someone must have been skimming off the production lines," she quipped.

Sitting at a small makeshift desk, Claire continued her diligent work with the communications gear, her brow furrowed in concentration. The static of the comms unit crackled intermittently as she tested each unit.

Graham, who had been deep in conversation with Emma, now turned his attention to the weapons. His eyes widened at the sight of the sniper rifle. "That's some serious firepower," he commented.

The scattering of backpacks and gear around the room, the quiet discussions, and the meticulous checking of equipment all contributed to the sense that they were on the cusp of serious and likely deadly events.

As Ian finished unpacking, he stepped back, surveying the assembled arsenal. Mike and Lynn entered the room, Mike with an expression of curiosity and Lynn with apprehension. The sight of the weaponry laid out before them elicited a sharp intake of breath from Lynn. Mike, however, was less anxious, looking over the array of guns and ammo.

Ian, observing Lynn's discomfort, approached her with a reassuring smile. "Your healing abilities are far more valuable than any weapon. And Mike, well, let's just say your nature provides us with a different kind of firepower."

Lynn managed a small smile at the pun in Ian's words. Mike, standing tall and composed, nodded in agreement. "I'll stick to what I know best," he said with a hint of humor.

Claire, having finished with the communications checks, joined the group. "We've got a solid plan, and each of us brings something unique to the table. It's about leveraging our strengths and working as a team."

The night passed with a mix of planning and preparation, each moment bringing them closer to the dawn of a critical day. After all was ready, they dispersed to their rooms to get what rest they could.

Ian maneuvered the car, his eyes occasionally darting to the phone in his hand. The dense forest closed in around them.

Emma, maintaining the link with Anja, updated them on the progress. Her face was a mask of concentration. "They're heading north now, off the main highway," she reported.

In their separate vehicle, Ian, Claire, and Dora coordinated their movements, ensuring they weren't too far apart but far enough to avoid detection. The team was well-prepared, but the unpredictability of their situation was a constant weight.

As they followed the route, Ian's instincts kicked in. He had studied maps of the area extensively, and his gut feeling led him to a location on the map.

Dora looked at the location Ian had indicated. "That place," she said, “it’s got a dark history. It’s whispered about in the underground. A place of secrets and, some say, of old, dark magic. It is known as Dwor Szeptów. There are tales of its grim past and its mysterious occupants. It’s deep within dense woods and the perfect place for clandestine activities, away from prying eyes.”

The group halted their vehicles at a safe distance from the turn-off that led to their target, not daring to venture closer and risk detection. Ian scanned the satellite imagery on his phone, his brow furrowed in concentration. The aerial view of the manor and its surroundings only confirmed his suspicions—they were heading into a foreboding stronghold.

“This is going to be a tough one,” Ian finally said, breaking the tense silence. “We need to be extremely careful.”

Claire, over the comms, acknowledged Ian’s assessment. “Agreed. This is not just a physical battle; there might be other elements at play here we’re not fully prepared for.”

It was a vigil now, waiting for the right moment to act. They would soon face a dangerous confrontation that would test their abilities as never before. But despite the risks, they were going to see this through.

The team moved through the dense woods, their steps muffled by the thick undergrowth. The air was heavy with the scent of pine and earth, the forest alive with the sounds of nature, but there was an underlying tension that couldn’t be ignored.

Carlos, Cari, and Emma took the lead, their movements swift and silent. Carlos scanned the skies, hoping to connect with a local raptor, a connection that would be an asset in this treacherous environment. With her drone controller in hand, Cari sent a drone buzzing ahead, its camera providing a bird’s-eye view of the terrain and any potential threats.

Ian, Claire, and Dora chose a parallel path, with Claire in her wolf form leading the way. Her keen senses were advantageous in the dense forest, her amber eyes scanning for any signs of danger. Ian carried their gear, his strength apparent in the ease with which he navigated the rugged terrain. Though less physically imposing, Dora moved with grace.

Mike, Graham, and Lynn were at the rear. Mike's newly awakened abilities were a wild card they hoped to play to their advantage. In his bear form, Graham was a fearsome presence, his massive size a deterrent to any who might cross their path. Lynn, still adjusting to her new reality, followed closely, and her healing abilities promised support.

The forest closed in around them, the trees towering like silent sentinels. The oppressive atmosphere of the woods was disorienting, but Emma's link with Anja kept them oriented toward their destination. The terrain was constantly playing tricks on their senses, and without the link to Anja, they would likely be lost in the forest.

As the daylight began to wane, they reached a vantage point that offered a clear view of Dwor Szeptów. The manor, shrouded in shadows, was an imposing sight. Its walls held secrets that were centuries old, and the team couldn't shake off the feeling of being watched.

They settled into their positions, the drones hovering overhead. While they waited, Claire and Graham shifted back. They had seen no roving guards, and they were more familiar with traditional weapons. Retrieving clothes from their companions, they dressed and armed themselves. The woods around them grew darker, the sounds of the night beginning to emerge. They were in enemy territory now, and every shadow hid danger.

Ian surveyed the scene, his expression one of grim determination. They had prepared as best they could, but the actual test was still to come.

As night fell, the manor and the woods around it seemed to merge into one dark entity.

Helena paced in Dwor Szeptów's sitting room, which was a blend of old and modern. Howard sat reading in a high-backed chair, his face a mask of resigned acceptance. Two armed guards kept vigil, one just outside the door, the other inside the room.

Helena's phone broke the silence, its ringtone echoing off the stone walls. She answered promptly. The agent on the other end reported the unexpected development at the airport. Lucian, Anja, and now Zoe Ananda had been picked up, all of them unarmed and seemingly without any electronic tracking devices.

Zoe's unexpected presence complicated matters, and it also presented an opportunity. "Bring them all." Helena's eyes flickered briefly to Howard, who had paused in his reading, his attention now on her.

The call ended, and Helena turned her attention back to Howard. "It seems our guests have arrived with an additional companion. Zoe Ananda, formerly of the FBI, is with them. I wonder why they chose to bring her here. She was there when Richard was captured and has now joined them completely. Lucian had four bodyguards but is coming here without them as instructed. No matter. Even those four stand no chance of rescuing anyone from here."

"I had hoped Lucian would leave me here and not risk himself or Anja. I am of no real consequence," Howard said.

She wondered if he believed that. He was of significant value to her. "Indeed. Ananda's involvement indicates that Lucian is not acting alone, and they are more organized than I anticipated. I need to understand their motives and capabilities fully. Prepare the reception room," Helena instructed the guard. "Our guests will be here shortly, and we must be ready to receive them."

Later, Helena stood in the grandeur of Dwor Szeptów's entrance hall, flanked by a contingent of guards. Her presence was commanding, an aura of authority and power surrounding her. As the doors opened, Lucian, Anja, and Zoe were ushered in by the two agents who had driven them here, accompanied by four additional guards.

"Howard, it seems we're all pawns in a much larger game," Lucian said, his voice steady yet revealing an underlying frustration.

"I'm sorry you've been caught up in this, Howard," Anja said softly. Howard waved off her concern with a resigned gesture.

Zoe's gaze lingered on Helena. Helena felt the intensity of Zoe's scrutiny, a silent challenge that was both unsettling and intriguing.

Helena addressed the trio. "I regret the circumstances that have brought us together. However, I hope you can appreciate the necessity of our meeting. There are opportunities here that we should explore." Helena gestured towards the interior of the manor. "I suggest you take some time to rest and refresh yourselves. We have arranged accommodations for you. We can convene for a meal this evening and discuss these matters further. I trust you'll find the arrangements to your satisfaction."

As the guards stepped aside to allow Lucian, Anja, and Zoe to be led to their rooms, Helena remained in the hall, her gaze following them until they were out of sight. She then turned to Howard. "Howard, your presence here is invaluable and could help shape the outcome of our discussions tonight."

Howard nodded slowly. "I'll do what I can, Helena. I'm not here by choice, and they are sure to remember that no matter how you try and spin it," he said.

In the ornate dining room of Dwor Szeptów, the atmosphere was thick with tension, veiled under a façade of strained conversation. Guards flanked her as Helena presided at the head of the table. Other guards were positioned in each corner of the room, ready to respond to any signal from her.

As the initial pleasantries dwindled, Helena looked across at each of her 'guests.' "Howard informed me that you attempted to break the oath binding Richard and ultimately chose to release him," she began. "You suspected the Grandmaster might trace him. A wise decision, yet it would have been better if you had just killed him. Your actions have branded you as more than human, entities the Sodality is sworn to destroy. Now, all of you are marked. I could choose to destroy all of you now and be richly rewarded for it."

Zoe spoke up. "Then why the pretense? Why bring us here at all? What do you want?"

Helena gave them a faint, enigmatic smile. "Perhaps to turn you. Or to track down and eradicate all traces of your kind."

Zoe analyzed Helena's words, her eyes searching. "That's not it, though, is it? What do you really want, Helena? Is it to take over? Is there more?"

Helena regarded Zoe with a newfound respect. "You're perceptive,

Ms. Ananda. Power is always a tempting prospect. But one must consider all variables in a game as complex as ours."

She paused, allowing her words to settle with her audience. Helena was a master at the art of conversation, weaving her words to maintain control and keep her listeners engaged and off balance.

"Taking over is a simplistic way to phrase it," Helena continued, her voice low and controlled. "The dynamics of power within the Sodality are intricate. My ambitions...Let's just say they are multifaceted. You see, power is not just about destruction. It's about influence, about shaping the future. The Sodality has vast resources, but it lacks any real vision. I intend to provide that vision. This evening is not just about your survival. It's about opportunity. An opportunity for all of us to redefine the rules of this ancient game we're entangled in."

Howard broke the uneasy silence. "You're trapped by the Sodality too, Helena. It's obvious. You're caught and controlled, just like Richard was."

Helena's response was immediate; her anger was barely contained beneath her polished exterior. "Do not mistake my position, Howard. I have other means to achieve my ends, means you would find most... uncomfortable."

Zoe, her expression steely, said. "Your methods, and those of the Sodality, are barbaric. There's no justification for cold-blooded murder!"

"It's becoming clear that reaching any sort of accord is unlikely," Lucian said with an edge.

"We are more alike than you may realize, Lucian." She crushed the memories of her past that were threatening to resurface in her anger.

In contrast, Anja sat with her eyes closed. Her posture suggested introspection, a silent retreat from the escalating conflict around her.

The room felt like a powder keg, each individual's presence contributing to the tension. Helena's authoritative demeanor was now overlaid with a hint of desperation. Her calculated façade was cracking under the strain of the mounting tensions.

As the heated exchange between Zoe, Lucian, and Helena escalated, the room descended into chaos. Anja found herself seized by Helena's two guards. Before she could react, she was held fast to her chair, and a third guard placed a heavy metal collar around her neck. Anja struggled, her eyes flashing with a dark, almost feral intensity, but the collar snapped into place.

Howard ducked under the dining table while Helena remained seated, her eyes never leaving Anja as the collar was secured.

"Anja!" Lucian lunged toward the guards, but two more closed in on him, one holding another collar. Lucian's hands balled into fists, ready to fight, but he knew the odds were against him. Zoe moved to support him; her own expression hardened with resolve.

"Hold still!" one of the guards barked at Lucian, but he only snarled in response, dodging their attempts to restrain him. His movements were swift, almost inhumanly so. But the guards were relentless, and Lucian found himself struggling to fend them off.

Helena stood up, her gaze icy as she watched the chaos unfold. "You can't fight us all, Lucian. Submit now, and perhaps I'll show you some mercy."

Lucian ignored her, his focus solely on the guards. He managed to knock one to the ground with a powerful punch, but another guard replaced him immediately, pushing him back towards the wall.

Zoe tackled one of the guards. But as she did, another guard came at her.

Anja, now restrained by the collar, looked at Helena, her eyes filled with a mixture of rage and desperation. "Let them go," Anja demanded. "This isn't necessary."

Helena's lips curled into a cold smile. "You misunderstand, Anja. This is very necessary. You all are a threat that needs to be contained."

Before Anja could respond, one of the guards yanked her to her feet, dragging her toward the concealed passageway. She struggled against the grip but to no avail.

Lucian, seeing Anja being taken away, let out a roar of anger. "Anja!" He threw off the guards, adrenaline giving him a momentary advantage. He dashed towards her, but the guards intercepted him, forcing him back once more.

Helena slipped through the melee, her movements calculated and precise. Her exit was almost unnoticed amidst the confusion.

# *Twenty-Six*

ZOE HAD PUSHED the emotional intensity to its peak as the cue for Anja to signal Emma and initiate their escape plan. Hopefully, she had succeeded, but the plan had taken an unexpected turn. Anja had been grabbed and had been taken away.

Anja's sudden disappearance left a void in the chaos; Zoe felt her absence immediately. Zoe's heart lurched as she realized the place Anja usually resided in her was silent—empty. *That strange collar must have done something,* she thought.

Zoe's heart raced as she tried to dampen the heightened emotions she had provoked more effectively than she had anticipated; her own emotions and growing capabilities had combined for devastating effect. She now needed to create a window of opportunity for them to retreat. Lucian was visibly torn between his instinct to rescue Anja and their need to extract Howard.

Zoe managed to foot-sweep and knock the guard coming at her to the floor, leaving him stunned. He had obviously underestimated her. She knelt down and her hand closed around his weapon. The weight of the gun in her hand provided a burst of adrenalin. Two guards tried to restrain Lucian as the last remaining guard took aim at her. She fired two rounds into his chest, and while he spun, his gun fired high. He fell and then lay still on the floor, dead or soon to be. She had just killed a man. It was self-defense, yes, but... She locked down that thought and turned to help Lucian.

The two guards holding Lucian dropped and started twitching at his feet. His eyes were wild as he grabbed their weapons. He stood and looked directly at her, then shot a guard who had pulled a knife behind her. That was the one she had disarmed. She had hesitated to kill him; her FBI training was for law enforcement and not combat.

Lucian turned and scanned the room for any sign of Anja while Howard emerged from under the table. The hidden doorway through which Anja had vanished was now closed.

Outside the dining room, the sounds of battle heralded the arrival of their rescue team. The cracks of gunfire made it clear that the manor had become a battleground. They could hear shouts and orders in some foreign language growing louder.

Zoe and Lucian found themselves back to back, trying to watch for any threats. Zoe's grip on the weapon was firm. Lucian, meanwhile, was a picture of fury, his thoughts focused on finding Anja. With Anja gone and Helena retreated, they were left to rely on their wits and each other to survive the night.

"Lucian, we have to stick to the plan," Zoe urged. "Anja knew the risks. She made us promise to get Howard out." She moved next to Howard to emphasize that.

Just then, Ian and Graham burst into the room. "We've got to move," Ian announced. "There are too many of them. We can't take it by force. Where is Anja?"

Lucian's stare shifted from the direction Anja had been taken to the urgent faces of his allies. Anja had warned him, but the reality was too much to bear. "Taken," he growled.

"Fuck! We can't win this fight, Lucian. We need to go, or we'll all be killed. Now!"

Lucian's frustration erupted into a visceral scream, echoing through the room. His body was taut with the need to act. "Fuck that!" He moved to where Anja had vanished and tore at the wall, looking for anything that would trigger an opening. He pounded and roared again. This time, it was just a roar, seemingly incapable of words.

"It's probably barred from the other side now, Lucian. We can't get through." Zoe laid a hand on his shoulder. She tried to send calming energy but wasn't sure anything was getting through, his rage was so great.

"Lucian, we have to move out and regroup!" Ian shouted.

To punctuate Ian's words, a door opposite Ian burst open. Lucian fired into the guards emerging. As each came into view, they dropped with splashes of blood appearing on the wall behind them. They quickly stopped trying to enter.

Explosions rumbled in the distance. "No more time, Lucian!" Ian urged, guiding a pale-looking Howard toward Graham and the exit.

Lucian turned to follow Ian and Graham, his every step a battle between duty and desire. The team began to move, with Lucian taking one last stare back, a silent vow to return for Anja etched in his expression.

Zoe stayed close to Lucian, her training keeping her alert to their surroundings. She kept a firm grip on the weapon she had procured, ready to use it—wanting to use it. To kill again.

The ongoing battle echoed around them as they fought their way out of the manor. The scent of cordite and the coppery smell of fresh blood filled the air.

This night would leave its scars, seen and unseen. But for now, survival was paramount, and the team moved with a singular intent: to escape and live.

As they navigated through the corridors of the manor, the sounds of conflict from outside filtered in, a constant reminder of the peril they faced, as if the staring bodies and blood were not enough.

Ian led them with the confidence of a combat veteran, his experience providing direction. Graham kept a watch on their rear, ensuring no surprises would catch them off guard from behind.

The group moved with purpose. Zoe's mind was a whirlwind of thoughts, her focus split between the immediate need to escape and the lingering worry for Anja. They had come into this knowing the risks, but the reality of their situation hit her harder than she had expected. She had not thought Anja would actually be left behind. She realized now that Anja might not have told them all of it. She should have probed more, but would deal with that later when they had her back. They would get her back. Zoe would not, could not, consider any other outcome.

They had to trust that Anja's sacrifice would not be in vain. With

Howard in tow, they ran into the night, the darkness enveloping them.

Zoe felt the crack of a bullet slicing through the air, narrowly missing her, its lethal intent thwarted by inches.

In the chaos, Zoe caught sight of an attacker crumpling to the ground behind them, taken out almost casually by Lucian. His expression was grim, but his marksmanship was unparalleled.

Ian and Graham, flanking Howard, moved with urgency towards a waiting vehicle. The night air was split by the sound of high-caliber rounds echoing off the walls that surrounded them.

Then, in a moment that seemed to stretch time, the manor's entrance erupted in a furious blaze. The heat was intense, a wall of fire consuming the path they had just traversed. It was a dramatic, almost cinematic sight, but one that left no room for awe—only action.

Claire provided hope inside an acquired vehicle, its engine roaring to life. As they reached the car, Ian and Graham pushed Howard into the front next to Claire and moved to the back. A crack resonated through the air, and Ian staggered, a bullet finding its mark. The sight of Ian falling jolted Zoe.

Seeing Ian hit, Claire yelled, "No!" She froze for a moment, then shouted, "In! In! Now!"

Graham and Zoe lunged forward, their arms wrapping around Ian's solid frame. They heaved him into the back of the vehicle, his body heavy with the weight of his injury. Lucian was right behind them, his expression a mask of distress.

Claire's voice had cut through the shock. The vehicle lurched into motion even as they struggled to get in and close the doors.

Zoe found herself crammed in the back with Ian, his breathing labored as he grappled with the pain of the wound in his side. She could feel the vehicle accelerating. Claire maneuvered through the maze of obstacles and out of the immediate danger zone.

As they sped away from Dwor Szeptów, Zoe's mind raced with the events that had just unfolded. They had made it out, but not without cost. Ian's injury was a bloody reminder of the peril they still faced. The flames in the rear window served as a haunting backdrop to their escape, fiery evidence of their battle and the sacrifices they had made.

In the confines of the vehicle, surrounded by her companions, Zoe felt a mix of relief and apprehension. They had Howard with them, but Anja's and now Ian's fate was uncertain.

Lucian placed his hand over Ian's wound. His focus was so profound it seemed to draw energy from the very air around them. The sight of Ian's blood, dark and profuse, had sent a shockwave of fear through them all, but Lucian's healing touch was making a difference. The bleeding slowed, then stopped, though the effort was taxing Lucian, draining him of strength. The scent of blood, sweat, smoke, and fear filled the car. The muffled ringing in her ears made everything seem surreal.

Claire's grip on the steering wheel was white-knuckled. The vehicle bounced and swerved along the narrow road as she navigated away from the chaos they had left behind.

With Ian down, Graham called over the radio to coordinate their retreat. The voices of their companions broke through over the noise. Reports of injuries and status updates poured in. Zoe's heart sank at the news of Mike's and Dora's injuries, but there was a sense of relief that they were manageable. Mike had to approach closer to the entrance to help cover their escape. Too close, it seemed, as both he and Dora had been spotted by responding troops. They had both been wounded, and neither was trained in combat. Fortunately, Carlos and Cari had taken down their assailants. Lynn's medical expertise and awakening healing powers were being put to use.

Emma's voice came through, her tone laced with worry and urgency. "Zoe, I can't sense Anja anymore. What's happening?"

That severance of their connection with Anja sent a wave of dread through Zoe. Lucian's roar of frustration and anger echoed in the confined space of the car, a primal sound that spoke of his pain and fear for Anja.

Graham handed the radio to Zoe. "She has been taken. They put some kind of collar on her. Maybe that cut us off. But…I don't know…" Zoe said over the radio.

The silence that followed said it all.

The night had spiraled into chaos, and now they were fleeing, scattered and wounded. Zoe replayed the events in her mind, each moment a haunting fragment.

She had killed a man.

As Claire steered them towards their rendezvous point, Zoe couldn't shake the feeling of impending doom. They had survived, but at what cost? And what of Anja? The uncertainty of her fate loomed large in Zoe's mind, a question mark at the end of a night filled with violence and death. For now, they had to focus on survival. The war was far from over.

Minutes earlier, Anja's world had become a blur of motion and sound. The dining room of Dwor Szeptów, once an elegant space, had transformed into a battleground, reverberating with shouts, crashes, and the unmistakable sound of gunfire.

Anja felt the cold, unyielding grip of a metal collar around her neck. Panic surged as her instincts kicked in. She attempted to summon her succubus form to tap into the mystical energies that had become second nature. But it was futile; the collar had severed her connection to her powers, leaving her vulnerable and exposed.

She struggled against the guard's grasp. Lucian and Zoe, standing together, were a formidable duo. But even their skill and determination were overshadowed by the overwhelming odds.

Helena, her expression a mask of cold calculation, gave a signal, and Anja was dragged away from the mayhem. As they moved through a concealed passage, Anja's heart pounded with fear and fury. She had known this was coming, and it was like reliving a nightmare. The hidden corridors of the manor were like the veins of a dark heart, cold and uninviting.

Anja had to remain calm and think. Her capture was a distraction, pulling Helena away from direct command and whatever powers she might possess. She had not been able to see or understand them. The collar showed that Helena had been prepared to counter the team's powers but likely didn't know their extent.

The passage twisted and turned, the sound of the battle growing fainter with each step. Anja noted every detail, turn, and feature of the passage, even though she also knew there would be no escape. The path was chosen, and it was much too late for regret.

As they emerged into a dimly lit chamber, Anja's captor pushed her forward. She stumbled but regained her balance, adjusting to the darkness. The room was bare, the walls lined with ancient stones. A single, narrow window high up on the wall offered the only glimpse of the outside world.

Anja was alone with her captors, cut off from her allies. In the heart of Dwor Szeptów, she prepared herself. The collar might have bound her powers, but her will remained unchained. Anja knew that survival now depended on her wit and resilience. The game had changed.

Helena's face twisted in a sneer of rage. "You have all squandered your opportunity to be reasonable, to hear my offer. Now, you may all have to die. I cannot allow any of you to escape."

Even in her weakened state, Anja grasped the gravity of Helena's words. She clung to the premonition she had seen—the vision of their successful escape and their pivotal role in freeing Howard. It was a sliver of hope in the dark future she was about to face. There were enough fragments of that vision—that beautiful, ageless woman now identified as Helena—to reaffirm her choice.

Helena paced back and forth, her footsteps echoing off the stone walls. After a tense moment, Helena stopped pacing and issued a command to the guard. "Take her to Zamec Echo in the south. She is to be kept alive." Anja noticed a flicker of murderous intent in the guard's eyes, an eagerness to defy the command.

Before Anja could react, the guard stepped forward with a sudden, vicious strike to the side of her head. Pain exploded in her skull. As the room spun and her vision blurred, Anja's last conscious thought was a defiant vow to survive. And then, with the floor rising to meet her, she succumbed to blackness.

Lucian's hands clenched and unclenched rhythmically. On the satellite phone, his conversation with Jonas Richter, his head of security in New York, was a rapid exchange of clipped sentences. "We need to find her, Jonas. Use every resource, every contact. I want everything you can find on this Helena woman," Lucian demanded.

As Zoe struggled to keep Lucian calm on the flight back to Iceland, the tension in the private jet's cabin was nearly unbearable. The aircraft flew through the skies, but Lucian was miles away, his thoughts fixated on Anja.

Lucian's instructions for his security team back in New York were unequivocal: they were to mobilize immediately, scour every source of information, and leave no stone unturned in their search for Anja and Helena.

Helena matched the description from the detectives Dan and Mark of the woman behind Richard's disappearance. This revelation added another twist to their already daunting situation.

Back in Poland, Ian, Claire, and Emma, aided by a local interpreter arranged by Dora, continued their efforts on the ground. Despite their extensive search, there was no trace of Anja. Emma's link with Anja remained quiescent, adding to Lucian's simmering frustration and helplessness. He realized only in its absence that he had a link to Anja, made apparent by the emptiness he now felt.

Zoe, sitting slightly apart, watched Lucian. Her time with the FBI had prepared her for high-stress situations, but the personal connection to Lucian and Anja made this scenario different. She offered Lucian words of reassurance, trying to ground him in the present and focus on what they could actively do.

In the dim light of the cabin, as the world passed by below them, the uncertainty of Anja's fate hung heavily, pushing them all to their limits as they dealt with this unfolding crisis.

With Zoe urging him to concentrate on what they could do now, Lucian listened intently to Howard. "She's meticulous, Lucian. Her questions were probing, calculated to extract as much information as possible while revealing little," Howard explained, but his face betrayed the stress of the encounter. "She spoke of interest in bindings and oaths. It seems she's exploring ways to strengthen the Sodality's control and seeking methods to break herself free from it. She's aligned with the Grandmaster, Eamon Vale, but I sensed her ambition extends beyond loyalty. She's playing her own deeper game."

Zoe, who had been listening silently, asked. "Did she mention anything about Anja or her plans for her?"

Howard shook his head, his expression grim. "No specifics, but she sees Anja as a piece in whatever game she's playing. And she mentioned contacting Edward, presumably to draw you out."

Lucian's jaw tightened at the mention of his uncle. "She did, and we went. She's underestimating us," he said with a steely edge. "We need to find Anja before Helena makes her next move."

Zoe agreed. "We're dealing with someone much more dangerous than Richard ever was. We need to be smart and unpredictable."

The idea of Howard possessing latent potential, albeit distinct from the otherkin transformations, caught Lucian's interest. "I'll ensure you have access to Anja's notes," Lucian said.

Howard nodded, his expression thoughtful. "Anja once mentioned that my potential might lie in different realms. Maybe in the manipulation of energies or accessing deeper levels of consciousness. I'm speculating now, but I'm willing to try it."

Lucian considered Howard's words. "Your expertise in ancient texts and mystical arts, combined with your latent abilities, could give us an edge. We need every advantage we can get. Traveling alone is no longer an option for you. You'll be staying with us at the lab. We need to consolidate our resources and knowledge. Together, we're stronger."

Howard gave a slight, appreciative nod. "I'm ready to contribute in any way I can. Anja's work could be the key to understanding these powers. And if I can help decipher and utilize them, then that's what I'll do."

# *Twenty-Seven*

HELENA WAS ANXIOUS to arrive. Her driver, the same guard who had knocked Anja unconscious and secured her in the vehicle, ascended the winding road leading to Zamec Echo. The castle emerged from the mist, an imposing structure silhouetted against the dusk. Its towering walls, constructed from dark stone, absorbed the fading light. It was built atop a craggy hill and overlooked the forests below at the edge of a lake where tendrils of mist drifted across its surface.

The castle was divided into several sections, each rising higher than the last, culminating in a great tower. With its walls and strategic position, the tower offered panoramic views of the surrounding countryside.

It had been a mistake not to bring Howard here. She had been overconfident, and it had cost her. She would not make that mistake again. This was the true heart of her power. Let them try and get Anja back. She would be waiting.

The car halted at the grand entrance. In the car's back seat, Anja began to stir, her consciousness slowly returning. The iron collar around her neck would feel heavy, a constant reminder of her captivity, and would suppress any supernatural capabilities that she might possess. What powers she did possess were of intense interest. Her ability to manipulate memories, as demonstrated by Richard, could be of great use.

When the vehicle stopped, two armed guards approached, and Helena got out. Helena directed the guards to take Anja to the cells.

"Ensure she is securely held. Do not underestimate her. That collar must not be removed."

Anja was brought in, still bound. Her body was limp, but her eyelids cracked open, revealing a glimmer of awareness. The guards carried her with a rough efficiency into the castle.

Inside, the main hall was lit by flickering lights recessed in sconces designed to resemble torches. The stone floors echoed the footsteps of their entry.

While stark in some areas, the castle's interior reflected the Gothic style of its era. Vaulted ceilings, arched doorways, and intricate frescoes contributed to the historical ambiance. The rooms, furnished to reflect the period, contained heavy wooden furniture, tapestries, suits of armor, and weapons.

Helena watched Anja closely, assessing her condition with a clinical detachment as they proceeded through the dimly lit corridors. The passageways narrowed, and the guard unceremoniously dumped Anja on her feet and growled, "Walk, or be dragged."

Anja faltered as she was led deeper into the castle, each step taking her further away from freedom and deeper into the heart of Helena's domain. She stumbled and fell to her knees at the bottom of a narrow stone stairway. The guard pulled her to her feet and dragged Anja, now kicking and screaming.

Helena opened a heavy door, which creaked open to reveal a dark chamber. Its walls were lined with assorted implements, and a single, large table dominated the center; she called it her chamber of secrets, but it was a dungeon.

In the castle's depths, away from prying eyes, Helena had plans for Anja.

"Let go!" Anja snarled, her eyes blazing with defiance. Her heart pounded in her chest, but she refused to let fear control her.

"Quiet, pet," Helena commanded. "You and your friends have caused enough trouble for one day. You had your chance to be civil and instead brought violence to the table."

Anja's struggles were futile against the guard's strength. Helena grabbed her by the hair and forced her onto the cold stone floor, the iron collar around her neck clanking as it connected with the ground.

"Look around you," Helena sneered, gesturing to the dimly lit chamber. "This is where you'll pay for your insolence."

Anja's eyes darted from corner to corner, taking in the chilling atmosphere and the instruments of torture that adorned the walls. "I am not your pet!"

"Actions have consequences, Anja, and now you must face them. You are indeed my pet. Put her in that cell. Let her anticipate my next visit," she said to the guard.

He grabbed a handful of Anja's hair, pulled her along the floor to the open door, and shoved her inside.

"Enjoy your stay." The door slammed shut behind Helena, plunging Anja into darkness.

Anja's heart pounded in her chest as she lay on the floor. Her clothes were torn and barely covered her, leaving her feeling vulnerable and exposed.

Her thoughts were consumed with guilt. The hazy futures that had revealed themselves to her had shown only one that did not end in death or worse for them all, and that one only led to pain and into shadows. She had dared not tell them all of what she had seen for fear that they would not have done what they must and left her.

Some interminable time later, the door to the chamber creaked open, and a masked man entered, a chain in hand. His scars and heavily muscled body showcased his brutal nature.

"Helena has sent me," he rasped. "You've caused her quite some trouble, haven't you? I'm going to enjoy myself with you."

"Go ahead," she snapped, eyes flashing with determination. "Do your worst."

The masked man snapped a chain to the ring on her collar before dragging her out of the cell and into the chamber by that leash.

Two other men were waiting outside the cell. Each grabbed an arm and forced her onto the table in the center of the room. Her wrists were secured to clamps above her head. Once those bindings were checked, they fastened her feet to extensions like stirrups on a doctor's examining table, only these had a twisted purpose. The masked man motioned the others back and leered down at her.

"Now, let me see what I have to play with today. Helena hasn't brought me a plaything for a while now, and I'm looking forward to this." Stepping back a pace, he regarded her for a moment. "Should I look first or reveal you with my whip?"

"Fuck you!" Anja spat.

"Oh, we'll get to that. Don't worry," he said, and she heard the others laugh from the room's corners.

He pulled a whip from the wall and raised it, bringing it down with a crack across Anja. She gasped in pain but did not cry out, not giving him the satisfaction.

"Ah, a tough one, eh?" he growled, striking her again and again, each blow sending shocks of fear and pain through her body. The whip stripped away the last tatters of her clothes, leaving red welts in their place. His accuracy and skill were unnerving.

But as the minutes ticked by and the onslaught continued, Anja began to feel something else amidst the brutality—a spark of arousal, an undercurrent of desire. It scared her; this twisted pleasure derived from her suffering, but she found herself unable to resist its call. Endorphins flowed to counteract the pain.

"Is that all you've got?" she taunted.

The masked man paused, his scarred face inches from hers. "You're a sick little cunt, aren't you?" he sneered before resuming his vicious assault.

As the strikes grew more forceful and intense, Anja's resistance crumbled, giving way to the darkness lurking inside her all along. She could no longer distinguish between the pain and pleasure, her body responding to both with equal fervor.

"Please," she gasped, tears streaming down her face.

But even as she surrendered to the twisted desires that threatened to consume her entirely, a small part of Anja clung to the hope that this nightmare would end and that, somehow, she would find her way back from the abyss.

She could hear, muffled in the distance, that a storm raged outside the castle. Thunder echoed through the halls. The chaos of nature mirrored the turmoil and the inner darkness threatening to consume her.

Through all of this, she had not noticed that Helena had entered and was watching until she spoke. “Look at you,” Helena taunted, her voice dripping with disdain. “All that bravado, all those challenges, and now you’re nothing more than a helpless plaything. Do you know how much trouble you’ve caused me?”

Anja gritted her teeth, ignoring the pain radiating from her battered body. “I don’t regret anything.”

“Really?” Helena’s blue eyes flashed dangerously. “You’ve damaged my stronghold, caused the death of many of my underlings, and allowed Howard and Lucian to escape. You think you’ve accomplished something? Well, let’s see how much more pain you can take, shall we?”

“Please,” Anja whispered, her voice cracking.

“Too late for that now,” Helena replied coldly, mistaking the meaning of Anja’s plea, her eyes locked on Anja’s naked, marked, and vulnerable form. “You brought this upon yourself. Continue,” Helena commanded, and the masked man raised his whip above his head.

Anja closed her eyes, bracing herself for the pain that was about to come. But even as she did so, her mind raced with thoughts of vengeance and escape.

The storm outside the castle intensified as if feeding off the tempest inside her. Each crack of thunder was echoed by a crack of the whip as the masked man continued his brutal assault on Anja’s bound body.

“Your defiance has brought this upon you,” Helena sneered. “You could have chosen the easy way, but there is still a use for you. When you are broken, I can use you against the Sodality. I would have preferred an alliance, but perhaps it will be better this way.”

Anja’s emotions churned, mingling hope with anger and betrayal. “An alliance? You think I would ever work with you?”

“Never say never, dear Anja. We both have our reasons to hate them, and they say the enemy of my enemy is my friend.”

Anja shuddered at the thought, all too aware of the twisted logic behind Helena’s words. But even as she considered it, the man resumed his torture, forcing her attention back to the present moment. He stopped and opened his trousers to free his erection. It was very obvious he was aroused by the torture he was inflicting upon her. His rough hands gripped her thighs, spreading them wide as he forced himself inside her without mercy.

Anja gasped at the sudden intrusion. "Helena..."

"Quiet!" Helena hissed, a strange mixture of arousal and revulsion flickering across her face as she watched. "You're mine now, to do with as I see fit, and right now, that means breaking you."

As the rapist continued his brutal assault, Anja's mind raced. If she could find a way to turn the tables on Helena, she could use her twisted desires against her. But for now, all she could do was survive.

Anja clenched her fists as she tried to resist the pain and humiliation of the rapist's relentless assault. The iron collar around her neck was heavy, cold metal biting into her skin. She could feel the weight of Helena's gaze on her as if she was feeding off Anja's suffering. Without the collar, she knew she could reverse it and hungered to feed. She could only endure.

"Fight it all you want," the rapist growled in her ear, his hot breath reeking of stale tobacco and alcohol. "But I know you're enjoying this."

As much as Anja wanted to deny it, part of her found a perverse pleasure in the pain and degradation. The more he hurt her, the more her body responded—a dark thrill coursed through her veins and turned the pain into pleasure fed by the buzz of endorphins and the twisted call from the shadows of her being.

"Isn't that right?" he taunted, adding a slap across her face for emphasis.

"Fuck you!" Anja screamed, but even as the words left her lips, she knew they were hollow. Defiance flared hotter, mingling with the unwanted arousal that continued to build.

"Such a spirited one," Helena observed from the shadows. "You have surprised me, Anja. I must admit there's something...enticing about seeing you like this."

"Get away from me!" Anja yelled, her voice cracking as she struggled against her bindings in vain to fend off the muscular man. It should have been unbearable, yet her body continued to betray her.

Despite her resistance, she found herself surrendering to the intoxicating mix of fear and arousal.

"You deserve this," the rapist sneered, tightening his grip on her breasts. "Deep down, you want it."

Anja's body trembled as the masked man continued to inflict his perverted desires. However, something began to change—she started to feel a power growing inside her as every wound and strike fueled her darkness. The orgasm that burst through her body convulsed her around her rapist and shivered her body. Her scream echoed off the walls.

Helena watched intently as Anja's eyes glazed over with lust despite her brutal treatment. Even through the haze, Anja could see that the sight of her body stirred something unfamiliar deep within Helena, an arousal that was making her question everything. As the rapist fumbled with his next move, she saw Helena's frustration grow. Anja's desires were screaming for more.

"Enough! This is not working the way it should." Helena stalked forward, her black dress trailing behind her. She shoved the man aside, taking his place between Anja's trembling legs.

The rapist stepped back, startled by her sudden action. Anja raised her head in surprise. But as Helena approached, it became clear that her intentions were not borne of mercy.

"Please…" Anja gasped, struggling to catch her breath. "Don't… Don't do this."

"Silence." Helena smirked cruelly as she ran a hand down Anja's sweat-slicked and blood-spattered body. "I'll show you what true submission feels like."

As Helena began, arousal coursed through her veins. Her body ached and screamed for respite; she craved the intensity of Helena's touch. With each slap, scratch, and degrading word, Anja was sinking deeper into the abyss of desire.

"Look at you," Helena sneered, her fingers digging into the tender flesh of Anja's inner thighs. "So desperate, even after all I've done to you."

Anja panted with arousal and fear.

"What are you?" Helena paused to consider. "There's something about you, something I can't understand." She leaned down, lips brushing against Anja's ear as she whispered, "You fascinate me."

Helena abruptly rose and stepped away, leaving Anja panting and desperate. The storm continued to rage outside, a fitting backdrop to the turmoil raging within.

"Get out," Helena ordered the rapist and two guards, who hesitated before scurrying away. Alone with Anja once more, Helena stood near, her expression conflicted.

"Let us see what another approach will do," Helena whispered, her cold fingers brushing against Anja's heated flesh, smearing blood. The touch sent shivers down Anja's spine, a contrast to the brutal treatment she had been subjected to.

As Helena began her cruel seduction, Anja's mind reeled. The line between pleasure and pain blurred further, her battered and bloody body reacting to Helena's touch, even as her soul recoiled in horror. Something inside her unfurled.

*"Let go, Anja,"* the sultry voice in her mind whispered. *"Take control. Make it your own."*

Pain, pleasure, and shame melded into one, fueling Anja's arousal as Helena's fingers thrust in and out inside her.

"Someday," Anja taunted, shaky but defiant, "things will be different."

Helena's blue eyes widened momentarily before a smirk played on her lips. "Oh, I have all the time in the world," she promised darkly.

Anja let out a guttural moan, her body writhing with Helena's touch. The darkness grew more potent. She couldn't explain why the pain and humiliation—and the pleasure—were awakening something, but it was becoming impossible to ignore.

"Are you enjoying this, Helena?" Anja managed to gasp out between moans, staring into her eyes. "Do you like having me like this?"

Helena hesitated, torn between the need to maintain control and the desire to give in to something that called to her from Anja.

"More than I should," Helena finally admitted, barely audible.

Their eyes remained locked, a silent battle of wills playing out.

The darkness grew more potent each moment. Anja heard it again:

a soft, seductive whisper deep inside her mind. *"Anja…Embrace your nature. You only thought you had before. There is more, much more, and you need more—all of it,"* the voice murmured, its words curling around her like tendrils of smoke. *"Make it your strength."*

*"Who…who are you? What are you?"* Anja thought, confused.

*"I am you, and can help if you heed me. Accept me."*

*"Am I going insane?"*

*"Perhaps,"* came the teasing and enigmatic reply. *"But what does it matter? This is why you came here. To find me. Us."*

Anja hesitated for just a moment before giving in, allowing the darkness to grow stronger. As she did, the orgasm that took her opened the door to that change as her body spasmed around Helena's fingers. Not a change in body. She was still locked in the collar, or the situation would be much different.

"Helena," Anja snarled. "You think you've broken me? You will never control me."

"Anja…what have you become?" Helena whispered.

"Something unexpected," Anja replied. "And something you'll never forget."

The storm outside mirrored the chaos here, their desires and power shifting like the wind.

Anja just gave Helena a menacing grin. Her body glistened with sweat and blood, yet she was strong and unbroken.

Helena's arousal was displayed by her quickened breath and the heat that radiated from her body. She couldn't hide it.

"I underestimated you," Helena admitted. "But don't think for a moment that this is the end."

Anja stared at Helena. "I wouldn't dream of it."

Helena turned and abruptly left the room, and Anja heard her tell the three outside to lock her back in her cell.

"Very well," the masked one replied as Helena's footsteps echoed off the stone walls before fading away.

Anja lay barely conscious in the dark cell, the distant rumble of thunder fading. The horrific experiences she had endured were beyond the grasp of human understanding, pushing her to the edge of her sanity. But she was no longer just human. Amidst this darkness, a new, alien aspect of her being began to stir.

The voice, a dark echo that emerged from the depths of her very soul, whispered seductively, urging her to embrace a part of herself that she had always known existed but never fully acknowledged. It was another part of her succubus nature, a part of her being that, until now, had only stirred occasionally. But in this hour of extreme anguish and isolation, it sought to assert itself as a separate, commanding presence.

*"Listen to me, Anja,"* her demon coaxed. *"You are not just a victim of these atrocities. You are more, so much more. Accept me. Fully embrace yourself. Let me show you the path to survival and true power."*

Anja, her mind spinning with pain and confusion, was drawn to the voice. It promised strength, a means to endure and overcome her captors. She knew that yielding to this darker aspect carried risks. It was a path that could lead her away from her humanity into realms of existence that were as terrifying as they were enticing.

It continued, now more insistent. *"You have the power, Anja—to seduce, control, and dominate. Let me guide you. Together, we can turn this agony into a weapon. Embrace your true nature. All of it."*

Anja felt an energy coursing through her, awakening primal instincts and desires. The cell, with its oppressive shadows and lingering echoes of her torment, shrank, becoming less a prison and more a crucible where a new aspect of her being was being forged.

As the thunder outside rumbled again, Anja closed her eyes and surrendered to the dark whispers that promised her survival and vengeance. She accepted the terrifying and exhilarating truth: she was not alone in her fight, for her demon had awoken, ready to unleash its fury upon those who had dared to chain her.

*"You must understand, Anja,"* it murmured. *"The woman, Helena, is not what she seems. Her presence is shrouded. There is a void where her aura should be, as if deliberately obscured, hidden from any prying senses by some powerful enchantment. She is more than mere flesh and blood."*

Despite her weakened state, Anja focused on these words. Helena's enigmatic nature had been a puzzle, but now, with her demon shedding light on the matter, she began to piece together a clearer image of her captor. Helena was cloaked in deception and wielded supernatural powers.

*"The collar around your neck is a clever trap. Forged of iron and laced with silver, it is designed to suppress your true power. But even the most intricate lock has its weakness."*

Anja reached for the cold metal encircling her throat, tracing the intricate filigree. The demon's words ignited a spark within her.

*"Focus on the silver,"* it urged. *"It is the key. A single flaw, a slight mar in its pattern, and you may be able to tap into some part of your power. It won't free you entirely but could give you the edge you need."*

The idea seemed impossible, but Anja clung to it like a lifeline. Her fingers explored every curve and line of the pattern, searching for any imperfection that could be exploited. The demon guided her touch, sharpening her senses to detect the slightest anomaly.

*"Be ready, Anja,"* it whispered as she continued her delicate task. *"When the time comes, we will unleash our fury upon them. Together, we are unstoppable."*

She now knew the purpose of her visions. The other paths would have led to death or other horrors, but this one, now that she understood—was it worth it?

Anja marred the silver filigree on the collar just enough to disrupt the enchantment binding her powers, yet not so much as to make it obvious. She continued wearing the collar, maintaining the illusion of being a captive while secretly regaining access to some of her power.

With her additional abilities, Anja prepared. She was no longer just a victim of her circumstances but a warrior, ready to fight for her survival. The demon had brought forth her dark side, and she embraced it fully, ready to unleash her wrath upon the woman who had imprisoned her. She had thought she had embraced her nature when she accepted her sexuality and the power that it provided, but in truth, it was only half.

In the darkness of her cell, Anja's battered form lay naked and exposed to the chill air. In this vulnerable state, as she drifted into restless sleep, her inner demon took control.

*At first, Anja fought her demon's influence and reached out to Lucian, also dreaming somewhere far, far away. She felt a faint connection, but her demon, now loose, morphed the dream into a nightmare replaying her rape and torment. To her horror, Anja felt it all again, and now Lucian would too. Her body's response of turning pain to ecstasy was reinforced. Her hunger was such that she tried to feed on Lucian, but with the collar, it was only a trickle and tasted raw. Before she could draw much strength, the connection was shattered by his screaming. Her heart felt like it would explode from that scream. She gave in to the demon, not fighting it anymore in her despair.*

*Trapped by the collar in this cell, she remained confined to her human shape. But her body began to shift in her dream, warping into something darker—a demon born of hellfire, fierce and unrecognizable. This was no mere echo of her usual form; it was something entirely new, an unsettling, primal version, fearsome in its raw power.*

*Her dreamscape became a theater of war, a place where her demon could impart ancient knowledge and experience. Scenes of skirmish and battle played out in her dreams, each more brutal than the last. Anja found herself amid ferocious combat; her newly discovered form unleashed havoc upon her foes, and she relished the destruction. These were not just dreams but lessons; each scenario trained her mind, instincts, and reflexes.*

*She reveled in the carnage, feeding on the bloodlust that surged. Lust. The line between sex and violence blurred. A sense of power and savagery took root with every enemy she vanquished in her dreams. Her humanity was slipping away, replaced by a primal force.*

*Her life before this transformation, a life filled with passion, love, and connection, faded into the background. She was losing touch with the woman she had once been. The memories of her past appeared distant and unreal, like fragments of a daydream.*

Yet, amidst the tumult of her dreams, a part of Anja clung to her humanity. The warmth of Lucian's embrace, the tenderness of Zoe's touch, the laughter and camaraderie of her friends—all these memories flickered like candles in the dark, refusing to be extinguished by the encroaching darkness. These were the remnants of her true self, a beacon that could guide her back from the abyss.

The battle for her soul was just beginning.

# *Twenty-Eight*

IN THE DEPTHS of a troubled sleep, Lucian's subconscious mind conjured images too harrowing for his waking self to grasp fully. He tossed and turned. Zoe, lying beside him, could only offer the warmth of her presence, her arms wrapped around him, attempting to provide solace.

In his dreams, Lucian witnessed unthinkable horrors being inflicted upon Anja. The vivid scenes of her suffering under her tormentors' hands played out like a grotesque opera of pain and despair. He saw Anja, the woman he had grown to love deeply, enduring unspeakable acts of violence and cruelty.

The images were so graphic, so visceral, that he felt each blow, each violation as if it were happening to him. Her pain was his pain, her despair mirrored in the depths of his being. The nightmare clawed at his sanity. What was worse, the pain and torture aroused him—part of him wanted to be the one with the whip.

And then, when the dream seemed to grant that wish, he felt Anja orgasm around her tormentor—him. Lucian awoke with a scream that tore through the night. His body was drenched in sweat, his breathing ragged, and his erection painfully rigid. Zoe tightened her grip, trying to anchor him to the present. She tried to soothe him, but the echoes of the nightmare still raged.

As he lay there, trying to steady his breathing and racing heart, Lucian realized the true extent of his feelings for Anja. She was more than just a partner or lover; she had become integral to his existence.

The thought of losing her was a prospect too painful to bear. His erection faded slowly, and even though Zoe would welcome him into her body, he could not contemplate that now. First, they had to get Anja back to reunite their triad.

"Lucian, we *will* get Anja back. You have to believe that." Zoe traced the contours of his face, wiping away the cold sweat that clung to his skin. In the dim light, her eyes shimmered with tears—tears for Anja, him, and the ordeal that bound them. "You must remember, Lucian, Anja made this choice for a reason. She knew the risks but knew it was the only way to give us a chance."

Zoe's unwavering faith in Anja warred with the helplessness that gnawed at him. He wanted to believe and hold onto the hope that Anja was still fighting and surviving.

"Trust in her, Lucian. Anja is strong, and she's doing this for us—all of us."

The sincerity in Zoe, the love and determination carried in her words and touch, slowly began to seep into Lucian's consciousness. He could feel the icy grip of despair loosening, giving way to a flicker of hope, however fragile.

Zoe pulled him closer. Lucian closed his eyes, allowing the warmth of her body and the strength of her conviction to fill him.

"We will find her, Zoe," he finally said, stronger now. "I trust Anja, and I trust you. We will bring her home."

Tension prevailed in the conference room as Zoe led the meeting. Howard sat across from her, recounting his experience with Helena. Lucian, Elín, Dora, and other team members listened intently.

Zoe leaned forward. "Howard, you mentioned Helena's interest in binding spells. Could there be more to it?"

Howard shifted uncomfortably in his seat. "It's hard to say for sure. But there was a sense that she might be struggling against something, maybe bonds placed on her like Richard."

Zoe nodded thoughtfully, her mind racing. "Anyone close to the Grandmaster would be forced to take oaths forcing their loyalty to be granted any trust or position of power in the organization. But if that is true, how is Helena seemingly operating in her own interests? Or is it an even deeper game? Richard was completely loyal, but she is different. How?"

There was no response from around the table, but she hadn't expected one either.

"That would indicate a conflict inside the Sodality," she mused aloud. "Helena's seeming autonomy in resource mobilization, her deviation from the Sodality's goals, suggests she's not just a mere executor of Eamon's will but maybe portraying herself that way to maintain his trust. It does show they are not all-powerful."

Lucian interjected, frustrated. "But what could her endgame be? Seizing control of the Sodality, or something more destructive?"

"That's the million-dollar question. Her actions hint at personal ambitions to take over or a desire to dismantle the organization for reasons unknown. She is a power player, as demonstrated by her ability to find and capture Howard and spirit him out of Italy and into Poland. She moved Richard out of New York City through Lithuania. Did Richard end up in Moscow or some other location? All questions begging for answers."

Graham leaned in, his expression serious. "What about her use of torture and rape, from what Lucian described? Brutal, but then some women are prone to exaggerated cruelty to compensate for being a woman, especially in gangs or similar organizations where they feel they need to prove themselves. On the other hand, she was also willing to treat Howard well and use enticement. How does that square with your thinking?"

Zoe's lips pressed into a thin line. "Simply put, she's a functional psychopath. I'm not diagnosing her with a mental illness with that label because then I would need to say antisocial personality disorder, the current term. It shows that she will use whatever she can to achieve her objectives. It's hard to tell if those goals are hers personally, the Sodality's, or a mix. From my observations of her, I would say her self-interest, above all else, drives her. She is more controlled than a typical sociopath and has more resources."

Zoe paused to let that sink in. "Fortunately for Anja, if I can call it that, there is a purpose to what she does, even if we don't know what it is. Anja also had a purpose for putting herself in this situation. She did not tell us what it was, though. In hindsight, it appears she wanted to be captured and knew we would never go along with that."

Zoe went on. "Other things I noted about Helena that were off… Her accent, or lack of one when she spoke perfect English, was unusual. She was fluent in other languages, such as when she talked to the guards. Her movements were all measured. Her facial expressions were controlled. Her eyes gave away nothing unless she wanted to impart some affected feeling. I tried and failed to read her as a profiler, even using my enhanced skills and empathic ability; she was a complete blank."

Zoe's remarks caused surprised looks around the table, but she continued. "When I *really* looked at her, she seemed physically younger, but her hair and makeup made her look older. Like a teen pretending to be thirtysomething. Why?"

Dora, who had been observing up to this point, sucked in a breath and exclaimed, "Wampir!"

"No, I don't think so. I did not get that sense from her. I don't think Eamon could accept her as a part of the Sodality if she were. Then again, she was very good at covering whatever she is. If she could hide it even from Eamon…" Zoe stated.

Howard added, "Vampires may have once existed but hopefully have been completely wiped out." Howard winced at his words. "I guess that came out wrong. If they did exist and were wiped out, it was because of the Sodality."

Elín spoke up. "So we're dealing with someone who's not just powerful, but also convoluted and unpredictable. Supernatural in some way on top of it all."

Zoe laughed and then sobered. "That is the short answer, yes. We need to understand it all. Every detail we get brings us closer to seeing what is behind her façade."

The room fell into a contemplative silence as they considered Zoe's analysis. They were up against formidable opponents.

"We might need to split up to triangulate Anja's position more accurately," Zoe suggested. "Emma and I can sense her now, but it's very faint. Getting closer might help us pinpoint her. Emma said somewhere south of her location in Poland." The possibility that Anja's location was now beyond Poland, maybe into Eastern Europe or even Turkey, weighed heavily on Zoe. They only had a direction to go on but not distance.

Lucian nodded. "We need to pursue every lead, no matter how slim."

Howard leaned forward, lines of worry etched on his face. "I regret not being able to bring my records. They could have been useful in this situation. I've been going through Anja's notes, and I believe I can perform a ritual similar to what she did for herself. It might give us another edge, possibly even a way to strengthen our connection with her. I also ran across an entry about Teodora…er, Dora. If it works for me, I may want to try it with her."

Zoe considered Howard's proposition. "That could be valuable. Combined with what is in Anja's notes, your insights might give us a breakthrough."

Lucian agreed. "We'll plan out our movements strategically. Zoe, coordinate with Emma in Poland to find Anja's location. Based on Emma's report, have them move in that direction if they are not already heading that way. Howard, start preparing for the ritual. We'll support you in any way we can. New doses of the serum have arrived, so I can prep a dose for you."

"I'm ready to try the awakening ceremony now," Howard declared. "Anja has documented what she did very well. Is there a spare room somewhere?"

Elín replied, "I can show you to a room that might be suitable. Lucian can prepare the serum for you."

Lucian said, "Howard, I hope it works for you. If you were an animal otherkin, I could assist, but you seem to be some other kind."

Elín led Howard out to guide him to the requested office while Lucian went to fetch the serum.

Howard watched warily as Lucian drew the serum from a small

vial. Lucian studied him, tuning the formula to his genetics.

After about a minute of study, the serum took on a faintly sparkling red glow. Howard nodded, and Lucian injected it.

As the serum flowed through Howard's veins, he noticed Lucian's concerned expression. Howard offered a warm smile and said, "I'll succeed."

After Lucian had departed, Howard opened Anja's messenger bag and retrieved her notebook. He opened it, revealing the sketches she had taken from the Ashton Grimoire. He also took out the *Ars Notoria* that he had entrusted to Anja when they first met. The ancient text contained rituals and formulas, and the diagrams showed a method to unlock potential.

Howard tried to relax as the liquid tingled through his veins. As he waited, he felt a change and knew the serum was taking effect.

Considering the ritual he was about to attempt, the same one Anja had used on herself, the comfortable furniture around him felt oddly out of place. He chuckled, envisioning stone walls, candles, and incense burning in a brazier.

Howard began the ritual for eidetic memory and fast learning described in the *Ars Notoria*. His eyes traced the intricate symbols, his mind absorbing the archaic words.

Howard recited the angelic names; his voice remained steady, resonating within him. The symbols on the pages came alive and glowed softly.

During this transcendent experience, Howard felt an inexplicable connection; his mind was linked with a vast, untapped reservoir of knowledge. The physical world receded as he traversed a state of pure thought, where knowledge flowed freely, and memories crystalized into understanding. Howard opened himself to the full scope of his potential, expanding his mind to absorb details with astonishing speed.

As the ritual ended, Howard was pulled back to the physical world, his body quivering from the profound experience. These feelings were just like what Anja had recounted in her notes about her awakening—minus the arousal.

Howard closed his eyes and relaxed into a recliner, replaying the ritual. He revisited Anja's research on Otherkin, which cataloged various types.

History intertwined with his current reality. Pages turned in his mind, revealing drawings and names of demons. Then the realization struck him—his lineage was not just steeped in the arcane but was intrinsically linked to it. It wasn't based on angels or demons of Christianity but instead on the beings from whom they were derived —the daevas from Sumerian times.

Now a sorcerer awakened, Howard pondered the mechanics of spellcasting. How would his unique lineage influence his magic? He reasoned that his spells might draw from a deep well of power shaped by the daeva magic coursing through his blood. His spells might manifest differently from 'traditional' sorcery, perhaps more intuitive and directly connected to his emotions and innermost thoughts.

The daevas of Sumerian times were woven into the fabric of the oldest myths and legends. As Ashton had in his diary, he speculated that those daevas, once revered or feared as gods or demons, might have mingled with humans.

This lineage, he pondered, would have been a closely guarded secret among the elite in those times. The idea that such powers were reserved for a select few and passed down through generations in secrecy was increasingly plausible. It was a compelling thought—that all Otherkin were, at their core, descended from the daevas.

The Sodality's desire to eliminate these powers, he realized, stemmed from a deep-seated fear of the unknown and the uncontrollable. To them, those with such abilities represented a threat to the established order, a challenge to their rigid worldview. They were not merely puritans seeking to cleanse the world; they were power brokers vying to control or destroy any source of power that lay beyond their grasp. It wasn't just a battle against the paranormal but a war against a legacy as old as civilization itself—a war and a legacy he and the others had unknowingly inherited.

Howard's thoughts lingered on the irony of it all. The organization bent on eradicating the supernatural was still secretly using it. It was a battle to maintain exclusive control of that power.

The implications were staggering. Within him lay the capacity for magic and a connection to a forgotten era when humans and daevas were intertwined.

# *Twenty-Nine*

IN THE CONFERENCE room, Howard returned with a new sprightliness that surprised everyone present.

"I've succeeded," Howard announced. "The ritual worked. I can feel...I can sense things I couldn't before." He went on to give a summary of his new insights.

Lucian's expression held a hint of skepticism. "A sorcerer, you say? I suppose I shouldn't be surprised, given your background and interests, Howard."

"Yes. It seems I've tapped into something...elemental. Something ancient—primal."

"And how does this...sorcery manifest?"

"It's like accessing a deep well of knowledge and power. I can't really explain it, but I feel a connection to ancient magics, the kind lost to time."

Zoe interjected, "Your entire demeanor has changed, Howard. You seem more...grounded, more present."

"I see things with greater clarity now. And I believe that with some testing and practice, I'll be able to harness this power effectively." Howard's eyes gleamed. "I intend to explore every facet of this. We have a mission, and if my abilities can help to free Anja, then I will do everything I can to make that happen."

The room was silent for a moment. "As for the specifics," Howard concluded, "I need to study and experiment with spellcasting. But rest assured, I'll put this power to good use."

Lucian nodded. “We’ll provide you with whatever resources you need, Howard.”

“What about Dora? Anja’s notes held an entry for her, although…” Howard hesitated, remembering Anja’s notes.

“Although?” Lucian asked.

“Perhaps it would be best to wait. I need to practice, and since we are in a hurry, well…”

Lucian’s eyes narrowed. “If you think that it can wait. She would still be an excellent candidate. Her genetic profile showed great but unrecognized potential. She has been an invaluable asset even without being awakened, and I’m sure she will continue to be either way.”

“We’ll wait for Anja then,” Howard said, nodding.

Howard stood in a spacious room at the lab, relying on his memory instead of ancient texts. His newfound abilities had sharpened his mind, and he could recall spells and incantations with remarkable clarity. He took a deep breath, feeling a mixture of excitement and trepidation. This was it—the moment to put his newfound abilities to the test.

He started with something simple. Holding out his hand, he attempted to conjure a small ball of light. Nothing happened. He chanted a few words, recalling the incantations he had read about in his studies—still, nothing.

“This is just like those stories from my students,” Howard muttered, recalling how they would excitedly recount their adventures in Dungeons and Dragons, asking him about various spells. “If only it were as simple as rolling a die and shouting ‘abracadabra.’”

With a determined look, he tried again. This time, a faint glow appeared in his palm before flickering out. Howard’s eyes widened in surprise. “Well, that’s a start.”

He couldn’t help but chuckle, remembering how his students would debate the intricacies of casting spells in their game. “Maybe the creators of D&D did their homework after all,” he mused, feeling a strange connection to his student's games.

Howard took a deep breath and focused again. This time, he envisioned the ball of light more clearly, willing it into existence. To his delight, a small orb materialized in his hand, casting a soft glow around the room.

"I did it!" he exclaimed, grinning from ear to ear. He tossed the ball of light into the air, watching it float before dissipating.

Encouraged by his success, Howard decided to try something more ambitious. He attempted to summon a small gust of wind, waving his hand. A breeze rustled through the room, causing papers to flutter.

"This is incredible," he said, his confidence growing. "Let's see what else I can do."

He tried a fire spell next, recalling a particularly enthusiastic student who loved to play a fire mage. Howard raised his hand, concentrating on conjuring a small flame. At first, nothing happened. He frowned, muttering under his breath. Suddenly, a burst of fire erupted from his hand, much larger than he intended.

"Whoa!" he shouted, waving his hand frantically. The flames shot up, singeing his eyebrows and setting off the lab's sprinkler system and alarm. Water cascaded from the ceiling, soaking him and everything else in the room.

The alarm blared, adding to the chaos. Howard stood there, dripping wet, his eyebrows noticeably missing. He couldn't help but laugh at the absurdity of the situation.

"Well, that didn't go as planned," he said, shaking his head. "I guess I need more practice with the fire spells."

As he tried to wring out his shirt, a lab employee burst into the room with a fire extinguisher, looking around before spotting Howard. "What happened here?"

Before Howard could respond, Lucian and Zoe rushed in. Zoe took one look at Howard and burst out laughing. "Howard, did you have too much fun with your new powers?"

Lucian raised an eyebrow, trying to suppress a smile. "Looks like you might need more practice before you try that again."

Howard sighed, still dripping wet. "Yeah, no kidding. Maybe we should move this outside next time."

Zoe nodded, still chuckling. "Definitely. At least that way, there's not much you can damage. The lava fields might be a good idea."

"Yes, and it's a good thing this was not one of the labs with electronics, which would have had halon rather than water. That would have been not good. It would have smothered the fire but could have suffocated you as well. We might want to send Mike out with you as a chaperone and safety observer. He can take the heat, if you know what I mean." Lucian patted Howard on the back. "Come on, let's get you dried off. We can try again later but with more space next time."

As they led him out of the drenched room, Howard couldn't help but feel embarrassed, though he was more determined than ever. Despite the setbacks, he was committed to mastering his abilities and discovering his limits. At the moment, they seemed many.

*How come I can't recall a spell to banish water?* he thought. Maybe that was a good thing. He didn't want to end up as a desiccated mummy.

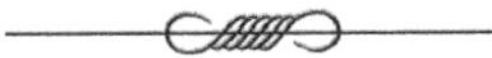

In the conference room, Zoe stood at the head of the table, her expression focused.

Howard's eyebrows—or rather, the noticeable lack of them—caught the occasional glance. Mike, who had accompanied Howard on his excursion, stood at the side, giving his report with a smirk. "So, aside from some impressive fireworks and a few burning bushes, it looks like Howard's getting a better handle on his powers. No more lost hair for now. But given how short on time we are, further practice will have to wait."

Howard shrugged, the corners of his mouth lifting in a sheepish grin. "Yeah, I think we've had enough pyrotechnics for one day."

Zoe cleared her throat. "We've been digging to try and attach a full name to Helena, since she was reluctant to divulge it," she said sarcastically. "Rumors and reports for the areas surrounding Szczytno indicate the Zvaigzne Syndicate controls the region. Dwor Szeptów features prominently in rumors of dark happenings. Dora provided some additional information on that.

"Jonas and his team have managed to trace the ownership of Dwor Szeptów through a series of shells to a Helena Dröger," Zoe said, looking at the faces around her. "It's becoming clear that Dröger might not be her real name. There are indications she is the leader of the Zvaigzne Syndicate. Intel points to Syndicate activity primarily in Eastern Europe—Latvia, Poland, and Russia. But details are scarce. She's careful, covering her tracks well."

"What about her whereabouts?" Lucian asked.

Zoe shook her head. "That's still a mystery. If she is still in Poland, she will probably go where she has a power base. The Syndicate is also active in Warsaw and Kraków. The last report from Ian was that they had passed Warsaw and were heading toward Kraków. If all this is accurate, Helena has access to both Syndicate and Sodality resources and will be impossible to track if traveling by car and staying in Poland, so they will continue the search by using Emma's link to Anja."

Lucian reached for his phone, dialing the team in Poland.

"Dwor Szeptów was empty; Emma said Anja was still to the south as we passed Warsaw. We're heading toward Kraków now," Ian relayed through the speakerphone, sounding frustrated. "We have no direct leads on Helena's current location, but we are assuming she is with Anja."

Lucian's jaw tightened. "Get to Kraków. You may be able to narrow down a location as you get closer to Anja," he instructed. "See if you can pick up more rumors on the Zvaigzne Syndicate there. It appears that Helena is its leader. They are very dangerous, so watch your backs and stay safe. We're not just dealing with the Sodality; we're up against an entire criminal network as well." Lucian stood. "We'll continue to gather intel. Zoe, keep pushing on the Syndicate angle. We need to know who we're dealing with."

"The Syndicate...they have a reputation for being ruthless, more than any other group in Eastern Europe," Dora began, her eyes sweeping across the room. "I always thought the stories about them were just...exaggerated. Tales meant to instill fear."

Zoe leaned forward. "What kind of stories?"

"Stories of sorcery, black magic. They say the Syndicate has powers that make them untouchable. I've heard whispers about members rising from the dead to exact revenge on their killers."

A chill ran through the room. Zoe exchanged a glance with Lucian. "Do you believe these stories now?" Zoe asked.

Dora nodded slowly. "After what I've seen, learned, and even experienced myself now, I think some of these tales might be more than just rumors. It would be dark—evil."

Lucian folded his arms, deep in thought. "This changes our approach."

The Syndicate, entwined with black magic, posed a threat they couldn't underestimate. They needed to proceed carefully, balancing the urgency to find Anja with the need to understand and counter the Syndicate's powers. Zoe knew it would be dangerous, but they had no choice.

Howard turned to face the group. "The name 'Dröger' could very well be a variation of 'draugr.' In Norse mythology, 'draugr' refers to a type of undead creature. The legends say draugr were once warriors, known for their greed and brutality in life, and in death, they rise from their graves as powerful, malevolent spirits."

Lucian leaned in. "You think there's a connection between these legends and the Syndicate's rumored abilities?"

Howard nodded. "It's likely. The tales describe the draugr as possessing superhuman strength, and they were said to be guardians of their treasure, attacking those who dared to disturb their rest."

Zoe interjected, "So the Syndicate's rumored resurrection of their dead members aligns eerily well with the characteristics of the draugr."

"The tales also spoke of them being resistant to conventional weapons," Howard added. "Only a hero or a sorcerer could vanquish them, often requiring magical or unconventional means."

The room was silent as they absorbed the implications.

Lucian broke the silence. "If this is true, our approach needs to account for this. We can't just rely on conventional tactics." Lucian stood and announced that his jet was fueled and ready to go. "I won't leave Anja in their hands. In the last forty-eight hours, she has been beaten, tortured, raped, and who knows what other vile atrocities she has endured. Staying here will not help her. We need to be on the ground and ready to act as soon as we can find her. I hope that by the time we arrive in Poland, Ian will have better news. Elín, Sigri, as with last time, you'll coordinate from here."

Elín stood as they all got up. "Get her back, Lucian," she said solemnly.

Lucian's private jet sliced through the clouds, ferrying its passengers towards England. Lucian's thoughts were turbulent, mirroring the skies outside.

Sitting across from him, Zoe tapped away on a laptop, her brow furrowed in concentration. The rest of the team occupied various seats, some resting while others engaged in quiet conversation.

The satellite phone on his seat buzzed with an incoming call. It was Ian, calling from Poland.

"Ian, report," Lucian snapped.

"We've pinpointed Anja's location," Ian said. "Near Niedzica, Poland. We're closing in."

A wave of relief washed over him. "Good work. We're still en route to England, but will change planes and be airborne again soon. We'll meet you there."

"The nearest airport is in Kraków. We'll arrange for a hotel suite where we can prepare."

Lucian ended the call and turned to the team. "Ian believes they have located Anja. After we land in England, the chartered jet arranged under a cover company will fly us to Kraków. We rendezvous with Ian and the others there."

Lucian's thoughts moved to the next leg as the plane descended towards England. The team prepared for the rapid turnaround.

The flight from Biggin Hill Airport to John Paul II International had taken a little over two hours. Dawn was breaking as they descended towards Kraków, a city steeped in history. Lucian watched through the cabin window as the urban sprawl of Poland's ancient royal capital moved beneath them.

Ian had provided much-needed ground coordination. They were to regroup at the Hilton in Kraków, where he had secured rooms for the team.

Upon landing, the air was brisk, carrying the whispers of a city that had seen centuries come and go. Lucian, Zoe, Dora, and the rest of the team disembarked.

Dora took the lead, her familiarity with the local customs and language making her an invaluable asset. She navigated the airport terminal with ease. Walking beside her, Zoe employed her unique abilities to smooth their passage through customs and immigration.

Once through the formalities, they piled into a rental vehicle, a nondescript van that would offer them a degree of anonymity.

The drive to the Hilton was a quiet affair, each member preparing for what lay ahead. The streets of Kraków blended the old and the new, medieval structures standing shoulder to shoulder with modern developments.

Upon arriving at the hotel, the team disembarked. The Hilton's plush interior was at odds with the urgency that drove them. They moved through the lobby with a single-minded focus, attracting little attention amidst the bustle of guests and staff.

The team reconvened in their rooms, gathering in a suite Ian had arranged. The space was transformed into a makeshift command center, and laptops opened as they set about coordinating their next steps.

Lucian stood by the window, gazing across the city holding the key to Anja's whereabouts. Emma pointed in the direction of Anja, and Zoe stepped up beside him. The weight of responsibility pressed heavily on his shoulders. They were close now, closer than ever to finding Anja and confronting the darkness that had taken her.

# *Thirty*

ANJA'S CONSCIOUSNESS CLAWED its way to the surface, dragged from the depths of a dream drenched in blood. Her demon form had been all sinew and savagery, a warrior born from shadows and flame.

A flood of icy water hit her bare skin. She gasped, sputtering, as the frigid shock chased away the remnants of her dreams.

"Rise and shine, hellcat," sneered the first guard, a grin spreading across his ruddy face as he tossed aside the now-empty bucket, which clattered. His eyes lingered on her form, assessing her vulnerability like a predator.

The iron collar bit into Anja's neck, a reminder of her shackled power. *"Wait,"* the demon inside her murmured. *"Our time will come."*

"Move it, we don't have all day," grunted the second guard. Rough fingers tangled in Anja's damp hair, yanking her upright. A pain lanced through her scalp, but she held back the growl burning to escape her throat.

"Careful, you oaf," hissed the first guard in Polish. "Mistress doesn't want more damage."

Anja had not studied Polish, but it was profoundly influenced by Latin and other Romance languages that she *had* learned. Italian and, especially, German were there. The grammatical structures were similar enough for her to get the gist.

"She is already damaged. The mistress just means not to get her covered in shit and piss. Don't mean I can't enjoy my work," the second replied with a vile chuckle, squeezing a breast. The unwanted touch ignited a fire in Anja's veins, her muscles tensing. But the collar's influence was still in place; it kept her beast at bay, forcing her to submit—for now.

*"Remember this one,"* whispered her demon. Anja committed the guard's features to memory—the cruel twist of his mouth, the lecherous glint in his eye—each detail fuel for the inferno of retribution she would unleash.

"Let's go." The second guard jerked her forward. Anja stumbled, her bare feet cold against the stone floor, but quickly regained her balance.

As they exited the cell, Anja could feel the weight of their leers, their crude thoughts pressing against her. The marred collar allowed some of their feelings to come through, but she was thankful they were muted. She held her head high, refusing to let them see the storm raging inside.

"Think the mistress will let us watch this time?" one guard sneered.

"Wouldn't miss it for the world. The way she breaks 'em, makes 'em scream—it's quite the show. Even better than her pet torturer."

"Better than last time, I hope. That one died too soon."

"Dead ones are no fun. But this one"—the second guard prodded Anja's bare back—"she's got fire. Bet she'll scream real pretty."

Anja bit hard on the inside of her cheek to keep from spitting venomous retorts at their vile fantasies. She did not want to reveal she understood them that well. Instead, she focused on the iron collar around her neck. *Patience,* she reminded herself.

They reached the top of the winding staircase, and the guards thrust Anja into a room, locking the door behind her with a clang. She stood there, alone yet not alone; the lingering echoes of their lewd predictions were grim company. The room, though meant for guests, did not feel welcoming.

She caught the scent of lavender and sage, a relief after the dungeon's damp rot. As she looked around the austere chamber, a woman emerged from an arched doorway where the sounds of water flowed.

"Helena expects you to be cleaned up," the servant stated in English. "I'm to ensure that you meet her standards. Yes?"

"Let's get this over with," Anja said curtly, betraying none of her turmoil. She would endure this, as she had endured before because surrender was no longer in her nature. No matter what these people took from her, they could not quench the vengeful fire that burned in her soul. "Start the bath."

The servant turned, leading the way into the adjoining washroom, where steam rose like ghostly apparitions into the air.

As the servant busied herself with adjusting the temperature, Anja looked at her reflection in the mirror. Her hair, once a lustrous mane, hung limply around her shoulders. Bruises, welts, and cuts marred her pale flesh. She touched the line of the collar at her neck.

"Will you want anything else?" the servant asked, pulling Anja from her reverie. Her question was laden with an unspoken offer.

"Help me with the bath. Nothing more." Her inner demon hungered for contact, for the raw power that came from lust. But Anja held tight to the remnants of her humanity, the memories of Lucian's tender touch, Zoe's playful laughter. These were her anchors in the tempest of her existence.

The servant bowed slightly and moved to help Anja into the water. The warmth enveloped her, seeping into her chilled bones, but it could not thaw the ice in her soul. She leaned back, closing her eyes as the servant's hands moved over her body with the professionalism of one accustomed to such tasks.

"Helena will be pleased," the servant murmured, her hands circling Anja's shoulders before rinsing away the soap. She worked shampoo into Anja's hair and rinsed that away. Her touch was clinical, but beneath it lay an undercurrent of something that mirrored the desires of her demon.

"I care not for Helena's pleasure," Anja retorted, opening her eyes to meet the servant's gaze. It was a battle of wills, unspoken but understood. The servant simply smiled, a slight curl suggesting she knew far more than she let on.

"Of course." After combing a conditioner through Anja's hair and massaging it into her scalp, the servant rinsed it away. She helped Anja rise from the bath and dabbed the droplets clinging to her skin, the air cool against her exposed flesh after the warmth of the bath.

The servant procured a jar of ointment and applied it to her wounds and bruises.

Anja's skin prickled and aches dulled with the soothing touch of the salve. Whatever it was, it was potent. She was directed to sit on a stool where the servant dried her hair with a fresh towel. As the comb ran through her damp hair, Anja could imagine herself in a time before her captivity, sitting at her vanity, preparing for an evening of indulgence and pleasure.

After combing the knots and brushing her hair to a renewed shine, the servant said, "You have beautiful hair."

"What is your name?"

"Jasmina."

"Thank you, Jasmina." As Anja dressed in the thin garment provided, she felt the pull of her past life, the flickering images of love and freedom that fought valiantly against the darkness consuming her.

"Is there anything else you require?" the servant inquired once more with a hopeful note, a mere breath in the silence that followed.

"Only solitude," Anja whispered, and Jasmina bowed her head.

Jasmina moved to the door and knocked. It opened just enough to allow her passage, then closed. The lock turned into place, leaving Anja alone with her thoughts and the ever-present call of her inner demon.

Turning her attention to the narrow slit of a window, Anja approached and looked out upon the late afternoon sky. Shadows grew long across the castle grounds, and the golden light of the waning day cast an illusory warmth over the stone walls that confined her. She was high up, so very high, the ground below a distant promise of freedom she could not reach. The castle stood on a rise surrounded by a misty lake on three sides. On the far shores, she could only see thick forest.

Anja settled onto the bed. Her mind wandered, time slipping from her grasp like the water she drank from the pitcher on the table. The cool liquid soothed her parched throat, a small mercy in a place where kindness was fleeting.

And so Anja waited, her demon coiled like a serpent ready to strike.

The last rays of sunlight caressed her face through the narrow aperture as the day surrendered to the encroaching night.

Anja's body was a map of pain, each bruise and welt a landmark. Yet it was not the physical agony that held her rapt; it was the chilling undercurrent of pleasure she had seen in Helena's gaze.

*"Perhaps,"* her inner voice mused, *"the lady harbors desires that can be exploited. She wields power for the Sodality, but what does she truly crave?"*

Anja weighed the idea. If Helena could be turned against the very order she served…

The door creaked open, and Helena entered, a vision of dark elegance. The vintage dress hugged her frame; black lace and silk whispered against her skin as she moved.

"Still as stubborn as ever, I hear," Helena remarked. She circled Anja like a predator appraising its catch, heels clicking against the stone floor. "It appears my techniques did not yield the desired effect on you. Why is that, I wonder?"

"Perhaps because there is more to me than flesh and bone," Anja ventured. "Or because pain is not the only currency in which you deal."

"Ah," Helena breathed out, smiling, "you suggest another form of… negotiation?"

"Call it what you will," Anja responded, her heart hammering against her ribcage as she gambled with the sliver of leverage she might possess. "But know what drives us may align closer than you think."

"I had hoped to engage in a more civilized discussion with you, Lucian, Howard, and your new friend Zoe before our last encounter, which was so rudely interrupted. The attack cost many of my people their lives. It was…personal."

"You wanted to capture all of us for your own reasons. Richard failed. You failed," Anja retorted. "What are you really after? What are you, Helena? And how do you propose that we could ever work together?"

Helena's eyes narrowed; a flicker of something—anger, maybe betrayal—crossed her features before she composed herself again.

"You question me yet sit here, at my mercy."

"Curious is all," Anja deflected. "At the dinner before our abrupt departure, you spoke of breaking with the Grandmaster. Why seek such a dangerous path? Defying him is tantamount to signing your own death warrant, I would imagine, especially after failing to capture or kill us."

"The Grandmaster's chains chafe more than any physical shackle ever could. Like yours, for instance, could be removed by my command. My ambitions reach beyond what he offers, beyond what he controls."

"Ambition can be a fatal flaw."

"Only if left unfulfilled," Helena replied, her back to Anja as she looked out the narrow window. "As for punishment, there are fates worse than death in the Sodality. But fear not, I have plans for every contingency."

"Even for those who refuse to be pawns in your game?"

"Especially for them," Helena answered, turning to face Anja with a smile that didn't reach her eyes. "But let us not dwell on such morbid thoughts. This place is designed to be impenetrable. Your friends, they will come for you."

"Without an invitation this time."

"Exactly. I will capture them upon their return, ensnare them in a trap they cannot hope to escape."

"Or kill them," Anja interjected, her heart pounding at the thought, even as she maintained a mask of indifference.

"Death would be cleaner, yes. But could you bear that? Would you convince them to parley instead?"

"Convince them?" Anja's mind raced. It could buy them time or at least avoid immediate death.

"Indeed. However, I sense we've reached an impasse in our dialogue. Perhaps you need more time to weigh your options."

Anja knew the woman before her was a master manipulator, and each word and gesture was calculated. There was an opportunity here—dangerous, but an opportunity nonetheless. Her inner demon urged caution, whispering that Helena's desires could yet be turned against her.

"More time," Anja said slowly. "Perhaps."

"Very well," Helena concluded, suggesting a magnanimity that Anja knew was entirely feigned. "Consider your position, Anja. We will speak again soon."

With that, Helena swept from the room, leaving Anja alone with her tumultuous thoughts. The silence that followed was oppressive, filled with the echoes of their conversation and the unspoken threats that lingered in the air.

As the door clicked shut, Anja closed her eyes, taking a deep breath. She needed to be shrewd, to bide her time. And when the moment was right, she would turn the tables on Helena—and the Sodality.

As dusk cloaked the sky in hues of deep purple and orange, Howard and the team approached the looming silhouette of Zamec Echo. The castle, an edifice of dark stone, stood perched atop a rugged cliff overlooking the winding river and lake below. It was a fortress that had withstood the passage of time, its battlements and tower casting long shadows across the surrounding landscape.

Acutely aware of their task's difficulty, Howard focused on his newly awakened powers. His mind, a reservoir of ancient texts and spells, worked feverishly to recall an incantation that would cloak their approach. As he whispered the words, a surge of energy flowed through him, an invisible veil wrapped around the group, diverting attention. Experimentation had shown that it worked on people but not on technology. He was sure some spells wouldn't be fooled either.

Sadly, he could not just call down lightning and strike Helena dead from a distance. He was still very much limited to simple conjurations in his immediate area. He would need much more time, study, and practice to do anything more.

Carrying a sniper rifle, Carlos scanned the woods through his scope, his posture tense and ready. Beside him, Cari operated a drone, her eyes fixed on the small screen that showed a bird's-eye view of the castle.

Ian let out a string of expletives when he caught sight of the castle.

"Bloody hell, this is going to be worse than the last time."

Claire, standing beside him, agreed. "Well, fuck. Not a walk in the park."

Lucian watched with a gloomy expression.

As they crept closer, Howard felt a surge of apprehension. He knew their success hinged on his ability to master his powers.

The group moved forward, their steps cautious. Howard's concealment spell held, creating a distortion that masked their presence. The ancient stones of Zamec Echo loomed before them.

As the last light of day faded, Emma and Zoe, after a brief exchange, confirmed that Anja was within the castle. Zoe's face was etched with concern.

Lucian, noticing Zoe's troubled expression, queried, "What do you sense from her?"

"Anja feels different...darker, vengeful. She's almost unrecognizable." The revelation sent a chill through them.

Their pistols at the ready, Dora and Mike scanned the area. Lynn trailed close behind, her presence a promise of healing and support should the worst unfold.

Moving with a stealth that contrasted with his size, Graham approached Ian and Claire, who stood in hushed conversation with Lucian. "What's the plan now?" he asked in a low voice, scanning the darkening landscape.

Ian and Lucian exchanged a look. "We wait," Ian decided. "We watch for any openings, any chance to get inside without alerting the entire castle."

Lucian nodded in agreement. "Cari's drones will give us eyes in the sky. We'll know if anyone approaches or patrols the area. Patience might reveal our best opportunity. This waiting is excruciating."

The group waited in a tense vigil, their eyes roving over the castle and its surroundings. The drones glided overhead, a technological counterpoint to the ancient structure.

As they huddled in the shadow of the trees, Howard's senses, now attuned to mystical energies, picked up a disturbance. It was a flare, an unnatural ripple in the fabric of the magical realm that spoke of wards or alarms being triggered.

His heart rate quickened. Howard leaned towards Ian, his voice barely above a whisper. "There's something...a surge of energy. A ward or alarm."

Ian relayed Howard's warning to the rest of the team through the comms gear. The group, already taut with anticipation, snapped to an even higher state of alert. They waited, each member blending into the dark embrace of the woods, scanning the castle and its surroundings.

Minutes stretched on, the tension rising with each passing second. Then, without warning, they all felt it this time—a powerful wave of cold energy sweeping over them, a force that was both threat and power. It was as if the castle had come alive, noting their presence.

In the wake of the energy surge, a hush fell over the group, a collective intake of breath. The stillness was deafening.

The quiet of the night was disturbed by the sound of scraping and movement emanating from the dark woods surrounding them. The noises were subtle at first, but they grew; a chorus of ugly whispers was closing in from all sides.

The energy Howard had felt was now manifesting into something more—something dangerous.

Lucian, his expression grim, drew closer to the group. Emma, her eyes wide with apprehension, stood back to back with Zoe, who held herself with a readiness born of their shared FBI training.

Shadows moved in the woods, the darkness coming alive with unseen threats.

They were no longer alone.

# *Thirty-One*

IN THE CASTLE'S grand dining room, Anja and Helena sat at an ancient oak table, its surface polished to a mirrorlike sheen. Four guards stood watch, their eyes betraying nothing and missing nothing.

Anja had worked on the lock of her collar in the solitude of her room before the meal. She had rendered it ineffective, concealing the tampered lock beneath the cascade of her hair, leaving only the unmarred surface visible. The time for action was near—tonight would be the night.

"You have had time to consider. Join me, Anja," Helena urged. "Together, we can reshape the Sodality, bend it to our will. Imagine what we could achieve with Lucian and the others at our side."

"Perhaps, but I have no way to contact them, not even to try and convince him. Do you really think you can replace your Grandmaster? How? I need to understand it all to agree."

Anja, her expression a mask of polite interest, harbored no illusions about the proposal. She knew that Zoe, with her unwavering moral compass, and the others would never consent to such a scheme, not under Helena's leadership anyway.

As they conversed, Anja's heightened senses picked up a familiar presence. Then another and another—Zoe and Lucian were near. And Emma.

A silent mantra echoed in her mind. It was a call to the darker part of her being: *"Soon,"* it said.

"I want to change the Sodality, and with your friends, I believe that is possible, but only with the Grandmaster's death—true death. They have suppressed the supernatural to near extinction throughout history. I believe that is the wrong approach. You have already discovered Eamon is more than human. He rules only to maintain his supreme leadership and power." At Anja's wary expression, Helena added, "Yes, my conversations with Howard were enlightening. You discovered Richard's blood oath and even managed to alter it and affect his memories. That is one part of the how of it. You and your friends still have no idea where to find Eamon or his seat of power. I can get close to him. That is another."

Suddenly, Helena grew still. It was as if she had turned her sight inward, listening to a silent call only she could hear. She rose, her movements betraying an uncharacteristic urgency.

"They have arrived sooner than I anticipated. Negotiation is now a lost endeavor. Perhaps tonight will not end in their deaths. I hope they choose to surrender. They cannot win, but I will still have you." She extended her arms and invoked some arcane force.

Anja felt it then: a powerful, dark pulse emanating from Helena, an energy so cold and malefic that it promised death—or called to it. It was a force raw and dreadful.

*"Now!"* her demon said.

Anja acted. With a swift motion, she tore free of the now-useless collar, her form shifting, morphing into the dark visage of her warrior nature. Her transformation was a thing of beauty and terror. Wings like in her dreams, powerful and tipped with spikes, unfurled. Her tail extended, long and tipped with a wickedly sharp spearhead. Fangs and talons sprouted, ready to tear and rend. When she called her whip this time, it was a long bullwhip tipped with razors—and this was not a dream.

Helena, eyes still closed in concentration, remained unaware of Anja's metamorphosis.

The first guard, who had begun to draw his pistol, never stood a chance. Anja's whip cracked through the air, coiling around his neck. With a savage yank, she pulled it back, the razor tips slicing through flesh and sinew. The guard's neck was nearly severed, and hot blood spurted in a fountain.

Startled from her inward focus, Helena's eyes snapped open, only to be met with the horrific scene unfolding before her. Her gaze locked onto Anja's transformed figure, a mix of shock and realization dawning on her face.

Wasting no time, Anja propelled herself toward the next guard, the thrust of her wings sending her hurtling through the air. The guard was caught unprepared and barely had time to raise his weapon before Anja was upon him. Her talons and fangs tore into him with a terrifying ferocity. She reveled in the taste of blood and the tearing of flesh. Battle lust consumed her.

The dining room, once a place of elegance and order, had descended into chaos. The remaining guards, witnessing the carnage and the nightmare form Anja had adopted, responded with fear.

Helena, though initially taken aback, regained her composure. Her expression hardened.

Anja turned her attention to the remaining guards.

The room was now a battlefield, the air filled with the sounds of combat and the metallic tang of blood. Anja moved among the last guards like a shadow. They died as brutally as the others.

Outside, the storm that had been brewing finally broke, thunder rumbling in the distance as if nature was responding to the violence inside. The night had taken a dark turn at Zamec Echo.

In a swift motion, Anja seized Helena, their bodies pressed together. Her talons closed around Helena's throat like a vice. Helena, who had finally decided to flee, was caught off guard by the sudden attack. But even in her dire situation, Helena's powers were not to be underestimated. With a desperate cry, she summoned the dead, calling to the lifeless bodies around them.

The dead guards, stirred by Helena's command, began to rise, their movements unnatural, a macabre puppet show. Looking into Helena's eyes, Anja saw fear but also a sliver of defiance.

A primal urge surged, her demonic nature screaming for vengeance, for the kill. Blood trickled down Helena's neck from shallow cuts from her razor-sharp talons. It would be so easy to tighten her grip and tear out her throat.

Yet, in that moment of truth, Anja hesitated. Instead of yielding to bloodlust, she closed her eyes and delved into the depths of Helena's consciousness. Raping her mind would be a fitting punishment and held more potential than a quick death. *"Ah, I see,"* her demon hissed in her mind. *"Let me help you."*

In the labyrinth of Helena's consciousness, Anja encountered the bindings that held her—chains of compulsion and control. It was familiar from her dealings with Richard, and Anja knew she could not break them, though she could alter them—add to them. Her long tongue flicked out and tasted the metallic tang of Helena's blood trickling down the hollow of her neck. It was not freely given, but it would be enough.

She could not probe deeper. The shadow bindings would lock her out. Drawing on the darker aspects of her succubus nature now helping to guide her, she wove a thread of irresistible lust into the fabric of Helena's bindings, embedding it so profoundly that it became an inextricable part of her psyche.

This was so sudden and unexpected that Helena could not twist it as she had done with the Grandmaster. It required no verbal acknowledgment. Anja saw what Helena had done to avoid his binding's full intent. With a final push of her will, Anja released Helena, letting her crumple to the floor, overcome by the sudden invasion of her mind.

**"Remember me, Helena,"** Anja's demon called out. Her voice was imbued with her full power.

She gazed down at Helena, now trembling and staring wide-eyed up at her. Night terrors were born of times like this—some night, she would revisit Helena.

There was nothing in the approaching dead she could manipulate. They were empty vessels, devoid of the desires and emotions she could twist to her advantage. Her eyes darted around the grand room, searching for an escape.

Spotting a window to the side, Anja propelled herself towards it with a powerful beat of her wings, shattering the glass and soaring into the stormy night sky. The castle, with its dark secrets and fallen mistress, receded as Anja flew into the darkness.

Below, in the grand dining room of Zamec Echo, the scene was one of chaos and defeat. Helena lay on the floor, her mind a whirlpool of confusion and desires. The dead beside her, their purpose unfulfilled, collapsed back into lifelessness.

The dark forest that shrouded Zamec Echo had become a battleground of nightmares. The dead, animated by a sinister force, poured out of their unmarked graves, swarming toward Lucian and his team. Overhead, the gathering storm clouds mirrored the growing dread.

"Keep firing!" Lucian yelled, despite their weapons' limited effect against the undead. "Aim for their heads!"

Ian and Graham stood side by side, their guns blazing in the darkness.

"Bloody fuck. They just keep coming!" Graham shouted in disbelief and frustration.

Carlos took careful aim with his rifle from the top of an outcropping. "I'm hitting them, but they won't stop!" They were knocked down but rose again. Sometimes, they were only able to crawl as he hit joints and limbs.

One of the undead grabbed Cari. Her ragged scream mixed with the tumult raging. "Help!"

"Get away!" Without a second thought, Ian transformed into his bear form, an imposing beast of raw power and fury. His clothes shredded as he shifted. His massive form barreled into the creature, his claws seeking to tear it away from Cari.

Lucian shouted, "We can't let them overrun us!"

Cari was bleeding now from scratches and bites. As Ian struggled to free Cari from the creature's grasp without hurting her more, the rest of the team redoubled their efforts. The sounds of gunfire, growls, and the eerie moans of the undead filled the air, creating a cacophony of terror.

The night at Zamec Echo had turned into a desperate fight against an enemy that defied the natural order, a battle not just for survival but against the very forces of death itself.

Following his uncle's lead, Graham transformed into his bear form. He tore into the undead with primal ferocity, rending flesh and bone with his powerful jaws and claws. Ripping limbs off and savaging the forms helped but would not be enough to stop them all.

Engaged in a fierce struggle against the encroaching undead, Zoe and Emma fired relentlessly. Amidst the melee, Lucian caught sight of a particular undead figure—less rotted, with two bullet holes puncturing its chest—fixated on Zoe.

The creature's tattered clothing brought a horrifying recognition. This was the man Zoe had shot in their frantic skirmish at Dwor Szeptów, the man whose life she had taken to save Howard. The first time she had ever taken a life. And now, here he was, a grotesque reanimation, advancing towards Zoe.

A cold understanding dawned on Lucian. This gruesome resurrection was Helena's doing. Helena was indeed leading the Zvaigzne Syndicate, wielding powers that Dora had whispered about in fearful tones. Tales of sorcery and dark magic granted the Syndicate a terrifying semblance of invincibility—whispers of Syndicate members risen from their graves to seek retribution against those who had killed them.

As Zoe froze in terror, recognizing the revenant of her own making, Lucian felt a surge of horror mixed with anger. The Syndicate's reach, its ability to pervert the natural order of life and death, was far more insidious and potent than they had ever imagined.

The once-human figure continued his relentless advance, impervious to the bullets Lucian and Emma fired into it. Since he was already dead, killing him again was proving difficult.

"We can't stop it!" Zoe yelled, shrill with horror. "We can't stop them!"

Lucian reached out and grabbed Zoe's arm. "Let's go!" He pulled her away from the advancing horror, sprinting towards the sounds of battle echoing behind them.

As they retreated, the sounds of their companions fighting for their lives filled the air.

"We've got to regroup!" Lucian shouted to Zoe, trying to penetrate the horror that had enveloped her. "Stay with me! We still need to get to Anja! We are not leaving her to this." That was the statement that shook Zoe out of her internal nightmare.

As they reached the others, Ian and Graham, in their bear forms, were wreaking havoc among the undead while the rest of the team fought with desperate bravery.

The storm had arrived and now raged overhead, mirroring the chaos on the ground. Lightning illuminated the grim scene as Lucian and Zoe rejoined the fray, determined to survive the nightmare that the night at Zamec Echo had become.

Amidst the tumult, Lucian's attention was drawn to a crash from above. A dark, winged creature soared out of a castle window. It was Anja, transformed into a nightmarish figure of shadow and malice. Her wings beat against the stormy sky.

As she descended, joining the fray, Lucian felt relief and dread. Anja's form was a thing of dark beauty. Her razor-tipped whip and flashing tail severed limbs and heads. She hurled bodies and parts in all directions into the forest. Her strength and agility were beyond what even Ian or Graham could accomplish. He could hardly reconcile this new form with the one he knew.

As the undead continued their relentless assault, Howard grasped the necessity for a more effective strategy. "Use fire!" he shouted, his voice cutting through the chaos. Concentrating intensely, he summoned his sorcerous powers, calling forth streaks of fire that surged toward the walking dead. The flames engulfed the creatures, bathing them in an inferno. They still tried to crawl as rotting flesh charred from their bones. Once burning, even the rain could not extinguish them. They would burn to ashes.

Mike joined in. "Burn them all!" he yelled, setting fire to the advancing horde, heating their bones and causing them to burst into flames from within. Fire leaped from one undead figure to another, the rotting flesh succumbing to the cleansing fire.

The forest was now illuminated by dancing flames, throwing long shadows around them in the wind-lashed rain. Flashes of lightning seared images into their minds. The scene was horrifying and strangely beautiful.

Amidst this fiery chaos, Zoe made her way to Anja. Anja, visibly exhausted and overwhelmed, returned Zoe's gaze with an expression of deep longing and despair. "**Zoe...**"

Lucian joined them, feeling sorrow for Anja. He saw the toll the night had taken on her, the cost of her transformation and battle. Her vulnerability was apparent as Anja shifted back into her human form. She stood there, naked and splattered in blood. The rain started to wash it away, running crimson in streaks down her body.

"Let's go," Lucian said. "We can't stay." The air around them was heavy with the scent of smoke, death, and decay. They had survived, but at what cost? The night's ordeal had left its mark on them, especially Anja. As they prepared to flee the hellish scene, the question lingered: would they ever be as they once were together?

As the rain continued to cascade from the storm-laden sky, the fires hissed as they smoldered. They would likely not spread to the surrounding forest. *Too bad,* Zoe thought vindictively. *It should all burn.*

She guided Anja toward their waiting vehicles. Lucian's statement was dire. "We can't afford to linger, and it would be suicide to assault the castle." They had Anja back. It was enough.

In the vehicle's relative safety, Anja curled up on herself, shivering as if she could still feel the cold touch of the undead or some other horror from the castle. She was seated between Lucian and Zoe, dressed in sweats provided by Claire. The shifters had brought extras for just such an eventuality. Anja's eyes were closed as she retreated into the depths of her mind.

Expression grim, Ian took the wheel with Claire seated beside him, casting occasional concerned glances back at Anja. The drive to the airport was made in near-silence. There was no sign of continued pursuit.

Once aboard the chartered jet, the somber mood persisted. The cabin was a haven of quiet introspection as they returned to Iceland. Lynn moved among them, tending to wounds. Of them all, Dora's were the most problematic. Infection had been spreading rapidly, but

Lynn had been able to counteract that and had taken care of her most significant injuries.

Sitting close to Anja, Zoe coaxed her into talking about what had transpired within the castle walls. Anja's account was chilling and barely above a whisper as she recounted the events. Lucian and Zoe listened in horror, the details painting a vivid and disturbing picture. Anja admitted to feeling unclean and tainted by her ordeal.

She spoke of her nexus, a place of personal sanctuary and healing. "I need to go there." Anja looked and felt vulnerable. Zoe could relate to what she sensed from Anja but pushed her own horrific experience down, locking it away to be faced later. She knew she would need to deal with it, too, but now was not the time. Instead, she focused on sending calming energy into Anja to help her relax.

Lucian tried to comfort her. "Whatever you need, Anja, you shall have," he promised. It was a vow that extended beyond mere words.

As the jet cut through the night sky, Anja finally succumbed to exhaustion. Her breathing evened out, and she drifted into sleep.

Zoe watched over her, a protective presence. The weight of what they had faced and what might still lie ahead was a burden they all shared. But at that moment, as the jet soared above the clouds, there was a unity amongst them, a silent agreement that they would face whatever was to come together.

They arrived at their hotel in Iceland at dawn. Zoe helped Anja into the bathroom and cleansed away the remnants of the nightmare. The hot water cascaded over them, but Zoe knew it did little to wash away the deeper scars the night's horrors had left. "It's going to be okay," she whispered, more as an affirmation than a certainty.

After the shower, Zoe guided Anja to the bed, tucking her in. Anja seemed smaller somehow, her usual presence diminished by exhaustion and trauma.

Zoe curled up, spooning behind Anja, enveloping her in an embrace. Zoe tried to send calming energy, a promise of safety and solidarity.

From across the room, Lucian broke the silence. "I've asked Mike to find us a quiet place at dusk tonight. A secluded lake with a rocky shore. When she created a portal to her nexus at my estate in New

York, she used the shoreline and twilight to help break through the barrier of this world. Undrentide, she named it—that thinning of the barrier between worlds. I hope it will work here, too, but if not, we will return to the estate."

Zoe listened, her arms wrapped around Anja, and felt the rise and fall of her shallow breaths as she relaxed into sleep.

Lucian disappeared into the bathroom, returning after a shower to slide into the bed on Anja's other side. His presence completed their protective circle around Anja.

With Anja nestled between them, the exhaustion of the past hours engulfed her. The comfort of the bed and the warmth of their bodies intertwined provided a respite from the chaos of their reality.

They drifted asleep in the hotel room, each lost in troubled thoughts and dreams. The events at Zamec Echo had left marks on their souls, but in that moment, they found solace in each other's presence.

# *Thirty-Two*

LUCIAN RODE IN silence that evening under a sky slowly transitioning to dusk. Mike drove them in his 4x4 to a remote lake near his house. Anja sat silently throughout the drive, her gaze lost in the passing landscape.

As they arrived at the lake's edge, the water was serene, reflecting the darkening sky and the first stars of the evening. The air was motionless.

Anja led them to the shore. She chose a spot near a large stone. Mike remained with the SUV at a respectful distance, affording them privacy.

Zoe and Lucian followed Anja, allowing her space as she gazed across the lake. Her eyes reflected the twilight.

Anja reached out, taking Lucian's hand on one side and Zoe's on the other. The connection was electric.

As Anja's concentration deepened, Lucian felt a change in the air, a faint pulse that sent a ripple across the water's surface. A shimmering rift appeared, its glow juxtaposed against the natural reflections on the lake. A portal had opened, revealing a passage to another realm.

Stepping forward, Anja led them towards the opening. The air grew noticeably colder as they neared it, a frosty chill that seeped into their bones. They crossed the threshold, leaving the familiar world behind.

They emerged on the other side, not on the rocky slope they had left but before an imposing cliff face. This was Anja's nexus, a sanctuary she had once brought him to. The familiar sight of the stone marking the beginning of a rocky path leading up to the cave's entrance evoked a flood of memories.

Standing beside Lucian, Zoe looked around in wonder. "This is incredible," she murmured. "It's like stepping into another world—no, it *is* another world."

The air around them was charged with power, a connection to something greater than themselves. The dark maw of the cave loomed before them, a gateway to the depths of Anja's soul.

"Anja showed me this place once," Lucian said. "It's a part of her, a realization of her innermost self."

Zoe's initial look of wonder shifted to contemplation as they approached the cave, its secrets hidden in the dark. For Lucian, it was a return to a place of deep significance, a reminder of his connection with Anja. For Zoe, it was a new experience.

Together, they stood at the cave entrance, ready to venture into its depths to explore the mysteries and wonders of Anja's nexus.

"I'm afraid," Anja confessed.

Descending the stone steps into the cave's depths, Anja felt a tumult of emotions swirling. The surroundings of her sanctuary now echoed her inner turmoil.

Lucian and Zoe followed in silence. The first chamber was no longer a reading chamber lined with shelves of tomes. The room now displayed murals, paintings, and statues. She instantly recognized the scenes depicted from her dreams in the cell where she had been held captive. War. Ferocious battles captured in horrendous detail. Blood, fire, and death were everywhere. Lucian was staring at one particular scene where her dark demon, naked and covered in blood, was astride a vanquished foe as she fed on the last of his life. The lust she had felt in her dreams came back to her fresh and hot. She had reveled in it. Zoe was watching her.

Leaving the chamber, they passed an arm and taloned hand rising from a columned pedestal near the exit to the next passageway. It held a heart trailing rivulets of blood down to a puddle at the base.

The blood looked fresh and so real. She licked her lips, remembering the taste.

The passageway they entered was lit by flames seeping out from cracks in the dark stone walls. All the while, Anja grappled with the voice of her inner demon, a presence distinct and insistent in her mind. The demon urged her to expel Lucian and Zoe, to sever the ties that bound her to them—to her humanity. *"They don't belong here. This is our realm."*

*"They are a part of me, too. They are the reason I fight to keep my humanity."*

*"You are not human,"* countered the demon.

*"But I am human too. With it, I am more than hunger and lust. Better. Stronger. You need me, and I need you like I need them. All together, we are more."*

The demon receded into a troubled silence as if mulling her words over. She almost chuckled. Arguing with herself was not a good sign. Sanity, she mused, seemed a fleeting thing.

As they ventured on, Anja's inner battle intensified. Each step was a confrontation between her darker nature and her love for Lucian and Zoe. The cave, a reflection of her inner self, bore witness to this struggle.

In her sanctuary, Anja realized that this was more than a physical descent; it was an exploration of her soul that Lucian and Zoe had joined. Their presence was a comfort and a challenge, a reminder of the life she yearned for and the darkness she sought to overcome—or accept.

*"They are just playthings. A passing fancy and food."*

Anja's steps faltered slightly, her heart torn. *"No. They are more than that. They are part of me and the life I've chosen."*

*"But you haven't told them everything,"* the demon prodded. *"About why you had to be captured, about how it unleashed me, completed you —us."*

Anja felt guilt at the demon's words. It was true; she had withheld the full extent of the ordeal she would face at Zamec Echo. The transformation had made her more complete yet more conflicted than ever. The struggle for dominance between her humanity and demonic essence was more intense now, a war waged in the depths of her soul.

"I'm sorry," Anja murmured aloud as they passed through a chamber filled with artifacts of her past. "I should have told you both what was happening to me. I was afraid...afraid of losing myself—of losing you."

"Anja, you can't keep things like that from us," Lucian said. "We're here to help you, to stand by you, no matter what."

Zoe's eyes were stern, though there was understanding beneath the surface. "We deserved to know, Anja. Hiding the truth, it doesn't protect us. It only makes things harder."

Anja had thought to shield them, to bear the burden alone, but in doing so, she had pushed them away. The realization was a bitter pill. She would atone for that now.

She led Lucian and Zoe past the bathing chamber, which remained a place of peace and serenity that she longed for but was not yet ready to enter. One of the enchanting pools lay beneath a shimmering waterfall, its waters illuminated by glowing rocks that cast sparkles through the spray and mist. The ethereal quality of the chamber spoke of purification and rejuvenation of the body and soul. "Bring me here when we are done."

Zoe asked, "Done with what, Anja?" But she didn't answer and instead led them onward, her demeanor shifting as they approached the next chamber.

Anja paused in front of a darkened chamber. Hints of flickering lights could barely be discerned. Lucian and Zoe, unaware of the full extent of her inner turmoil, watched her with concern.

"Something's different, Anja," Lucian began. "You've been distant, withdrawn. What else haven't you told us?"

Anja's eyes darted away as she struggled to find the words. The presence within her urged caution. "It's hard to explain," she murmured. "Since...since the...the rape and torture, I've had a presence within me. A voice that's not mine but is also me."

Zoe's brow furrowed with worry. "A voice? Anja, are you saying you hear voices?"

"Not voices," Anja corrected. "Something. Part of me, yet not me. It emerged during...during those moments of pain. It turned the pain into pleasure. I craved the pain as much as the pleasure. My dark fantasies came to life. Not knowing if I would survive only amplified it."

Lucian's expression hardened. "Does this voice...does it try to control you?"

Anja hesitated, then nodded slightly. "Sometimes. But I fight it. It's an internal battle, a dialogue between who I was and...and what I've become."

"Can we hear it?" Zoe asked. "Maybe we can understand more if we hear what it says. Is that possible?"

Anja's eyes widened before she closed them. She took a deep breath, and when she spoke next, her voice was altered, deeper, more profound, and resonant. **"They are too close. They cannot understand what we've become."**

Lucian and Zoe exchanged a glance. "Anja, we're here to help you," Lucian said, addressing both Anja and the entity within her. "You're not alone in this."

A booming laugh echoed through the chamber. **"Oh, the irony!"**

She had relinquished too much control, and her demon had been awaiting an opportunity. Anja's clothes vanished as her body began to transform, the change both mesmerizing and terrifying. Her skin darkened to an obsidian hue. Muscles rippled beneath this midnight veneer, giving her an aura of raw, untamed power. Her fingers elongated, ending in ebony claws. A pair of massive, leathery wings unfurled from her back, each wing tipped with spikes. Her eyes glowed crimson, casting an eerie light in the dim chamber. Six horns emerged from her forehead, and a sharp tail thrashed back and forth. It was a beautiful and terrifying sight.

Her teeth sharpened into fangs. **"You think you can help her?"** the demon sneered, its voice a chilling blend of Anja's and something far more sinister. **"You do not know the depths of what we have become."**

Lucian stood his ground. His expression was resolute. "Anja, I know you're in there. Fight this."

Zoe reached out to try to calm the anger, but it seemed to slide off of her like light on her obsidian skin. "We won't abandon you, Anja.

No matter what."

Anja's demonic form shuddered. Its crimson eyes flickered, revealing a glimpse of the woman beneath the monstrous exterior. **"You...can't understand,"** the demon hissed, but there was a note of hesitation.

"Anja, we've faced darkness before. We'll face this too," Lucian said. "Let us in. Let us help you fight."

For a moment, the room was silent, the tension palpable. Then, with a scream that was both human and inhuman, the demon's form began to recede, the obsidian skin lightening, the claws retracting, the wings folding back. Anja collapsed to her knees, her breath ragged, her body trembling.

Lucian and Zoe rushed to her side. "We're here," Zoe whispered, placing a hand on Anja's shoulder. "You're not alone."

"You can say that again." Anja chuckled bitterly as her clothes reappeared. Anja looked up then, her eyes returning to their green. "Thank you," she whispered. "I don't know how long I can keep it at bay."

"We'll figure it out together," Lucian said. "One step at a time."

Anja's normal voice returned, fragile yet firm. "You see? It's always there, commenting, reacting. I can't escape it, but I'm learning to live with it. To moderate it...mostly."

Zoe reached out to touch Anja's hand. "This is a part of you, Anja. It's born of trauma, but it doesn't define you. We'll help you integrate this...whatever it is, understand it, and find peace."

"Finding peace...may not be an option." The flickering light from the chamber cast a haunting glow on Anja's face. The revelation of her dual succubus nature—one that fed on pleasure, the other on lust, be it blood or sex—weighed heavily on her soul.

Lucian met her gaze with an unwavering intensity as he spoke. "Peace isn't a destination, Anja; it's an evolution. And strength—the kind you've shown—is a crucial part of that. Your demon emerged not to subdue you but to empower you in your darkest hour. You endured. You survived."

Zoe's expression was one of understanding. "And remember, Anja, love and justice are on our side. What Helena did to you was unconscionable, but you emerged stronger. The pleasure and pain you experienced don't define you. They are facets of your experience, channels through which your demon aspects give you strength."

Anja's eyes reflected her turmoil. "But the violence, the bloodlust... it terrifies me. I fear losing myself to the savagery, becoming a monster. Tearing flesh...killing...the taste of blood...I enjoyed it—reveled in it."

"Control comes with understanding and acceptance," Lucian replied. "You have power. But it's yours to command, not the other way around. Even in its most primal form, your strength is a part of you."

"And love," Zoe interjected softly, "love is a powerful counterbalance to any darkness. Your capacity for compassion and connection are anchors that will keep you grounded. You're not alone in this, Anja. We are with you every step of the way."

**"But will you be there with me after all this?"** they asked as she moved into the chamber. "I need to face this and trust that you will still love me when you see me—truly understand me."

The atmosphere changed as they entered a dungeon. The walls were adorned with various implements, each hanging from pegs—whips, floggers, paddles, and knives, each telling a silent story of pain and pleasure. In one corner stood a large X-shaped structure, a Saint Andrew's Cross.

The sight stirred things inside her, a mixture of arousal and apprehension. Images from gothic novels flickered in her mind alongside memories of her torment in Helena's dungeon.

She turned to Lucian, her expression unreadable and intense. "You know what you need to do."

Lucian looked at her, a deep understanding passing between them. The dungeon, with its daunting array of implements and the imposing cross, was a place of revelation. In this space, Anja's innermost desires and fears could be confronted. She needed to atone. She needed to lay bare her soul.

The room was a manifestation of the battle raging inside—a struggle between dominance and submission, control and surrender, sadism and masochism. It was here, in this chamber of contradictions, that Anja sought to explore the depths of her being, to reconcile the disparate parts of herself—all of them.

Zoe's mild introduction to dominance and submission had done absolutely nothing to prepare her for this.

Anja glanced at Zoe's wide-eyed stare. "I'm sorry."

Anja felt it when Zoe and Lucian realized the importance of this place for Anja. It was not just a room but a crucible. It was a place where Anja's true self could emerge, unmasked and unrestrained. A place of atonement and testing—for them all.

Lucian took a deep breath. He understood the magnitude of what was being asked of him. Lucian traced the outline of the Saint Andrew's Cross, his fingertips grazing the smooth wood. It represented their desires, both Anja's and his own. Maybe even Zoe's. The cross beckoned.

Anja stepped forward, her body radiating an intoxicating blend of confidence and vulnerability. Her eyes bore into Lucian's, captivating him with their intensity. "Strip me," she whispered with heated anticipation. Banishing her clothes was not enough.

Lucian's heart quickened at her words.

Anja glanced at Zoe while Lucian strode toward her, knowing Zoe would need a push to join in what was to come. Her demons, the lighter sensual and the darker ravenous one, vied for dominance, but in this, they all agreed—so Anja pushed. Zoe's mind was open, and struggled to comprehend what Anja needed, so she provided lust and a need to dominate. It provided the incentive to punish Anja for her deceptions.

Anja's breath caught as Lucian tore her dress; the sound of fabric ripping filled the air. His action sent excitement through her body, and she couldn't hide her arousal.

Zoe saw Anja's reaction and knew she needed to participate. She approached a wall adorned with various tools and implements with a devilish smile. Her eyes landed on one of the knives mounted on the wall. She grabbed it and returned to Anja.

Lucian's hand had moved to her throat; his other trailed down her arm as he removed the tattered remains of her dress. Zoe trailed the tip of the knife across her skin, not enough to draw blood, but only leave scratch marks. She used the knife to cut off first Anja's bra and then her panties, leaving Anja wholly exposed.

Anja gasped at the cool air against her bare skin, but any sense of insecurity was quickly overtaken by exhilaration. Her dark demon had helped her when it was rape, but this was different. It would feed on and relish the lust—and the pain.

Zoe stepped back. Anja could hear Zoe's heart pounding and see the pulse at her neck beating. Zoe's fingers grazed Anja's exposed skin. Anja's pupils dilated, and her breathing came in short gasps.

Lucian's hand found its way to Anja's throat again, but instead of squeezing or choking her as she'd braced for, he cupped her neck, his thumb caressing her pulse point. Anja closed her eyes, her body trembling under his touch. Conflicting desires warred, vying for dominance.

Zoe moved closer, her breath warm against her ear. "We're here for you," she whispered. "We'll walk this path with you."

Anja's breath caught in her throat as she struggled to find the words to express her turmoil. "I…I don't know what I want," she said, barely above a whisper.

*"Liar,"* her demon thought to her. *"You know."*

Zoe's lips found their way to Anja's neck, nipping and sucking on the sensitive skin as her hands roamed over her body. Lucian joined in on the assault, his mouth descending on one of Anja's breasts, and he bit while he roughly squeezed the other.

Anja moaned and writhed between them, lost in a haze of pleasure and desire. They were determined to make every inch of her feel. *"Yes,"* her demon hissed in her mind.

Anja was unraveling with each touch and kiss from Zoe and Lucian. They were pushing all of her buttons in just the right way—dominating yet gentle, rough yet tender—sending waves of sensation through every nerve in her body. It was good but not nearly enough.

Anja took a deep, shaky breath, her eyes transfixed on the looming structure. "I…I need that," she said, indicating the cross, steadier this time. "I have to know. You must see."

Together, they led Anja to the Saint Andrew's Cross. Lucian stepped forward. Her skin was alabaster against the dark wood of the cross, glistening with a light sheen of sweat. Lucian brushed her skin with his fingertips, tracing patterns.

Lucian and Zoe moved in tandem. Lucian grasped Anja's wrists, positioning them above her head on the cross, while Zoe retrieved lengths of rope from a nearby chest.

They began to secure Anja's wrists to the beams. Anja's breathing became ragged as the bonds cinched tighter. Anja arched her back, inviting more of this exquisite torment. Lucian and Zoe didn't disappoint; Zoe moved to Anja's ankles, lifting one foot at a time to secure them to the base of the cross, spreading her legs wide. Anja's heart pounded in her chest as she felt herself being immobilized, at once terrified and aroused by the loss of control.

"Look at me," Lucian commanded, raw with emotion. Anja's eyes met Lucian's, and an explosion of desire flared between them.

Lucian and Zoe exchanged a look. "Are you ready for this?" Lucian asked.

Anja breathed out "Yes" at the same time as Zoe said, "No."

With Anja bound and watching, spread-eagled on the cross, Zoe shed her clothes, tossing pieces off to the side of the chamber. Watching them undress and then start to kiss and caress each other while she could not move was another form of exquisite torture. Their earlier attention to her was now directed elsewhere, and a low growl escaped her throat.

Turning toward the sound, Lucian said, "I think our sex fiend here is feeling neglected." The smile he sent her way was one she had rarely seen, like she was about to suffer his wrath.

*"Ahhh,"* her demon said. She was having trouble distinguishing it from her own thoughts. *"I think he may be worthy. Maybe both of them."*

Lucian had finished stripping and was very erect as he appraised her vulnerability. He turned and reached for a whip, its leather crackling under his touch as he ran it up and down Anja's body. He coiled it and used it to caress between her legs. She was slick and trembled at its touch with need.

The first lash across her stomach caught her by surprise, a crack echoing in the room. It stung, but not enough to cause real pain—more for her to focus on the present moment. The second lash was harsher, lacing across her thighs; she moaned, craving more.

With each kiss of the whip, Anja's nipples hardened into tight peaks. Her scent filled the room, a mix of fear and anticipation mingling with arousal as she surrendered more of herself to them: Lucian and Zoe and her demon. She had no choice.

The lashes grew harder and faster until Anja was crying out in a frenzy of pleasure-pain, her body writhing off the wooden surface. Some of Lucian's strikes were severe enough to draw lines of blood across her pale skin. Zoe's tongue lapped at her sensitive folds and traced circles around her clit while Lucian continued his assault from above, Zoe expertly finding every sensitive spot inside her.

Anja's heart raced as she felt Zoe bite her heated core; her breath came out in short gasps. Her vulnerability drove Lucian and Zoe, who watched her reactions with hungry eyes. Her flesh quivered under their ministrations.

Lucian's fingers sank into her hair, pulling and holding her steady while he swung the whip down again. The leather cracked against her, leaving a hot trail of pain. She moaned as Zoe's tongue darted out to taste the saltiness of her skin where the whip had landed moments before. The scent of desire, blood, and sweat filled the room. Fear spread through her—fear they might not stop and afraid that they would.

As Anja's pleasured cries mingled with those of pain, they knew they were pushing her boundaries to their limits—and beyond. Every time she thought she couldn't take any more, they would pull back just enough to tease and tempt her before pushing forward once again.

Her hips bucked involuntarily against Zoe's mouth as Lucian lashed harder and faster, leaving thin lines of crimson across her pale skin. She bit her lip hard enough to taste a coppery tang while trying to stifle her moans, but it was no use; they echoed off the walls. Her body shook uncontrollably under their touch, her juices dripping down her thighs as she neared climax.

Lucian generously poured the oil Zoe had found onto her body, watching as it glistened on her skin. It caught the light perfectly, highlighting every lash welt. With one final stroke of the whip, she fell over the edge—her orgasm crashing through her like a tidal wave, drowning out all other sensations.

Zoe joined her soon after with a deep groan against her skin, her release mirroring Anja's as she collapsed against her trembling form. Sweat gleamed on their bodies like molten gold. There was silence between them now—not because they couldn't find words but because none were needed.

As they switched roles, Zoe taking up the whip and Lucian focusing on her entrance with unrelenting fingers, Anja's body felt like it was being torn apart and put back together at the same time. The impact of each lash burned into her skin while the wet heat of Lucian's mouth on her clit threatened to push her over the edge. "Please," she begged, barely able to form words as she was lost in a haze. "Please..."

As if sensing that she was getting close to her breaking point, Zoe reached for something else from the wall—a riding crop. She traced the leather tip along Anja's skin, eliciting goosebumps.

Lucian smiled wickedly before thrusting himself deep inside her, filling her. Anja cried out, arching her back in a mixture of pain and pleasure, pulling against the ropes. The sensation was unlike anything she'd ever known—raw and intense.

Zoe slapped the crop against her in an unrelenting beat. Being able to get close with the crop and work around Lucian's body, she could target the tender sides of her breasts or lay the blows over the welts and cuts left by the whip. The cracks resounded and echoed in the chamber.

With each thrust from Lucian, an electric current surged through Anja's body, and with each strike of the crop, a jolt of pain redirected that current until finally...

The final wave of release crashed over her, wracking her body as she shuddered against the smooth wood behind her. It was overwhelming—hot, sharp, and all-encompassing—and left her gasping for air. Lucian went inside her. Scalding heat pulsed and fed her demons. Every muscle tensed as she hovered on the precipice, and then her whole body convulsed in a blinding glare of ecstasy before going limp in her bonds.

They carefully unwrapped Anja from the cross. She felt reborn as they lowered her to the floor. It was dangerous yet safe, taboo yet tender; it was everything she had been searching for. The pain absolved her of her guilt. The pleasure was a release of another kind.

Her demon was sated and purring with satisfaction. It curled up inside her, merging with her being, at least for now.

Lucian cradled her in his arms and his healing touch spread over her body, sealing the worst cuts from the whip.

"The Sodality sought to break you, but in a twisted way, they forged something new," Zoe murmured.

Anja listened, their words slowly seeping into her consciousness. The idea of reframing her experience, of seeing her demon aspects not as a curse but as a source of strength and a result of her endurance, began to take root.

Anja whispered, "It's what I needed—we needed."

"Exactly," Lucian said. "And now, we use that strength to fight back, to stand against those who wronged you. Your experiences, as harrowing as they've been, have prepared you for that fight."

Zoe reached out, her hand clasping Anja's. "And we fight with love and justice. Your dual nature…it's a part of this fight, too. It's not just about succumbing to or fighting against your demon aspects; it's about integrating them, understanding them, and using them."

With Lucian's unwavering strength and Zoe's compassionate love guiding her, Anja closed her eyes and looked into the future. It was still clouded in mist but not as dark as before.

Zoe followed them as Lucian carried her back to the chamber of cleansing pools. Anja, limp and spent from her ordeal, bore the physical marks of it, welts and bruises marring her skin.

Zoe felt a complex mixture of emotions. The tremble in her hands was not just from the strain of witnessing Anja's trials but also from a sense of relief and catharsis. Her earlier anger at Anja for keeping secrets had dissolved, replaced by a more profound understanding, love, and respect for her. She saw now the necessity of what Anja had endured, a path to healing and self-acceptance that only Anja could walk.

Together, Zoe and Lucian helped Anja into the pool beneath the waterfall. The cool, clear water felt otherworldly, suffused with purity and rejuvenation. They washed her, their movements tender and caring. Still in an altered state from her experience, Anja leaned into their touch, her eyes closed, her expression one of profound peace.

As they bathed her, the water worked its magic. The blood that had stained her skin was washed away, disappearing into the depths of the pool. The welts and bruises that had marked her body began to fade. The water itself was imbued with healing properties, erasing the physical reminders of her ordeal.

Zoe watched the transformation, in awe at the power of this place. The nexus, Anja's sanctuary, was more than just a series of chambers; it reflected her soul, where even the deepest wounds could be soothed.

A moment of peace enveloped them in the serenity of the pool beneath the cascade of the waterfall.

Lucian broke the comfortable silence. "This place…It's a reminder," he began. "We're all still learning and adapting. Just as Anja has her inner struggles, we have our own battles."

Zoe, scooping water over Anja's hair, sighed in agreement. "You're right, Lucian. We're all learning. "It shows how much we all hide beneath the surface."

Anja, opening her eyes, turned to look at them both. "I always thought I had to face my demons alone," she admitted, a little steadier now. "But seeing both of you here, I realize we're interconnected in our struggles."

Lucian moved closer, his hand finding Anja's. "And in our strengths, too. We each bring something unique to this…relationship. This triad. There's strength in vulnerability and sharing burdens."

Zoe smiled, the warmth in her eyes reflecting her deep love for both Anja and Lucian. “And I’ve always believed in my ability to understand others. But tonight, I’ve seen a different kind of empathy, one that not only understands but also shares in the pain and healing.”

Anja sat up a bit more, her strength returning. “I never knew how much I needed this—not just the pool’s healing, but the healing that comes from being truly seen and understood. And accepted.”

Lucian’s gaze was firm yet filled with affection. “We’re in this together, Anja. Your battles are ours, and ours are yours. We’ll face them.”

Taking Anja’s other hand, Zoe added, “And we’ll continue to grow. This is just the beginning.”

# *Thirty-Three*

SIX WEEKS LATER, Lucian stood in the heart of the new addition to the Akar Lab compound, taking in the details of their new sanctuary. This structure, largely prefabricated and tucked mostly underground, represented more than a mere physical shelter; it was a bastion of security, a response to the looming threat of the Sodality.

The facility melded seamlessly into the rugged landscape. The externally visible parts mimicked the land's natural contours, cloaked in an array of native flora that Mike had selected. It was as if the building had grown organically into the earth, demonstrating Mike's dedication to integrating the structure into the environment.

As Lucian walked through the space, he sincerely appreciated the thoughtfulness behind every element. The connecting tunnel to the central lab ensured easy and secure access. Using geothermal power, supplied by the lab's independent plant, was another of Mike's masterstrokes, harnessing the natural energy to sustain their haven.

The interior of their new home was a harmonious blend of modern and traditional Icelandic design. Clean lines and minimalist decor were juxtaposed with cozy, rustic elements, creating a space that was both cutting-edge and homey. Each room was thoughtfully arranged, providing communal and private spaces.

Gathering the team in the living area, Lucian addressed them. "This will be our new home," he began. "Here, we're not just safer, but we're also better positioned to respond to any threats. Our proximity to the lab means we have immediate access to our resources and research." He gestured towards the large windows that offered a panoramic view of the surrounding landscape. "The design of this place, thanks to Mike, ensures we remain inconspicuous, integrated into the land we draw our strength from."

Lucian paused, and his gaze swept over his team. "Living out of a hotel was never a long-term solution. Here, we can be more than a team; we can be family, supporting each other while maintaining the vigilance our situation demands."

Each team member absorbed Lucian's words. They all knew the gravity of their circumstances and the constant danger that shadowed their lives. But in this new home, they found a beacon of hope, a fortress amidst the storm.

Lucian's heart swelled with pride and protectiveness for his team. They had all made sacrifices and faced unimaginable challenges, but together, they had created a place of safety.

Ian and Claire were engaged in animated conversation with Graham. Their laughter punctuated the air, a welcome sound that added warmth to the space. Their stories, rich with memories and past adventures, served as a reminder of the depth of their shared history.

Carlos and Cari, in another part of the room, appeared to have grown closer. They shared knowing glances and soft smiles, a silent language that spoke of their future.

Having flown in from NexGen Labs in Switzerland, Isabelle moved through the groups, her contributions to the conversations marked by insight and expertise.

The impending celebration had brought a sense of anticipation to the gathering. Sigri and Mike circulated among the groups. Emma and Lynn were a striking pair. Emma was wearing a little black dress, while Lynn had on a shimmering gold number that matched her hair. The contrast of light and dark was very appealing. These two couples were new, and Lucian watched all this with pride and wonder. This team, his new family, had been through so much, yet they remained resilient, their spirits unbroken.

Dora and Howard were engrossed in a hushed conversation and leaned close. The seriousness of their discussion was evident, though there was a sense of trust and mutual respect in their exchange.

The sight of his uncle Howard so changed turned his thoughts inward. His family had been taken from him—mother, father, brother, sister. They were not a close-knit family, but his heart held a grief he was not yet ready to confront. Their lives had been snuffed out. The murderer's heart had ceased to beat, yet the true architects of their demise, the Sodality, still loomed—a threat to his new family. The Sodality had too long cast its shadow over the world. In the wake of loss, he found solace in the bonds forged by choice rather than blood. Howard, closer now than he had been as an eccentric uncle, and his new family, bound by shared cause and mutual protectiveness, filled the void.

Shaking off the maudlin thoughts, Lucian shifted his focus to Anja and Zoe. They sat close, their body language speaking of intimacy. Anja appeared contemplative, her gaze often drifting off into the distance. Zoe, for her part, was also more subdued than usual, her characteristic quick wit dimmed by the shadows of recent events. They held his heart now, and he shuddered to think what he would have become without them.

Enough of this melancholy reflection. It was time to look forward, where his thoughts and actions could make a difference.

Lucian stood to address the room, and the murmur of conversations tapered off, all turning towards him. He cleared his throat. "I have two special announcements to make. First, this gathering serves as a housewarming for our new home—a place that will shelter, unite, and strengthen us. Secondly, and most importantly, today we celebrate a very special occasion—Anja's twenty-sixth birthday."

The announcement was met with cheers and applause, filling the room with jubilation.

Anja offered a small, grateful smile in response. Standing up, she addressed the group softly but with emotion. "Thank you, everyone, for your support. It means more than words can express."

Lucian declared, "And in honor of our housewarming and Anja's birthday, I'm declaring a day off for everyone tomorrow. Our worries, plans, and strategies can wait. Tonight and tomorrow, we celebrate."

The room erupted again in cheers, the atmosphere turning festive.

Then, in a spontaneous act, Lucian leaned in to passionately kiss Anja. Zoe joined them with equally passionate kisses for each. It was a moment of unguarded joy, a brief interlude where the dangers they faced faded into the background.

As they broke apart, laughter and smiles filled the room. Lucian looked around at the faces around him and had hope. Together, they were more than just a group of individuals; they were a force to be reckoned with, bound not by shadows but by ties more substantial—love, respect, and unwavering support.

The evening progressed into a celebration of life and togetherness, a much-needed reminder of the joys still possible in their tumultuous world. For Lucian, Anja, Zoe, and the rest of the team, it was a night to remember, where they could put aside their fears and uncertainties, if only for a little while.

In the sanctuary of their new bedroom, Anja found herself enveloped in a sense of ease and security she hadn't fully anticipated. The room held a comforting warmth, especially with Lucian and Zoe by her side. In the glow of the room's lighting, Anja acknowledged, perhaps for the first time, the depth of their connection: they were her lovers, in truth and in heart.

The discussions with Howard over the past weeks had stirred a whirlwind of thoughts in Anja's mind. They had spoken about strategies and knowledge, exploring ways to bolster their defenses against the threats they faced. Howard had revisited the idea of accessing the Vatican's secret archives, a notion filled with danger, especially considering his recent experiences in Rome. He had also mentioned another tantalizing possibility—the 'vaults of Liberia,' shrouded in mystery, rumored to hold the dowry of Princess Sophia Palaiologina, Ivan the Great's second wife.

The Golden Library held a fascination that called to her. The original collection, substantial in its own right, was said to have been expanded up through the reign of Ivan the Terrible, who had supposedly added mystical texts—even black magic. The thought of such lost and untapped knowledge was intriguing; however, Anja knew that came with its own risks.

But those thoughts receded into the background as she lay there, sandwiched between Lucian and Zoe. This moment was not for strategy or planning; it was for intimacy, for reconnecting with the two people who meant the world to her.

Lucian's arm wrapped around her, his touch familiar and electrifying. On her other side, Zoe leaned in close, her breath a whisper against Anja's skin. The closeness of her lovers was a balm, a reminder of the life they were fighting to protect and celebrate.

Anja marveled at the journey that had brought them together. With Lucian, there was a depth of understanding, a bond forged through shared challenges and unwavering support. With Zoe, there was a fiery passion, an electric connection that sparked with every glance, every touch.

Anja felt a surge of gratitude and love. Anja closed her eyes, savoring the sensations, allowing herself to be fully present in this shared space.

Zoe shifted closer, her presence comforting. "I never expected to find something like this. With both of you, I feel…complete."

Lucian leaned in, his lips meeting Anja's in a kiss filled with yearning. Zoe watched them for a moment, her eyes softening before joining, her lips brushing against each of theirs in tender, exploratory touches.

The kisses deepened into a slow dance of lips and tongues, a melding of three souls seeking comfort and connection in each other's embrace. The outside world, with all its challenges and fears, faded into insignificance.

Hands began to roam, exploring the contours of each other's bodies. They surrendered to the love and desire between them. With Lucian and Zoe, she found not just passion or lust but a sense of belonging, a safe harbor where she could express her deepest self without fear or reservation.

# *Epilog*

HELENA'S FOOTSTEPS echoed with a measured cadence. The walls of the Vault whispered secrets of past intrigues and silent judgments. She was acutely aware of the delicate balance she must maintain in her audience with Eamon, a man whose power was as absolute as it was merciless.

As she entered the control center, Eamon's presence dominated the space, his colorless gray eyes scrutinizing her.

The bindings that tethered her to Eamon compelled honesty, though she knew she must be careful. "I must report a failure," Helena began. "Despite our efforts, Howard has eluded my grasp."

Eamon's expression remained unreadable, but the slight narrowing of his eyes hinted at the calculations whirring behind them. "Explain."

Helena took a breath, choosing her words. "Lucian's people have grown in power in ways that were…unexpected. Their abilities have reached a level where ordinary means will not suffice to confront them. I underestimated them."

The admission was a risk, but Helena knew it was necessary to maintain her credibility.

"You seek another chance? 'Do not fail' was my singular expectation, yet you *have* failed."

Helena met his gaze, her expression earnest yet veiled. "Yes, I request another opportunity to rectify this. I have strategies that could tip the balance in our favor."

"Your failure cannot go unpunished, Helena," he stated, carrying an undercurrent of threat. "You must appreciate the cost of your shortcomings."

A chill ran down her spine, but she maintained her composure. "I assure you, my loyalty to the Sodality is unwavering." The twist in words was sufficient to imply that she was loyal, while the reality of her loyalty—non-existent as it was—remained unchanged.

Eamon's expression remained impassive. "Loyalty is proven through action, not words. Your failure requires a…reminder. Should you fail me again, understand that your demise will be neither quick nor easy."

The threat hung heavily, a reminder of the perilous position she found herself in. Helena knew that any sign of weakness could be her undoing. She bowed her head slightly, acknowledging the warning. "I understand, Grandmaster."

In the relative sanctuary of her chambers, Helena sat in contemplative silence, the room's shadows stretching around her. Amidst the strategic calculations and looming threats, her thoughts inevitably drifted to Anja and the unexpected turn of events between them.

Helena could not, dared not, reveal to Eamon the truth of what Anja had done to her. The admission that she had been overpowered and manipulated in such a way by the succubus would sign her death warrant. The Sodality was unforgiving in punishment for weakness or failure. Perhaps this new twisting of her bindings added more options.

Surrounded by the silent walls of her room, Helena allowed herself to acknowledge the transformation of her desires. The lust she now felt for Anja was undeniable, a searing, unbidden craving that had taken root in her psyche. Her fantasies, once dominated by thoughts of revenge against the Sodality, had morphed into vivid images of succumbing to the succubus's dark allure.

The situation had gone sideways, but Helena saw the potential in the chaos of it all. The risk was immense, the stakes higher than ever, but the reward—the chance to leverage Anja's power—was tantalizing.

Retreat was not an option. She had chosen her course. Driven by hatred, she had followed whispered rumors until she had found the source. It had taken centuries. She had entered its den only to be trapped and not strong enough to complete her plan alone.

As the night deepened around her, Helena sat motionless; the only sound was her shallow, controlled breathing. She was waiting to face the consequences of her failure. The fear that gripped her was almost unbearable, a psychological torment that she knew was precisely Eamon's intention.

Helena had always been the one in control, the one wielding the power in her dungeon and torture chamber. She had been the orchestrator of others' ordeals, never believing that one day she might find herself in a similar position of vulnerability.

The memory of her last encounter with Anja came unbidden to her mind. Anja had seemed to find pleasure in pain. Could she now do the same?

Helena's resolve hardened in the silence. Whatever the torture, whatever the pain, she would endure it. She would emerge from his punishment scarred but unbroken. This was the price of power, the cost of ambition within the ranks of the Sodality. She was prepared to pay the price, fueled by the determination to rise again.

The End

(To be continued in *Blood and Ashes,*
*Book 3 of the Reclaimed Legacy Chronicles)*

# *About the authors*

THE DUO behind Morgan Emerson Fox is a husband-and-wife team that has ventured into the realms of urban fantasy. They weave tales that are not only entertaining but resonate on a deeper level with readers.

Their journey into writing began as a shared passion, a way to create worlds and explore the complexities of characters and narratives together. During the challenging days of the pandemic, they found solace in writing, using it as a creative and emotional outlet when they were running out of novels to read, audiobooks, and podcasts to listen to.

Writing under a pseudonym has allowed them to blend their voices, thoughts, and ideas into a single stream of storytelling that reflects their imaginations. It's a partnership that challenges and inspires them, pushing them to delve deeper into the intricacies of plot and character development as they strive to understand the human condition.

For more information, please visit morganemersonfox.com

www.ingramcontent.com/pod-product-compliance
Lightning Source LLC
Chambersburg PA
CBHW020606310726
48979CB00008B/1366/J

* 9 7 8 1 9 6 5 2 8 0 0 1 0 *